# The Beckwith Brothers

## By

## Ivana Sanders

# Dedication

To my biggest supporter, my mommy!

For The Vardey Family!

Thank you to my most excited and darkly lovely Beta-Reader, Michelle, who contributed to my confidence in this story!

# Contents

# From Whence They Came...

Young Eric Beckwith could hear the clack, clack of her heels on the tile floors in the kitchen as she paced back and forth monitoring the Chicken Parmesan in oven to make sure it didn't burn. The smell of marinara, cheese, and meat wafted on currents of warmth emitting from the avocado green oven. Eric didn't even have to take his eyes off the nature show on elephants he was watching on the television box to know that his mother was pacing with her arms folded over her narrow frame. Tiny wrinkles in her forehead determine not to fail herself, fail her sons. If the food burnt even a little there would be hell to pay.

This hell probably worse than other days. Her husband, Carson, would not be in a good mood soon anyway. They were expecting a follow-up phone call about the health of the twins: Lyle and Luke. Ever since they were born two years earlier, June, knew her sons were different. Too quiet. Too withdrawn. Too much of a target for a father who would grow increasingly antagonistic towards the boys if he could not use them to get a leg up in life. She feared the pressure he'd would put on Eric once that phone rang. Eric would no longer be his son, he would be the meal ticket. Could she let that happen? She wondered if she had already let too much happen.

*Ding.* The oven timer shook her from her thoughts. She shoved her hands into the oven mitts positioned perfectly on the stove for quick entry and pulled the hot baking dish out. She could hear the bubbling under the foil lid she had wrapped over the top of the dish. She removed the foil. A face full of hot steam. Staring at the chicken Parmesan as if she could see straight to the bottom she grabbed a spoon dig it all the way to the bottom of the red bubbling liquid and lifted up a piece of chicken. Golden brown. *Oh sweet Jesus, merciful Savior. Thank you.* She breathed a heavy sigh of relief. Tears burning her eyes.

Eric's ears could hear things others couldn't. Prophetic listening. He could hear the mailman driving up to their neighborhood before his mail truck even reached their block. He could hear the scream of the little girl who fell and scraped her knee playing outside seconds before she had even tripped. He could hear when a raccoon was peering at their garbage cans in the backyard. Knew when she was there. Could almost smell her before she made her presence know using a black paw to lift the metal can with a clink and shove her intrusive little nose in for discarded food. He could hear June wiping away her tears of nervous relief as she often did when she did well enough - according to his father's standards - to avoid a beating. The phone? It was ringing. Oh wait...*not yet*. Eric had to remind himself. *Not yet was it ringing for the others. Others...not like me.*

He waited for the upcoming ring. Hair on his thin arms raising at the anticipation as it often did when he knew something was coming before it had even happened. The bull elephant's on the nature show were calling into the night. The long drawn out horn/trumpet left the biggest bull's mouth a flash of pink palate and tongue visible. His penis engorged, dangling near his feet.

"The male is courting the female." The narrator said his voice robust and breathy. "He picked her for a specific purpose for he has been watching her and knows that she has not been mated by another male. He wants to be her only one because then there will be no mistaking who her baby is. Soon his courting will pay off and soon she will give in to his advances."

There is a time lapse of the bull courting the female chasing her from behind, fanning her with his ears, and nudging her with his thick trunk. Eventually he mounted her. His long penis reaching out like an arm to deliver his seed.

"The bull will mate the female many more times within this day to insure fertilization. If he is successful the female will become pregnant with a member of the next generation of these majestic gentle giants. Of course only after a gestation period of nearly two years for the elephant species. Her bump will gradually grow as will the herd. And this bull's genealogical code will be passed on. A feat most important to him as it is the continuation of his life and establishes him as the alpha male. Dominant. Conquering. King amongst his peers."

Eric watched intently. Drinking it all in. The telephone finally rang..*as expected.*

Carson answered the phone. His gruff voice etched with dread. He didn't want to have this conversation with the doctor. June's footsteps to the bedroom made a soft crush, crush every time her kitten heels made contact with the shag carpet. She readjusted her camisole over the bruise on her forearm where he grabbed her the day before. She didn't want Carson to see. Didn't want him to get upset. Accuse her of flaunting it for sympathy and pity. Make him lose even more respect for her. She passed by Eric his head curiously tilted watching some nature show on television. She was glad that old box could occupy and entertain him especially during this time. It was not like he could go to school anymore. Not after *the incident* a year earlier.

June eased into the master bed room Carson's thick chestnut brown eyebrows threaded together creating deep wrinkles between them. *Muscle memory.* She thought. His wrinkles may not have been so deep if he did not shout and frown so often.

"Mute?" He spat into the receiver with a shudder. A mix of anger towards the doctor speaking to him on the other end of the line and fear for his youngest sons and simultaneous disgust at the thought of them being...disabled.

June eyes fell. She knew there was something different about them. They were always less verbal and expressive with her than Eric was when he was their age. No babble. No normal cries or screams to strengthen their little lungs. Just escapes of air and breath no voice of their own. This explains it. They didn't have voices. They wouldn't speak. They would always be treated differently by others, but not her. She would make sure they knew she loved them for who they are and that they could be anything they wanted. She had decided all this before Carson uttered his next sentence.

"You will burn in Hell for suggesting my boys are retards!"

*Retards?* June squinted glad Carson's back was turned so he would not see her expression to his idiocy.

The doctor assured Carson that his sons had no mental defects. They were simply missing their voice boxes. From the womb this was a problem in the neck region not the head. The doctor also insisted that one day science might enable them to speak. That one day maybe they themselves might be a gift to science.

Carson heard none of it. He took in a breath and roared, "My sons come from me! That means they are normal and they are strong!"

Ironic Carson would declare such a notion since he was far from being either of those things.

"And they will be too. They will NEVER be handicapped little worthless, shitty, piss-ants. Shameful. A DISGRACE TO MY NAME! HOW DARE YOU!"

*Oh God.* June caught her breath. She'd never seen him this angry. He'd certainly take it out on her and the boys. She should take them. She should run. This wouldn't end well for any of them.

"Sir!" The doctor shouted into the phone. "The sooner you accept what is wrong with your sons the sooner you will be able to help them adjust in a very verbal world in which they cannot speak." The doctor was a master at enunciation.

*Elitist, whore.* Carson immediately judged silently. *Thinks he's better than me. Lying on my boys. He hates me. And I hate him. I want him dead!*

June saw the veins in Carson's neck bulging so much she feared they would rupture. For a split second she thought about how that wouldn't be such a bad thing. *Her husband dying.* She clinched her teeth together and scolded herself for entertaining a vicious, malicious thought. She really didn't want him dead...she just wanted peace.

He was flushed red in his round face and the visible color of his heat and fury traveled down his neck and chest. He shouted into the phone, "There is nothing wrong with my sons!" Then he growled, "They will speak. I'll prove it. I'll show you. And when they do, I'm gonna bring them up to your office and show you how wrong you are."

"You cannot make those boys speak. They do not have the organ necessary to do so. It is possible they can find alternative forms of communication–"

"And when I bring them up there they will be singing daddy's praises when I shoot you! You motherfucker! Teach you to label my sons...disabled!" With a loud grunt Carson threw the phone into the window. The glass shattered. The sound loud in their home. June stood with her hands slightly clasped. He looked her way. Her eyes met his gaze. He squinted.

She knew he'd seen it. Her disdain for him. It would be the final straw if he made her boys feel less than because of the way they were born.

His eyes filled with rage. She took a step back and he charged for her. Smacked her right across the face. Once. Twice. Three times. Four times. She squirmed away from him with a whimper and a yelp. Eric heard it and came running. He stood in the doorway of the master bedroom. Watched his dad slap his mother two more times in the face. Her hair jolted with her shoulders every time. Her legs were limp underneath her the only thing keeping her at chest level of his father...Carson's fist clamped around her left bicep.

"I ought to rip out your damn tubes! Prevent you from having anymore misfit failures! This is your fault you know that?" He let go of her bicep. She collapsed on the floor. "Cause it sure in hell ain't mine!"

She couldn't help, but remember the time Carson took her to his family's backyard barbecue when they were newlyweds. She ended up meeting many of his cousins that day. Two of which were mute. Then she met his uncle also a mute. This anger was his guilt seeping through, but to her he didn't need to feel guilty. There was nothing wrong with their boys that he needed to blame himself for. She just wanted to love him and for him to love her and their children. Why couldn't it all be just that simple?

Eric ran to his brothers' room. From the doorway he slowly approached their crib. He knew not to interrupt them.

He watched them sitting facing each other eyelids fluttering over eyes rolled into the back of their heads. They were talking. Silently. The only way they knew how to talk. They did it more and more often. Eric figured they probably had more to say than he did. Sometimes he could hear their thoughts, but most often not with words instead it was like he and his brothers could feel each other's thoughts, emotions, hopes, fears, and personalities. Eric could lock eyes with them in order to join into their actual conversations. But, he couldn't do this all the time, for this was their gift. Their waterfall of telepathy which he could only dip his toe into.

"Get them!" Eric could hear their father shout from the master bedroom. Lyle and Luke stopped talking amongst themselves. Looked at and past Eric and to June trying to smile through twitchy and bruised cheeks. "Kids, we're going on a little drive, okay? We're going to go fishing!"

Eric turned to June cutting his eyes at her the same way he did as a newborn and an infant. The same way the twins did now. "Why?"

"Because daddy wants to takes us all to have some fun." She walked over to a dresser on the right hand side of the room and pulled out a pair of overalls for the twins. "Help get your brother's dressed. And then I want you to get your big heavy jacket. It's a little cool out."

Eric's eyes caught a dribble of blood running from June's nose. She quickly used the back of her hand to swipe it away. Smiled again and gave Eric a tender forehead kiss. "Darling, we're going to go to the lake and then come back and everything will be okay."

"How do you know?" He said quickly in his childlike voice.

"Just trust me. It will." She whispered into his ear. He could feel her breath wiggle through his chestnut brown locks and heat his scalp.

Eric loved his mother. She was gentle, humble, and kind. She represented everything he loved…purity. Wished his father could be that way. Didn't see it ever happening. No. Daddy was too set in his ways of violence and perversion.

Soon the family was packed up with fishing rods, bait, hooks, tackles, a hacksaw, knives, and jerky in two tackle boxes. Carson lugged two stools to the car. June with shoulders dropped, carried two pairs of little boys boots to the passenger's side. She situated the boys in their seats after that.

The family backed out of the driveway of their quaint little one story home surrounded by other one story homes filled with families some as broken as theirs was others much more unified and joyful. The neighborhood looked like a little in-between-ville. Families and single mothers settled in this space in-between some low point in their lives to some future success. It wasn't a neighborhood one moved to, to stay forever and set up roots. Closer inspection would bring a more accurate summation of the value of this neighborhood. The streets had potholes, the wooden stairs leading up the home's were bent, some of their railing rotted and crumbling. Patches of the sunburnt grass in the lawns.

But still true to form the residents tried to decorate their common abode with carved jack-o-lanterns, artificial spider webs, toilet papered trees, and the occasional zombie statue. Halloween was tomorrow and the holidays were Downers Grove's particular specialty. A time when all villagers could come together and find commonality in seasons of change and also tradition. This coming Halloween would be the twin Beckwith brothers second and Eric Beckwith's sixth. His mother had mentioned something about "Trick-or-Treating". She explained the whole concept of them getting dressed in costumes and going door-to-door to get free candy. She seemed so excited for him. He didn't find it all that amusing to be honest.

June wanted to encourage the boy to be less…inward. Participating was never much his thing. In all his six years on earth he usually observed. Watched others intently. Glaring at them from afar. Nature piqued his interest the most. Only when the family went fishing did Eric ever step forward to participate. But, then he could watch the fishes propel their bodies forward with the flutter of their flippers, dance just beneath the surface of murky waters. Turn up his rod with a jerk, send the line reeling backwards, then he'd throw it forward shoulders already stronger than most children his age, and cast his line many yards ahead. Then wait in silence. Wait for the nudge of a fish. Maybe that was what he liked…the silence. No shouts or yells, no angry tones or fists pounding his mother. Fishing was quiet. Nature was beautiful. Nature was the most beautiful thing.

They drove towards the mountains. Nothing but autumn colored foliage covering the cluster of vertical ascensions which looked down over their small town. June watched as the buildings of their community members pass by in a blur. Carson's lead foot lunging them forward too fast to be safe. She knew better than to correct him. She would just pray for her family's safety. God had always kept she and her boys safe even under Carson's fist. As backwards as it may have sounded to an unbeliever, June did believe that God had favored the four of them despite the pain that surrounded them. God had shown them His grace in the mist of the storm. It could have killed them, but it didn't. Now she knew it was time to listen to the quickening in her spirit. It was time. She couldn't keep holding on.

The family's old two toned '78 Ford Station Wagon bounced and rocked up the mountain. A leaf covered dirt road surrounded by the trees of the forest. Carson was driving wilder than usual. Taking turns as wide as he did when driving his 18-wheeler back before the crash took away his ability to sit for long periods of time without being in excruciating pain. He was speeding even on slick mud. June felt the tires spin on the wet soil and soggy leaves. Hit rocks peaking from the mulch so hard she'd thought the tires would pop. A dark sense fell over her and rose from her soul almost simultaneously. It was an unmistakable feeling of doom. She swallowed her anxiety back hard. Trying to stabilize herself. She needed to remain level headed her boys needed her. She glanced over at Carson. His eyes locked on the road. Little wrinkles formed around the corner of his eyes from his intense squint. It was like he was possessed.

"We can slow down and enjoy the view." She said as softly and as pleasantly as possible. She needed to calm him before he did something he'd regret.

He had no reaction. Gave no response. Only accelerated faster.

He white knuckled the steering wheel all the way to the lake. Miles and miles into the middle of nowhere. The leaf covered dirt road opened up to an open field littered with leaves and the lake in the middle. Carson sighed gruffly and put the car in park. Turned it off. Hopped out and got the fishing gear leaving the children to June. June and the boys watched him walk to the lake.

Eric glanced over at his mother. Something was wrong. He tasted blood. Wait no...*not yet*. He squeezed the hand of Lyle. He could hear him crying. Wait...*not yet*. What was coming? The fine hairs on his arms stood up tall.

June stared at Carson. Concern etched her face. She'd take a few glances around the area before stepping out. Bears were known to be in this area. Wolves and Mountain lions too. She'd didn't know which one she feared the most. Probably the Mountain Lions. Notoriously fearful of loud noises, Brown bears could be scared off as long as they didn't come as a surprise. Mountain Lions will rip you to shreds regardless of how much noise you and your group made. And the Wolves Hunt in packs. Corner prey and trick them into traps. They too were a threat up here.

She put boots on each of her sons and got them out of the car. Gave them each a kiss on the forehead. Eric watched her intently. Almost like he could see through her.

"What is it honey?" June smiled warmly.

"What's going to happen?" He replied with a seriousness of someone much older than he.

She looked slightly confused. She had gotten eerie vibes from her eldest since he was old enough to be aware of his surroundings. Even in his stroller as an infant he always seemed to look at the world deeper than anyone else she had ever known. At times she was tempted to think he had a gift that could not be described. A discernment like no other. The ability to see the unseen.

"Nothing, dear. Nothing is going to happen. You and me and your brothers are going to enjoy eating the fish you catch. Because I know that you'll catch a lot of fish! And when we get back home we're going to sleep in our beds. And then tomorrow...now this is a secret...tomorrow the three of us are going to go stay at grandpa's."

"Will it be forever? I think it should be forever. We'll be safe then."

"Oh Eric. My dear sweet child. You will be safe. As long as you remember that you are smart, special, and…you are a king my darling. Never forget. You are and your brothers are the best thing that ever happened to me."

"Why?"

She smiled and responded, "Because you're my babies. My pride and joy."

"Is that how all mommies feel?"

"All the good ones." June smiled.

"Even the animals?"

"Yes, them too."

"What about daddies?"

June dropped her head and then looked up at her son with her same quiet humbleness and replied, "All the good ones."

"Bring the boys over here, June." Carson said his tone implying a threat.

Eric watched her expression change. Her smile fading, eyes falling to the cool soil below his feet her knees, a hard swallow preludes her helping Lyle and Luke into their boots and walking the boys to the lake's edge. Carson helped thread Eric's line. June did her own after handing the twins some orange slices she wiggles loose from the rind of the orange she had in her purse. She kept watch for bears, lions, and wolves. Snakes too although it was probably to cold out for reptilian life.

Eric tasted blood again. His hair stood on edge it was coming for real…soon. He stared at the still shining waters. The tip of his nose cold. Fear aching his chest cavity. He looked over at his brothers. He didn't sense that something would happen to them. He wouldn't allow it anyway. He'd kill his father before he let him hurt them the way he'd hurt mom.

Maybe that was why he was tasting blood. He considered. Maybe he was going to bite his father. Lick the blood that oozed from his daddy's wounds like the alphas of the animal kingdom. Beastly it was and beastly he'd be…if need be. Like the animals a means to an end was worth brutality. Protecting the young was as good a reason to be violent as any.

An hour passed and there was pure silence. The only sound the chirping of a Robin in a tree somewhere nearby. She sang her heart out and her sisters joined in making their own chorus of synchronized sounds in sets of threes. The origins of musics are often traced back to the birds of the air, but where else did they get their musical talents from, but mother nature?

Carson sat on his tree stump forehead wrinkled. His face etched with concern and anger. If he didn't hate the world before he surely hated it now. He was sure of it. He hated life because he hated his existence. He hated himself. He hated his sons. Caught June's eye while taking a swig from his flask. He gulped it staring at her brazenly. When he turned the flask back down he already had an insult ready to fire.

"Can you cook up something for your husband and your sons to enjoy? Or are you too lazy to do even that?"

*Lazy*? Did he suddenly forget everything she did to clean up after him not to mention the boys. Carson was the Tasmanian Devil causing a mess no matter what he did and when he got drunk he only got worse. Breaking lamps, furniture, dishes, glasses, beer bottles, vomiting…anywhere he was passed out and she cleaned up all of it. Not him. Her. It was because of her that their entire house wasn't in shambles.

On top of that she was practically a single mother. Carson had never even changed a diaper for ANY of their three children and he had the audacity to call her lazy?

"There isn't any food." She replied.

"I put hot dogs in the car. You must not have been paying attention. Not surprising."

*Huh?!*

"I was dressing the boys so they wouldn't get sick sitting out in the cold for hours fishing in October."

"Get. The. Food."

She swallowed the retort she had in mind, stood up, walked back to the car to find the hot dogs. She opened the rear door behind the driver's seat and dug into a duffle bag. Then another. She found them. She sighed dreading having to ask Carson to help her start the fire. She knew well enough he'd use it against her for being ignorant to fire starting as some cockamamie piece of evidence of her uselessness as a mother and a wife. If not today then he'd do it another day somewhere down the road. She mustered up her strength to go back to him and politely ask. Maybe if she was polite he'd have a little mercy on her at least for today. She was doubtful of that though considering she could already see him turning that flask back up to his mouth even now. He was steady getting drunk.

As she stood up hot dogs in hand she made sure she had the car keys when she heard a branch snap behind her. She whipped her head around. Eyes wide as saucers she tired looking as deeply as possible into the forest in the direction she heard the snap. A bear? A mountain lion? What if a blood thirsty beast charged at her, pounced on her, and ripped her to shreds while she was still fully awake and alert? She felt terror overtaking her. She eased a foot to her right, slipped on some wet leaves, an ended up falling up against the side of the car. Tears stinging her eyes she tired to spot the culprit of the snapping the branch. Maybe it was a raccoon she told herself. *But, what if it wasn't,* a voice in her head immediately told her.

She had to get her boys. Then she remembered Carson had his rifle with him. She remembered something her father once told her about carnivorous animals, they have a trigger sense. When they stalk prey and their prey runs they run after their prey, but if they stalk prey and the prey stands his ground stares down the predator and his sharp teeth and vicious eyes the predator is likely to flee. She dared not to turn her back to the direction of the branch snapping that would be like giving the green light. She wouldn't run either for the same reason. Instead she slowly back up towards the direction of Carson and the boys. Keeping her eyes peeled for any shadowy figures in the thicket.

Her trek a mere 20 feet felt like eons, but eventually she made it.

"Carson." She said calmly keeping her back to the lake and her eyes on the thicket. "I think there's something in the woods."

"Woman, there's a lot of things in the woods. Did you get the hot dogs?"

"Carson, something big is out there."

"Leave it alone. It'll leave you alone." He said gruffly not ever once taking his eyes off his line.

"Carson, please. I want you to see if it's a bear or-"

"June." He interrupted. "Is this your ridiculous way of getting out of making the boys something to eat?"

"I have never been too *lazy* to cook for you or the children." Her tone was much sharper and much louder than she intended. Her patience was warring thin. After today it wouldn't matter she had made up her mind. He wouldn't be her husband for much longer. All she needed to do was make sure her boys were rid of this stress and abuse. Herself too. She was done. He wouldn't even help her make sure they all weren't about to be attack by a wild animal! What a shitty excuse for a man! What a small dicked little parasite. Small dicked little.....Was that another tree branch snapping?

Carson looked back. Eric too. June stared into the trees thinking of escape routes. The water? Could she keep all the boys above water if something were to happen to Carson?

"Do you believe me n-"

"Make the boys some food." He glared at her out the corner of his eye. Was he trying to get her and the boys killed? Keep his gun to save himself, leave them in the forest, and drive back to town pretending like he was the poor widower who lost his wife and sons to a fishing trip gone wrong?

She tried not to piss him off any further maybe she and her sons still had a chance. She asked him to start the fire for her and started making the hot dogs on the open flame. Eric put down his fishing line to help her plate and put the hot dogs in their buns. She kissed him on the forehead. Stroked his hair softly. He'd put himself between the bear and her. Maybe that was why he tasted phantom blood. He was going to be mauled. As long as he didn't die in vain he was ready. What better way to die than to die saving the angel that was his mother?

June served the hot dogs. She cut the twins' up into little pieces that they could not choke on.

Eric heard a woman screaming. His hair stood straight up. It wasn't happening yet. Who was the woman? Was it mom? He couldn't eat or fish. His lungs were tight. Throat too. All he could do was pant short breaths. His heart was pounding. June was watching the thicket intensely. Eyes shifting left and right rapidly. Blinking at minimum. She thought she saw the leaves of a baby tree move up ahead a little to the right. Maybe it was just the wind.

Carson washed his hot dog down with some whiskey from his flask. Looked over at Eric not eating or fishing. Got insulted almost immediately. "I bring you up here to fish and you can't even participate?"

The words didn't even seem to register with Eric. All he could hear was the woman screaming. His heart pounded irregularly. Beat his rib cage so hard and violently he could feel the reverberations all the way up in his esophagus.

"Did you hear me, boy!" Carson shook with rage.

Eric snapped out of it. His mouth hung open like he was lost. It annoyed Carson even further. Carson stood up his face twisted in anger. He immediately knew he'd stood up too fast. His back caught and the muscles around his spine tensed. It made him angrier. June stood up. He was not going to attack her boys. Carson didn't take his eyes of fire and lighting off Eric. Eric's expression changed to something cool and docile. He was ready. Carson snatched Eric's hot dog out of his hand shoved it down the boy's throat. "IF YOU CAN SIT THERE WITH YOUR MOUTH OPEN JUST STARING THEN EAT DAMN IT!!!" Carson's back locked up. He screamed, "Damn it!!!" He kept shoving the hot dog further down Eric's throat. Choking the air out of the boy. June wrapped her arms around Eric and pulled his body away from Carson. Carson beat his fists into her side and waist. The blows weakened her core and she couldn't help, but drop Eric. He landed into the soft leaves with a dull thud. He picked himself up catching his breath and put himself between Carson and June.

Those screams he'd heard must have come from his mother. For the first time he'd try and stop his premonitions from coming true. He'd try to stop his father from killing his mother. Carson continued to beat June in the head. Grunting and screaming with each blow. Hitting as hard as his back allowed him. She clenched her teeth to stay quiet. She plucked up Eric and spun around trying to put some distance between herself, her son, and Carson. In the blur she thought she saw a shadow in the trees. The twins cried silently by the lake. June didn't want her youngest by the water alone. They were supposed to be with her or their father, but their father was too busy acting like a maniac. This time she questioned if he'd stop. He came towards her for more. Eric grabbed ahold of her tighter squeezing his arms around her waist. She pried his arms loose and shoved him towards the lake. Carson back handed her in the face. Then he doubled back and grabbed Eric. He punched the boy in the face. Eric saw stars. Carson then slapped him twice across the face. Eric finally tasted the blood he expected. June elbowed Carson in the jaw. Then the nose as he stumbled backwards. She heard another tree branch snap. She had to get her sons out of here before they too were attacked. June punched Carson in the nuts. Bleeding from the nose and mouth, he was able to shove her to the ground and kick her again and again.

"No! No!" Eric screamed. Trying to get up and get away from Carson June saw the twins now holding each other standing in the water at the edge of the lake. Water surrounding their little shins.

*Why are they in the water? They need to get out of the water! J*une thought. Her hands sticky with blood. *Whose blood is that?* Then something thick ran into her eyes. She wiped it away in between kicks from Carson. Her hand came away slathered in fresh blood. He kicked her in the head again.

Eric watched as his mother was beaten. Knew he had to do something. His fight mode kicked in, in full drive. He looked to his left silently commanded his brothers to *get out to the water and go to safety* and they obeyed. He spotted the rifle and the ax next to the tree stump. He didn't know how to work the rifle, but he'd used the ax to cut the heads off fish before. He knew just the right pressure needed to chop meat with that blade. He turned to pick it up, saw Luke and Lyle hide behind a thick tree to the right, and turned back to his parents.

Carson was on the ground with June her face covered in blood. It looked like some of her fingers were broken from blocking his blows, crooked at a degree that couldn't be natural, but still she fought him. She tried scratching his eyes out as he attempted to strangle her. Eric saw all this out of his peripheral because his gaze was on the brown bear standing by the family car. The bear licked the air dramatically. Eric knew from watching nature shows that a bear licking the air meant he was trying to sniff out food. Was it the smell of mom's blood or the hot dogs that he was tasting in the air?

Eric didn't want to find out. He silently commanded his brothers to *stay quiet* and they obeyed cowering behind the tree holding hands and squeezing their eyes shut as tightly as possible.

Eric ran towards his father who had not even noticed the bear, and axed him in the arm. Then the face. Carson managed to stand, his legs wobbly, a gash in his arm and flap of flesh connecting his ear and cheek to his skull hanging by his chin. There was more blood than Eric expected. He had only axed fish before and they didn't have as much blood. Then he remembered when animals hunted on the nature shows there was always a flood of blood. This was him…hunting. Just like the animals.

Carson let out a delayed groan. June's eyes were almost swollen shut from the beating, but she had seen what Eric did. Then she saw the bear. Terror and adrenaline gave her enough strength to let out that scream Eric was expecting. Then another as the bear roared and stepped closer.

"Oh Goooooooooodddddddd!" She shrieked. Then she shrieked the same thing again and the bear roared again. Then she screamed again and the bear roared again.

Eric screamed at his mother, "Shut up!!" He knew she was agitating the bear almost challenging him to a duel.

Carson bumbled towards Eric dizzily, "Give me that!!" His voice shook as he wrestled Eric for the ax. Eric held on for dear life. Carson's skin flap wagged by his face slinging splats of blood with it. Eric felt his face get splattered with Carson's blood, but his attention was on the bear inching closer and his mother backwards crab crawling towards him ever so often looking back at him forcing her swollen eyes as open as they could go to see her son without turning her back to the animal. Carson finally got ahold of the ax despite being weakened by the pain in his back and the ax injuries. He panted, "I'll kill you, Eric! I'll kill ya! Just like I killed the others!" Carson took the end of the ax in both hands and raised it above his head ready to hack away at his little boy's flesh with all his might. Eric's instinct kicked in and he dodged the first attempt by his father. He knew he had just dodged death by the sound of the blade slicing through the air much harder in Carson's hands than his 6-year-old upper body strength had managed moments earlier. Eric backed away slowly not putting his back to the animal either.

Carson grunted frustratedly. Raised the ax above his head again following Eric deeper into the thicket. Eric tripped on a fallen tree limb. He fell in sprouts and damp soil with a small grunt. He heard the bear roar again. Couldn't see his mother. Couldn't see the car. The camp site. Nothing. Just his disfigured father standing over him five times as big as he raising that ax above his head again. This time he'd get him. Eric just knew it. This time he'd die. Carson inhaled and brought the ax down harder this time. Eric shut his eyes and clenched his teeth bracing his body for the impact of the ax. He tried not think about how much it would hurt. How scary it would be to look down at his own body and see it disfigured too. How similar being axed to death would be like the fate of the wilderbeast he'd seen eaten alive by lions in Tanzania on the animal shows. He heard rustling and the sound of the blade slicing through the air again. *Here it comes.*

Suddenly he heard a thud and his mother cry out. His eyes flew open just as she flew on top of him. Blood spilling over her right shoulder.

"Mommy?" Eric whimpered.

Like she was powered by electricity and gasoline she picked herself up and slung Eric to his feet all in one swoop. Then before Carson could hit her again she kicked him in the stomach in the direction of the bear. Carson fell at the bear's paws. The bear roared hungrily over Carson's head. It was the first time June had ever seen him frightened, but there was no time to stick around and observe. She took Eric's hand asked where were the twins. For some reason…she was certain he knew. Not only that she was certain he had told them where to go and that they would still be there in utter obedience to their brother. Because that was what they did all the time. That was Eric's relationship with them. Eric pointed her to the tree he silently commanded them to hide behind.

Carson, now soaked in blood from his ax wounds, crawled away from the bear screaming. He wobbled to his feet and staggered left and right. "Eric!" He screamed. "Eric you little shit!"

Eric turned back to his father as June collected the twins. Her shoulder spewing shining, burgundy bodily fluids. He saw his father stumbled into the leaf covered road they drove up the moment on. "I'll kill you, Eric! How could you betray me like this!"

The bear roared at Carson following him into the road.

*Betrayal?* Eric thought. All is fair in the battles of the alpha males. There is no such thing as betrayal in nature. Only survival.

Carson screamed as he felt himself getting weaker and unable to stand as the bear approached him. Carson panted trying to think when no thoughts seem to stand out among the thousands of thoughts he had at the moment. Left? Right? Up a tree? Wait, bears can climb trees. Run? No energy? No balance. He stumbled. Down to the ground he went. June, Eric, and the twins ducked behind the thicket. He screamed again as the bear climbed on top of him.

Eric could hear a familiar scream. The scream of some creature being eaten alive and even though he knew that creature was his father….he still liked it.

June's breathing was getting choppy as blood saturated her blouse and pants. The ax in the shoulder went down to the bone, sliced her lung, and nicked an artery, but she was happy because she was alive and able to care for her boys at least a little while longer. Two thoughts plagued her as she and her sons trekked along the river bank. Other wild animals were lurking in these woods and going back to the family car wasn't an option because that was apparently in the bear's territory. She needed to find them some shelter and try to stay awake despite her blood loss. She considered the trees. Could she climb with her shoulder? If they found a tall tree and rested above the canapé they just might allude Mountain Lions and Bears for the night. What was also good is being that high above the forest she might be able to spot the closest route back to Downers Grove. Or anywhere that was close…she didn't know how long she would make it. She was thankful that the only one of her boys who come make a sound knew best to be silent in the forest.

"Eric." She said softly. The ringing louder in her ears than the sound of she and Eric's footsteps in the leaves. Louder even than the trickle of the river right beside them. They need to find a tree because like this she could not even hear if a predator was stalking them. "Do you think you can climb a tree honey? You haven't done it on a tree bigger than the little one in the backyard, but I want you to be honest and tell me if you think you could-"

"Yes." He answered already predicting her next words.

*How exactly did he do that?* She caught her breath.

"Which?" He asked.

"Well…" she looked around.

"That one." He marched ahead confidently.

She followed close behind. Pushing herself forward never wanting to be far away from her children particularly in the mist of lurking dangers.

Eric zipped baby Luke in his jacket.

"Wait." He felt his mother pull at his arm. Her eyes on Luke.

"He won't fall." Eric proceeded up the tree not waiting for another objection.

June tucked Lyle into her shirt as best as she could with one good shoulder blade and one axed one. She bared the pain of holding onto Lyle's little leg to make sure she had him with her right hand and began to climb the tree behind Eric.

They got far enough up the tree that the leaves below them headed them blend into the foliage. June considered the smell of blood she left on the bark, but she decided not to worry. Just trust God. He had protected she and her boys thus far and against all odds. They'd done the best they could. God would make their flawed, ordinary efforts perfect and extraordinary.

Eric straddled a thick branch beside her. She admired his calmness. But it was nothing new. Eric always seemed to live with one foot in earth and one in another realm. His soul roamed. His eyes seeing things beyond the visible, natural world since infancy.

As her boys rested June stayed awake for fear she might die if she slept. Her breathing labored. She tried to be as quiet as possible. She squirmed straddling her tree branch trying not to wake Lyle in her arms. Shooting pains rang out in her body like fireworks. Coagulated blood drying on her body made her clothes stick to her skin and hair. She was miserable. A small groan left her lips into the cool night. She sat up and tried to expand her lungs. The sharp gasp of pain from June woke Eric, who was barely sleeping. He cuts his eyes over at his mother. Lyle awoke. Eric silently told him. *Don't cry. Go back to sleep.*

The infant stared at Eric. Then yawned and closed his eyes again. June tilted her chin up to the sky. Saw all the stars out. Saw smoke bellowing up from the trees. Wait, what is that? She thought.

A chimney? Her eyes widened.

The tree branch snapped on the ground below. Eric examined what he could see of the forest floor lit only by the moonlight. "Daddy?"

"Eric." June whipped her head his way. "What did you say?"

Eric looked confused and shocked by himself.

"Daddy's gone." She reminded him without an ounce of loss or mourning.

"He said he'd come and kill me. He took an ax to me." Eric had a rare moment of childlikeness. June wanted to wrap her arms around him, but she couldn't.

"He's not here, honey. He's gone."

"Well…the bear?" Fear building he leaned to see what he could see down below. Luke almost slipped out of his jacket. Eric caught him just in time glad June hadn't noticed the close call.

"No. It sounds smaller. Like a raccoon." Her eyes peering to that smoke.

"Bears can climb trees." He whimpered.

"Eric, sweetheart. Calm yourself. Just breathe. We need to be quiet." She said softly.

That smoke must be coming from a chimney. June was sure of it. It didn't look that far away just a day's walk further up the mountain. There they could find help and shelter. She had lost a lot of blood. She was lightheaded. Her right lung might have collapsed. Her legs numb and her body cold. She didn't know if she could make the trip. They would just have to try. She swallowed hard willing herself to remain conscious through the night. She listened closely to see if she heard rustling on the ground below or any creature climbing up the tree.

By morning only Luke and Lyle and actually gotten any rest Eric quietly helped his mother keep watch and quietly watched his mother to see if she was holding on alight.

He readjusted himself on the tree branch. She looked over at him. The small tilt of her head made the tree canopy spin like the propeller of a plane. She wobbled on the tree branch trying to straighten herself. Felt herself lean too far and squeezed her thighs tight around the branch to keep herself and little Lyle from falling out the tree. She shut her eyes as tight as someone would who had an intense light shone in their face. Eventually the spinning got better, but did not completely subside. She wiggled back onto the branch.

Blue jays and macaws chirped in nearby trees and their mates responded from a distance. The sun's rays twinkled through the leaves of the tree canopy. The slight breeze that passed making the leaves and light dance on the forest floor below. The floor became a ballroom for dancing and prancing natural light.

"We should go." Eric said.

"Why now?"

"I haven't heard anything in a while."

It had to have been about 7 o'clock in the morning. June sighed. "Okay. I'll go first."

June clutched Lyle close to herself and started making her way back down the old spruce. Moving was pain. Moving was dizzying. Moving was shaky and uncertain. She felt at any moment her body would give out. She expected all of her muscles to just give up and relax right when she needed to hold up her own weight, but they didn't. She saw Eric maneuvering his way down above her. "Be careful, Eric." She said softly.

"Okay." He replied.

Almost to the bottom. There was a relatively wide space between the branch she was standing on the last branch to the bottom. When they climbed this tree the night before she realized this was a problem then. They had to elongate their bodies and reach above their heads and pull themselves up past this wide space, but she wasn't as dizzy then and now she had to drop herself down to the branch below without collapsing under her own weight. She wiped sweat from her brow. Teeth chattering and body shivering from the morning chill or was it because of the radiating pain and consistent blood loss?

For the first time she considered trying to go back to the car. Maybe the bear was roaming around a different part of his territory. Maybe they could slip into the car and she could drive them back to town instead of going deeper into the forest?

Eric watched June struggle to ease her body down to the branch below without crushing Lyle between her chest and the branch she was using to steady herself. In the light, Eric noticed for the first time how pale June was and how dark the area below her eyes had gotten between the night and the morning. Her form didn't look right. Her arms were shaking. The muscles in them hopping and jumping under her skin. She couldn't hold her weight. She pointed her tippy toe towards the branch below trying to find her footing. Dizziness overtook her. She felt like she was going to throw up. She was wet with fresh blood again. All this moving must have put stress on her wound somewhere. Her eyes rolled into the back of her head and Eric gasped watching her falling backward out the tree. She landed on her back with a sickening thud onto the lumpy and hard roots of the tree. Eric rushed down. Almost lost his own footing, so quickly he spotted a pile of what looked like soft autumn leaves and he leaped out the tree and aimed for it. He expected to land on his feet without falling over. Instead he landed one foot in soft leaves and one wedged in between tree roots hidden underneath a thin layer of autumn leaves. The pain of scratches, scrapes, and a gash on his right ankle from the tree roots lead him to straighten and lock his legs mid-fall resulting in the impact of his body on a hard surface cracking his right knee. He yelped, dropped Luke, and collapsed against the tree. He let out a pained groan, but clenched his teeth with all his might to keep himself from screaming like he wanted to. He needed to stay quiet. Gasps of agony left his body. It hurt. It hurt so bad. He grunted hard willing himself to check his mother. She was so quiet. Too quiet. *Stand up, Luke. Stay quiet. Stay close to me.* Eric kept a look out for predators. *Help me look out, okay? Please. If you see something wave at me.*

Luke sucked his lower lip looking into Eric's eyes. Then turned and looked off into the distance. Eric winced and eased over to June who bled unconscious.

"Mom? Mommy! Get up."

Lyle begin to silently cry. The silent cry turned into a silent wail. His arms flailing about. Eric ignored him. Took him out of June's arms and propped him up against the base of the tree.

"Mom, you have to get up. You have to." He stated calmly. "Mom." He said firmly.

Her eyes opened. Lids fluttered. "Lyle?" She whimpered.

"He's fine. Get up." Hurried.

"Eric." She breathed. "Eric, I…" A sharp intake of air cut off her words.

"You…you have to."

"Eric, there's a house. It's not that far."

"Mommy, no." He fervently fought tears.

"Eric. You have to follow instructions. I know you can do it." She extended her arm in the direction of where she saw the smoke plume. "It is right that way. You can make it there today, honey. Just a few hours walk. There'll be help there. You have to find it."

"I want you to take us." He cried.

"Oh Eric." She breathed weakly. "You don't need me. Remember that as long as you can survive everything will be okay."

"Mommy I need you."

"One day Eric you'll have children of your own and you'll realize how fulfilling that is to just know that they're okay. You'll see that it will become the meaning to your life. When you have cubs I'll be there with you. I'll see it. You just won't see me."

Eric rested his head on her chest and cried. "I can't do it. I can't do it."

"Of course you can."

"Take me closer."

"I'm too weak, dear. I can't."

"Just try. Try to stand up. Try to take me closer. I can't leave you out here. Something will come and get you."

"I'll be alright honey. Death is nothing to be afraid of. It happens to everyone and everything. We all experience it. But, you have to make it because I'll live on through you and your brothers. You are my life now. That's how important it is that you make it."

"We need you to get up and take us. Because I'm hurt. I'm...I'm hurt. I hurt myself. I feel out the tree. I didn't mean to, but I did. I can't get there alone...Move your legs." He demanded.

She grunted as she squeezed her thighs together before releasing them slowly with a grunt that ended in her gurgling and choking on blood which dribbled down her chin. She hid it from Eric's eyes. Wiped it away quickly before his gaze met her face.

"See. You can walk." He stood propping himself up against the tree avoided putting weight on his right leg. June realized that she needed to muster up enough strength to get her sons just a little farther.

"Honey...Okay. I'll...I'll try." June rolled over to one side and stifled a cry. Eric wrapped his arm around her shoulder. She sat up trying to hide how painful it was from Eric. Her entire body rattled, but it wasn't a rattle from pain, but of expiration. She could feel her body shutting down. Teeth chattering again, she pushed herself into a stooping position. Propped herself up on the tree with her butt and stood as straight as she could. Still crooked over. She could taste fresh blood in her mouth again. She couldn't have had no more than a few hours left, if that.

She and Eric both plucked up a twin and hobbled to the river's edge following beside it as far as they could in the direction of the house leaning on each other for support. They crept along keeping watch for wild animals. Keeping quiet to not bring attention to themselves.

Eric noticed the glistening babbling waters, heard the macaws still communicating with each other, saw the beautiful meadow of flowers peeking out from behind a hill some ways to the left. He thought he could see a deer frolicking away after munching on some of the flower blossoms. The leaded into the distant thicket like it was galloping airy and effortlessly on a cloud. Eric loved nature. The beauty. The quiet. He'd like to spend peaceful time out here. One day. Some day.

June could feel herself getting weaker. She was surprised she had made it this far. She knew the house must be close. She had to get her boys there she had to make it now. If she could just hold on they wouldn't have to be alone. She could look over them through this and through life. If she could just hold on she could still be their mother for years and perhaps decades more. Have the guidance of someone who loved them more than life itself. They deserved that. They deserved for the sins of their father not to mar their future. They deserved to have a mother. But, she just didn't feel right. She hoped Eric was listening enough for them both because the ringing in her ears was deafening. He hoped he could see enough for both of them because her vision had blurred considerably.

She hoped they were near the house. A few more yards and her prayers were answered. They could see the front of a three story log cabin surrounded by a white picket fence just around the bend of the river. Eric sighed relieved. It looked lived in. There was a small garden out back. A trellis of pink roses up the front of the cabin. It was tranquil and lovely. An elderly man with a watering can in one hand and a bushel of freshly picked strawberries in the other, and smoking pipe hanging from his mouth strolled around the side of the cabin. His gaze settled on the broken family. His expression immediately shifted. From all the way on the other side of the river, Eric could see the old man's bushy eyebrows shoot up. Create a ripple of wrinkles in his sunbaked forehead. His mouth hung ajar so much so his pipe flipped out. He dropped his watering can, leaned forward, and took a reluctant step towards the sight before his squinting eyes.

"Hello?" He said like he wasn't sure June and the boys were actually real or if the constant solitude of the forest had finally cracked him up.

"Please…" June croaked nowhere near loud enough for the man to hear over the sound of the river.

Suddenly, as if his eyes were miraculously opened, the old man noticed the blood all over her clothes and the ends of her hair. He threw his strawberries to the ground, went threw the gate of the white picket fence, outstretched his long arms, and marched into the river until he was waist deep. Eric clung tightly to Lyle, squeezed June's hand in his, and lead her into the pristinely clear waters. She shuddered at the coolness of the river. She and Eric waded into the river trying desperately to keep the twins heads out of the water. Eric kicked towards the old man. His cracked knee hurting worse than he realized until he realized he was having to swim and kick harder against the current because June wasn't carrying her own weight. Eventually he made it to the man. June kept Luke's head above water even as she felt the cool liquid filling her chest cavity from the ax wound in her back. She gasped sharply again and again bobbing up and down like a buoy. Her head dipped under the river. The old man stood firmly in the sediment of the river, used one hand to usher Eric to shore and another to hold onto June. Next, she handed him Luke who he turned and handed to Eric. She struggled to stay afloat. Gasped for air. Told her legs to move. Kick! Try to find the floor of the river to stand on! Something! But, her limbs ignored her commands like a disobedient child. Limp they served no purpose. She took in more water. Choking gasping. She pawed at the old man's arm, tried to grip his bicep for support, but it was no use her arms failed her as well. Quickly she noticed the water was taking her away. There was nothing she could do, but flip over to her back. Choking on water and blood, her vision faded. She heard Eric cry, "Mommy!" before blacking out.

The old man gasped seeing June be taken away by the river. "Stay there, son!" He shouted back to Eric as he swam powerfully with the current to see if he could catch June.

Eric watched as he came within inches of June many times without catching her as the current whisked them both around the bend and out of sight. Eric stood in shock. "Mommy? No." Without the man or his mother there was no one. He and his brothers were alone. His little heart was pounding. Veins pulsating in his skull. His eyes burned. He left Luke and Lyle at the river's edge and ran around the bend of the river with hopes that the old man and his mother had washed ashore there. They weren't there. He ran further down the bank. Maybe they washed up somewhere further down? He couldn't see them, but he could hear someone rapidly, thinly gasping for air. *Hyperventilating*, but he didn't know that word. Was the rapid thin gasping from the Old Man? His mother? He ran further and was able to see a long stretch of the river. There was no sight of the Old Man OR his mother. Not seeing anyone he still heard the hyperventilating. Then he realized it was him. He couldn't breathe. Then he gasped. The twins! He'd left them on the bank.

He ran back twice as fast wheezing deeply. A dozen frightening thoughts churned violently in his mind, coursing thoughts that felt like they chipped away at his brain. Somehow they hurt and made his head ache like never before. *The twins may have fallen in by now. A wild animal may have gotten them by now! They may have run off and gotten lost! I'll never find them! I'll truly be all alone now!* He made his way back around the bend and there Luke and Lyle were huddled together on the skinny little porch just wide enough for the Old Man, his rocking chair, and a chopped off tree stump that he apparently used for a small table. The coffee he was drinking still steaming in the mug on the stump. The twins were shivering their way through strawberries they'd plucked up off the ground.

Eric panted approaching them. They looked at him curiously. Seeing them was a relief. He caught his breath dragging his feet up the porch. He gave the perimeter a visual once over before opening the heavy front door made up of small narrow trees debarked and nailed closely together with moss shoved in between them for insulation. The handle was smooth and curvy like who ever had built the house, probably the Old Man himself, had carefully and meticulously whittled it until it was just the right smoothness and just the right shape. *Inside*. He told the twins and they obeyed him. He walked in behind them. Shut the door. Was pleased to find a lock on the inside of the door. It was a bolt lock and a flat lock which folded over the width of the door. He locked it.

Mom always taught him to lock the door behind himself. There were bad people out there…

Eric leaned his back up against the door, swiped wet curls out of his eyes. Looked around the cabin. The inside was simple, woodsy, and rustic. A true woodsman's abode. There were exposed beams, low ceilings, hard wood floors through and through, a bear skin rug in the living room, antlers over the fireplace, and a red flannel throw over the well used tweed, green sofa. He looked to his left, a full kitchen. He looked to his right, the living room. Eric could see another room behind the staircase directly in front of him and the twins, but for once he wasn't feeling curious enough at the moment to go check it out. Scents like coffee, tobacco, dust, and nameless musk joined together in the air to make a new combination of what could have been the official woodsman's cologne. The floors creaked and whined underfoot. Lyle and Luke squished, squished in their soaking wet shoes and soggy Fall clothes towards the sofa and crawled on. Lyle tugged at his clothes, an uncomfortable wince on his face, wrinkles folding his baby soft forehead. Eric calmly walked over to the windows and drew the green curtains which were nothing more than scraps of fabric. For the first time in his life he didn't want to see the sun, the nature, nothing.

He turned back around to his brothers. He could sense their confusion.

"It's okay. I'm here." He said softly. "I'll protect you."

Eric climbed the steps somehow his knee didn't hurt as badly. Maybe he couldn't feel the pain in his knees as much because adrenaline was still coursing through his veins. Maybe it was because the pain of losing his mother hurt worse. Or maybe...

Eric reached the second floor two furnished bedrooms. Navy blue sheets in both rooms. A lamp in both rooms. The style of lamps were different, but each resembled the type that Eric's grandmother had in her house. Round knitted rugs lay under each four poster bed. There were closets. Eric didn't look in those yet. Down the hall was a shady deck with two more rocking chairs on it and a rain guard.

Third floor. Eric found it practically empty. Just a wide open space. A loft almost, but he didn't know that word. The ceiling here was much higher and vaulted. There was a skylight on both sides of the vaulted peak and an oval window which looked over the front yard. Eric walked up to the window. His gap effected by his subtle limp. He looked out the window. No sign of mom or the Old Man outside. There was a small bed of flowers hooked onto the outside of the window. He would have closed the curtains, but there were no curtains to close. *Besides flowers always deserved to be seen,* Eric thought. *Even on a bad day.* So, he opened the window. Reached his wet arm out, cool air receiving it with a bite. He brushed a thumb up against a single delicate petal. The beauty, the soft daintiness of it reminded him of his mother. Once, when he was much younger, he remembered classical music playing on the top table over at grandma's house. The three of them had just finished baking a big batch of snickerdoodle cookies. Eric had to have been barely three at the time. At some point they all went up to the attic where there were old clothing and jewelry and June changed into a pastel pink gown and started twirling in it. The gown flowed for ages and as she turned round and round it enveloped her, blossoming like a tulip around her waist. Her smile wide and her hair healthy, long, and flouncing. It was one of the few memories he had formed of her actually being happy. He named the flowers outside the window, June. They deserved to be seen and if they had awareness they should be honored to name after his mother.

He swallowed hard already missing her. That's what bothered him so. Missing her. But, he wasn't scared. The task at hand didn't feel daunting. Raising his brothers in the middle of nowhere among beasts and the natural elements. No. For this was a world which he was familiar with. Kindred spirits: the soul of nature and he. It was a thing he loved and enjoyed. A thing that inspired him beyond anything in town. Anything among the humans. In their old lives. He didn't assume boredom would overtake their minds or drive them insane. There was plenty to do. This was their new home and it would be perfect. They would take care of each other and it and have dominion over the soil and the creeping creatures. They would survive. Be fit and be wise. They would be the alpha males of the forest. They had to be. There was no way out.

Then he realized why his knee had stopped hurting as badly. He was adjusting to his environment. His fight mode already in full drive and with no chance of stopping. This time he wouldn't dissolve into whimpers or fear that his daddy's ghost was coming back to attack him with the ax. This was an environment where only the strongest survived and resilience was key and he had what it took and he would teach his brothers to have it too. They were alpha males.

Eric looked down at the flowers, the June Flowers. Could hear his mother's voice echoing in his head to the sight of her twirling happily and freely in the gown like a tulip:

"One day…" She echoed. "Eric you'll have children of your own and you'll realize how fulfilling that it is to just know that they're okay. You'll see that it will become the meaning to your life. When you have cubs I'll be there with you. I'll see it. You just won't see me... As long as you remember that you are smart, special, and…you are a king my darling. Never forget. You and your brothers are the best thing that ever happened to me. You'll understand that type of love and passion one day."

The words would echo in Eric's mind for weeks, then months, then years. Years that morphed into a decade plus some. They were among some of the last words he would ever hear and never forget. And it might have stayed that way…

Additionally, there was another voice he simply couldn't forget. The nature show narrator and his robust voice capable of making one feel the warmth of his breathe through the television screen. There was just a way about the way he spoke. And what he spoke with all its essential meaning to life. Such as, "The miracle of reproduction. The meaning of life and living for the alpha male."

Eric knew in every meaning of the word he and his brothers would embody the characteristics of the alpha male…for life.

No matter what.

# Chapter 2: I Wanna Feel the Heat with Somebody

*14 years later ~ October 15, 1994*

In a quaint little town, revitalized and renovated from the ground up was the city center, the town Plaza, made up of a collection of shops, cafés, eateries, diners, baby stores, a dance studio, and the five Screen movie theater was just opening for business for the day. Owners of the cafés were already in preparation to feed the caffeine addicted of Downers Grove.

It took 14 years to spruce up the old town-of-the-in-between, Downers Grove, and yet here it was brightened and lightened like restored photographs in a scrapbook. The city still had its landmarks: the old textile mill in the south, the historic Heisenberg High School in the east, the never changing billboard for the world's best costume designer Downers own Angelica McCord to the north, and of course the Halo Mountains to the west. Other than those tells Downers had been given a glow up that took it from the land of in-between to the city of wholesomeness, quirky artistic charm, a respite topped with cozy, small town pleasantries.

The baker in the back of the house of Ashley's Café who made all the pastries for the breakfast crowd and French loafs for the paninis for the lunch crowd was elbow deep in her second batch of dough for the third and fourth batch of sticky buns. The bubbly British borne baker would be kneading for another six minutes. To get the dough nice and smooth just like the morning Grovers on the go wanted. The shop keepers would be making there way over soon for the morning Sip and Dip Delight which was a special the café had every morning for years. It offered a $2 off discount if anyone bought a café drink with a pastry to dip in it.

Strolling down the glossy, charcoal colored cobblestone road known as Sweet Pique Lane, the main vein of Downer's Grove, a route she had taken since childhood, 16-year-old, Seraphim "Sierr" Ruth Blake made her way into town. She often went by a shorthand anagram of her angelic first name. "Sierr" which was pronounced *See-air*. Brushing a lock of her naturally curly two-tone chocolate brown and golden blond hair out of her face, she was glad her thigh high boots, chestnut leggings, thick and loose sweater dress the color of the fallen gold autumn leaves, and plum colored scarf for added accent all managed to keep her snug in the nippy Fall breeze. The cool air bit her thighs, only the little bit of them that were only cover by leggings not stuffed into her boots or covered by her dress.

She smiled at fellow Grovers she passed on the road. Bowed her head and said "Good Morning" to Mr. Jennings the Carpenter and home improvement man who gave her a friendly waved as he swept the welcome mat in front of his housewares stores, smiled at Mrs. Carter who was shining the windows of her tiny antiques store from the inside, and waved to Tabitha Swoon, 17, who did what she did second best, exercise religiously.

Tabitha did yoga by the water fountain on the park lawn across the street from the town Plaza. Tabitha was a busy body if there ever was one, but lacked the attention span and patience for high school which is why she recently dropped out with only her senior year left. She was only 1 1/2 years older than Sierr, but always seemed the same age every year. She spent the same amount of time and energy, if not more, obsessing over the latest celebrity gossip, keeping herself up to date on the hottest trends, and chasing after handsome men may they be fellow Grovers or visitors. In fact chasing men no matter how available or unavailable was the thing she did best. No man she ever pursued, thus far, ever made it past her glance without first being pulled in by her aura.

Sierr couldn't help, but chuckle at the sight of Tabitha quickly sashaying in her Jane Fonda style workout ensemble and a pair of fuzzy socks across the street. Her natural ruby red hair flouncing with every step.

"Hey! Femme Fatale."

Sierr sighed. She always kind of hated the nickname Tabitha gave her in school, but she didn't have the heart to tell Tabitha to stop. With Tabitha's sensitive disposition and emotionally fragile nature. Sierr could remember a time when Tabitha broke down in tears when she couldn't make the perfect batch of cookies for a long gone boyfriend who she insisted was "The One". Then there was the notorious breakdown of '91 where Tabitha wailed and sobbed at the realization that she wouldn't be able to get the pencil pager from the En Vogue Music video with savings from her allowance.

*Just then it dawned on Sierr, didn't Femme Fatale loosely mean lesbian? Good heavens as if the male gender didn't ignore her enough. The last thing she needed them thinking was that she swung the other way.*

"Good morning, Tabs. Stretching?"

"Absolutely. You know my hip flexors just drive me aaabsolutely crazy. Tension never does me any good no matter what form or location it's in. I need a tension free existence! I need a clear mind and physical flexibility. I want my hips to move from side to side without catching or popping. I mean how much good would that be if when I finally get married and I can't even manage to ride the hubby like a horse? What a disappointment I'd be as a wife! He'd probably have an affair. I swear I'm not going through all the effort to find my soulmate just to disappoint him as a wife and have him cheat on me! I mean what good is it to have experience in the bedroom if you can't even used all you've gathered on your own husband!?"

That was the other thing about Tabitha. She was endlessly worrisome and lacked a basic verbal filter.

Sierr found herself sighing again, "Tabitha."

"Oh that's right you haven't yet have you. Ha! You probably don't even know what I'm talking about!" Tabitha laughed.

Sierr blinked away the sensation to roll her eyes. She wasn't nearly as naive as people thought her to be just because she hadn't shared herself with anyone yet. Irritated the hell out of her that they thought she was. The truth was she might have known more about sex and thought more about it than her peers, but that was her little secret.

Tabitha continued to ramble on about something. Sierr scolded herself for not listening, but then again she had to choke back a laugh. This girl literally never stopped talking. The last thing she heard Tabitha say was something about trying out aerobics. "Well they say that water exercises do help your mobility and provide a certain buoyancy that is good for your joints while working out and still getting resistance." Sierr rejoined the conversation seamlessly.

"Oh I know! But, if I do water aerobics I'd have to drive all the way to Wilson county which is the only place nearby that actually has a water aerobics center. Do you know that, that's more than 50 miles away from here? Oh, it's too much. Too much. Uh-uh. I can't do that. Can you imagine? I'd have to drive there for almost an hour. Work-out. Loosen up. Then sit in my little LadyBug for an hour back." Tabs loved calling her Ladybug car "My Little LadyBug". She did it all the time. Thought it was cute. If Sierr had to decide if it was cute she would say, *yes*, as opposed to *no* it wasn't cute, but Tabitha had done it for so long that it had gotten slightly annoying. "Anyway, if I had to do all that driving I'd be all tense again before I even reached Downers! Besides you gotta pay for those classes."

"Well…I think you can do aerobics workouts on your own in a below ground pool, right?"

A look of eureka flashed across Tabitha's face, "OhMehGawd! Sierr you're a genius!"

Sierr couldn't help, but laugh as they both stepped into Ashley's Café. Sierr swung open the squeaky glass door with a steaming hot coffee mug and the words Ashley's Café painted on the front in pink, blue, and green. Sierr always though some shade of brown would be befitting for a coffee shop logo, but whatever. As long as the brew was strong Ashely could have had a soiled monkey as the café's logo and Sierr wouldn't have batted an eye.

"Good morning, Sierr!" Ashely said in her silvery voice studded with the pronunciation traits of her Puerto Rican accent. Her oval face peaking out behind the frame of chestnut brown smooth as butter hair, a lush fluff, which swept her knobby elbows covered by a burnt sienna cardigan. "You're usual?"

"Yes, please. Good morning." Sierr walked up to the counter. By force of habit she subconsciously dug in her purse for the $3.20 needed for her daily breakfast on the go.

"And what can I get for you, Ms. Tab-ee-tha?" Ashley said crooked over, looking almost upside down, eyeing the most jumbo sticky bun to grab with her tongs for Sierr. She tap, tap, tapped the tongs together as she always did without even thinking about it as she peered into the goodie box. Reached her arm into the glass case where all the baked goods lie in wait for hungry customers. Some customers were on the go like Sierr and others where easing into their day like the patrons delicately sipping from slightly steaming colorful mugs and reading from novels and newspapers in window seats around the panoramic building. On the weekends Sierr was one of the others. Sometimes she had a novel in hand – something inspirational, mysterious, fantasy, or urban fantasy – or some class work she was finishing up on.

"Oh um nothing for now. I think I'll come back la…oh is that snickerdoodle cookie cake?!" Tabitha perked up spotting the cinnamon sugar cookie vanilla buttercream icing coated cake under the glass dome of the edge of the ledge on the outside wall of the kitchen.

"Oh yes it is." Ashely said following Tabitha's eager gaze.

"May I have a slice?"

"Sure." Ashely went to cut into the cookie cake.

"So *aerobics*!" Sierr tried to spice up the word aerobics hoping to somehow make it seem like she was just as excited about it as Tabitha was.

"OhMehGawd. Is that Kerry Thomas?" Tabitha whispered subtly pointing at a young handsome man sitting at a booth alone. Two different coffees by his side.

"Who?"

"Son of Uber successful Dr. Horacio Thomas psychopathologist, of course." Tabitha eyed the dashing young man a few years older than she studying something on his open laptop with laser focus. She hisses the words "of course" as if Sierr had studied up on all the men in a 100 mile radius with an annual net profit of over $300,000 the same way that she did and was somehow having a brain fart.

Sierr looked at the son of ~~Mister~~ *err* Dr. Whoever and thought his eyes looked used to squinting at things with laser focus. He couldn't have been anymore than 24-ish and yet he had crows feet already to set up house and assume the permanent zip code of his upper facial region. "I don't know. I don't even know who Dr. Whoever is. Who's that?"

"He lives here. He became one of the main investors that changed Sleepy Hollow from a dingy old trailer park into the quaint little town we know and love today."

"Wait Sleepy Hollow?" Sierr frowned.

"Downers Grove." Tabitha said slowly. "Gawd, it's like you don't even live here."

"I've never heard this town be called Sleepy Hollow."

"Girl, you are kidding. Angelica McCord costume designs supplies all the best Halloween costumes around the country and we are known nationally for being one of the most standout towns to turn *Halloweentown* in October."

"Is…Is this Sleepy Hollow nickname something Angelica came up with? Cause you know the closest that she lives to earth is up in the clouds?"

"Uh, Yeah?"

"I see now." Sierr sighed. "So, whose the son? What's he do? Is he training under his father or something?"

"No, I bet he's a journalist. I heard that Dr. Thomas, you know Thomas, Sr.-"

Sierr couldn't help, but notice that Tabitha called Dr. Thomas, Thomas, Sir., as if Kerry Thomas was a Kerry Thomas, Jr., but he wasn't. Dr. Thomas' first name was

Horacio which means Dr. Thomas was not Dr. Horacio Thomas, Sr. at all he was just Dr. Horacio Thomas whose son's name was Kerry. Which means there is no Kerry Thomas, Sr.... Sierr felt herself frowning. *Pay attention, Seraphim.* She told herself.

Tabitha was still talking, "....So, anyway I heard that even though it was against his father's wishes, Kerry just graduated with a degree in journalism from Howard University and now look. He's here!"

"Sooooo?"

"Soooooo, this comes as we approach the 14th anniversary of the Beckwith Family going missing on that faithful day when they left their home and never returned."Tabitha said in the same creepy voice of a Horror movie trailer narrator.

"Oh I've heard about that family."

"Well of course! Some used to say that they had gotten glimpses of abusive, alcoholic father Beckwith's ghost standing in the window of their old house before it was demolished in the 80s to clear the land for the Mangroves. Others say they saw mother Beckwith weeping among the weeping willows of Dorlows pond, mourning the death of her boys at the hands of her tyrant of a husband."

"I though the boys were never found? I thought none of them were ever found. Alive or dead?"

"No one ever claimed to see the boys ever even leave the house that faithful day. The oldest, Eric Beckwith, was just six-years-old when they all went missing. He and the twin two-year old boys Luke and Lyle are all presumed dead. Legend has it though that father Beckwith was abusing them and that is why mother Beckwith always seemed to be hiding something and that the boys finally got tired of the abuse, lured both of their parents into the Woods by sneaking away and hiding there earlier that morning, and when the parent finally found them the boy's systematically tortured and killed them both as revenge for their tragic childhood."

"Oh come on the two-year-olds too?!" Sierr laughed. "Little twin killers in diapers?"

Just then Ashley returns with Sierr's coffee and Tabitha's slice of cake.

"Thank you. All the Best!" The girls echoed to Ashley before going on their way. Sierr got another glimpse of Kerry Thomas before exiting the café. She didn't know that he'd noticed her, but just the same...he did.

The girls wait to cross the street periodically nibbling from their pastries. "They say Eric was always the leader and that even though the twins were unable to speak that somehow they always managed to communicate with each other and their big brother. Recently, two unkept men who looked exactly alike were seen standing together on the other side of the mountain. They were about the age that Lyle and Luke would have been by now and just like that the old tale of the lost Beckwith family is piquing the interest of journalists and reporters again. This time they say they they'll get to the bottom of the case, but who knows. I bet that's why Kerry Thomas is here. Cut his chops on bringing clarity to a local mystery."

"You don't supposed those boys are really alive do you? I bet their parents took them somewhere far away from here."

"Where? And why is there no record of them? Some say that father Beckwith has some kind of deep dark murderous secret. He had all these bizarro cryptography writings on the wall of the basement of their old house and no one knows what they mean to this very day!"

"You sure do know a lot about this."

"Well yeah. You know what the headline on the story was where I got all this info…Muscular Lumberjack Men Lurking In Forest. And all I could think was how hot would that be? You could imagine doing something like camping and or skinny dipping in the lake and suddenly some sexy woodsmen are there standing, waiting suddenly aroused by your nakedness? And suddenly erotic thoughts and urges are awakened in you, you walk towards the hot, sexy wild men and start kissing one of them as sweat drips down his chin and onto his hard nipples. All the while other one takes you from behind…."

"Okay. Okay. Okay. Okay. I have one objection. Do you really think Muscular Lumberjack Men Lurking In Forest mean anything good? I hear serial killer. Serial rapists even. I see violent rape ending with your head on a stick somewhere and maybe cannibals eating what's left of you."

"Oh geez you are morbid!"

"I'm being realistic!" The girls stroll across the street and stop in front of The Heat Dance Studio. Michael Jackson's "Beat It" could be heard blaring inside.

"Just allow yourself to fantasize. Dirty wild men. Attracted to you. Horny as hell. No other women for miles. Three of them ready to control and satisfy all at once. It's pretty friggin' hot."

"I wonder how they could have killed both of their parents being so young?" Sierr pondered thoughtfully.

"Abused people are capable of many drastic things if those things could set them free. I mean what would you do if you were being held captive by an abusive person?"

"Hmm. I guess six-years-old is old enough to commit desperate acts, but why disappear into the forest?"

"I can find all of this out when Kerry and I go out on our date."

"Excuse me!?"

"Our date."

"I'm sorry you haven't even spoken to him yet."

"Oh but I will! And he'll say yes I mean c'mon. It's me. I have to go home and get ready."

"For what? Your *unplanned* date?!"

"Noooo, I have to get ready to come back and ask him looking impossibly fresh looking and in bright colors that compliment my red hair! He'll have to say yes to me. He'll have no other choice." Tabitha flipped her hair and bounced back towards the Carrs Development where she lived. It was a housing development with nearly identical skinny three story tall red brick row homes. Carrs was closer to the city center, than the Mangroves the upper class housing development where Sierr lived with her family, and it offered affordable and also temporary housing options to newcomers and those on a budget.

Sierr couldn't help, but shake her head in awe of Tabitha. That girl got any guy she wanted. Sierr had never been confident enough to pursue guys and felt she had never been desirable enough to be pursued. She peaked at her skinny wrist watch and opened the door to the studio "Beat It" was just going off as she stepped inside.

"Heyyyy! Tried to wake you up earlier to say "bye," but noooo as always somebody ignored me." Luxury "Lux" Judith Blake, Sierr's older sister who was as unique as her naturally tightly curled naturally tan and sandy blond hair so big and full it was twice the width of her shoulders and hung just above her tiny waist. She was future choreographer in her head and had the moves, long legs, and education in public relations to make that dream a reality. Although, she had plans to be an entrepreneur she never quite planned on moving away from home that would mean she pay rent and that would mean less shopping money which is why at 21 she still occupied her childhood bedroom next to Sierr in their childhood home. She did a jig across the hardwood dance floor in four-inch high stilettos towards Sierr. She threw a leg straight up in the air and did a twirl all just to turn the volume down on the stereo.

"I needed my beauty sleep." Sierr said like a dramatic, old Hollywood actress.

"Yeah cause *that* sounds like you." Lux laughed.

"I have the $15 I said I would pay you back for." Sierr dug in her purse for it.

"Girl, keep your money." Lux said slipping out of her heels and massaging her feet.

"But, you bought that book for me the other day when I didn't have enough."

"I know."

"I said I'd pay you back."

"I know. I bought it cause you're my little sister not for you to pay me back. *Dizzy girl.* So, what are you up to today?"

"Well first and foremost I satisfied my caffeine addiction. Most important thing."

"Totally."

"Then school. Choir rehearsal with Carmen and Willow. Then back home."

"Cool. I'll be here giving the best of myself to the privileged few in Downers Grove who get to see me at my best."

"Dancing?"

"Not just dancing, dancing to my girl, Whitney!" Lux turns on "I Wanna Feel the Heat With Somebody".

Marnie Hilton, co-owner of The Heat with Lux, strolled onto the dance floor in leggings and a loose sweater throwing her hair into a messy bun. She and Lux sang along with Whitney for the first few lines of the song. Sierr watched and smiled. They try to get her to join in, but she just shakes her head. She hated being so shy, but she just couldn't help it. She always somehow felt naked in public. Tried not to let it dictate her every move, but sometimes she could feel how hot her cheeks got with embarrassment if she ventured too far outside of her comfort zone. It made her even more uncomfortable and timid.

"We're offering a new set of classes to newlyweds and married couples and the whole boot camp will be bookended with the music of Whitney!"

"Love songs." Marnie said with a dance.

"Dance songs." Lux said doing a random split.

"And everything in between." Marnie did the t pose in a twirl.

"All to highlight the romance in love!" Lux said.

"Well I bet it'll be fun." Sierr chuckled.

"Oh it will. If these courses go well. I'm sure Marnie and I will introduce more courses for different groups of people! College students! Exotic Dancing! New mommies like a offer a mommy makeover workout regimen sort of thing."

"Ooh! College student discounts!" Marnie exclaimed.

"Oh write that down." Lux growled playful.

"On it."

"Put me down for Exotic Dancing!" Sierr winked.

"Don't think I won't, sis." Lux arched her eyebrow.

Sierr chuckled, "Hey, I gotta get going."

"Sure, use your $15 and get yourself something new to read." Lux suggested stretching on the floor, effortlessly laid on her left side, brought her right leg up parallel to her head, hooked it behind her neck, and lazily threw her arm over her impossibly limber limb just kind of hung out in that position for a while. Looked so chill like she could taken a nap just like that..

"Maybe I will. Toodles." Sierr threw the door open.

"Toodles." Lux replied.

Hours later scarfing down lunches made by their mothers, or in Willow Koi's case her stay-at-home father, Sierr caught up with her closest friends. Both Willow and Carmen Cameron Danahue were fellow Downers, members at the local Living Waters Baptist Church, and avid readers.

"You're not really considering it are you?" Carmen winced at Willow in her silvery high-pitch voice.

"Why not?" She replied. "It's a part-time job and I need experience in some kind of a fashion house if I am every going to be a designer in New York like I've always wanted. This could be a good opportunity for me. Who knows where it could lead?"

"When do you start?" Sierr asked.

"Mid October." Willow replied biting a blueberry in her lunch perfectly in half.

"But, that woman is so….odd." Carmen sighed.

"Angelica McCord is fascinated by her own imagination. That's all. She's just a lonely old lady who wants to feel amazing, and dazzling, and important." Willow said.

"I think she's just 50." Sierr pipped up.

"Right. An *old* lady." Willow responded with the utmost innocence.

"She is important. She was once the costume designer for The Lord of the Rings! Elijah Woods knows her name. She doesn't have to act like a quack to get attention. She just really *is* a quack!" Carmen added.

"I heard that she's trying to turn Downers Grove into some kind of Halloween town. At first I couldn't figure out why, but after I thought about it I realized what her intentions are. She wants this place to be in a constant state of Halloween so that people will wear her designs all year long." Sierr suggested.

"That fame whore." said an annoyed Willow.

"Congrats. You already sound like a disgruntled employee." Sierr grinned.

"Don't say "whore"." Carmen scolded. "Think of the hypocrisy."

"Lord, forgive me." Willow shut her almond shaped eyes tight. Exhaled through her shapely, full, pouty lips. "It's hard striving to be Christ-like this early in the morning...and around other humans."

"It's noon." Carmen, the natural early bird if there ever was one, replied.

"And I'm still asleep." Willow wrinkled her blemish free fair forehead skin.

"It's always easier to be Christian in solitude. Much less temptation." Sierr nibbled an orange slice from her lunch box. "To be fair. Angelica does live and breathe off attention."

"No, *that's* someone who lives and breathes off attention." Carmen said.

Just beyond their table the girls' gaze fell upon Abby Windsor. Petite and pretty, blond and buxom, she was the most popular girl in the school. Not because of her rancid personality or her penance for throwing away supposed friends and even boyfriends for not making it their life's mission to serve her. No, she had what the boys called "The Goods." Even more than that she was willing to share them. Rumor has it she gave up The V in middle school which had given her plenty of time to get good at the act of sex. Rumor had it she gave great head.

Seraphim steered clear of her not for fear of her passive aggressive behavior and all the subtle daggers she threw to her peers, but because she and Sierr were like oil and water. Sierr knew that no good could come of her getting tangled up with the likes of Abby Windsor. There was no outcome involving he two of them socializing which could end well. Sierr couldn't look past the seediness of Abby Windsor or the multitude of disagreeable things that Abby was not above, such as bullying, like many of the boys and girls of her school could. Sierr knew those people in her school only looked past Abby's behavior because they wanted to be a part of the in-crowd which was something Sierr never needed or desired. Even if she did she'd never sell her soul to Abby for it. Although Abby's in-crowd, also known around Heisenberg as The Controversy Crew, had already claimed its share of souls.

It would have been nice; however, if only the boys were not so absorbed in getting head from Abby and maybe noticed her at least once. Not that she'd bite, but the mere opportunity to bite would be nice. Why was it Abby was considered the hot one just because she put her boobs on display when Sierr had bigger boobs than most girls in her school? Abby was curvier in the hips than Sierr was, but Sierr was long and lean. Granted Sierr's hips just did not move the same way that Abby's did when she walked. From side to side like a wave of soft flesh dancing slowly from left to right ever so seductively. Abby was beautiful sure, but so was Sierr. Yet Abby always got attention and all Sierr ever got was ignored.

*Just a little attention would be nice.* Sierr thought to herself. Watching everyone else watch Abby walk by. Then she had a thought that gave her the resolve she needed. She remembered what her mother had told her over the years that, "Not all attention is good attention." Here she was craving thirsty male eyes to be all over her and there was a good chance she wouldn't even know what to do if she had it. Furthermore, she didn't want to do anything even if she had the chance. Not right now at least. She had plans for her life. None of which involved getting distracted by the opposite sex. She needed to stay focused.

Soon lunch was over and Sierr was sauntering into her Critical Thinking (CT 2470) class. Other students gripped about the class which demanded that they actually think further than manning controls on their Nintendos or picking out shoes to wear that matched their outfits. However, Sierr thought it to be interesting when her classmates were not making it a point to be stupid or antagonistic. The main instigator of problems in CT 2470 was Damian Getchum. The current other half of Abby Windsor. *Abby and Damian the Reigning Queen and King of The Controversy Crew.* He would make it a point to rub his relationship with Abby in the face of Mr. Windsor...the teacher of CT 2470.

Damian would always put his arm around Abby's shoulder or rub her inner thigh when Mr. Windsor was looking in their direction. If only Damian knew that while he was jumping through hoops to satisfy Abby's wishes to assert herself over her dear old daddy that she was cheating on him with Jedediah, his teammate on the football team. If only Abby knew that her dear old daddy could care less about her childish games or any of her oodles of off-putting personality traits. What a monumental, mind numbing waste.

Hailey Francesca, the school anti-social outcast, waltzed into the classroom late and did not even seem concerned. She always looked like death incarnate with all that black on. She identified as a Romantic Gothic, everyone really just considered her the school's sexy goth girl. Her black tops were either tight while covering everything, loose enough to hang off her bare shoulders, or low cut enough to tempt, but leave the details of her tits up to the imagination. Her black bottoms were either flowing skirts, skirts with a split up the back, front, or side, shorts, or jeans with holes in them in all the right places. It was possible that she dressed that way because it made her feel confident or maybe she just liked to tempt the boys to get hot for a girl they would never have a chance to bed. Either way she had no desire to make friends with anyone at school and certainly was not a participant of hookup culture. Some said she was asexual. A lesbian even. She never gave her peers the satisfaction of thinking that she cared about their opinion of her and never intended on offering an explanation. The truth was she just wanted a man who challenged her, an intellectual, who had heart and soul, and artistic interests like herself. Not one of the goofy, unkempt, overgrown little boys she was constantly forced to be around at Heisenberg High.

Sierr was surprised to see that Mr. Windsor didn't bat an eye when Hailey entered his classroom late. Usually tartiness was his ultimate pet peeve. Instead once Hailey's black fabric covered butt touched her seat in the back of the class, Mr. Windsor silently stood from his chair. Sierr always noticed how good looking a man he was especially to be a middle aged father. Even more to be a middle aged father of a stressful child like Abby Windsor. Daddy Windsor's muscles were obvious through his button downs. Broad shoulders, a tapered waist, and strong back all looking as good as ever. His thick quadriceps popped in his trousers as he lifted his body from his chair. That deliciously well-endowed flaccid penis bulging in his pants like always.

Sierr was definitely a habitual cock gawker. Did not have a clue what the exact age was when she started noticing men from the waist down, but knew it had been since childhood. There was something ticklish and comforting about seeing male genitalia in some form or another. Watching men's penises move inside of their pants as they walked, adjusted their hands in their pant pockets, or sat gapped legged made her feel all bubbly inside. In addition to that, there was something rather empowering about knowing what a man was working with even if she'd never have a piece...not even the tip. In fact, Sierr had unintentionally mentally cataloged the penis size of almost all the men she frequented in life from school, to the Arboretum, to church. It was a lovely catalog indeed. Perhaps there was something in the water around Downers? One thing was certain, to Sierr, Daddy Windsor could have easily been the catalog's centerfold. She considered for a moment if he was the reason why she liked CT 2470 so much?

The somehow relaxing hollow tap, tap, tapping of Daddy Windsor's chalk hitting the chalkboard filled the room as he introduced the lesson for the day by writing its title on the chalkboard.

Slowly he wrote the words: *Irrational Fear?* He had the swirliest letters. The most beautiful penmanship Sierr had ever seen. Hers was pretty too, but only if she kept a steady hand and gave each letter aesthetic attention.

"What are your initial thoughts on irrational fear?" He sat back down in his chair, leaning back the way he always did. His abs flat with every exhale of his breath and curved out with every inhale. His glare was always sharp and his inhales always stifled like he was only tolerating the teenagers, his job, his life. Like he never quite wanted to be where he was at, at any given time. Like he was always right on the brink of saying, "To hell with it all" and walking off into the sunset with he, himself, alone finally at peace and away from the drama of high school, a dull life, a loveless marriage, and a daughter who made it a point to show him that she did not care about him or herself for that matter. Why else would she make it a point to cause such unrest around herself? Why else would she isolate herself from true affection in return for fake pleasantries from jealous peers? Why else would she subject herself to the likes of Damian Getchum?

Daddy only ever seemed to find solace in teaching the most teachable students of the class. Sierr and Hailey were two of those most teachable students and he always managed to have the patience for them.

"Alex?" Daddy Windsor asked.

"Huh? Oh, um. Irrational fear. I, uh, I guess phobias would constitute an irrational fear." Alex replied.

"Okay. Well, if someone has experiences a venomous snake bite for example and they have a phobia of snakes. Would you really consider their fear irrational?"

"Uh is the answer no?" Alex said a look of fear crossing over his broad features.

"Alex." Daddy Windsor sighed readjusting his legs behind his desk. "I've said in this class before I'm not trying to get any of you to feed me a "right answer" I just want you to develop your ability to think critically and logically. What do *you* think?"

"Well why did you come back with...."

"Why did I come back with what? What did I come back with?" Daddy Windsor threaded his hands together on his lap.

"With...with...." Alex stammered nervously beginning to sweat.

"A challenge? Your own opinions should be able to survive a challenge....unless..." Daddy Windsor trailed off.

"Unless?" Alex asked confused.

"Unless." Daddy Windsor tried to coax the revelation out of the poor boy.

"Unless. Uuumm." Alex's voice quivered. "I…I…I change my mind. I…I agree with you now." He surrendered pitifully.

"Can anyone explain why I said "Unless"? Please." His 'please' was a please of desperation.

Hailey crossed her legs in her slinky black skirt a split up the side. She tilted her head to the side and her jet black hair most of which was pulled up in a tight, slick bun, besides two pieces that hung deliberately in her face, caught the gleam from the afternoon sun as it came through the west facing windows of the classroom. "You said 'unless' because a person's opinion should be able to withstand a challenge unless their opinion is flawed or under evaluated."

"Yes, Hailey." Daddy Windsor replied softly also crossing his legs. "Anyone else have any ideas?"

"I think an irrational fear would be a fear that came to be from believing in rumors. You know things that people say that have no bases." Seraphim stated.

"Oh like believing in God?" Damian smirked.

"No, that's not what I'm talking about." Sierr squinted already annoyed by the implication that she was not rational for being a person of faith.

"Oh, Damian stop you'll make the Jesus freak get her panties in a bunch." Abby sneered.

"Abby, a person can believe in God and be perfectly rational." Daddy Windsor asserted.

"You see I disagree with your thinking Mr. Windsor. Because you see there is no proof that God exists so then a person who believes in God shouldn't be taken as serious. If anything they should be taken as seriously as fortune tellers or the house at a casino. They portray and believe in a façade." Damian said.

"You are wrong on so many levels." Sierr said.

"Oh yeah?" Damian snorted. "Oh and I guess you're going to tell me how I'm wrong now? You?"

"Why yes I am. You just stated that there is no proof that God exists, correct?"

"Uh yeah! That's the truth."

"Well now why would you assume that that's truth? You must not be entirely familiar with the scientific research surround proof of the existence of God."

"Yes, I am."

"You are!" Sierr exclaimed surprised he would accidentally admit that there is proof of God.

Hailey snorts in the background.

Damian corrected himself, "I mean yes, I am aware of the *pseudo* science that so-called "believers" have used to say that there is proof of a god."

"So, do you know that Sir Issac Newton, Stephan Hawking, and Albert Einstein are all in agreement that the universe could not have created itself?"

"The Big Bang actually aligns with scripture so that should help you sleep nice and comfy at night." Damian mocked.

Abby laughed.

"The Big Bang does align with scripture you're right! But, that still doesn't explain why renown scientists cannot explain how the universe is in existence if not for a force outside of the universe."

"What about the Wormhole Theory?" Jax another student with shaggy blond hair interjected.

"The WormHole theory doesn't explain how the Big Bang happened. How Matter which has no thought and which has no decision making ability just "decided" to make something, as in the massive Cosmos, in a matter of seconds rather than remain nothing forever. The Big Bang nor does science explain why any of that happened."

"The Multiple Universe Theory?" Jax suggested.

"That's so far out." Hailey said her chin in her palm.

"Well if we are willing to consider an infinite being we should also consider infinite universes. Should we not?"

"What does one have to do with the other? And one infinite anything doesn't make it more plausible that there are billions and trillions of different universes all operating under different laws of nature."

"What if everyone would be blue!?" An eager voice sounding like Skeeter the Skateboarder said from the back of class.

"Well what about *life...uh...uh...finds a way.*" Another skater dude said in his best, dramatic Jeff Goldbulm as Dr. Malcolm from Jurassic Park impersonation. He and Skeeter crack up in snickers.

Damian turns around in his seat facing the skater dudes. "Actually that's a good point. Nature knows how to support life by itself who's to say that nature didn't begin life by itself?"

Sierr squints, "And itself too? It chose to begin...itself? Since when does that happen even in nature? Since when do things *decide* to come into existence?"

"Since when do people bring their imaginary friends into high school?" Damian snorted.

"Damian..." Sierr began.

"Damian. Lemme ask you something. Where do you believe morality came from?" A dark skinned thin and lean black male student said sitting sideways in his chair. His shoulder length skinny dreadlocks all swept to the right. He was known by his initials, JSF, which were often pronounced as if the letters were a name or word in and of themselves. So not J. S. F., but Jay-ess-ef. In fact most people did not even know JSF's actual name except for his family surname, the Fitzgeralds. The Fitzgeralds were known for providing 30% of the home security systems for the American West. Coming in just third to Maximus Security Company and Secure Me Force Security. The family usually lived well under their means yet even their "cheap" was luxury. Despite that, JSF often dressed like a homeless man, ate leftovers for lunch, and refused to buy anything that wasn't already on sale. He had taken the Fitzgerald frugal to a whole different level. Part of this was because of his constant distrust of the stability of society. To him all resources should be saved for later because he was sure the world was bound to fall apart either economically, biologically, environmentally, or otherwise. Suspicion was a dominant trait in his personality.

"Morality is a farce."

"Ah, so if I came over there and took your belongs and tossed them in trash that wouldn't be wrong?" JSF remarked with a grin.

Damian smirked. "How about this. Why don't you come over here and try and I'll show you how I feel about it."

"Oh Damian. I try to challenge your limited intellect and you resort to your brawny little threats. Explains so much." JSF grimaced.

"Intellect. This coming from the conspiracy theorist!" Damian laughs with Abby and Dallas.

JSF clasped his finger together between his gapped open legs. Sitting one row behind JSF and to his left, Sierr could see him grinning to himself with his full shapely pink lips the color of a bruise on a pink rose, lighter than red, but darker than salmon on his profile. He had a nose on the thicker side that ended in a sharp edge, a narrow bony face, and eyebrows so thick they looked like they could have been braided. They were straight across his forehead with a small break in the middle. He was a little more than a centimeter away from the only the third boy in the whole school with a unibrow. Sierr had always been taller than him through their elementary school years then middle school and 9th grade, over spring break JSF sprouted up like a little brown weed. Now he towered over her at 6'2 and he probably wasn't even done growing yet. Sierr wondered what else on him had grown since spring break than she scolded herself. This was the one male in her life that she felt deserved not to be ogled by her like everyone else. Besides he wasn't her type and...

"You know what I think is an irrational fear, Mr. Windsor?...The fear that the common people have against questioning the stability of our society." JSF finally said.

"Oh Meh Gawd, please tell me this isn't about that Y2K thing?" Dallas Parker, an extended member of The Controversy Crew, rolled her eyes and head all the way around in the front row.

"The whole world could literally be on its last leg and you want to blow it off like it's nothing or it's a fallacy." JSF said bewildered.

"Because it is. Just because we are entering a new century in six years doesn't mean the world is ending." Dallas replied.

"What if I told you only had six years left to live?" JSF tilted his head towards her.

"The year we should really be worried about is 2012. Do you really think the Mayans, people who had every insight into the future possible and the ability to comprehend math better than any other ancient civilization, just decided to simply STOP making calendars past the year 2012? I don't believe it. I'll never believe it! Never. That's the year we're gonna die." Tyler said with the utmost certainty in a tone that bordered on hysteria.

"Any of us could die tomorrow." Hailey hunched a shoulder her brown skin literally glistening like edible gold in dark chocolate under the glowing sunlight coming through the blinds in class.

"Well I mean those of us who are left by 2012." Tyler responded.

"The question is if the Mayans were right about the world ending in 2012..." JSF started.

"We don't even know if that's what they were saying, JSF." Sierr interrupted. They had all known JSF since kindergarten, but she and JSF had always been close living in close proximity as neighbors in The Mangrove and ever since they discovered their shared interests in astronomy and similar dry humor as small children.

"Hang on a minute." He put his palms up in surrender. "IF that's what they were saying then it puts the whole Y2K theory into a whole different perspective. What change will be taking place in the year 2000 and beyond that we have simply misinterpreted as the coming apocalypse?"

"Like are we going to be experiencing some kind of awakening or revelation in the new millennia?" Sierr asked.

"Yes!" JSF snapped his fingers, eyes wide. "Oh or some kind of devastation economically, socially, naturally, politically. Are we going to experience some sort of moral bankruptcy? Is our security going to be shaken? Is our country, as one of the world's superpowers, going to be rattled? Are we going to recognize the world as we know it ten years from now? Will what we are getting frighten us? Or will it be glorious? And if it's glorious will it be glorious for the right reasons? Will we allow our greed and selfishness to brutalize others just to benefit ourselves?"

"I'm sure 'Cherubim' hopes the awakening will be spiritual that way we'll just start doing the t pose up to the sky and worshipping imaginary friends like her." Damian smirked. Light laughs ensued from Abby and a few of her ~~worshippers~~ err ~~followers~~ err "friends".

"Dude, why are you so damn rude?" JSF snapped and shot daggers Damian's way.

"I agree. Let's be mature for once, Damian." Daddy Windsor sighed glared at the boy gently stroking his daughter's knee under her desk.

"Mkay, Mr. Windsor." Damian arched an eyebrow and sarcastically smirked at Daddy.

"And that'll be the last time you call Seraphim outside of her name in this classroom." Daddy added.

Damian was silent until he and Abby shared a snicker directed at Daddy Windsor.

Those two were truly the most disgusting people Seraphim had ever met. She couldn't help, but wince at the back of their heads. The putrid stink of their collective rotten souls seemed to eventually fill whatever room they occupied and she couldn't stand it.

"Continue with your thought, JSF." Daddy tilted his chin up at JSF uncrossing his legs and then crossing them the other way.

"Well I just think that people fear being afraid so much so that we leave ourselves vulnerable."

"What do you mean?" Daddy pushed.

"I mean that we have to be willing to face horrible truths in order to have power over our lives. The powers that be want us to remain stupid and uninformed, but we have the power and resources to make ourselves knowledgeable we have to use it.

We have to question that status quo, we have to question societal norms, we have to question the government!"

"Through conspiracy theories?" A boy in the back asked with a wrinkled forehead.

"No. Not only, but it's a start. 'What does a man who is already looked at like a fool have to loose by telling the truth?' And we should ask ourselves why are conspiracy theories written off outright? What does the media and the government have to loose by examining them to the best of their abilities?"

"Well they would never do that if the source that provided the conspiracy theory was untrustworthy. And a lot of conspiracy theorists have sketchy pasts." London Riley offered.

"And sometime mental health issues." Dallas added.

"Do they?" JSF pressed.

"Yes!" Dallas said exasperatedly.

"Or is that just what the government and the media just want us to believe so that we question the real truth and accept the lies they tell us framed as the truth? Even a mentally ill person can be rational sometimes, some of them even *most* of the time. Do you really think that I should question something a mentally ill person says?" JSF asked.

"I'm doing that right now." Dallas nodded slowly with a grin.

"I'm not mentally ill. You see!" JSF threw his hands up.

"See what, JSF?" Sierr asked trying to show him that she at least didn't think he was a nut...most of the time.

"That people with insight are pushed aside for a reason. And that's your irrational fear Mr. Windsor." Daddy Windsor grinned and silently drummed his thick fingers on his desk. "Fear of the truths that could truly set us free. Free from the bondage of corruption, deception, and potential danger. To be afraid of that IS irrational! Knowledge is power my friends."

The room was silent.

"So, I bet you think the ghost of The Beckwith Brothers are haunting Downers Grove too?" Abby remarked turning around in her chair to face JSF.

"No, I do not." JSF replied. "I don't believe ghosts or any kind of hocus pocus. But, lemme point this out to you. Why is it that all these years after those boys went missing people are still claiming to see figures moving inhumanly fast through the forest up in the mountains? Why is it that the wolves of the Halo Mountains are never seen venturing outside the thicket to hunt deers and the like around this time of year to store up food for the winter anymore? Why is it that the deers don't even venture that far from the forest anymore? Why is it that two unidentifiable, disfigured bodies washed up on the banks of a river fifty miles south of the Halos just days after the boys went missing? And finally why are reporters suddenly all interested in the disappearance of Eric, Lyle, and Luke? What is about those three that the media have been tipped off about in order to come all the way to Downers Grove? What all validity did the tips have? All questions have answers. I just think people should demand to know what they are."

"Stop it. You just want to *sound* cryptic." Abby turned back around in her chair.

"The truth doesn't need to try to sound cryptic. Most of the time it just is. Life isn't always Lip Gloss and Rose Petals, sweetness." JSF threw and arm over the backrest of his chair and slouched with his legs gapped wide.

Abby glared at him from the corner of her eye. Her lips quivering with pure hatred and anger.

# Chapter 3: The Beckwith Brothers

*O*utside a geometric shaped, contemporary home on a hill in west Downers Kerry Thomas drove his forest green, shining 1965 Cadillac Coupe Deville, named C.C., up the long winding driveway up to the front door. All the stars were visible in the night's sky. Night was setting in and the air was perfect. Kerry stepped out of C.C. one black loafer out of the driver's seat then the other. Lifted his briefcase out of the passenger's seat, shut the driver's side door, and walked towards the house.

The glow from the cylindrical lights leading up the driveway made his perfectly slicked back hair shine. He shared many traits with Dr. Thomas. His tall stature, strong bone structure, twinkling green eyes, straight eyebrows, and poor eyesight. Unintentionally they had both picked out the same black rimmed glasses which made them both look like Clark Kent at different stages of his life: handsome young Superman and handsome middle aged Superman.

Just as Kerry raised his finger to stab the doorbell, Dr. Thomas threw the door open. "Kerry." He said with anticipation.

"Dad, hi." A hint of a smile grew on his face before he reminded himself that he and his father weren't really on speaking terms or smiling terms.

"Come in, son." Dr. Thomas stepped out of the way.

Kerry stepped in. Took in the interior of the home. It was a split level with two-story high ceilings and apricot and cream colored marbled floors which his loafers made a satisfying clop, clop sound on when he walked. Through the foyer and he was in the living room. He could see the dining room to his right through an open archway. Stairs to the second floor and the first floor were just ahead of him, but he veered off into the living room.

A cream colored saude sofa and loveseat greeted him a black, brown, and cream cow hide accent chair was to the left of the glass coffee table in the middle of the floor. He sat his briefcase down on the floor with a thunk.

Dr. Thomas walked towards him. Sat down in the seat closest to him and gestures for him to sit down next to him. All animosity between them seemed to be nonexistent. Kerry sat.

"Dad."

"Son."

They spoke at the same time in the same pitch. Kerry pursed his lips allowing his father to speak first.

"Kerry, I want you to know that I'm glad that you're back."

"I am too, dad. I…I've wanted to talk with you."

They sat in silence for a while. Kerry watched the crescent moon slowly reveal itself in the fading blue sky through the floor to ceiling windows. No other lights were on in the room except for two low light lamps on a clown table on the other side of the room and it was rather shady.

Horacio was the one to break the enduring silence. "Kerry, I need you to know that the only reason I was so against what you're doing is because…there is a lot more to this story than you know. I was just trying to protect you."

"What on earth kind of dangers could be coming against me investigating the disappearance of The Beckwith Brothers?"

"You have no idea." Horacio sounded close to the pitch and delivery that Scar had when talking to Simba in The Lion King.

"Well then please give me an idea, dad. Tell me why I should just take your word for it when my entire career could depend on getting answers about the boys. Tell me what the big secret is. Because I know you know. You met them. You knew the family. You have answers, dad, and I need them. Is there some kind of conspiracy here? Some bigger picture? I've looked at the known facts and they've never added up." Horacio repositioned himself in his seat. "Dad, those boys had mysterious ways about them even before they went missing."

"I know."

"I interviewed Eric Beckwith's kindergarten teacher, Mrs. Branch."

"Dear God, Kerry. Why can't you just leave well enough alone?" Horacio huffed in an annoyed and heavy voice.

"Why?!" Kerry begged exasperatedly.

Horacio stood up and walked to the window. Sighed digging his hand deep into the pockets of his tan slacks.

"When I went to Mrs. Blanch's home in Monroe county she greeted me in a pleasant tone. Everyone always said she had a pleasant tone. As soon as I mentioned the name "Eric" the blood drained from her face. She was sitting near a window at the time and the glare of the sun allowed me to see her pupils contract in fear. Terror even. I asked her about why she left Downers Grove. She told me, 'It was just time.' But, I knew not to believe her. I knew she was dodging my question so I asked again. She dodged some more. Finally, I asked her what was her relationship with Eric Beckwith? She paused. Her eyes went blank as she seemed to relive a moment in time, long ago."

Horacio dropped his head before turning it to his son.

"She began. She said Eric was always a behaved child. Said that's what made what happened so much more confusing to her. She said he had the discipline of a much older boy. Much older. He was naturally intelligent. Insightful. Attentive. Calm. One day she said she had seen the school bully push Eric down the stairs at the front of the school. Put a nasty cut on the front of his head. Left a scar too."

Horacio shook his head and pained look crossing his face.

"As she ran to comfort little Eric she said he stood calmly licked away a trickle of blood that ran past his mouth from his brow. Stared the school bully down and started shuttering violently. She thought maybe he was having a seizure or something, but almost immediately the school bully's eyes rolled into the back of his head, he dropped his school books, marched into on coming traffic and was struck by a vehicle. Was dead on impact."

"Kerry, you do not need to get closer to this boy or this story! Don't you see. There are forces involved here that we cannot control and that we cannot pursue. If the media ever found out about Eric…"

"Eric needs to be found out about. Eric is either a danger to society or one of the greatest gifts to mankind. He may be the answer to mental illness, night terrors, Post Traumatic Stress Disorder, Schizophrenia, Sadism. He could be the thing that we have needed to bridge the gap between the subconscious brain and world peace. The difference between the deplorable and the honorable. The cure to corruption in high places and the opening of floodgates of decency and grace all over the globe. All of the horrible things in this world originates in the brain of men and women who Eric's gift could make better. Eric could be the key to making the new millennia a time of renewing and restoration all from the minds of men!"

"How? That damn boy killed his classmate with the blink of an eye…or a stare actually! He is no answer to peace. For all we know he took over his parents minds that day. Commanded them into the forest and slaughtered them like dogs."

"Dad." Kerry stepped towards his father a shadow cast on the bone structure of his face. Made him look suddenly skeletal in the darkness. "The fact that Eric was able to control another person's brain and actions is as significant a discovery as Penicillin, the Dead Sea Scrolls, the secret languages of the Nazis of WWII. This will change history. For better or for worse."

Thomas turned to him peered deeply into his soul. "Kerry, if the world found out that natural mind control exists in the brain of Eric Beckwith and his twin brothers do you really think that the powers that be would wield that power for good?"

Kerry's eyes shifted. "Why do you think his brothers can do it too? No one ever said that before."

Horacio pursed his lips and exhaled. "Because I met Luke and Lyle. Just once."

"Did…did they hurt someone too? When did you meet them?"

"I met them when they were taken for the scans of their brain and neck to check out the structure of their vocal cords. It was one of the many tests they had to diagnose why they could not speak. I was in the same building after an appointment with a different very sick child. As I was leaving I was pulled into an office by a friend of mind, their physician. He said he saw some interesting brain activity in their scans and wanted me to take a look. The twins verbal communication abilities are nil without vocal cords, but somehow the Branch's and Weiner's language processing and language production centers of the brain were 1,000 times more active than that of an average human being. Luke and Lyle were separated for the round of their next tests. And those sections of Lyle's brain remained hyperactive even while he was alone. We couldn't figure out what language he could be producing or processing in a room all by himself. Luke's brain revealed the same thing. The Branch's and Weiner's sections of his brain also remained hyperactive while in a separate room also alone. Then we realized that Lyle was talking to Luke and Luke was responding to him. From the other room. All in silence."

Kerry looked fascinated. "Had Luke or Lyle ever shown violent tendencies?"

"No, Kerry, but they were just infants then! If those twins are alive they are 16-years-old right now and plenty equipped to be violent. Eric, who has clearly shown us that he can be violent, would be 20. You are playing with fire. If you even find these boys and reveal their abilities, before you know it the government will have turned those three into test subjects, extracting their gift, mass producing it, and eventually using it against us. You, me, the people we love. For the most part our government doesn't want "the power of the people". To an extent they need you docile enough and stupid enough to serve them and believe what they tell you. For now they keep us out of the loop as much as they can, they lie to us, they feed us stories they want us to believe, they classify what they never want us to know, but if mind control is a thing of the future they won't need you uninformed all they will need is The Beckwith Brothers."

"Dad. We cannot shudder on the cusp of discovery."

"Kerry!" Thomas growled with frustration and desperation. "When I was in Vietnam journalists tried to exposed the U.S. Government for our actions testing Agent Orange on the natives and POVs of Vietnam and do you want to know what happened to the majority of those journalists? They mysteriously ended up dead or missing. They had good intentions just like you to help the world, to help suffering and struggling people, but greater forces beyond them silenced them forever. Not ten years ago Chernobyl Nuclear Power Plant exploded poisoning the land and poisoning the land's people. But, if those in charge over there had their way the lie that Chernobyl was contained incident with few casualties and few consequences would have continued to have been believed. The few brave soldiers who've tried to and managed to tell the truth about that nightmare have either been killed, died under mysterious circumstances, or have their name on lists."

Kerry knew his father was just trying to warn him, not scare him. Still he felt the need to say, "I won't be afraid to tell the truth."

"Kerry your good intentions just aren't enough. I'm trying to protect you! I've been trying to protect you. That's why I've fought you so hard about not pursuing this story. I know the stories about Eric. I know he was…is special. But, sometimes special things like a beautiful but poisonous flower in a rainforest just need to be left well enough alone." Kerry sighed inaudibly, his conflicted gaze settling on the stars. "He's gone. Let him stay gone. Do you understand? Please. Say you understand."

"I cannot do what you're asking me." Kerry shook his head slowly, tried to break it to his father as gently as he could. He knew this was painful for his father. What he was asking of Thomas was not to let the argument go, but instead to allow his son go up against the powers that be. "I have to investigate the disappearance of The Beckwith Brothers because it will lead me to Eric and it will give me the answers that we need as a country and that science needs globally. He could be the key to our future. Even if he is dead and gone I still need to know where he is. His brain could still be viable. Some enzyme. Some special neuron or protein could still be useful to science and medicine. He just might save us all, dad. Is that not worth the risk? What if my life's work is just beyond those trees?" He tilted his head to the Halo Mountains. The same direction Carson Beckwith's station wagon was last seen driving towards with the boys in the backseat.

"Maybe he doesn't want to be found. Downers formed a citizen's search party to help locate the boys when they went missing. They never found Eric or his brothers. Or their parents."

"But, the sightings. The sightings of mysterious figures in the trees…they are becoming more…common. The boys are up there. I know it."

"And just where are their parents? What have they done with them?"

"What happened to their parents we don't know. Maybe a wild animal got to them and the brothers had nothing to do with it." A hopeful smile grew across Kerry's face. "I want to believe that and it is possible."

"So, they could leave if they wanted to."

"Yes, they could."

"Then why don't they?"

"Maybe thus far they've had everything they ever needed in the wild."

"Why stay so close to home?"

"Could be fear. Could be comfort. Could be a small connection to the life they once had slowly fading into the past like the ashes of a burning tree. So real and so true at one point. After some time ashes float away in the breeze just like the memories of lost children often do."

"Like the memories of *normal* lost children. You shouldn't fool yourself into thinking that you will ever understand The Beckwith Brothers or anything about them or their nature until you know what they did to their parents and who or *what* they are now."

Thomas shook his head slowly, wearily at his son. He hoped, he prayed Kerry wouldn't live to regret his decision to seek out the lost boys of the forest. They were born different. Strange. They hid themselves under the cover of the forest where people like them belonged. Kerry was so sure The Beckwith Brothers held the key to healing and medical breakthroughs, but Thomas knew that sleeping dragons should be left to lie.

# Chapter 4: Untamed Nature

There was still just enough from the sun to see and just enough shade to shield. A doe took cautious steps further out into the meadow. Her head extended low in front of her body. Wide eyes studying the details of the thicket beyond her and behind her flank. Any movement and she would dart back into the cover of the trees. Prance away as quickly as her hoofs could take her. The only reason she had strayed this far, dewy grass. Like a meal and drink all in one. The perfect morning treat.

In her peripheral, she thought she saw a flash of fur dart to her right. She whipped her head in that direction and froze mid-step. Her giant long ears high above her head listening intently. Her heart pounded. Suddenly her instincts were buzzing with alarm. She had ventured too far. She was sure of it. She heard a twig snap in the distance in front of her. She elongated her neck high above her shoulders and stared in that direction ears even more sensitive to stimuli with adrenaline flowing like a river in her veins. The twig snap was light as if it was far in the distance. Too far for immediate danger she calculated.

Movement to her right, but she doesn't see him or hear him. Her senses, refined like a sword of steel from her life growing up in the wild with danger after danger lurking around every corner, blew his cover.

A figure creeping in the thicket. A mere shadow with quick legs and cat like reflexes. He could kill with his bare hands and had the strength and resolve to do so. Blood did not deter him and challenge did not intimidate him. For he was king of the forest. The wolf skin he wore swung with his movements. Helped him blend into the brush. The hollowed out cranium of the animal covered the top of his head and half of his face, but he could still see through the eye sockets. The animal skins left him in shady darkness perfect for stealth stalking and hunting.

With his bow and arrow made from the vine and bark of a once mighty oak, he eased towards his prey. Heel-Toe. Like a cheetah tracking a gazelle his eyes were quick. Cut to the left to make sure the rest of his pack was in place. Cut to the right. No predators hunting him...for now. Cut to the forest floor, he couldn't be foolish enough to step on any branches or twigs and give away his position. Cut to the doe alone in the meadow.

He reached up to retrieve his bow and arrow from the pouch on his back made up of an old, worn, and torn satchel. His back was rippled with muscle his neck thick and hard sweat trickles down already sweat slicked chest hair that covered his strong pectorals and continued down his abdominal muscles and cut lines sculpted by wilderness living. Running for prey, running for his life, observing the nature around him, raising his brothers, teaching them how to forge for nuts, seeds, and berries, perch in a vantage point high in the trees, and how to tame the forest which always tried to overthrow their home. Twisting vines, chopping lumber, tending to the old man's flourishing garden, it was all very physical work. All in the days work of an alpha male.

He could tell she knew he was there. Could feel his presence stalking her in the shadows. He had to act fast. He place the triangle end of the long blood stained arrow into the bow. Took his place. Instinctively he knew…a perfect place. As a boy he could barely fish. Was intimidated by the thrashing of a desperate soul, the red spill of pain felt, and the possibility of failing to accomplish what he set out to do. Kill. Yet, now hunting was a natural act. He did it only when necessary for feeding him and brothers and the pack and that was often. He readied his aim. Closed his left eye. The arrow was an extension of his line vision. Like a part of his right eye. Aim for the heart. He would happily gift her with a quick and painless death.

He drew in a strong, deep breath pulled the arrow back in the strong curve of the bow. Just then the whimper of a puppy dog to his far left. The doe heard it too. She paused frightened. Then bolted to her right.

*Ah Shit.*

To the far left twin Beta Males, named Pedigree and Atlas by their doting and dominating Alpha Male, of the wolf pack of the Halo leaped from the thicket and charged after the doe across the meadow. Grey paws with fur which gradually blended to white, pounded the soil behind him as the predominately female wolves of the wolves pack followed closely behind tongues hanging out the side of their mouths, the sound of short, quick pants and snorts surrounding their cluster.

Eric Beckwith packed away his bow and arrow and silently told Luke and Lyle, *She's coming. Go get her.*

Nearly 50 yards away Luke and Lyle sprang to action in ripped jeans and wearing nothing else, but body hair, sweat, and soil from the earth under their fingernails from foraging for mushrooms the day before. They both ran toward the same direction in hopes of cutting the doe off when she least expected it. They smiled and had belly chuckles with each other never once making a sound or breaking stride and in fact getting faster and faster. Until their legs were just a blur of dull blue denim and beige feet meeting dirt and leaves. 20 mph. 30 mph. 40 mph.

The younger Beckwith Brothers always loved to run. It was freeing somehow. Exhilarating and exciting. Mellowing and Meditative. They would run as fast as they could until they were unable to breathe and collapsed in angel positions in a pile of leaves somewhere struggling to catch their breath. Gasping for air and wiping sweat from their brows. Until one day they grew tolerant of the speed, their lungs expanded further than before, they became more agile, and even quicker. Faster until they were able to run so fast they could have outrun a falcon. They could go on for hours. Days even. Only stopping to replenish with a drink of cool water from the fresh stream.

They could hear the Doe's hoofs galloping through the trees over the sound of their own pounding hearts and steady, controlled breaths. They stopped dead took their places on either side of her path and waited for her to leap between them. Lyle pulled a hunting knife out of his back pocket, Luke would immobilized her.

They waited for seconds in slow motion. She was getting closer as was the pack howling, barking, and panting. Forcing her into the trap. Out of the shadows of the tree canopy she leaped through the air right in front of the twins. Luke lunged for her throwing his arms and legs around her body and throwing her and himself to the ground. She bucked and brayed. Tried to stand, but he was too heavy for her delicate body. He tied a scarf around her eyes to calm her. A mere two seconds later Pedigree charged for the doe and took her from Luke by the teeth. Dragging her a few feet from the force. She bucked. The rest of the wolf pack howled and barked as they went in for the kill.

The doe cried with terror and fear on her side helpless and defenseless.

*Hoooooooooowlllllll.* He called gently. Towering over his brothers and the wolves.

The pack instinctively obeyed their leader and backed away from the crying doe. Eric walked towards her his right shoulder dipping lower then his left with each limping step permanently effected by his childhood fall out the tree. He stroked her head, whispered into one of her giant ears softly, "Shh, my love. Hush, my darling." She stopped crying. Then he began to sing into her ear a song from his mother. A song he never let himself forget from long ago. Pedigree and Atlas both snarled at the doe drooling with anticipation for her meat. Eric hiiiiiiiisssssssed at the male wolves and sat protectively in front of the doe. Pedigree backed up with an antsy whimper. Atlas paced wanting blood. The shuttering doe breathed heavily into Eric's chest. Eric rested his forehead flat on hers. Still singing softly he remove an even longer and wider hunting knife than Lyle's from his tan leather satchel.

He didn't have to open his eyes to know where the knife needed to go to be as humane as possible. He moved his forehead further down her long snout. Extended his arm out and above them both. He kept singing to calm her. Not wanting her to suffer. He gripped the knife in his fist and brought it down hard into her brain. Felt her go immediately limp in his other hand, her snout fell away from his forehead. He gave the knife a good shake just to make sure that she was gone. He removed the knife from her brain and the scarf from her eyes and thanked her. Rested her head on the ground. Lyle approached and kissed her snout. Luke too. Eric stood with his brothers handed Luke his scarf back ran a hand through his tussled chestnut brown, loose curls which framed his face and rested on his bare shoulders. Eric gave him a little smile and he smiled back. *Good work my brothers. We all shall eat for many days now. We have provided for ourselves in a natural way, for which we have been gifted, but like leaders and not followers we took a beautiful life in the most humane way possible. Keep that in your minds forever. Here?*

Luke and Lyle responded by bowing their heads respectively. Their eyes glowing with pride and joy.

*Very good.*

Just then Lyle noticed July, the fluffy white mother wolf of the pack, approach the group with a tiny white ball of fluff curled up and dangling from her mouth. Eric stepped towards July. Knelt down to her. "Sweet girl. My sweet July flower." He patted her head and took the ball of fluff from her mouth. He stood with his back to his brothers and the rest of the pack for a moment. Stroking her fur. So tiny in his arms. He wondered where she could have come from.

Turning to Luke and Lyle. *What do you think we should name her?*

Lyle's eyes got wide as he gnawed at the corner of his finger. He knew Lyle wanted to say, *Puppy!*

*That's not really a name.* Eric replied to the unspoken suggestion. *And stop scratching with your teeth. We talked about this.*

Lyle stopped gnawing, tilted his head to the side curiously. Eric could still only dip his toe into the flood of telepathy that his brothers shared with each other. He had developed the ability to sense some of their occasional unspoken words. Their emotions, responses to his questions, their sneaky little ideas as adolescents to venture further away from the old man's cabin than they were allowed or gorge on all the fresh strawberries in the garden unable to control their urge for more sweet fruit despite the fact that some strawberries needed to stay in order for the plant to keep growing. Eric figured he had adapted to his environment. An environment where his young brothers who could think cognitively, plot successfully, and be lead by curiosity into dangers, but could not speak out or get needed protection from themselves by the only other person who could tame them and teach them the ways of the wild. He knew early that he would have to freely offer and force that protection from themselves upon them.

Beta Female wolf, simply named "A" by Eric, growled hungrily at the corpse of the doe.

*Let's get the deer back home.* Eric said to his brothers.

Luke and Lyle both heaved the doe onto their strong right shoulders and her torso formed a bridge between them. Her limp neck and head flopped around on Lyle's chest as he was in the front taking the lead. The twins carried the doe back to the old man's cabin where the butcher block awaited her. Eric carried the lost pup in his arms. Made her feel safe and warm in the nippy fall air.

Wolf sisters Bee, Cee, Dee, and Eee, all named by young Eric years prior, framed the perimeters of the group and kept watch for bears with their keen sense of smell, tuned ears for hearing even the smallest of sounds, and laser focused eyes. They slinked through the layer of autumn leaves on the ground with their heads on a swivel. Their noses sniffing feverishly through the air.

About a half mile away, the twins entered the gated fence surrounding the cabin first, the pack second, Eric third and last making sure his entire family was together and safe before himself. He locked the gate behind himself. They all then entered the cabin in the same order, subconsciously ducking under the top of the door frame which they had not cleared standing fully erect in years. The boys were far taller than the old man built this place. Their shoulders almost too wide to fit through the door frame without turning their bodies slightly to the side to fit through. After Eric entered he locked the door to the cabin. Two deadbolts and a Bear hatch which he reinforced with extra wood over the years.

The newest member of his family, the little white pup, he knew it had to be lost because no one in the pack was with child. None swollen. None fatter. Like other animals in the forest often got around the time they were about to give birth. Besides none of the females not A, not Bee, not Cee, not Dee, not Eee, and certainly not Mother July had been mated. Mother July's reproductive abilities had seemed to cease when the original wolf pack's alpha male had....*died.* The smell of elevated sexual hormones had not yet wafted on the breeze so Eric knew that none of the females were in heat. He had also noticed that Pedigree nor his tiny brother, Atlas, were particularly frisky. No this could not have been a puppy from this pack.

Luke and Lyle threw the doe on the thick wooden table in the room off the kitchen. Pulled out their hunting knives and started to break down the doe. The pack antsy and salivating scurried, with flurry tails wagging, to surround the table eager for drippings and lost pieces. Tiny tastes of warm, fresh blood and tiny pieces of meat and bone, lost through the butchering process, to savor until the alphas had gotten the top pickings that they were worthy of.

Eric started a fire in the fireplace with one of the old man's many fire-starters. For it would be dark soon and with the chill in the air he, his brothers, and the pack would need light and warmth. He stoked the flame with kindling and a collection of dried moss which he and his brothers had learned, soon after being abandoned in the forest, was best when set out in the summer sun on top of the roof of the cabin for weeks on end. They had also learned to collect and dry as much moss as possible through the summer to keep the fire going all winter long and continued to regimen each year. Young Eric came up with the idea after remembering how the skinny, unwashed subject of a documentary focusing on survivalist living used the same technique to survive the arctic winters of Russia. He had not seen the entire documentary, but paid what attention he could to it one night while trying to tune out the beating of his mother in the other room. Between the distracting sound of each blow and yelp from her lips, he could remember how the man in the documentary made use of everything in nature that was at his disposal to live and find comfort in...unconventional circumstances.

As the fire grew its strength, Eric sat crossed legged on the floor and used the glow to finally get a good look at the puppy. Looked into its eyes and wanted to feel its soul. He lifted the puppy up to eye level. The first thing he noticed was that she was a girl. Eric was glad. The female wolves were always more docile and friendly. Unlike the rest of the wolves in the pack who were mostly grey, speckled grey and white, or dirt brown, this girl was almost pure white except for the small light grey spots only on her back. Her fur soft as a newborn bunny curled up just slightly at the ends on her back, up the sides of her neck, on top of her head, and down her long tail, but went smooth and glossy on the underside of her body, her face, and down her legs. Her ears just as large as a fawn dangled by the cheeks of her narrow elongated face. Everything on her was remarkably thin, narrow, and elongated: her trunk, face, forearms, tail, and hind legs, but not in a sickly way. She didn't seem underfed she was just long especially to be a wolf. Just then it dawned on Eric that this little one might not be a wolf at all. She could be a dog.

"Why did you come find us all the way out here, hmm?"

The puppy squirmed in his hands so big they swallowed her whole. She yawned revealed tiny teeth that made Eric grin. "You'd never survive out there alone."

He cradled her in his arms and smiled down at her. "I'll protect you." She tilted her head curiously at him and looked into his eyes for many moments.

Her gaze held a haunting comfort. Her soul held words unsaid and unknown and carried with it a presence to be felt. The light of the fireplace flame flicked off her eyes making her brown irises appear hazel and translucent all at once. "Pretty Brown Eyes. I think that's what I will call you." He remembered first hearing a song with the words Pretty Brown Eyes in it and a robust melody that he would never allow himself to forget. He had heard it during one of his many trips to the outskirts of other towns surrounding the forest. He and his brothers often ventured into those towns in secret, under the cloak of night, for supplies. His new puppy would be named after the lovely song that he heard on one of those excursions into civilization.

Pretty Brown Eyes held her gaze and with the eagerness of a puppy perked up, hopped to her feet, stood on her hind legs in Eric's lap, put her forepaws in his chest, and examined his face seeming to smile. He kissed her forehead and patted her head.

After a dinner of venison and potatoes from the garden Eric, his brothers, and the pack prepared for bed. Eric threw water on the flame from water Luke and Lyle collected from the stream in an empty flower bed.

Lyle closed all the heavy curtains using the opportunity to look out and inspect the perimeter of the cabin while he did. No giant beast lurking at the moment. At the moment, they were safe and because they were safe he was at peace.

Luke threw salt on blood stains soaked into the wood of the butcher table and any blood stains not licked near clean from the pack as they waited the be fed their dinner.

Luke also placed all the remaining cuts of the doe into the underground cold place under the kitchen. He always thought the old man was rather intelligent for thinking to put a cold place in the floor to keep meat good for a good long while. Of course he wouldn't know what to do with the cold place or the cuts if not for Eric. Luke felt a pang of regret for not being able to get more salt from the old mill in that little old town towards the side of the mountain where the sun rises. Lyle thankfully spotted the old men seeming to notice them and they were able run away as fast as they could, but now it was not clear how they would get more salt to stave off the smell of meat rot. He'd simply never forgive himself if his brothers and the pack would be endangered because a bear or a mountain lion found their little sanctuary all because of his failure.

Just then Luke could tell that his brother was attempting to sneak up on him. Had Lyle not learned that Luke could always feel his close proximity to him? That silly boy. Luke thought. Lyle had the same sense for heaven-sakes! Luke spun around quickly. Lyle grinned approaching his twin with an old, tattered copy of Grey's Anatomy. He opened the book to a page of the sexual reproductive system of a human female with a devious smile.

Luke's eyes rolled in the back of his head. His eyelids fluttering rapidly. Lyle subconsciously did the same in response.

"*What is with you and that picture?*" Luke telepathed like a question and with a laugh.

"*It's beautiful.*" Lyle responded in his mind. "*The giiiirrlll person.*"

"*It's just different.*" Luke casually hunched a shoulder. "*No, hanging organs for reproduction like us. That's all.*"

"*They seem to have balls like we do. They're just on their chests and detached in the middle. I like them there instead. They make me feel good inside.*" Lyle said with a giddiness. "*These are what female people look like. Doesn't that interest you?*"

"*Yeah, I guess. But, meeting a human female would mean leaving home. Going into the city where we'd never be accepted. They all talk you know.*"

Lyle's eyes stopped fluttering. His face dropped along with his shoulders.

"*We know we're happy here. The animals are our friends and we have Eric!*" Luke telepathed.

"*I'm curious about the human females. What if we courted then like the bull deer do towards the doe? They should like that.*" Lyle telepathed with hopeful eyes.

"*I have a feeling people aren't like the animals. You remember daddy.*"

"*Yes. A little. But....how will we ever breed? We're not true Alpha Males until we breed.*"

After a long pause Luke finally said, "*I really don't know about that. Perhaps it's not impossible. Maybe.*"

"*Two males cannot do breeding.*" Lyle frowned.

"*Yes. But, maybe there is a solution here in the forest where we belong and will fair better off that we simply haven't thought of yet. We just need a little...uh...*" Luke sought his memory for the new word Eric had taught him by reading to him from the selection of books from the library. "*Innovation.*"

Eric made it a point to read to his brothers. Teach them how to read. Learn what all they could with limited means and try to make since of all the words and messages in the words. They had what seemed like endless things to read; yet, together they had already burned though each book in the library and the old man had many books. He was a bibliophile although the boys didn't know that word. He was also a philosopher with books on philosophy, sexuality, the cosmos, biology, medicine, nature, gardening, and botany. He had photography books of nature from every hemisphere and ecosystem. Beautiful vibrant pictures showcasing the beauty of life in all forms. Then there was his books on the cosmos featuring colorful pictures of massive, ominous figures lurking out in the depths of space and time. He had story books with fantastical stories including great adventures, memorable characters, striking and powerful beasts, and displays of great strength from other Alphas. All these stories the boys had decided were too vivid not to be true like Moby Dick, Huckleberry Fin, The Iliad, Hamlet, Dr. Jekel and Mr. Hyde, Frankenstein, and The Chronicles of Narnia.

Eric taught his brother how to read with painstaking diligence and patience. This time also gave him the ability to carefully weed through what the twins should and should not be exposed to. Over the years Eric found most all the books necessary and useful to read to understand life, nature, how to survive, and how to understand themselves. However, even as a boy Eric felt the need to withhold some of the old man's books on sexuality. His books on mammal reproduction, his instructional books on various sex acts including detailed, graphic pictures and descriptions of said sex acts, and books on the history of human sexuality throughout centuries just seemed inappropriate to show to the twins as young as they were and still are. Eric didn't consider himself vulnerable to shocking material. He was the alpha male after all and the Alpha Male must put himself between his pack and all threats to their wellbeing. Sex wasn't meant to be corrupted in this way in people's minds. It was an act between a male and a female to produce future generations. Not pleasure. Not entertainment. Beautiful for what potential it held.

Life and Legacy.

Besides the twins didn't need to be thinking about sex. It would only be a distraction until they could figure out their place as Alpha Males. So, Eric hid the books on sexuality and merely allowed the twins to read about reproduction in Grey's Anatomy as well as other Biology and Botany books so that they could simply understand what the natural purpose of sexual organs are and what the act of sex is for in nature.

Upstairs Eric crawled into the old bed which creaked and groaned as it received his weight. He tugged at the covers and pulled them up to his waist. Still had to poke a foot out from under the corner of the blanket. He always had to do that really wasn't even sure why just knew it felt just right and seemed to regulate his body temperature. Pretty Brown Eyes was snuggled in his arm. She had fallen asleep after dinner. But, the transport from the kitchen to the master bedroom left her awake and once again curious about her surroundings particularly Eric. Her tail wagged playfully as she pounced on his face as hard as her tiny body could. A mere thud really. She sniffed around and eventually found the arm of Noah. Tugged on it with her nubs for teeth. Gave it a harder tug. Before long she was passionately wrestling with the skins like there would be winners and losers in the war. Eric watched as she fought with the skins yipping and growling, until Mother July slinked into the bedroom panting and sniffing the air. She climbed up into the bed with ease. She sniffed Noah's hide and curled up beside Eric resting her head on top of Noah's and curling her warm, fluffy tail around Eric.

Knowing that July had, had a long day and probably wanted some rest, Eric tried to calm Pretty Brown Eyes. Her energy was not matched in the senior wolf. Not by far. Eric held Pretty Brown Eyes to his chest on her back and stroked her belly whilst scratching her behind the ears. She seemed to like it and thankfully that kept her quiet.

Eric always had a soft spot for July. Her mothering nature was a comforting find when he and the twins were devastated by the loss of their real mother. Eric thought it fitting to name the Mother Wolf July because she was wonderful in her way, but she would always come after June. She nuzzled her narrow grey snout into the nape of his neck, right under his hairline.

July often found her way to Eric. He could move from here to there. The kitchen. The living room. The bed. The bathroom. The bed again. The garden. And all the way back and soon enough he would notice that she was never more than a few feet away. Following him back and forth. Most times July's choice to be in constant close proximity to him made him feel loved by her. Yet, occasionally Eric found himself wondering if July actually wanted to be close to him or if she was naturally drawn to the scent of the hide of her mate for life, Noah, on his back.

Thankfully she did not know just how he got Noah's hide. How he earned his place as top dog of the pack would be his little secret. July let out a hot yawn behind his neck. Steam from her breath glued hairs to his skin, but they cooled quickly giving him a chill. Eric rolled over in the creaky bed which would have smelled strongly of animal dander if Eric were not so use to the smell of animal dander being in his nostrils. He was able to wash the sheets in the flow of the stream outside his front door, dry them on a line attached from one of the front porches pillars to another, but animal scent had crawled through the mattress like a gopher in soil. He curled his body around July, placed Pretty Brown Eyes in-between them like a baby between a mother and father. Gave Pretty Brown Eyes a pat on her tummy as she finally quieted down and wrapped an arm around July. In the slight glow from the full moon, he could just see the gray on July's snout and he wondered how much time she had left.

She'd slowed in recent years, got tired eyes, napped more, took long strides, and changed from her chocolate brown to a wiry grey. Eric would never have known what grey hair meant if not for his years spent in human company. His mother had shown him pictures of his grandparents before he saw them last their grey hairs too coming through. He remembered June's colorful explanation to him that their hair had turned grey since the pictures were taken because they had done a lot of thinking since then and all their thinking made them wise and smart. And that thinking for as long as they had over the course of their lives had turned their hair different colors. She explained that thinking was a magnificent thing to do though and that he should do it whenever he could so that he could be wise just like them one day. So, Eric figured, July must be wise by now which is why she lead the pack beside him. He trusted her instinct because she had refined hers through her years so much so that it could be trusted. She was his sidekick in the forest. His backup intuition in times of trouble.

He appreciated her, but two thoughts gave him pause. How long did his sidekick have left? Would age send her body back to the earth sooner or later? He hoped later, but couldn't be too sure.

Also, he wondered how long he and his brothers could be masters of the land and the forest without having sired offspring of their own? The passing of a male's seed is key to his status as alpha male and that is what they were. Alpha males. The males of the forest would risk life and limb to earn the right to stalk and court the female until she submits. Until she turns in the direction he is facing and allows him to mount her. Eric and his brothers had seen the mating rituals of the animals avian, canine, feline, bovine, even fish kinds if they looked into the waters of the stream hard enough to see the spawning rituals of the scaly ones. The brothers often wondered when would it be their turn? Who could possibly take on their seed? If a human female, they would have to go down into Downers Grove, home, a city big enough where they would have an array of pickings over females with which to mate and breed with and where Eric was determined never to return. The horrors of the forest scrapping and scrounging for food, killing for life, mating for pride, and predators lurking near and far was nothing compared to the brutality of other people.

*Is mating worth that risk?* Eric thought to himself stroking Pretty Brown Eyes' belly lulling her off to sleep.

Suddenly his hair stood on edge. His breath was taken away. He gasped for air. July leaped  up, anxiously panting. His hands are covered in blood. But, when he frantically looks at his hands. They are clean. Wait, it hasn't happened yet. This was a premonition. Was it his brother's blood? No, wait then why could he not breathe? It must have been him. He steadied himself. Gave July a calming pat on the head. He may not die. He may just get injured somehow. When he had a premonition of tasting blood, the day his father died, he thought that, that day he might die, but he did not. He mustn't misinterpret the pictures he sees in his head. The things unseen. He was a survivor. He had learned to feel at peace knowing when something was coming. Either good or bad. With warning he could prepare. With warning he would have perspective. With warning he could plan and be ready for the inevitable.

But, what if the blood was not his in the vision? What if he was breathing heavily from angst? From the pain of witnessing something happening to his brothers? He tried to think back what did he see beyond his bloody hands? White dots. Spots? Snow flecks, he realized quickly. Snow flecks falling from the sky. The air around him is cold and is making the wet blood on his hands cold.

So, he had some clues now. Some injury was going to happen to either him or one of his brothers and it would be cold outside just before a fresh snow fall. Then Eric bit his lower lip…

It was just about winter already.

# Chapter 5: Baser Instincts

With his confidence higher than ever that he was on the right track to hunting down the answers to The Beckwith Brothers trail and the hidden secrets of their brains, Kerry drove down Sweet Pique Lane in his Cadillac Coupe which he called C.C.. As he drove through the chill of the night the air was biting and the unusual cold left him was periodic shivers and his glasses annoyingly fogged. He had to keep wiping away the moist haze from his lens. The town was dark;.yet, he could still recognize his old stomping grounds. The Park. The Plaza. Carrs. Heisenberg High's shadowy presence at the end of the road a few blocks ahead.

The streets were mostly empty. The only people who were out besides him looked like couples still strolling around wrapping up date night. To Kerry's right, a man and women sitting on a bench in the mini park star gazing probably starry eyed too. She laid her head on his shoulder. He pointed up at the stars. Kerry could tell he was smiling by the look of his rounded cheeks from behind. To Kerry's left, a middle aged couple strolled along the sidewalk hand-and-hand talking and laughing away like good old friends. Kerry often wondered if he'd ever have those sweet moments with someone special. Sometimes he doubted the possibility of love for himself. Work was his love, his life, the thing that consumed his time. What place did a woman have in his future, if any at all? If he really wanted love, by now he figured he probably would have pursued it.

He sighed and thought, *Oh well, if I unearth the secret to mind-control and become an internationally known journalist the women may line up for the picking? Ha! I probably still wouldn't make them a priority!* He chuckled to himself. He'd already been the heartbreaker for at least one women. Choosing work over her. A shadow of regret darker than the night sky came over him for a moment remembering how he'd hurt her so. He could never do something like that to anyone again.

The lanterns style street lights beside the glossy cobblestone roads dimly lit the path to the metallic colored diner. Metallic it was appropriately named. One of the hottest spots in town for greasy food, great pie, and even better coffee particularly for the late night crowd. Metallic was open for twelve hours daily from 3 to 3.

Kerry parallel parked C.C. in an open space on the end of the few cars in front of the building. It was the only place the car could fit without side-swiping, clipping, or bumping the other patrons' cars being as long and wide as it was. He turned off the old girl and stepped out. Entered the building which was surprisingly full and lively. The smell of burgers, coffee, french fry grease, and something that reminded Kerry of pickles engulfed him all at once. The black and white tiled floor added that old diner feel to the joint, the little red box car booths, and the line of round stools at the counter just enhanced the atmosphere. Of the twenty benches only five were available. The others were full of people enjoying small midnight snacks, couples together, singles just enjoying their moment out, and clusters of young adult females giggling amongst themselves about God knows what. More of the stools were available than booths so he picked a seat on a stool.

Almost immediately a buxom blonde waitress in a poodle skirt and matching skin tight sweater greeted him behind the counter.

"How may I take your order, sir?" She chirped in a warm southern accent.

"I'd love a cup of coffee actually." Kerry replied.

"Okay. We have a nice fresh Apple Pie just waitin' to be cut into if you'd like a piece."

"Uh maybe later. You make it sound so good."

She giggled scrunching up her nose. Scribbled his order onto her notepad. "I'll get that coffee for you."

"Thanks." Kerry opened up his copy of the local newspaper to the current events section. His eyes immediately went to a still shot of an older woman. Her scowl solidified into her deep wrinkles like the imprint of a shoe in cement. Pale skin pasty as raw, floured pastry dough. Barbie Pink lipstick far too pink for a woman of her age. Thin salt and pepper hair pulled back into a sleek and low ponytail. If it were not for her trademark tea length pencil skirt and elongated blazer jacket with extra long shoulder pads, Kerry might not have recognized so quickly that this was surely Downers Grove's other elusive specimen, Angelica McCord.

The article, done by a newcomer in journalism, Amber Marks, focused on the secretive businesswoman's plans to take the Angelica McCord's Haute Couture to new heights. A new line. A season. A new phase of her life. Who knew crossing the hurdle into the Big 5.0. could be so fulfilling, reassuring, and confidence boosting! She would have gushed in her gruff voice, the result of vocal cords smoked like brisket and burnt ends from the Fourth of July from decades of chain smoking.

Then she alluded to a "Top Secret" plan that she had to make Angelica McCord's Haute Couture a staple worldwide and year round.

"I have secrets. Downers Grove has secrets. Even the mountains have secrets. All of which will be known soon. One never knows what the winds may bring." Angelica would have purred taking a long drag from her pipe. A bony elbow dug into her thin thigh, crossed over the other perched on the edge of one of her many over the top sequenced chaises inside of her mansion sized house/Fashion House Headquarters combo.

Kerry couldn't help, but wonder what were these so called, "secrets" hidden in the mountains and in Downers Grove's past? And more importantly what did she know about it? Angelica had been a staple in Downers Grove since the 70s. She had more than enough time to learn the details of Downer's past and perhaps even the past of The Beckwith Brothers. Did she see them that day? Did she know of someone who did? Did she have any knowledge about the brothers sightings up the mountain and how true they were? If the truth was really in the wind it must come from some specific direction. Angelica lived up North in the very elite and exclusive Highland Park. It over looked the plains and a gorgeous sunrise in the East and the Halo Mountains in the West.

In his peripheral, a thin red head plopped down in the stool next to him. He looked up at her. She smiled right at him, seemed to peer into his soul.

"Hi." She said. "I'm Tabitha." She arches an eyebrow over her dark green eyes. Freckles barely noticeable on her cheeks. Her halter top leaving little to the imagination. The slit in her skirt so, so high.

"Hi." Kerry nodded another thank you to the waitress as she sat his coffee down in front of him.

"Hi." Tabitha said again.

"I'm...Kerry." He said getting the message. She didn't just want to be friendly in passing, she wanted more.

"Kerry." She initiated a handshake. "Nice to me you. Are you new here in Downers?"

"Well not exactly new. I lived here once. When I was much younger. Before my parents separated. I came back ever now and then for visits before going off to college. It's a second home."

"Ah, what did you study in college?" She leaned in.

"I have my B.A. in Journalism and my M.A. in Political Ethics."

"Wow, that sounds deep and serious."

"Yeah, I liked it though."

"Political Ethics that's pretty timely, huh?"

"Well I didn't get into it for the reasons you might think."

"Why did you get into it?"

"To prepare myself as a journalist for a world where politics and science may no longer consider ethics, but only relativism and ideology on the basis of circular reasoning. What if one day the branches of our government no longer kept a check on the presidency? What if one day ethics were disregarded in medicine and research? What if one day climate scientists were silenced?"

"Mm-hmm." She nodded slowly with a blank stare.

"What if our government was infiltrated by foreign bodies, what if the environment becomes more toxic and they start fudging data, keeping the truth from us? We could become the Soviet Union circa Chernobyl. It's just a matter of time if we do not persist."

"Mm-hmm." She nodded slowly again.

"I think it is imperative for us to know what has happened in the past so we know how to protect ourselves in the future."

"Oh. So, so deep and serious. I like that." She purred in a low voice.

He could tell she had no idea what he was talking about.

"Everyone's so deep now and days. You know the...like...AIDS Crisis!" She said like she was guessing answers to a question nobody even asked. "And no smoking campaigns. And you know refraining from sex until Y2K! Crazy stuff like that!"

"Crazy stuff? Like the AIDS Crisis?" He arched an eyebrow with a grin.

"Oh well no silly!" She laughed like a drunk. "That's important. Deep and serious. Ya know? Imperative like you said. Imperative and deep and serious." She nodded dramatically..

"Right." He nodded slowly. Took a sip of his black coffee. Continued with his newspaper.

The buxom blond waitress approached Tabitha with the same sincere smile. "What can I get for you tonight?"

"Ah, gee I'm not sure. What do you think I should get Kerry?"

"I heard they have pie. A fresh apple pie." Cutting his eyes up from his paper.

"Pie? Oh I think I want meat. A big piece of meat in me tonight."

*No, that girl did not even.* Kerry thought to himself.

"Gee, I don't know what I want. Kerry tell me what type of meat do you think I need to eat tonight." She sighed and purred all at the same time leaning towards him.

He took a moment and then looked up at her, "From what I remember they make this giant liver pudding, liver gravy, pancake sandwich thing. It is massive, but if you like meat it's a lot of meat." He was a master troll.

"Oh no, maybe not uh liver pudding. No, no. Any other suggestions?"

"Nope." Kerry said casually.

"I suppose I'll have a hot dog. I nice big and hot one. Lots of ketchup please."

"Sure thing." The waitress scribbled Tabitha's order onto her notepad before flouncing into the kitchen.

"Oh I'm so excited, Kerry."

"Are you?" He continued to read the paper not looking up at her.

"Oh I am. I'm soooo ready. You know why I didn't go to college, Kerry?"

"Nope."

"I'm just not a girl who can do all that waiting, Kerry. I like everything how I want and when I want it and four whole years for a degree just seems so loooong. I don't know how you did it."

"Sometimes the best things are worth waiting for." He took a sip of coffee. At least it was good damn coffee. Strong with floral notes, a sweet undertone, and rich chocolatey goodness.

"My goodness you are so mature! I like that."

"Thank you." He mumbled taking a sip.

"You care. You read the newspaper. How old are you anyway?" She dimmed her eyes.

She was desperately trying to get some.

Kerry took a deep breath and sighed. "I am 25. How old are you? You have a curfew you need to beat or anything?"

"Nooooo. Silly. I make my own curfew. I'm kind of a night owl to be honest. I am most comfortable keeping late hours."

"Hmm. Really." He took a sip.

The waitress flounced Tabitha's hot dog towards her. Sat the plate down at Tabitha's hands. It was drowned in ketchup.

"That's wonderful. Thank you."

"No problem. Just let me know if you need anything!" The waitress flounced away.

"Mmm, this is my kind of meal, Kerry."

"Uh-huh." He read his newspaper hoping that eating would keep the girl's mouth too busy to keep talking.

"Mmm." He heard her practically moan plucking the hot dog up in her hands. She tossed her red locks back, stretched her neck long, rolled her eyes into the back of her head, slowly brought the hot dog to her lips and kissed it.

Kerry turned his head, his wide eyes unable to look away.

She moaned again licking ketchup off each side of the soft round humps of hot dog bun on each side of the long meat. She then lifted the hot dog meat half way out of the bun, holding it only with the small part of the meat that was still stuck in the bun. She dragged her tongue along the underside of the meat. Licked her lips moaning louder, more dramatically. Ketchup dribbling down her chin.

Kerry couldn't help but cut his eyes at other patrons to see if they were noticing the…err…*show*? As if on queue Michael Jackson's "Dirty Diana" came on Metallic's radio.

Tabitha then went all in and started taking the hot dog meat all the way into her mouth and slowly pulling it out over and over again. Gave the tip a little suck every time she got to it. Kerry could see her tongue push past her bottom lip every time she took a long drag of the meat, licking at the underside while she sucked the rest. Slurping ketchup and moaning.

Kerry could feel himself frown. Involuntarily cut his eyes to the other patrons again.

She peaked at him out the corner of her dimmed eyes. Slowly pushed the hot dog further and further back into her throat, got some ketchup on her upper lip, retracted the meat, and licked her lips, licked the tip of the meat flicking her tongue up and down like a snake sniffing the air for prey, while eyeing Kerry. Tabitha sighed like a dreamy school girl and shoved the meat back into her throat again with extra gusto and eagerness.

Kerry unable to look away from the sexual, ketchup drenched, car accident unintentionally encouraged her to carry on. She felt rather complimented by his horrified staring. One of the ketchup dribbles on her chin ran further down her neck. Kerry found himself staring hard, forehead wrinkled, eyes wide, mouth tense, teeth clenched, but then he felt a stirring in his trousers. She was giving that hot dog a real good blow job. If she wasn't so ketchup covered maybe it wouldn't look so grotesque somehow.

His dick grew firm from base to tip. Damn. He hadn't felt someone lick his penis in forever. Not since his love loss. He'd been so focused on work, school, research, travel. For a second it crossed his mind to let her just straddle him in C.C. right outside. Just let her scratch his itch. She obviously wanted to so badly. She's young and probably so tight and so fresh. No! Kerry swallowed hard. Re-focused his mind. Just no! What he was thinking was unacceptable. For one, this girl could be a minor for all he knew and he didn't need to become a criminal before he even got a chance to be a serious journalist. For two, he needed to learn the who's who in this town and having messy connections with potential future witnesses or sources was the last thing he needed. For three, he was supposed to be a professional and a professional would not shit where he eats particularly not in a tiny small town.

Finally, just because this girl was young didn't necessarily mean that she was "fresh". For all he knew she was this fast from having lots of experience and as the news said HIV/AIDS was almost completely glo-bal in every demographic at this point and he just couldn't afford to get sick and die right now all for a blow job no matter how good it looked. So, that was that. He needed to get out of here. Now!

He folded his paper remarkably well for not taking his eye off of Tabitha and the hot dog. She was sucking and licking like there was no tomorrow now. His dick grew harder. He'd just have to hide it behind his paper. He patted his pant pocket for his wallet still watching Tabitha with a look of fright mixed with admiration. Pulled out what was either a ten or a hundred. He didn't even look to see. Didn't really matter he had plenty of money.

*Thank God dad was rich.* He randomly sighed in his head. The waitress would certainly benefit from the latter.

For a moment he wondered if it would be so wrong to have meaningless sex with the girl. *I mean how young did she look really?*

His inner voice screamed, *Fifteen years old at best!!*

Kerry quickly shooed that thought away. Sighed and decided to stick to his plan to leave anyway. Just as he was about to get up and carefully conceal his erection, Tabitha pushed the hot dog back down her throat and accidentally lost her grip on the other end sending the entire dog flying down the back of her esophagus. Her eyes flew open as what felt like a fatal panic came over her. She start flailing her hands around choking, gasping, and gobbling like a turkey. Just like that Kerry's penis went as limp as a wet noodle. Well, at least he didn't have to hide his erection anymore. Although, he was still a little hot. Glanced at Tabitha's breasts jiggling in her top with all the panicking movements and desperate heaving she was doing. Kerry was ashamed that was the first thing he noticed while the girl could be dying.

So, he jumped up and assumed the position of the Heimlich maneuver behind Tabitha. She, still trying to breathe, held onto his arms as he lifted her off the stool and applied pressure to her upper abdomen. One squeeze. Two squeezes. Three squeezes. And the hot dog dislodged and slid out of her throat fell on the floor with a rubbery bounce. The patrons erupted in applause and cheers of praise for the hero.

Tabitha wheezed a, "Thank you." Fingertips fluttering to her throat.

"You're welcome. You gotta be more careful with the things you put in your mouth." Kerry grinned.

"I'm just not used to anything so…so skinny that's all." She croaked.

*Wait, was she still trying to get laid? Good Lord.*

"You got a little ketchup…" Kerry trailed off motioning to his chin and neck area.

She wiped her chin and neck with a spare napkin. The waitress approached Tabitha.

"Do you need a doctor? Are you alright?"

"No, no I'm fine. I…I'm sorry. I'm gonna go." Tabitha dug in her purse for some cash.

Kerry fanned a hand in front of her and handed the waitress a ten dollar bill. "Keep all the change." He told her. Turned to Tabitha to tell her, "It's alright."

Tabitha sniffled and nodded red as paprika, eyes glossy as if they'd been shellacked. She turned to leave and exited Metallic. Kerry followed close behind. Caught up to her saying, "Wait, wait."

"Look. I...I owe you my life, but I really should be getting home." She interrupted no longer giving eye contact.

"No. Okay, just wait." He grabbed her bicep. He could use this situation to his advantage. It was useful having someone who owed him a favor in this town. Who knew her favor could come in handy later on in his investigation. He wasn't just going to let her disappear into the night. "It's dark. It's late. You can't go walking off into the night. At least let me take you home. I have a car. If you live close it'll be just a few minutes and then your home. Young women shouldn't walk around alone after midnight."

After a moment, she blinked and replied, "You'll just take me home?"

"Yes. That's all. That's my car right there." He willed her to agree. If they had a moment alone on the drive maybe he could get her to tell him about her life in Downers. He could get her phone number and also her home address plenty of information to come in handy if and when she could help his investigation.

Tabitha inhale deeply, "Okay."

Kerry walked her to the passengers side door, let her in, and closed the door behind her. He walked over to the driver's side feeling slightly rotten about using her moment of vulnerability to have an edge in the game, but he tried to tell himself that he was still doing the right thing by taking her home. It was late after all.

He started up the car and pulled off. She gave him simple directions to go towards her home. After that the car was silent for a while. He didn't want to start ~~picking her brain~~ talking too soon. But, he couldn't wait much longer either.

"So, Tabitha did you go to school around here?"

"Yes. But, I dropped out. I work odd jobs occasionally." She said looking out the window. She always said she worked "odd jobs" when anybody asked what she did for money. It was just easier that way.

"Well they say a lot of people in the new millennium won't pursue higher education. It doesn't mean you're any less intelligent or capable of making a life for yourself." Kerry smiled at Tabitha. "Not to say that it won't be harder."

Tabitha cracked a tiny grin, "Yeah. That's true."

"How did your parents feel about you dropping out?"

"My father is active duty in Desert Storm. He avoids saying anything to me that wouldn't sound ideal as his potential last words to me. It's morbid I know, but honestly I could say I was a crack addict and was headed to jail and he'd probably be like, 'Oh well, dear!' And probably regurgitate some philosophical quote from Rumi, MLK, JFK, or C.S. Lewis to put the cherry on top."

"Wow. Well that takes a lot of restraint."

Tabitha laughed, "Totally."

"And your mother?"

"My mom is so busy she hardly even noticed."

"What's she busy doing?" Kerry turned down a residential street.

"She's a full-time police sergeant here in Downers."

*Jack-pot.* Tabitha could be a significant connection between he and the town law enforcement. He was sure if Tabitha's mother was a sergeant she would probably have easy access to files and maybe even evidence lockers…with a little finagling.

"Well I bet she'd be just heartbroken if you died choking on a hot dog tonight." Kerry playfully pouted.

Tabitha whipped her head towards him with a smile. He laughed and then after a moment so did she. "That was pretty stupid, huh?"

"Ya think?"

"Ugh. I'm so embarrassed."

"Don't be. I'm the one who saw the most and I know how to keep a secret."

"Ha. Ha." She said dryly.

"Besides getting the applause from the audience made me feel like a local celeb for a sec-

"Wait!" She interrupted. "What. Do. You. Mean. "Audience?""

"Oh my fans? My cheering fans after they witnessed me save you, the damsel in distress', life? That audience my friend. *That* audience." He smirked.

She smirked too, "The patrons?"

"Who you so rudely interrupted by almost dying, missy." He teased in an almost parental manner.

She kind of liked it. "Okay. I relent. It was my fault. I *made* you a hero."

"Oh no you did not *"make* me a hero" I became a hero all by myself. I'm the one who knew the Heimlich maneuver."

"I was the one who was dying."

"By trying to impress me. See it all comes back to me." He smiles proudly pulling up the driveway to her house. "Let me give you my pager number in case you ever need anything. And give me your home phone so I'll be able to recognize the number."

"Okay."

Kerry had a pen and scribbled his pager number onto a blank corner of the newspaper. Then he handed Tabitha the pen so she could write down her number.

"What brings you into town, Kerry?" She asked writing her number down careful to make the zeroes look like hearts.

"I'm researching a town myth. You probably know what it is."

"The Beckwith Brothers?"

"Yeah. You wouldn't know anything about them would you?"

"No, they were long before my time. I guess a lot of people think they're still around though. Like their haunting us. They have a full blown cult like fan-club around here."

"They do?" Kerry arches an eyebrow. Another lead. "Isn't cult a bit of a strong word?"

"If it looks like a cult and smells like a cult…it's a cult." She replied matter-of-factly.

"What makes them cult like?" He watched the road and mentally logged Tabitha's every word.

"So, they are this really secretive group. Nameless. Faceless. No leaders just unified in their belief that The Beckwith Brothers are I dunno *"something other.""*

Tabitha did air quotes. "They have all kind of theories about the brothers. Claim they have magical powers. Claim they turned into werewolves. Claim they evaporated to escape their abusive father and somehow melded with the soul of the city. They are the ones who keep the boys name alive. They are the ones who give the interviews to the media about sightings in the woods. Whispers in the night. Ghosts of the boys in town."

"The Night the Howls Held Words." Kerry grinned a tabloid style headline that claimed the howls that can be heard in town had one night been actual words from a human disguised as a howl..

"Yes!" Tabitha laughed remembering that ludicrous story. "It's all pretty silly."

"Well hopefully that's as bad as it gets. Some silly fan-club. Do you think that Angelica McCord is part of the fan-club?"

"Angelica? That uppity costume designer? Everyone hates her. It makes sense that she would have to find friends in some fringe group."

"Ah, also pretty silly, huh? Maybe I can put an end to all the rumors."

"If you do that you'd be a lot more than just *my* hero." Tabitha grinned thoughtfully and stepped out of C.C.. she took a few steps then turned back. "Hey. Mister Patience and Mature Graduate what do you think is better going fast or going slow?"

Kerry looked at Tabitha for a moment a grin slowly creeping across his face, "Painfully slow, my dear. Makes the finale so damn good."

Tabitha smiled, turned, and walked all the way up to her house. She unlocked the door and gave him a small wave before stepping inside. He pulled off. Made a U-Turn in a cul-de-sac and made his way back to the Main Street.

He felt accomplished and badass. He'd gotten his first real connection to Downers. He did it with a girl who he knew wanted him in-between her legs...or behind her. She seemed like the kind of girl who liked it different ways. His mind flashed back to her using her tongue to tickle the tip of the hot dog back at Metallic. He inhaled. He could see her eagerly taking the length in and giving the tip a delicious little lick each time. He could feel his abdominal muscles tighten. He turned on his radio to distract himself as his penis got hard all over again. He could still smell her perfume in his car. He did always love red heads. They looked so vibrant and sexy. His penis got harder. He turned down Sweet Pique Lane on his way back to his father's house to turn in for the night. He was hard as a rock. He kept seeing her sucking on that hot dog. He imagined himself in its place. His dick in her mouth. His semen running down her chin and her neck instead of ketchup. Nobody was behind him. He slowed down and unbuckled his pants, gapped his legs, and accelerated again. Drove with his left hand and slipped his right hand around his hard-on. Squeezed his balls hard sending chills up his spine. He moaned out loud. He always felt the need to quiet his sounds of pleasure, but outside everything cried out exactly the way it wanted to. The animals had no shame and out here he didn't have to either. He pumped his penis. Felt muscles inside his thighs jump for joy and bliss. He moaned more. Squeezed hard until he felt himself coming hard. He cried into the night air the breeze from the drive muffling most of his noises. He caught his breath.

"Thank you, Tabitha." He mumbled under his breath.

Soon as he was back at his father's house. He eased back inside careful not to wake the old man probably already asleep. He locked the door. Retreated to his old room. Exactly the way he'd left it since the last time he'd returned from college. Probably summer break or winter break. He couldn't remember right now. His old Magnum P.I. paraphernalia finally gone out of style. Who knew he grow to not only get tired on the franchise, but also hate it with a passion?

That new Sci-Fi film, Jurassic Park, seemed like it'd be a good movie. He'd have to go see it sometime. Monster movies were always the best in the theater. He'd read Michael Chiton book years earlier in between semesters and internships. Always thought Jurassic Park would make a good movie. At least for cinephiles like himself, wonderfully enough Steven Spielberg had the same inclination.

He removed his shoes, socks, pants, shirt, and boxers ready to hop in the shower. Just then he got a message on his pager. It read:

Remember that mystery woman rumored to have been discovered below the mountain the day after the Beckwith Brothers went missing? She may not be a rumor after all. Let's talk.

Kerry didn't recognize the number. In fact he was curious why anyone would be contacting him this late at night anyway. Very few people even knew how to reach his pager. There was no doubt that he was curious. Immensely curious about the message. The rumor of the mystery woman found half-dead washed ashore the stream line the day after the brothers went missing in the mountains just above her always piqued his interest, but there was never any evidence of leads to confirm the story. The trail of the woman herself had long dried up. Records keeping could be better if it could be logged into a system that multiple sources had access to. *Oh technology. When will you benefit the crime field more?*

This person, whoever they were, claimed to have insight, clues, juicy information. He wouldn't be doing his job as a journalist if he did not pursue the lead. He'd reply in the morning and schedule a time to meet with this…messenger. See exactly what they had to offer and what, if anything, they could be asking for in return.

Kerry put his pager away headed to the shower. He turned on the water before stepping in. Allowed it to heat up first. The cold would be a shock to his system if he got in now and the Fall chill was cool enough. He finger combed his glossy hair in the mirror. Imagined what he'd look like with long hair for a moment. The sound of Eric's prolonged howl in the mountains broke his line of thought. A series of wolf howls accompanied the first. Howls which Kerry felt held all the answers he needed.

# Chapter 6: Fame Whore

Sierr's eyes were still shut even as her alarm went off. Not completely awake, not completely asleep. Somewhere in between. That delicious feeling of being so relaxed in your plush bed, in your plush sheets that were perfectly scented with ten drops of Lavender essential oils freshly out of the dryer, that you could just drift back off to sleep and stay in bed all day. Sierr could bask in that feeling all day and yet it was Tuesday. A school day. Even worse the mere second day of the whole school week.

Relaxation gone. She sat up. Her curls cascaded down her shoulders, tinkled the tops of her thighs, caught the gleam of the sunlight peering through the window blinds. She took a peak at her hard nipples. She sighed. Even naturally perky, Full-Cs weren't enough to make guys notice her. She threw her head back, resting it on one of her many pillows. Thanked the Lord for allowing her to wake up in this day. Thanked Him for her family. Her home. Their health and well-being. Prayed that they would be guided by His spirit to live in excellence in this day. That they would be blessed and be a blessing to others. She asked for protection from dangers seen and unseen as well as dangers known and unknown. She opened her eyes and hopped up.

She used her wrist to part the sheer curtain surrounding her mattress and slipped out of her white four poster distressed wooden bed onto the lovely silvery blue rug under her bed, walked from that onto the cold hard wood floors, and then onto the even colder tiles in her attached bathroom. She was greeted with colors of creams and golds as that was the color scheme of her bathroom and she reached for her Jumbo shower cap on one of the hand towel hooks and neatly tucked each curl of her head into the plastic.

She had way too much temperamental curly hair to risk getting it wet or allowing steam to make it frizzy just before school. She had a rule she only did her hair at night when she had the time to give styling it and defining each individual curl her undivided attention and even re-do it all if necessary. This way she could always have defined curls which would hold up through the night, as long as she slept on satin sheets which she did religiously, and they would always be effortlessly bouncy and shiny in the morning. Her jumbo shower cap was her last line of defense against the moisture that could easily ruin her hair. When she stepped out of the shower she left the shower cap on. It was necessary as the bathroom was still full of frizz causing steam. Until it dissipated, her hair had to stay sealed in the protective plastic. She padded to the window in her bedroom dripping wet and naked. Opened the window after making sure no one was jogging down on the sidewalk or walking their dog or something. She loved the morning air.

Afterwards she padded back to the bathroom brushed her teeth, dribbled Witch Hazel in her palm, rubbed her hands together, and coated her face with the cool, refreshing medicinal liquid. Sierr was always thankful she had never experienced the nightmares of teenage hormone driven acne. She occasionally had a zit or two, but other than that her skin stayed remarkably blemish free. Her sister did not have it so well in her teenage years. Lux's acne was not too bad, but it was certainly worse than Sierr's. Sierr did not know if she could credit her lack of breakouts to genetics or Witch Hazel, but she had enough faith in Witch Hazel that for years she made sure that she used it whenever she washed her face or stepped out of the shower just to make sure her skin stayed clean and clear. It was such an ingrained habit that she thought it to be ludicrous that she could ever forget to use it at this point. Forgetting to use it after washing her face or taking a shower now would probably feel as unthinkable as "accidentally" forgetting to put clothes on before walking out of the house. That's just how second nature it was.

She strolled into her closet and plucked out the two hangers her pre-selected clothes for the day hung on and laid them on her bed. Finally, the steam was dissipated enough. So, she whipped the shower cap off and gave her hair a toss. Reached into her nightstand and retrieved the glass container of her homemade Shea Body Butter. Removed the gasket sealed lid, with that oh-so satisfying suction release sound, and took out a glob which would be just enough to coat her arms and legs and rubbed it in her palms. Any residual butter left over in her palms would be shared between her face, neck, and tummy. She sighed. *The body butter always smelled so good.* She had like three different essential oils in the mixture: Lavender, Rosemary, and Peppermint. All healthy oils with countless benefits or at least that is what pop-science had informed her about them. After rubbing it all in she pressed the lid back on with another satisfying suction sound and popped the container back in her nightstand. She then got dressed in her outfit: thick, bell bottom tweed pants, with a mustard colored sweater that had puffed sleeves. The mustard color brought out the little flecks of mustard yellow in the tweed. She put on a choker collar necklace that her father gave her for her 16th birthday earlier that year. Used a rat tail comb to part her glossy curls to the left, the direction she subconsciously always tilted her head, grabbed her book bag, opened her bedroom door, and flounced down the stairs.

Sierr had always loved her families house. All the spare bedrooms were upstairs. Her bedroom was at the stairs while her sister's was diagonal to hers. Sierr did not mind that she had the smaller room because technically her sister was an adult and Sierr found it understandable that she should have the extra space. Beside she liked her room. It was perfect. Cozy. Perfectly lit. Had that absolute delicious silver, blue, and white color scheme she adored since her tween years. It had a relaxing quality. Just perfect for studying, reading, writing, praying, alone time. Just perfect.

She dropped her book bag at the foot of the stairs. Headed to the kitchen where she could hear her parents cooking together. The house was a quaint cottage style home. It was mostly white inside accented with color in creative ways. The accent pillows in the living room. Colorful pictures and lamps too. Antique, multicolored, and dark black, brown, and burgundy artifacts and souvenirs from all the places her parents had traveled in the past lined book shelves along with many books in the living room and the hallway. Still not even half the books in the house. There was the rustic library in dad's office, which everyone was welcome to stroll in and out of, and then there was Sierr's collection of books on bookshelves in her room.

Sierr made her way into the kitchen. Sierr's dad, Bryan Blake, was hugging her mom, Michelle Blake, from behind. Michelle was giggling about something. *Good Lord.* Sierr hoped it wasn't her dad's hard penis or something absolutely uncomfortable making like that. She made her presence known with a breezy, "Good Morning!"

"Hi, honey!" Michelle smiled warmly. "Are you staying with us for breakfast or you're going to get it out again? I'm making French toast?" Michelle sing-singed the words "French toast" trying to entice her youngest to stay for a family breakfast minus Lux unfortunately.

"I'd love some french toast, momma." Sierr slid into a bar stool at the island.

"Oh good." Michelle replied using a spatula to remove a fluffy piece of french toast from the pan.

Bryan walked towards Sierr and mouthed, "Aww" covering his heart with his palms. "You're wearing the necklace I bought you."

"I've worn it before." Sierr gave him a crooked smile.

"You have? I've never see you wear it."

"I have! Mom, haven't you seen me wear the necklace dad got me?"

"Yes, dear. You know your father's blind as a bat with the attention span of a moth." Michelle said as casually as could be serving Sierr her breakfast.

"I. Do. Not. Have. The. Attention. Span. Of. A. Moth." Bryan replied offended.

"Except ya do, dear. Ya do." Michelle smiled transferring a dot of maple syrup that was on her fingertip on the tip of his nose.

He went cross eyed trying to see the shiny, syrup, slick on his nose. Stuck his long tongue out to lick it. And successfully lapped it up.

Sierr laughed she and her father shared a lot of things. One of those things was their long lizard like tongues. They could both touch the tips of their noses with their tongues with no hands and no effort and do other tricks with them including twirling them upside down, folding them in half, an sticking them all the way out their mouths rolling them up into a circle to use them as straws to drink with. They also had extra tastebuds on the bottom of their tongues as well as the top. Sierr put a dot of syrup on her nose and licked it off too. Bryan than put a piece of french toast on his nose and tried to work it into his mouth hands-free. The family had a laugh.

Sierr took many things after her father. The golden half of her two-toned golden and milk chocolate colored hair was similar to his blond waves although the curly texture in her hair came from Michelle. Michelle was a first generation Ethiopian-American. She and Bryan met in Italy during a Queen concert.

They were steeped like tea in the cultures of the world. Sierr and Lux were the product of the two stages of their parents' lives: contemporary art and religious awakening. Their names represented both of these stages. Lux was born into the first half, Bryan and Michelle's main focus was gaining riches, status, and traveling the world. Luxury was the name of their game. It made life glossy. Smelled of roses and champagne. With money the weather was never too hot or too cold, the sun left perfect tans, the sands of exotic beaches were never far away, and the elegance of decadent foods were never out of reach. Luxury was raised as one of those children who was cultured. Learned the language of love and the West. Familiar with Beethoven and De Vinci and Maria Abramović Alike. The children who never laughed too loudly. Never played in the mud and clasped their hands together and crossed their feet at the ankles appropriately like Princess Di. She hadn't even tasted M&Ms until she was in middle school. Raised on treats such as Belgium chocolates, French Macaroons, and Tres Leches Pudding.

Sierr had, experienced, and enjoyed much of that same cultural exposure too, but when she came along the lust of luxury and materialism had waned on her family. Didn't have quite the same appeal anymore. Started to seem rather empty and unfulfilling. Items get dusty, clothes go out of style, travel doesn't heal the soul as it once did. Bryan and Michelle realized they needed something more.

Lux was around five when grandma, Diana, died. Lux could hardly remember her face, but she could remember the devastation that befell her mother in the face of heartbreaking loss. Michelle was inconsolable. No person could make her better. Death shocked her somehow. Sierr had heard stories about her Grandmother Diana. Michelle often said she wished her mother would have given her and her sister some kind of spiritual foundation. Some touch stone of some kind. Maybe if Diana had have done that Michelle would not have felt so lost for so long in life. Upon hearing the stories of Michelle struggle following Grandmother Diana's passing, Sierr knew what Michelle was so concerned about when her mother died. Her eternal destiny. What if? Michelle couldn't help, but wonder. Traveling had introduced her to so many different beliefs and worldviews. All the questions and questioning made Michelle want to give her children a more stable foundation in the abstract rather than just in the material. She wanted to give them something that would help keep them centered, hopeful, and secure spiritually. Preparation for life as human beings with a body, soul, and spirit.

Then came Sierr, named after one of the highest ranking angels. The Seraphim. Which marked the next stage of her parents' lives perfectly fit to the town of Downers Grove. Of course Bryan and Michelle's path was not forgotten or buried in fact it was all around. All around the house, their vocabulary, their work as art dealers and internationally known anthropologists. Their lives were like the rings of a geological structure. Years of change, transformation, and stories to tell all in one stunning slice of history.

Soon Sierr was on her same footpath to Heisenberg High. The nip in the air a little more crisp today as the seasons inched closer to winter. She did as she usually did. Strolled down Sweet Pique Lane towards school. She stopped by Ashley's to get her morning coffee. Continued onto school. Sierr often found her short interactions with the people of Downers in the morning the epitome of the perfect relationship with humanity in general. Pleasantries in passing. Not too much chatting. Not too much face-to-face time. Yet, kind, sweet, pleasant. A breath of fresh air, but not nearly as intrusive into her day as full conversations or unnecessary small talk. Not too draining, it didn't take up too much time. It really was perfect. Especially since when the waving and pleasantries were over she could walk on in silence and solitude. She had the patience to give more attention to her best friends: Willow, Carmen, JSF, but they were enough. Sierr savored all the rest of her time alone. The peacefulness of oneness. The quietness and calm of solitude. She sighed in absolute calm....

And then came the flash of red hair.

"Hey Femme Fatale!" Tabitha jogged up next to Sierr in a friggin' fuchsia pink fitness onesie and you-gotta-be-kidding-me glow in the dark neon yellow ankle warmers.

*Good Lord.* "Morning Tabs." Sierr said in the nicest grunt she could possibly muster up.

*Solitude ruined. Ruined!*

"I have news! I met with Kerry." She sing-songed.

"Who?"

"Girl, Kerry Thomas. Hot stuff. Handsome journalist."

"Oh yeah. That guy." Sier grinned and dredged up some feigned excitement.

"He's more than 'that guy'. He's investigating Angelica McCord."

"'Cuse me?" Sierr stopped and turned to Tabitha.

"He was asking about her."

"Whaaa?"

"And her relationship with The Beckwith Brothers."

"Oh Jesus." Sierr rolled her eyes and started walking again shaking her head.

"No really listen to me! He said that he wonders if Angelica had something to do with their disappearance!"

"Why would she be involved? Doesn't that put a stop to the idea that they killed their parents all those years ago?"

"Not entirely. Kerry makes it seem like that she is connected to their disappearance not that she specifically caused the parents to go missing. The boys still could have done that themselves."

"Has a crime been committed here? Because Willow is interning with Angelica right now? I want her to be safe."

"Dunno."

"Well what does Kerry think?"

"Kerry wants to talk to her."

"When?"

"Dunno."

"What's his angle?"

"Dunno."

"Does he think the brothers actually are alive right now?"

"Dunno."

"Where is Kerry right now? Can Willow talk to him?"

"I dunno."

"This has quickly become an infuriating conversation." Sierr stated.

"The only thing I know is that when I mentioned that people around here suspect that The Brothers are haunting the city and that fan-clubs have been formed to honor their so-called supernatural powers the first person he suspected of being involved with these groups is Angelica."

"Where is Kerry?"

"Haven't seen him since last night."

"Since your date?"

"Wasn't a date. He just took me home from Metallic. We can have our date another time." Tabitha had an eager look in her eye. "I think they're alive. I'm going to see if my mom knows anything about them." Tabitha was a fitness fanatic, sexually hyperactive, full of high energy, and just looking for something, anything to intrigue her mind enough to keep her attention and keep her guessing. This little sleuthing project might be just the thing she needed to keep herself occupied during the winter months. Having a connection to Kerry through it couldn't hurt either. She'd be his little source if that meant she could spend some time with her newest crush.

"Be careful, Tabs." Sierr started back towards her school. "If they are alive then that means they actually are lurking in the forest and are close to town and may have actually not been kidnapped, but were indeed the killers of their own parents."

"I know right?" Tabitha applied a fresh coat of her Pinky Glitzy Lip Gloss. Her tone of voice the same one she used to show excitement about the season premier of her favorite show.

Sierr glances over at Tabitha. "Do you really think they're alive?"

"Children have survived in the wild before. Anything's possible." Tabitha hunched a shoulder. "Hey, do you think Lux will allow me to work out at the studio if I show her my coupon? I have a coupon."

"Sure. Yeah."

"Great cause it expired like a month ago." Tabitha stretched her arms above her head. "See ya later Femme Fatale." Tabitha waved bye to Sierr over her head jogged back across the street to the park to presumably resume her workout regimen.

In the second tier of the parking deck of the office building adjacent to Heisenberg High, Daddy Windsor got a very special morning pick me up from his very special student, Hailey. She was still straddling him as they kissed basking in each other's scent and sweet afterglow.

"I love being here with you." She smiled.

"I love you." He replied gently tilting her chin up, to kiss her lips from a different angle with slick tongue slowly licking her upper lip.

She kissed him tenderly leaving him wanting more. A passionate deep kiss that made his muscles pulsate from within. She knew it drove him nuts. She liked driving him nuts. For it gave her a sense of control.

"I love you too." She replied.

"We should go away together." Daddy said.

"What do you mean?" She asked.

"Go. Leave Downers. Get away together. Get married. Be husband and wife somewhere else. Somewhere far away. Far from people who don't appreciate us."

"What about Mrs. Windsor? What about…Abby?" Hailey asked.

"I'm leaving Mrs. Windsor. You know I've wanted to for a while."

"But, you said divorce would be too expensive." She slid off his lap and onto the tan colored leather crossed her right leg over her left leg and his right leg. She ran her hand up and down his abs. Rested her head on his chest and he wrapped his arms around her. He was so much bigger than her and she felt safe in his arms. Like a tiny bird nestled in the palm of a gentle owner.

"I know. I did say that, but I may have come up with an idea to get freed from her without destroying myself financially."

Hailey whipped her head around to him. He gave her a long, tense look. Her eyes widened. "No." She breathed.

"What?"

"What are you talking about?"

"What are *yooouuu* talking about?"

"Hopefully something different from what you're talking about. What are you talking about?"

"I was talking about investing my savings to double what I have because I've been watching the markets. Then I can leave her and also pay child support for Abby until she turns 18 and make a good life for the two of us without being strapped for cash. What were you talking about?"

"Oh I thought you were talking about killing her." Hailey admitted.

"Who Abby?" He nodded with a devious little grin. "That would be almost full proof she does have a lot of enemies." He added thoughtfully still with that same twisted smile. Tiny wrinkles becoming emphasized in the corners of his blue eyes, and parentheses around his goatee.

"N…no, you're wife." Hailey arched eyebrow at Daddy.

"Oh. Oh no. I can't stand her, but I don't need to end up on an episode of Forensic Files either. They always suspect the husband."

"Where would we go?" She quickly changed the subject slightly unsettled.

"Wherever you like." He smiled warmly at her. "You are everything I need. Everything I want. I'll go anywhere as long as you're there with me." He brushed a lock of jet black hair out of her face.

They kissed again. "I have something for you." He crawled half way into the front seat and reached into the glove compartment his unfastened belt buckle jingling between his thighs with every movement. Hailey took the opportunity to check their surroundings. The parking deck was totally empty. It would be a little creepy if they weren't locked in the car and Daddy wasn't there to protect her and keep her company. He sat back down in the seat next to her with her present. It was obviously a book, but it was wrapped in a scarf tied with a ribbon around the top and bottom. Hailey smiled not even knowing what it was. She was just happy knowing that Daddy would think of her even when she wasn't in his presence. She sat up and unwrapped the present. Before she had even unwrapped the whole book she could tell what it was. She gasped with delight. Her fingertips fluttered to her lips.

"Open it all the way." He laughed.

"Oh my goodness. A first edition Charlotte Bronte." It was by Hailey's favorite author. The international known female author who assumed a male pseudonym in the early 1900s in order to bypass the discriminatory climate against women in publishing. Hailey had been fascinated by Charlotte Bronte for years. The gift was not only perfect, it was touching because it showed how much Daddy knew her.

"I love it." She whispered before giving him a hug.

"I knew you would." He whispered back gently kissing her forehead. "One day we will travel. One day we will be free to be together out in the open. No one will have control over us. No laws. No obstacles. Just us. Together."

Later the bell rang for lunch, Sierr met up with Carmen in the hallway from their different classes.

"Hey-ya." Carmen squeaked. Entering the combination for her locker.

"Hi." Sierr noticed Carmen's boots. "Oh what's happening south of your ankles? I love!"

"Oh nothing just a little something I picked out from the Delia's catalog!"

"Nice. Can I borrow sometime?"

"Sure. Uh, what is Willow doing?" Sierr followed Carmen's gaze to see Willow passing out flyers to students congregating the hallway.

"Get ready for the Halloween Town Bash of the century. A Night of Mystic & Mystery. The best one you've ever seen. The upgrade of upgrades. An entire tour through Halloween in the Plaza. Sponsored by Angelica McCord Costume Designs!"

"Oh." Sierr started.

"My." Carmen gapped.

"Gawd." They both said together in horrified awe.

Quickly Carmen prayed aloud not taking her eyes off Willow, "LordForgiveUsForUsingYourNameInVein."

"Amen." Sierr whispered. "It's like invasion of the body snatchers." Sierr winced as Willow approaches them, handed them both a colorful flyer featuring all the needed information for attending this annual Halloween Town Bash: A Night of Mystic & Mystery. The flyer was professionally done, probably designed by Angelica herself. The background was a royal purple color which gradually faded into a deep eggplant color. The edges were lines in sparkles which were colored matched to the background. Towards the center of the page, black gradient was filled with all the text information. It was done like a ransom note. Each letter like the clipping from a magazine or a catalog. But each was the same black lettering surrounded by a pumpkin orange color which matched the smirking pumpkin to the right of the letters. The pumpkin wore a dramatic black sparkling hat, red lipstick, and fangs dripping blood. Behind the letters a blurry image of the gazebo in the Park Plaza where the event was supposed to be held.

"Since when does Angelica McCord sponsor the Halloween Town Bash? It's just supposed to be a town…thing. We all come together and pool our money together to do it." Carmen pouted like someone had pissed in her Froot-Loops.

"Willow, sweetie. Are you in there? Has she taken away your soul and made you into one her minions now?"

Willow laughed, "Noooo, this is my first assignment for the job. I'm getting paid $24/hr too."

"Oh what? To pass out some flyers? Where can I sign up?" Carmen salivated.

"Carmen." Sierr's voice was saturated in shaming vibes.

Carmen lowered her head. "Sorry. You're so right. I will not sleep with the enemy."

"Oh my Lord. 'The enemy?' I though we agreed 'The Enemy' was Satan." Willow arched a thin eyebrow.

"There is something about her. Something I dunno sneaky. Underhanded. Like she does...what?" Sierr turned to Carmen for clarity.

"Insider trading." Carmen respond with a wince, a turned up nose, and a tone a person might use to say something like "human trafficking".

"Uh well I meant something abhorrent. Like I dunno. Cannibalism." Sierr replied.

"Wait, but why though? Do...do you think I'd be unsafe working there?" Willow's perfect, blemish free skin on her forehead wrinkled.

"Could be!" Sierr hunched her shoulders. "She has bad juju vibes to me. I just get this sense about her. And you know what Tabitha was talking to me about earlier-"

"Tabitha. What's she up to? Do you know? Is she a prostitute?" Carmen blurted out casually in possibly the loudest volume one could speak in without actually shouting.

"Is she a prostitute?" Sierr couldn't help but laugh a dry laugh as she opened her own locker. "I don't think so. She's just...fast."

"You mean a ho?" Willow stated casually reaching into her locker to retrieve her lunchbox. She noticed her friends' stares. "Forgive me." She looked remorseful, but her tone said otherwise.

"Cause I heard she dropped out of school because she was making hundreds of thousands of dollars pimping herself out to the highest bidders and that she felt like she didn't need an education because her vagina could carry her into wealth and luxury." Carmen concluded.

"It's amazing where our vaginas can carry us." Willow stated sarcastically and casually.

"No. No. Wait, if she was making hundreds of thousands why does she hang out around Downers all day doing nothing, but yoga?" Sierr questioned.

"What's there to do when you only job is to have occasional sex and rake in the Benjamins?" Carmen replied.

"I don't think she's a prostitute. No. If she's making that much money why would she be living in Carrs? If she had wealth she would be living in Mangroves with me and Carmen and JSF." Sierr rolled up her sleeves and retrieved her lunchbox from her locker. "She...she just doesn't like school and is a tad flippant." Sierr said in a even voice trying to set the record straight for her friend.

"You know just because Jesus hung out with a hooker doesn't mean you can. I mean He was Jesus, you're just a person you can get corrupted. He couldn't."

Sierr snorted, "Yes, Jesus could get corrupted He was fully God *and* fully man. He was perfectly capable of being tempted into darkness. He just stayed strong in the Father to not sin."

"How do you not know these details? Do you even read your Bible?" Willow said like a parent scolding their child. Her husky voice a few octaves lower than the average female voice making her words sound even more assertive.

"I do!" Carmen exclaimed.

"You shouldn't even be gossiping. My goodness." Willow added.

"Are you not the one who just spat that she was a ho 27 seconds ago!"

Willow couldn't help, but squint, "Was it 27 seconds ago specifically?"

"It was super specific?" Sierr nodded also confused by the number.

"Whatever. I am not gossiping. I just heard a rumor and I'm passing it onto you all to see if you think it sounds true." Carmen insisted.

Sierr smiled at Carmen with clenched teeth. It was the look she often gave when she was trying to find a way to break the truth to someone. "Honey, that is the literal definition of gossiping."

"In what way would it not be gossiping?" Carmen asked desperately. She was the Wendy Williams of Heisenberg High and it was almost pathetic how much a sucker she was for a wild story.

"Um if you were passing the story along in order to protect somebody from harm or pain or being mistreated. Like a whistleblower." Sierr respond as the girls stepped down the three steps into the bowl that was the cafeteria. As always the room smelled like cheap microwave pizza particularly the artificial cheese. The sound of scooting metal chairs, endless chatter, trays sliding across the bar at the food line, and metal spoons hitting the bottom of the glass fruit and soup bowls filled the trios ears.

They had to talk louder just to continue their conversation. Willow asked, "So, wait what did Tabitha say? Should I be concerned about working with Angelica McCord?"

"Well she met this journalist guy the other day. Son of some I dunno doctor, famous child psychologist guy, and she tried to hook up with him-"

"See?" Carmen said as if Sierr had made some sort of juicy admission that confirmed Tabitha was a prostitute.

"Well it didn't work. He turned her down flat. But, he asked her if she knew anything about Angelica McCord. Thing is he is here in town investigating the disappearance of The Beckwith Brothers."

"WHAT!?" Willow squealed. "That whole thing is a big silly joke!"

"I dunno JSF brought up some pretty good points about it. And why would an amateur journalist come all the way to Downers to cut his chops on some *silly myth* unless something about the story rang true enough to investigate? I mean why would he waste his time and potentially his fledgling reputation, right?" Sierr asked. Willow was thoughtful for a moment. "All I know is that he definitely suspects her of something. Otherwise why ask the questions?"

Willow sighed sadly. "I really need this job. If I don't work with Angelica I may never have another opportunity to get anywhere near a fashion house and I may never ever get anywhere near the New York fashion scene like I've been dreaming of my whole life."

"I want you to be happy. But, I also want you to be safe." Sierr's eyes fell.

"Girl, you just have to watch out. Report everything. To us. That way we can be your sounding board for anything shady or suspicious." Carmen leaned forward dramatically.

The girls tried to shimmy past the line of students waiting for their turn in the lunch line. Suddenly a thick, wrinkled black plastic wolf face appeared next to Willow and snarled loudly. She and Carmen yelped, jumping back. It was just,

Jeremy Trainer, an unofficial member of the unofficial skateboarder's clique in Heisenberg and biggest goof ball in the entire school, playing a prank. He was thin as a toothpick and pale as white rice. As if he wasn't incredibly annoying enough, him laughing like the prank was the funniest thing in the world made his presence even worse. Sierr was disgusted. Nothing about him was redeemable. Besides her crouch gawking habit had revealed to her that his penis had to have been micro at best. Everything about his person was unattractive and messy.

"Lighten up ladies, it was just a joke!" Pieces of greasy blond hair sticky to Jeremy's long flat forehead.

"What it was, was rude! We were having a conversation. You don't just go and interrupt us with your nonsense!" Willow spring into action. She had a short fuse and always seemed to be one spat away from finally socking somebody in the face.

Jeremy literally skipped away laughing with another friend who was skinnier than he. That dude, Kev Dune, was another one of the skateboarders.

Willow whipped her body back around to her friends. "Why do people have to be so...so..."

"Horrible? Totally." Sierr finished Willow's sentence casually while walking through and open gap between students towards the double doors to the front lawn.

Willow and Carmen follow closely behind. The girls made their way to the brick steps in front of the school and took a right on the third step from flat ground onto the connected brick boarded around the school's elevated flower garden and took their usual spot perched under a tree. After unpacking their lunches: a vegetarian sushi roll and homemade trail mix for Sierr, Jambalaya and a pear for Carmen, and leftover cheese pizza and blueberry pecan salad for Willow. They were the scent of three cultural foods all in one whiff.

"So, are you guys coming to the bash? I'd love if you were there. It is my debut after all." Willow chirped.

"Halloween is the devil's holiday." Carmen noted matter of factly.

"We help put together the bash every year?" Sierr noted.

"Sure we volunteer for the fundraising process because it's fun, but actually participating the Halloween celebration. Is that right?" Carmen genuinely asked.

"Well I will be there anyway. For work. I just wanted you guys to be there too cause I want your company." Willow said.

"Supporting a friend should be okay." Sierr said. "Even if it means participating in the Halloween celebration." Then Sierr added thoughtfully, "I'm sure Jesus will understand."

"Well...alright. Are we supposed to dress up? Are there rules for Angelica McCord's Halloween Bash?" Carmen asked Willow.

"No, you don't have to dress up. You can come as you are!" Willow grinned.

"Aww, it's just like church! Isn't that quite fetching?!" Sierr gushed playfully. The girls share a laugh.

"Oh no! I completely forgot. We have the Hollows Eve Play at church at the same time." Willow gasped.

"No wait it's earlier right? The flyer for the Halloween Bash said eight until midnight, right?" Sierr said. "And the church thing is at six until eight. When we finish our part in the play we can leave early, stop by Ashley's, and get drinks and then head to the Bash in the Park!"

"Perfect." Willow gave a sigh of relief.

"That works great because our part in the play is in the beginning!" Carmen bit into her pear happily.

Later on after school let out and the teenagers were off to digress with coffee at Ashley's or lunch at Metallic, JSF was getting his fix elsewhere. He passed his dealer a crinkled $20. It was new and crisp just hours before, but JSF always crushed new bills in his fist to give them crimps and crinkles. That way they would be less likely to stick together as new money often did. He couldn't risk losing even a dollar in an unfortunate mishap such as that.

JSF had a short exchange with the familiar face, the guy didn't have a name, not an official one anyway, just a title, The Deep Dish. The name was a pun. The word "Dish" was the only thing that applied to him as in he would dish out what clients, near and far, wanted. JSF wasn't sure if the "Deep" part had to do with how deep the drug took people or if it was simply just a reference to pizza. Either this was he only source of treatment at the moment and he'd honestly buy it from a serial killer if he felt the price was reasonable. Sure he could afford the expensive stuff, but expensively did not necessarily mean quality so why waste his fortune? He want to save as much as he could. Who knows the apocalypse could be right around the corner?

Soon JSF was walking away from behind Ashley's, stepped over a trashed coffee cup rolling from left to right on the pavement like a staggering drunk. He was pleased to know that he had a replenished stash. He knew better than to walk around with the stash on his person, but he just had one extra stop to make before hopping on his bike and going home. He unlocked his bike chain, unlooped it from around a light pole in front of Heisenberg High, stored the chain in his backpack, hopped on, and headed for church.

He paddled up behind the girls. "Hey laaaadies." He glided next to them in the grass as they walked on the sidewalk side-by-side. He forced the bike forward with the paddles. It was a little tougher on the grass.

"Hey. Where were you today?" Sierr asked.

"Ehh, around noon I got sick of that place and I just said, 'fuck it I'm done with learning today' and I just walked out." He hunched a shoulder with a smirk.

"Sometimes it gets like that." Sierr nods like she would totally skip school too if she had the nerve and if her parents let her do just about anything like JSF's parents did. It's not that they didn't care or that they were neglectful. They were just too busy running their own business to notice his existence beyond his immediate wellbeing. For example, they wouldn't notice if he was gradually becoming a drug addict, but they would notice if he happened to fall down the stairs or chop off a finger making dinner or something suddenly drastic like that.

"What on earth would you know about skipping school?" Willow grinned challenging Sierr's agreeing attitude with JSF.

"I'm just agreeing with the feeling." Sierr replies before turning back to JSF. "Hey, solve this riddle. *You may find me in the sun, and yet I'm never out of darkness. I am the beginning of sorrow and the end of sickness. You cannot express happiness without me, nor misery. I am always in risk, yet never in danger. What am I?"*

He thought for a moment, scrunched up his nose like he often did out of habit, it would easily qualify as his official thinking face. "Hmm, I'm gonna say the letter S."

"Bingo." Sierr in a monotone voice.

"Oh could you sound happier. I only solved a complicated riddle in under 30 seconds." He rolled his neck.

"Oh did you?" She replied as unamused as possible.

"Giiirlll, stop playin'. You two know don't cha?" He leaned over his handlebars stretching his neck to see Carmen and Willow in full, without Sierr blocking his view.

"I thought it was awesome, man. Just awesome. Bet you can do the Times crossword puzzle too?" Willow said with a hint of respect and admiration.

"Sure can. Those are easy." JSF gushed.

"I mean the Sunday one, you know." Willow insisted.

"Me. Too. You, know?" JSF said in the best mimic of her voice that he could muster up.

"Hey-Ya." She replied in the way someone would say "touché".

"Hey-Ya." He repeated.

"I'm still stuck on Sundays and Saturdays?" Carmen said perplexed.

"Okay so the answer is the letter S, right? So, think what starts Sunday's and what finishes Fridays?"

Carmen looked bashful.

"Isn't it cute when you see your little one finally get it?" Sierr teased like a proud parent of her little girl.

The foursome laughed together.

Soon they were walking up to the doors of the church. JSF walked his bike to a pole and chained it back up. Sierr waited on the porch for him as the other girls stepped inside looking for the choir lead. "Rebecca!" They called from a distance.

When JSF was done securing his bike to the pole, he charged up to Sierr like he was getting ready to mow her over. She shoved him off with a laugh. "Oh what you act like you don't want me nowhere near you? What the H? You don't like me no more? Is that it?" He got all up her in her face rolling his neck around. She turned away laughing. He stayed stuck to her like glue making false accusations that she wasn't a good friend until they got all the way inside the church.

"My goodness how do you come up with such outlandish stories kind sir?" Sierr put on her best southern belle "I Do Declare" accent.

"By peering into your eyes my love!" He said in a debonair voice much deeper than his own.

"Ooh, hot stuff. Been reading some harlequin novels kids?" Youth Leader Rebecca Hill said as she walked up behind Willow and Carmen from a conference room in the church.

"Nah, just watching some sappy porn." JSF stated casually.

"Whoa." Sierr blurted.

"Wasn't too bad. The cameraman really focused on bodily excretions which I appreciated." He hunched a shoulder with a nod.

"Well God Bless you in the house of the Lord too." Rebecca said briskly. She turned to the girls changing the subject. "Anyway, girls today we will be going over your part in the Hallows Eve play. So, c'mon let's take our places and begin reciting each line and tune." She gently clapped her palms together twice.

The girls sat down their book bags on the pews and made their way up the stairs to the alter. Sierr bundled her thick hair on top of her head and held it in place with a single stressed out bobby pin. It formed a crown of glossy curls and she took her place on the ~~stage~~ alter.

JSF took a seat in one of the pews, more to the middle than the front. He slouched in the chair and gapped his legs open like he did in every chair and threw an arm over the back. He couldn't help, but notice how supremely beautiful Sierr looked with a cascade of curls falling all around her crown of curls. He loved when she wore her hair up because it accentuated her feminine long, thin neck from shoulders to jaw line.

"Ms. Becca." Willow said. "I'm going to have to leave a little early from the play."

"Whaaat?" Rebecca breathed, clutching the collar of her blouse like the mere thought of anything coming in the way of her play would lay her out.

"I'll be here for my parts in the beginning, but I just have to leave a little early because I have an internship requirement that will...uh...require me to be there at a certain time on Halloween day too."

"But...But..." Rebecca trembled. "You won't see the finished play." She was nearly whimpering.

"I...I've seen it." Willow replied in a gentle voice for fear of pushing the woman all the way over the edge.

"Noooo, things have changed." Rebecca said.

"Well we still have two weeks of rehearsals. I'll see the end rehearsed and I'll see the costumes and the staging...stuff...backstage and I'm sure I'll get a very clear visual of what the entire play will look like."

"You promise?" Rebecca said like her life depended on it.

*Good Grief.* JSF couldn't help, but sink further into his place on the pews to keep from laughing out loud.

"Yessss. We...all...promise." Willow said as carefully as humanly possible.

"We all who?" Fear returning to Rebecca's eyes.

"Just Carmen and I." Sierr said.

"Her internship has requirements that requires you two be there too?" Her eyebrows shot up.

*Whoa, not this serious.* JSF clamped a hand over his mouth to stifle a rouge giggle.

"Noooooo, no, no. Carmen and I just want to be there to support our good friend, Willow. This is her first step towards her dream job and we just want to witness her mediocre rise to greatest!" Sierr chuckled throwing an arm around Willow's shoulder ignoring Willow's annoyed squinting at her cheek.

"Well, I guess that is a noble reason to miss the end of my play. Alright, I'd be happy to let you ladies leave the play early!" Rebecca smiled warmly.

"Well weren't really asking for permis...." Willow started.

"Um what Willow means is we thank you for your understanding. Ms. Becca." Sierr finished her thought by saying through clenched teeth only to Willow, "...the lady who we have to see every week during mass and even more during rehearsals and do not want any lingering hostility with."

Willow nodded firmly in agreement. "Exactly Ms. Becca!" She smiled like an angel.

"Okay, then ladies. Are we ready to begin? Good." Rebecca answered her own question not even giving the girls a chance to respond. "First, the opening which you know...whoops come grab your lyrics sheets, girls. Come. Come." Rebecca waves a hand.

The girls stepped forward as Rebecca handed them each a lyric sheet. They once again crush, crushed their way back to their places on the alter.

"Okay, let's try that again, girls. First, the opening which you know is the child pumpkins singing Stevie Wonder's Superstition which then succinctly transitions into, "Burn the Witches, Burn the Witches"."

Sierr couldn't help, but laugh. She leaned over a whispered to Carmen, "Child. Pumpkins!"

Carmen snickered in her hand. The thought of small children dressed up in round, bulbous pumpkins costumes waddling onto the alter to sing a song about successfully killing witches during the Renaissance era just gave Sierr a morbid little tickle.

Rebecca scooted across the floor to the piano. "And then of course you girls appear. In your shimmering gowns representing the "four buttresses of glory". Are you with me so far?"

"Um...who are we?" Willow's forehead wrinkled.

"The four buttresses of glory." Rebecca like it made perfect sense.

"Uh-huh. And...who are they?" Willow responded.

"I think we've cross into the extended fantasy part of the program." Sierr whispered to her friends.

"I thought it was supposed to be based on Biblical history?" Carmen whispered.

"Well there are no "buttresses" in Biblical history. So, this is...All imaginary. Think a Christmas magic or Santa Clause centered holiday tales."

"Oh my goodness." Carmen sighed.

"What you girls are is the heavenly servants come to earth to save the holy city after the rapture." Rebecca outstretched her arms dramatically while explaining the...tale.

"From witches?" Willow frowns confused.

"Are...are our lyric sheets even relevant anymore?" Carmen asked.

"Yes! Yes!" Rebecca replied excitedly.

"Wait, the holy city? The rapture? That's all in Revelations. Prophecies of future symbolic and/or literal events. But, Hallows Eve is about the past how does that match up?" Sierr asked.

"Well time passes, darling!" Rebecca gushed like she was offering some eureka moment type of information to Sierr.

"But, But…not this fast. Noth…nothing in the future pertains to Hallows Eve?" Sierr replied.

"Girls. Girls. You have to use your imagination. It'll be fun. It'll be fun. It'll be fun." Rebecca waves her hands and flipped a page to her sheet music. "Let's practice and see how it goes. She how we flow. Come on. Come on." She said in her peppiest voice.

Sierr caught JSF's eye. He stifled a laugh. So did she.

"Okay, let us begin. Follow the lyric and the musical notes. Okay, 1, 2, 3, 1, 2, 3." Rebecca motioned for them to begin by dipping her head just as she started playing the keys on the keyboard.

Sierr and her friends started singing all the while thinking. *This play was bound to be a mess.*

Later on Willow and Carmen walked to Metallic to get sandwiches together and Sierr and JSF made their way back towards the Mangroves. JSF let Sierr ride his bike, but she peddled slowly so he could keep up and they could talk.

"JSF." She said thoughtfully a clunky curl bouncing in from of her right eye.

"Yeeeesss."

"When we look in the mirror do we see ourselves as we are or how we were?" She smiled at him widening her eyes over and over again.

"How we were." He answered without a beat.

"Why do you think that?" She cocked her head to the side.

"The human eye is a curious thing."

"It is."

"It can bring the physical world into our brains as our memories."

"Uh-huh." They crossed over to the other side of the street.

"But, one must ask how does the eyeball work?"

"It flips the image we see upside and then right side up in a hundredth of a second which is the cause for the delay in which we are able to actually see the world." Sierr gave him an innocent smile.

"Oh so…so this was just a setup for you to broadcast your smarts is that it?"

"Possibly. Potentially. And Probably." She hunched a shoulder.

"You are reason I reason I smoke pot."

She whipped her head to him and hit the breaks on his bike. "JSF! Noooooo." She said disappointedly.

"I'm just kidding." He pinched her cheek.

"Wait. You're just kidding about me being the reason for you…doing what you just said." She whispered. "Or were you kidding about actually doing…w…what you just said?"

"I was kidding about you being the reason."

"J…S…F." She whined. "Why?"

"Because it makes me feel better."

"From what? Is something wrong at home?"

"Nah, my parents just...they're just busy. I know they love me. I'm not like alone. I know that. But, when I'm sitting in my room or something I just take a few puffs...mellows me out."

"If you feel bored or something get a hobby."

"I have school work. I'm pretty busy."

"Well then take a minute to pray."

"I pray before I go to bed."

Sierr stopped his bike again. Slowly looked over at him with a look that screamed that she thought he was insane or at least what he was doing, living a double life, was insane. "So, do you pray before or after you do the drugs?"

He exhaled and started pushing her along via the handlebars.

"And watch the porn?" She arched an eyebrow enjoying the ride.

"Sierr, I don't do these things because I want to compromise. I do them because I need to."

"You cannot be serious."

"It's complicated. It's getting me frustrated." He sing-songed to the beat of 'It's Complicated' by Avril Levine with a grin.

"This isn't that complicated, Avril."

"I just like distractions."

"What do you mean?"

"Things to keep my mind...occupied. When you're down you write. Not to pour feelings into, but to get away. Transport yourself to another world. I don't have stories to pour myself into so I disconnect in other ways."

"I understand that, but what's making you want to disconnect so much?"

"Just life. The world. Sometimes I just want it all to go away. Silence all the chatter."

"But not at the expense of your soul...or your health."

"I don't think I'm risking my soul. I understand it's not the best thing I could be doing, but I've deemed it my acceptable weak spot."

Sierr knew about acceptable weak spots. She had one for sure. "I want you to be happy, but I want you to look for another outlet too."

"Oh meh gosh, is this you talking me with finding another way to disconnect?" He grinned and arched an eyebrow.

"Uh-huh!"

"No."

"Yes!"

"No."

"Why?"

"Because right now it works for me. Give me a some time. Maybe I'll get past it."

"Is something else wrong?" Sierr said with concern.

"How could anything be wrong with me? I have a guardian angel."

She knew he meant her, but she didn't quite believe what he was saying. She had known JSF since...forever. She knew he was hiding something. She decided to give him a few weeks at best to tell her everything on his own that way she wouldn't seem pushy or insensitive and then she'd promptly start pushing some more.

"Well alright." She said. What she really meant was, *Alright for now.*

Meanwhile, JSF predicted that Sierr would only give him a few weeks at best to tell her the full story. He knew her quirks. Her intrusive habits in the name of "love" and "caring". He sighed. He didn't mind her ways really. In fact he kind of liked that he had someone in life that would actually bother to press him about his well-being beyond the physical. He was so used to the emotional detachment of self-employed parents who work 100 hours a week in their many at-home offices. He practically raised himself, was his own therapist, spiritual leader, chef, tutor, etc. Self sufficiency had become the rhythm which made him tick, but he had to admit it was a relief just to be considered for longer than a quick check-in during a quick breeze-by by those two strangers who provided his genetic code and the roof over his head. Besides he had just bought himself enough time to stave off her questions until he gathered more information himself. He just didn't want to worry her if there was nothing to worry about. Sure the pain was getting unbearable, but the weed helped… a lot. Sure he had symptoms, but maybe the test results would be negative. Maybe it was explainable by some minor cause that would go away on its own or was at least curable. Whatever his chances were he would get the test results back in two weeks and then he would let Sierr know everything.

Later that day, laying in bed, Sierr could feel herself still digesting the Alfredo Coated Vegetarian Fried Lasagna Frittas her mother made for dinner. It was the staple of a full Italian spread including: Italian Couscous Salad, Eggplant Parmesan, Grilled Asparagus, and Tomato-Feta and Balsamic Bruschetta; plus, Frosty Hibiscus Tea Gelato with a Sweetened Condensed Milk drizzle over the top for dessert. She had already finished all of her homework. Twirled a lock of her hair with her left hand while writing with her write.

She was finally able to write the character arc of her leading lady, Jessica Daffy. Named appropriately after Jessica Rabbit because that is what she was with a few carefully placed alterations. The beauty. That was what stayed. The attention grabbing looks that made all the girls envious and made all the guys swoon. She always wore red or some variation of it. Pink, Salmon, Magenta, Fuchsia. It was Jessica Daffy's thing. The alterations began with her height. Jessica Rabbit was long, curvy, and tall. Jessica in Sierr's untitled novel was petite and fit. Jessica Rabbit was sexy with all the confidence in the world. The sultry voice, the Victoria Secret model's walk, and the come hither eyes. Jessica Daffy was modest, a little too modest for her own good, but she hadn't quite figured that out yet. Daffy was confident only where she was supremely gifted. In being a young adult NARC agent for the LAPD.

Then came the age difference. Jessica Rabbit had to have been at least 30 hanging out with that rough crowd and all. Jessica Daffy was 18. Barely even legal. And experienced and wisdom oozed from her attitude and only added to her appeal. Jessica was always the smart one, the reserved one, but her pout lips and long eyelashes always seems to beacon the male gender. She'd only accept their call of it was necessary for her assignments from the precinct. Conflicted in the dirty details of her work, Jessica was an anti-hero. A rare breed in the literature of the time. Sierr could only hope television, books, and movies would dare to touch on the stories of the unforgivable and badass in the new millennia. Only time would tell. Perhaps she could write the stories herself? Anyway, Jessica Daffy was a Master manipulator in charge of any and all perps, always one step ahead, hip to the jive, and clever as a fox. Her confidence came from a deep sense of self and a deep sense of pride in her ability to do her job well.

She was never one to be distracted by such things like dating, but the budding romance between she and her superior had particularly intrigued Sierr. The dashing and debonair Supervisor Officer Oscar Vaschez, 35, was nearly twice her senior and staying true to the common cliché it was so wrong but it felt so right. As Sierr penned their forbidden romance on paper. She imagined herself with Officer Vaschez an older, beautiful man, to look at her like his queen and be here comforter and protector. Jessica Daffy sought Officer Vaschez's counsel even when she knew what to do and when. She always considered him before sleeping at night. She once thought it couldn't have been because of love or lust. No! It had to because of the case, the students, her friends whom she was betraying. She tried to convince herself that it was she that simply needed a sounding board for her thoughts, but deep down she knew it was more than that. It was more than an work relationship. But, it wasn't love that blinded the young agent. It was lust that kept her eyes on him. What would it be like to have a romantic interest who occupied one's thoughts day in and day out. To be so submerged, marinated, based, soaked, and saturated by a single person. *I want to be soaked in thee,* Jessica Daffy realized. For he was just around the corner. And why did he want to meet her here and now? Why at this hour? Why in this way? She hoped his intentions were also fueled by love, lust, illogical liberation from the logical and the desire to be soaked in her. She approached him in the darkness. His broad shoulders casting a shadow over her whole body. *What ifs* ran through her reeling head. What if I am fooling myself?! Jessica cried internally. What if he just thinks of me as some silly little girl? What if I am only a fetish that he thirsts for, for only a moment? An experience to be experienced once maybe even twice and then cast aside like open cans of soda gone flat? What if he thought we had too much too lose? What if....

Sierr put down her pen. She'd write the climax to the story tomorrow or perhaps over the weekend. She had to decide if she wanted her main character to get everything she wanted or build some more tension in her life. What type of tension would be best? What if Officer Vaschez is only playing her? What if he really does love her too? What if the case is compromised and Jessica needs to go into the witness protection program?!? What if the person meeting her who she thinks is Officer Vaschez is actually not Officer Vaschez, but some organized crime bosses setting a trap to silence her?

*Whoa, too many ideas.* Sierr sighed. She loved writing, but it was certainly work. Free work to make matters a tad worse. On the other hand it was fulfilling work too. Fulfilling beat out free. The free did not matter if the fulfillment was genuine and it was genuine. Writing genuinely kept Sierr company during her most lonely and quiet times. It offered her a calming outlet for her fantasies, daydreams, and creative nature. It was the gentle wave to her surfboard. It even provided lives that Sierr could vicariously live through where the narrative, the consequences, and the characters were free from critique because they were all under her control. It was a free space for her true self. It was a free space where she could be comfortable and know that there was already a level of acceptance, freedom, and competency already in place unlike in the real world. Acceptance of her lustfulness and cynicism. Freedom to speak without fear of being judged or shut down. Freedom to be clever and say the best lines because there is no pressure to think of them during face-to-face conversation. And her competency is always spot on. In the real world Sierr was always second guessing herself and her value, but in her writings she is everything and is definitely the most equipped for all the roles she has selected to play.

Even still her self-doubts still crept in. If only she could crank out something amazing like the great written works of the writers of the past. Those in the 20s and even the 80s. Those good works, with great words, meant for the smartest people. If she was capable of doing that. No, if she proved to herself that she was capable of doing that then. Then! She just might feel better about herself. Worthy and equipped for the world and life. Like her dreams were actually in reach like her life wouldn't be a lie. She just needed some assurance that she was indeed good enough. But, what if the assurance never came? She sighed sitting up in her bed.

Noticed her size nine and a half feet sticking out from under the duvet. She wanted to swat them away like flies. What teenage girl had a size nine and half foot? Worse case scenario she wasn't even done growing yet. Don't people keep growing well into their late teens? Dear God why did she have to be so ugly? At first glance she only seemed pretty, but it was little details like giant feet why no one ever really liked her and why she would never like herself. Boys notice small things like this. They are very critical. They try to pretend they are all laid back and easy breezy and it's us girls who are temperamental, emotional, and materialistic, but she wouldn't be fooled into believe that lie. Boys are like children they like a toy until they've had it for a while and then every little thing that is subpar or less than with their fav new toy become the first thing they think about whenever they pick up said toy again. Every little detail magnified. They make do for a little while try to still have fun with it, but then comes it upgrade which seemingly has no flaws. Nothing subpar or worthlessness that brings hatred and disgust out of them. Then they trade in. This wasn't just a mindset meant for middle age men this was the way of the male gender. Even the most beautiful girls were not safe from the tragedy which is their ever waning glances. So, how in the world did Sierr ever have a chance?

Sierr fell back on her bed. Her hair framing her entire thin body like a crinkled circle down to her waist. Staring up at the ceiling. She could hear Lux moving around something light in her room. A couple of them. Sierr set up propped up on her elbows. She frowned trying to identify the objects responsible for the noise. Kind of hollow sounding, but solid enough to make a noise that would travel much further. Then she figured it out. Of course. Hangers. Lux must be trying to find something to wear.

Sierr slid out of bed and padded to the door. Wrapped her hand around the glass doorknob of her bedroom door. Took a second to consider if she wanted to socialize again today or had she had enough for one Tuesday? She wanted to lay back down in solitude, but hunched a shoulder she was rather curious about whatever Lux was doing. She threw her door open and shuffled to her sister's room. Outside the door

Sierr could hear Jazz music from the talent of Boney Janes through the door. Lux had introduced Sierr to Jazz music years ago said it was the best music to dance a sultry routine too. Sierr was still in elementary school when she started requesting Jazz music in the morning car rides to school, but since then another wordless musical genre had called her name: Classical Music. One playback of Samuel Barber and she was hooked. Classical music had officially become her favorite genre of music. It was relaxing, inspiring, and sensual, but she could still recognize a few standout Jazz songs. Boney James was one of Lux's favorite artists. Sierr could pinpoint the song playing was....Balm? No wait...Cream? Luscious?

Sierr knocked on the door with a knuckle didn't give Lux time to answer before peaking her head in. "Hey-Ya."

"Hey-Ya." Lux replied walking a fitted skirt from her walk-in to her elevated sleigh bed angled from the far wall to give the room a more geometric and open feel. Sierr had to step down two wide wooden steps into Lux's room. Lux always joked that she had no reason to leave home because she already had a room the side of an apartment anyway. It was partly true. Her bedroom could shame some studio apartments. It was at least 750 square feet, unlike Sierr's 300 square foot room. It was wide open and because it was on the corner of the house it had two windows facing different directions and allowed concentrated sunlight to enter her room in the morning on the east side and the evening on the west side. Kept it rather warm making Lux's room the most expensive one in the house to keep cool, but the natural light it got daily was peaceful and beautiful.

The color scheme Lux choose was a light lavender, deep lavender, and white. The bed linens gave the room it's most striking pop of purple. Containing all the lightest and deepest shades of lavender present in the room the bed was the lead actress in the room and all other appearances of purple including the lamp shades, the sheer curtains on the window, the lavender crystal chandelier, and the lavender custom made ceramic chess board on the white tea table by the window, were all the supporting cast members.

Sierr pushed the door almost closed and walked further into the suite, "Where ya going? Whatcha doing? Who ya seeing?" Sierr threw herself on all the pillows on Lux's bed as if she was bellyflopping into a pool of water.

Lux snorted, "Well gosh lemme think. I am going to meet with an investor for the studio tomorrow, Graham. A local business owner." For as long as Sierr could remember her sister never missed an opportunity to call teachers, doctors, elders, businessmen, and businesswoman by their first name when she was around close family and friends. Sierr figured it was her small way of normalizing those whom she could have been intimidated by. This "Graham" surely had a last name, but she'd probably never hear Lux say it unless directly asked. "I'm picking out what outfit I am going to wear to said meeting, and who I'm seeing is the aforementioned investor."

"Ah-Ha. What's the investment for?" Sierr fiddles with a button on one of Lux's blazers laying on the bed.

"Advertisement for the new Co-Ed Classes. Two(t)-Sweet. You like the name I picked out for it? It's a okay in the term 'Toot Sweet' except two is spelled like the number two, because it will take two dance partners." Lux smiled laying a tea-length dress up against her golden skin, holding it up and in place as it would be if she were wearing it, with her chin and her hands, turned around and looked at her reflection in the full length mirror which hung on the back of the door of her walk-in. She pivoted from one foot to the other imagining exactly how she'd look walking into her interview with the dress and trying to judge what level of professionalism, if any, it screamed.

"I love it. Almost as much as I love that dress!" Sierr's eye twinkled.

"Aww, I know you love the tea-length style. You can strut in here and borrow it anytime you like." Lux laid the dress back down on the bed, plastered another one up against her body, and again watched herself in the mirror pivoting from one foot to the other thoughtfully.

"Thanks a bunches!"

"What do you think?" Lux twisted her mouth to the side squinting at the dress she was still pivoting with.

"Honestly?"

"Please. I need to know what your first thoughts are because that's probably what Graham will think, honestly."

"Okay, if you're going for girl leading with her breasts for money approach *that's* your dress."

"Hmm, okay done with that." Lux stepped into her walk-in and hung the dress back in it's proper place among the other dresses, skirts, pants, shorts, work-out, and exercise wear.

Sierr sat up, propped up on one arm, "Lux? Did you...did you...when you were my age did you ever wonder...or um think...actually...um..." Sierr trailed off nervously.

"What's going back there? You preparing to cough up a hair ball?" Lux stood in the mirror grooming her hair.

"No. I'm not sure how to say this."

"You finally killed Abby Windsor and I'm the first person your confessing this to?" Lux dabbed her lips with lip gloss. "Don't worry I won't tell if you tell me last words."

"No!" Sierr laughed.

Lux turned to face Sierr, "Well what is it?"

"Have you ever experience a great love?"

"Excuse me?" Lux gaffed.

"I'm serious. If you tell me I promise I'm not trying to use your experiences to excuse myself from having to be accountable for my own actions. No matter what you tell me I will be disciplined. I'm just...curious."

"Wasn't my concern FYI. I know you. You're the girl who when we were younger would hold yourself to the strictest limits about eating sweets even when mom and dad weren't home. You're the girl who when you are given too much change back from Mariah-who-can't-count-for-the-life-of-her at the grocer you always help her count out the money again and then give her back the extra so that she won't get into trouble. When you say that that you will be strict with yourself...I believe you."

"I respond well to limits." Sierr replied casually.

"I know." Lux smirked.

"What has been your experience with love and passion?"

"Passion?" Lux tore a shirt from its hanger. Then paused to think. "Have I had passion before? Lust, yeah. Passion, I dunno 'bout that."

"Because lust is based on sex and passion involves being enamored by a person?" Sierr asked making a mental note that Jessica Daffy and Officer Vaschez had that. They had unexplored *passion*.

"Yeah. What you said." Lux plastered the shirt across the front of her body and posed in the mirror. "I've not been in love, pipsqueak. Not yet anyway. Why are you asking though?"

"Curious."

"Curious, why?" Lux arched an eyebrow over her skinny, gold wire frame glasses that made her resemble a teacher.

Sierr thought before she spoke, "You know how I…" She sighs purposefully. "Like a little attention."

"A little?"

"Yeeeessss! Well I don't exactly just want attention. I want to be the sparkle in someone's eye. Ya know? I want to be made to feel special to someone who's special to me."

"Are you sure that you're 16?" Lux grinned cocking her head to the side her tiny, kinky curls following the movement of her head with a bounce.

"I see other girls in my school being pursued. Being fawned over. Being cared for in deep, beautiful, endearing ways, and personal ways. I mean the thought of being so close to someone that you can finish their sentences, almost read their thoughts, be one in spirit and in mind, have intimacy and love. It intrigues me so! I want that. And I feel like a complete lump because no one wants that with me."

It was at this point Lux needed to sit down and face her sister. She eased onto the bed, brought a boney knee up to her nearly flat chest, and looked her sister dead in the eyes. "Sierr, I don't think it would be healthy for someone, anyone, your age having a relationship that um…consuming."

"Why not? Love is the most perfect thing in the world."

"I think what you want is to feel desired."

"That would be great too." Sierr nodded.

"Sierr, those other girls in your school are not like you."

"Yeah, that's the other thing. Guys actually look at them as something to be desired. Not me because I'm really not that pretty."

"Sierr! Ugh! Okay, you are nuts!" Lux leaped up from the bed.

"I'm not! I mean look at you and look at me."

"Two beautiful brown Blakes. That's what I see."

"One beautiful brown Blake and one okay looking brown Blake. I am the okay looking brown Blake. I can never not see that and being ignored by all of my peers just reinforces the feeling."

"Ugh! You're one to complain. At least you have breasts! I'm standing over here friggin' flat chested!" Lux cupped her A cups over her shirt with tense fingers like she wanted to just tear off her sad tiny titties and replace them with a pair of boobs more worthy of her approval.

"You'd think my boobs are nice, but even they don't make any guys attracted to me. It's like I'm always wearing a sign that says, *"I'm Invisible. Don't Pay Attention To Me"* and I hate that. It makes me feel totally ugly. And I'm beginning to see what they see."

"You don't need attention from boys. All boys do is just spell trouble. Them and their demands and pressures and their penises. Steer clear of them. They are bad news! What you need is some confidence, girl. Get up!" Lux waved her sister towards her. Sierr dragged herself off the bed. "Hurry up!"

"Okay! MehGosh."

"Just march right over here young lady." Lux pushed Sierr to the mirror.

"Oh, I don't need silly affirmations." Sierr turned away, but Lux grabbed her skinny biceps and positioned her back in place.

"I'll be the judge of that. Now missy. No more talk of you needing the attention of men. Got it!"

"Not need just really, really would like it."

"Well forget about it. How you feel about you needs to come from you. It needs to be your genuine feelings about yourself with or without the approval of anyone else."

"But, what if I don't approve of me."

Lux exhaled sharply. "Girl, you are really testing my nerves. Standing here all beautiful and sounding like a complete nut referring to yourself as ugly."

"No, one ever looks at me. You can tell me all that matters is that I like myself, but it bothers me that I am never seen. Because a person who is truly beautiful would not have to go through that."

"You could not be more wrong! You loon!" Lux threw her hands up in the air.

Sierr sat back down with a bounce.

"Do you know how many supermodels are called ugly on a daily basis? Tyra Banks! Naomi Campbell! Kate Friggin' Moss! All of them! And do you know why? It is not because they are only "okay looking people" it is because their gorgeousness is not always appreciated and perceived by others." Lux spoke with her index fingers and thumbs pinched firmly and swirled them around in the air like Mrs. Martinez did when teaching Social Studies class. "Some people cannot see beauty when it stares them in the face."

Sierr sighed.

"Look if you walk out of here learning anything from this conversation let it be these two things at the very least: you need to believe that you are beautiful and the guy that is right for you will see that you're beautiful without even having to squint."

"Have you always liked your looks?" Sierr asked.

"No, not always, but I learned that I do have nice features and that I should embrace my natural beauty." Lux started back modeling her outfit choices for her meeting with Graham. This time a pea green sweater dress that swung to her ankles.

"Oh you can't wear that tomorrow."

"Why not?"

"Because I'm wearing that tomorrow." Sierr smiles from ear to ear. Lux sighed and tossed the dress to Sierr like a basketball. Sierr caught it with one hand. "It's nice." Sierr said admiring the soft, warm wool lined green fabric.

"I know. That's why I bought it." Lux said moving onto another outfit. She then let out a light chuckle. "You know what. I'm confused. You want boys to give you attention and yet you're not even interested in dating. You have never even went out on a group date."

"It's just confusing and annoying. I see all the other girls in school being pursued, but not me. It's always like the hot girls and then Sierr, the lump."

"Sierr, not all attention is good attention."

"I would just like to know that I could have some attention. Just to prove to me that I could be desired at least."

"You barely want to talk to people. You like your alone time. You're an introvert like me. Which is understandable."

"You'd still think that I'd be noticed…a little." Sierr hunched a shoulder into a bundle of freshly washed curls still a little damp deep inside. She washed her hair as soon as she got home from school, that was five hours ago, so that divided by the density of her hair probably equaled about another 12 hours for her hair to actually dry through and through give or take a few hours.

Lux chuckled lightly, "Sierr, what would you even do with male attention?"

"Give…give it back?" Sierr responded like she was trying to guess the right answer to a World History question in class.

"How?"

"Be…um….I would…uh…"

"Before you answer just remember boys your age will hardly appreciate you for your intelligence, your immense kindness, or your conversational skills so let's just get that out of the way now." Lux tried to shake the wrinkles out of something Polyester.

"JSF, likes talking to me."

"Well JSF is different. I mean obviously I don't even have to explain why. And also he's known you since childhood and he's grown…accustomed to you."

"Accustomed to me?" Sierr laughed. "He's used to my presence now, huh?"

"Yeah, you're a staple in his life at this point." Lux plucked up an apricot colored fitted skirt that reached that perfect tea-length and a matching long sleeved top with reached the high waist band of the skirt. If Sierr actually wore the ensemble the top would probably rise up to the point of being a midriff once it was stretched over her upper body and her breasts.

"Maybe if I didn't walk like a penguin?" Sierr wondered aloud.

"Welp, you've got giant feet whadda ya expect?"

Sierr gasped and then pouted, "Did you have boyfriends at my age? I don't remember."

"You were a little young back then. And no I did not have a boyfriend at your age. I had my first boyfriend at 18. Harry Leyden." She sighed his name. "We dated to two months before he got a college scholarship and moved away. He had beautiful red hair. Strong shoulders. Smelled like Carmel every day. Drank Crystal

Pepsi like us mere mortals breathe air. He was taller than me. Had a deep voice. It was fun while it lasted."

"Did you two ever have sex?"

"Oh God no. We were both virgins, but I wasn't ready. He never pushed. We knew it was just temporary anyway." Lux said plastering the apricot ensemble up against her body in the mirror.

"When did you lose your virginity?"

"Who says I have?"

"Look at how you dance?"

"Anybody can move their hips. Even children do dance class, interpretive dance, and ballet."

"You're old...er."

"E...excuse me!?" Lux gasped with a shocked smile.

"Well I mean older than the virgins I know."

"You know people who are the same age as you. 16-years-old. Ya know that age where you are waaaay too young be needing people to tell them they're pretty FYI."

"Well when was it?"

"My twentieth birthday."

"Go on."

"Don't tell me you wanna have sex now too. You're just throwing all brands of *shite* at me I can't even handle today." Lux used the Blake word replacement for "shit" by saying "shite."

"No, shite. I'm not looking to have sex. I promise."

"Do you swear?" Lux darted her pinkie finger in the air towards Sierr.

"I swear. Cross my heart and hope to die. Or at least hope to suffer some sort of hard fall or tragic accident or something."

Lux dry laughed. Sierr smirked.

"Why did you do it though?"

"I was feeling a bit rebellious that day. Or maybe it was that whole year." Lux admitted thoughtfully. "I drifted from the tenets of our upbringing. But, I came back. The puppy always finds her way home."

"Was it temptation? A certain guy? A special guy?"

"He was handsome. Sure. I didn't think we'd be getting married or anything. It was spontaneous." Lux hung some of her clothes back up in the closet. "Honestly, I could have waited longer."

"Are you just saying that because you don't want accidentally encourage me to indulge in the sin of fornication?" Sierr leaned forward with a grin.

"No, I truly think you pressure yourself to be pretty much as *angelic* as possible."

"It's truth." Sierr sighed pleased with herself.

"I'm being transparent with you. It was nice, but after it was over I realized that I would always have a notch of my bedpost that wasn't my husband. My future husband. And I wasn't fond of that. My sexual history could've just been between me and that one special guy and now it will never be that way. And I kind of wish it was." Lux paused for a moment in thought then she said, "But, there's no changing that now."

"Well I guess my looks will help me stay untainted for sure."

"Did…did you just imply that I was *tainted*?"

"I mean no attention surely means no sex for *this* girl."

"So…so you did call me tainted?"

"I'm just saying one of us in this room is still pure and the other has a notch on her bedpost." Sierr grinned.

"Who said it was just one?" Lux blurted.

Sierr gasped, "Whaaaaaaat."

"Hey-ya." Lux arches an eyebrow.

"How many?"

"How many doesn't matter now. What matters is that there won't be anymore until that special guy comes along."

"You. Hussy. You."

"And by the way you are nuts for wanting those stupids boys at your school to be fawning over you. I mean they are the epitome of overgrown children."

"Well except JSF. He's smart."

"He's a kook! A quack! A nutter-butter! But, yeah I'm sure there's some smarts in there somewhere. Sure." Lux took a sip from her big glass of lemonade on the nightstand. The Blakes were always big citrus fans. Sierr too.

Sierr looked dreamily, "Maybe I will focus all my energies on being the best at my craft: The female Stephen King of Thrillers and the female James Cameron of Film. And then when I am at the height of my sprawling multi-million dollar career, at a ripe 22-years-old of course, suddenly a tall, handsome, gentle older man, who is of course also a fellow millionaire artist, will just come along with his dashing, dashingly, dashingness and take me under his wing, adore me, love me, and I will overlook the fact that he is probably in the beginning stages of age related Erectile Disfunction and call him, "Daddy'."

"It sounds like you've thought about this before." Lux said.

"Only a little." Sierr chuckled.

"This fantasy guy sounds a bit old."

"Not very just seasoned. Like Abby's dad. Mr. Windsor."

"Oh Mr. Windsor. Yep, he has some Mack Daddy mannerisms. All that big dick energy. I had a crush on him when I was attending Heisenberg too."

"He's sexy without even trying. Gosh, he's just…he's…" Sierr tried to find the words to describe him.

"Lickable." Lux states plainly.

"Ugh! Yeah!"

"What do you mean, 'Ugh! Yeah!'? What do you know about licking men?"

"I know that the tip is suppose to be very sensitive!"

"You…"

"Aaaaaand that men and women share the same erroneous zones so that's a good place to start, huh? To learn how to do ya know…*the sex*." Sierr nodded slowly like she was informing Lux of some secret, special information.

"Enough with all your sexual knowledge, kid!" Lux popped the wrinkles out of a pair of pants. "But, in all seriousness there best not be no *old ass mens* coming after you with their bad intentions. Or I will…" Lux trailed off.

"You will what?"

Lux whipped her body towards Sierr and said dramatically, eyes dimmed, hair tussled, nostril flared, "Or I will slowly karate chop them."

Sierr cracked up and Lux joined in.

Over the next two weeks the grip of fall took hold on Downers Grove. The trees were bare except for a few crispy orange and browning holdouts on their branches. Bare bark wrenched and curled up to the sky like they were praising the heavens for the opportunity to shed the old in preparation for the new. All their shed material littered the ground. What was a burden for homeowners was a joy for the young. Crunchy crispy leaves was a priceless joy that could last hours. Warm clothes were required to shield from the chilly air. Some days the forecast was sleet and the others sunshine, but the grey of coming frost didn't seem to let up.

Ashley's had re-introduced their seasonal menu items. Pumpkin spice donuts with buttercream glaze, gingerbread loaf, peppermint chocolate chip cookies, peppermint coffee, crème brûlée lattes in vanilla, hazelnut, and chocolate, and pumpkin spice coffee with a pumpkin spice whipped cream.

Her café had scary Halloween decorum. A ghoulish, ghostly hooded figure stood in the back corner by the bathroom looming over the patrons. Some claimed it would turn its head ever so gently to watch them walk to the bathroom and sip their coffees. The windows were covered in fake spider webs pinned up in two places in each window frame to allow patrons to be able to look out on the Plaza. Different species of poisonous and frightening spiders were interwoven into the strands. Some looking a little too lifelike for comfort. A smoke machine ran all day long and plastic headstones were sprinkled around building. With the headstones and the fog the floor looked like a cemetery. Ashley loved the spook quality of Halloween and she especially got a kick out of scaring her customers by dropping a robotic centipede from the ceiling on an invisible string in front of them as they waited in line. The robotic centipede twirled around itself, flexing its hundred legs back and forth. It looked both like a giant flying insect and a giant flying snake all at the same time. The reactions of victims or this prank varied from terror, to anger, to giddy laughter, and fascination. Sierr was present for a time when a furious and hysterical prank victim threatened to sue Ashley for "undue stress" and "attempted homicide". Ashley apologized giving the woman coffee and an entire cake no charge plus a coupon for free coffee for the rest of the year. When the woman left in a huff, Ashley retorted, "Bet she's just ready for winter since she's such an ice queen."

The majority of the time Ashley's pranks were well received by customers, probably because she was prone to giving out free coffee to customers who loved Halloween just as much as she. Once a day in the week leading up to Halloween the walls of Ashley's would bleed dark red blood from ceiling to the floor. The walls were actually fitted with a gel covering in which the red running fluid was contained and recirculated through a system of tubes and pumps. The blood was said to be that of dead hunters and huntresses of seen and unseen mystical creatures such as Chewbacca and the Loch Ness monster. The story behind the blood was so random and confusing, still in this week leading up to Halloween customers would "camp out" in Ashley's maintaining booths and tables from open until close to be present for the moment the blood ran down the walls. When it did the café would erupt in cheers and applause! Celebrating the recognition of the dead and the promise of the future.

Outside Sweet Pique Lane was decked out in Autumn embellishments. What looked like orange Christmas lights were spiral wrapped up each light pole on the street and two-sided Autumn reeves hung over the bulbs one side facing the street and the other side facing the pedestrians on the sidewalk.

Colorful Mums hung from the facing of "ma and pa" shops, some included scary Halloween decorations with their Mums such as a skeleton holding a "Welcome" sign propping open the door of the entrance to Mr. Jennings Hardware and Construction store. Some included cartoonish Halloween decorations more targeted at the young such as a sticky plastic Casper the Friendly Ghost plastered in the inside of each window pane of "Trinkets and Crickets" the cozy antiques shop which always smelled like warm cookies and played insect nature sounds particularly cricket chirps. Some others took the Hallows Eve approach stacking hay squares by their store entrances with a stack of creamy colored, green, orange, and burnt sienna gourds and fake multi-colored corns, maybe even a smiling scarecrow or two propped up together the best of friends. Or at least friends of the scarecrow from The Wizard of Oz. This was the Halloween style that Rachel's took, the shop for off the rack clothes that was perfect positioned in the Plaza for frequent foot traffic.

Sierr, Willow, and Carmen walked purposefully in step with one another singing the intro to Living Single bumping their hips up against each other. They clutched onto condensation coated green-tinted bottles of spiced, non-alcoholic Ginger Beer in their palms slightly shielded from the cold by fingerless gloves. Carmen forgot the third verse leaving dead silence in the middle of their three-person audience-less concert and the girls burst out laughing. Willow folded over laughing and her fuzzy cat-ears headband fell from the crown of her head to the top of her nose. She snorted throwing them back up on her head and readjusting the headband back into her silky straight hair.

"So, that's where the 'queen,' herself, is going to grace us with her presence in just a few hours, Willow the Footswoman?" Sierr said in her best English accent after taking a crisp, cold gulp of her Ginger Beer and catching a shiver.

"Why yes Kind Sierr! Her eminence will be here in this very Plaza in or little town promptly at 9 pm! She will probably present herself to us in some royal, regal, colorful attire that will be a delight to our eyes when she arrives!" Willow declares in her best English accent.

"And then Her Majesty will address the crowd!" Carmen pronounced with her own best English accent.

"From her royal litter carried by handsome shirtless hairy male peasants." Sierr added in her same English accent from before.

"Absolutely, her handsome shirtless hairy guardsmen!" Carmen agreed.

"Wait, hairy?" Willow wrinkled up her nose in disgust.

"YES!" Sierr and Carmen replied eagerly nearly salivating at the thought of men covered in smooth yet untamed bodily hair.

Carmen continued, "And she'll address the crowd, mere peasants that we are, and devote her Kingdom to us tossing rubies in a prayer of good health and good fortune!"

"Hallelujah!" Willow pumped her non-alcoholic beer bottle up to the heavens.

"Preach sista, preach." Sierr cheered, before initiating a toast in fluent Spanish.

"Si, si, Mona Lisaaaa!" Carmen exclaimed as the girls toasted.

Sierr and Willow both made a face, "Huh?" Sierr asked.

"Excuse. My Espanola is not so good!" Carmen squeaked.

"I could've figured that when you called me 'Mona Lisa.'" Sierr laughed.

"I meant, My Friend, the Angel!" Carmen said like surely the blunder would make sense now.

"Wha...? That's not even close!" Willow laughed. Sierr and Carmen ended up laughing along too.

They passed the Park on the Plaza it was shrouded in a barrier of white curtains draped between poles. If Grovers took a peak through one of the openings between each section of curtain they would see the Gazebo being outfitted with Ghoulish Halloween decorations wrapped around its width, fog machines being rolled into their perfectly hidden places behind serving tables, caterers with dirty aprons zipping back and forth between their many white vans with a variety of labels and logos and a tent where they were cooking up all the hors d'oeuvres for guests of the Halloween Bash. Also, any peaking Grover's would see construction workers from Mr. Jennings feverishly putting the final touches on Halloween structures and statues throughout the Plaza and Park.

Sierr and her girlfriends arrived at Baptist Church. They were greeted by fellow congregation members walking with them up the pathway to the front doors. A set of African-American twin girls about three-years old dressed as angels, wings and glowing halo and all, made their way into the double doors hand-and-hand with each of their parents. They were going to angels in the play. The girls had met the twins during rehearsal. They were polar opposites in personality. They were half sweet, half polite, half obedient, half quiet, and half delightful. The problematic half, also known as Lola, was every bit an embodiment of the terrible twos turned unruly child as can be. Lily was the perfect half and liked being dolled over though so perhaps she would do well in her part as the "floating angel baby."

The girls were greeted by Mrs. Ginsburg and Mrs. Haven. Two of the most idyllic, older ladies. They were like the great-aunts a person never had. They baked cookies, pinched cheeks, gave unwarranted dating advice, had inappropriate sense of humor which they let loose anytime they were not in church, smoked like chimneys, and smelled like cigarettes dipped in the lemon essential oils that both women both managed to use in the humidifiers in their homes. True, it was highly probable that either Ginsburg or Haven suggested the lemon essential oils to the other, but why would they both settle on such a shocking smell such as lemon? Did it even have holistic benefits like other essential oils? It mostly smelled like cleaning products.

"Hello dawrling." The hunch-backiest of the two, Haven, said looking up at the girls above the top brim of her wire rimmed glasses. Her thick Jewish accent always noticeable.

"Good afternoon, Mrs. Haven." Sierr said with a smile.

"Hi honey are you wready for the play tonight, deear?" Haven blinked with her trademark expressionless presentation.

"I am. I am. We're so excited. The play is so um…" Sierr paused thinking of the right word to say, "…imaginative." She finally settled on.

"Inventive." Willow plastered a fake smile on her face.

"Incoherent." Carmen cheesed proudly.

"Really?" Willow tucked a lock of hair behind her ear turning her upper body around to Carmen.

"Uh cha?" Carmen replied with a single nod.

"Well we've made everyone some snickerdoodle cookies and Pumpkin Pie, dear. So, feel free to help yourselves." Ginsburg said.

The girls echoed a long, "Thank you" for both ladies and stepped inside the church. Among the pews they observed which of their neighbors, classmates, and which play members had arrived.

Sierr trotted over to her parents and gave them a hug. Her dad gave her a boisterous, "You go, Kiddo!" Giving her hair a fluff. Lux couldn't be there. She was doing a Halloween Themed Dance Session at The Heat.

Willow greeted her dad and Carmen was smothered by her parents who were both covered in jewelry and Burberry.

Backstage err actually behind the alter Sierr spotted JSF clutching his stomach trying look normal. "Hey. You Okay?"

He tried to play it off, "Oh Hey I didn't see you there."

"I saw you." She said.

"Oh well it's hard to miss a black guy in a small town."

"I'm a black girl in a small town." Sierr said innocently.

"Ehh. Barely blondie. But okay."

"I…ex-cuh-uuuuuuse me?"

He chuckled at her with a devious grin.

"You football." She said.

"Hey-ya." He said like someone would say touché.

"Why do we do that?" She asked.

"I dunno."

"You don't know anything."

"Nope."

"That's why you claimed that I'm not black."

"Are you?" He snorted.

"Shut up!"

"*Well!*" He put extra emphasis on the word to make himself around as outraged as possible. "God bless you in the house of the Lord *too.*"

"Dude. Sit in the pews and be a good boi!"

Soon enough the ridiculous play was starting. Sierr, Carmen, and Willow after the little butts off and uttered every preposterous line of the outlandish script in front of the audience who only sucked up the play because they were the proud parents of all the actors and actresses. The ending came with toddlers Lily and Lola becoming duo floating angels who told of the coming favor of the Lord. Soon enough the play was over. Everyone was off to eat at the Hallows Eve meal. It was common in Christian communities to keep Hallows Eve festivities going on until after most of the *evil* Halloween celebrations were over. As distracting believers during Halloween was the supposedly most effective way of keeping them away from sin. *Out of sight out of mind*, Sierr supposed.

Walking out onto the street made it all the more clear why Downers Grove was getting nicknamed "Sleepy Hollow". Not that anyone would ever want to agree with Angelica McCord. It was dusk now and the freaks were just beginning to emerge from their dens and bunkers also know as homes and condos in the area. A Penguin crossed the street just as Michael Myers wielded his trademark butcher knife at a group of teen girls he opened the door of Ashley's for. Sierr and her friends trotted towards Michael Myers, he held the door open for them too, and he raised his knife at them. They screamed, cowering playfully. To their surprise the usually silent Michael Myers screamed bloody murder back. The scream took on an eerie hallow pitch muffled inside of his Shatner mask. Patrons inside of Ashley's flinched at the other worldly noise.

Sierr stepped in the door first, but not before giving Michael Myers a high-five. "Awesome everything dude."

"Thanks." He replies breaking character and speaking in his surprising friendly, non-threatening voice. "What are you?"

"Just me." She flipped her curls unintentionally.

"Nice." Michael Myers nodded, his words barely audible.

Carmen and Willow shared a look closer to the pseudo slasher than Sierr now and the only people who heard his pleased response to their friend.

They wait in line. Willow notices Carmen checking over her shoulder, up at the ceiling, in the back corner of the café, back up at the ceiling. Her teeth clenched, forehead wrinkled, and eyes full of fear.

"What are ya doing?" Willow asked with an arched eyebrow.

"I'm terrified of being in here. Knowing Ashley she's probably plotting some elaborate way to make us jump out of our skin all for a good laugh, but I swear if it was me I would NOT find it funny!" Carmen hushed yelled.

"If you don't like her jokes she usually gives you free coffee." Sierr whispered.

"If you do like her jokes she usually gives you free coffee too." Willow added in a whisper. "You know come to think of it someone's always getting free coffee here. You'd wonder how this place stays afloat?" Willow concluded thoughtfully.

"W…." Sierr started, but almost immediately her sentence was cut off as blood ran down the walls of Ashley's. The entire building exploded in cheers, screams of joy, and applause. Ashely herself started jumping for joy and laughing with no one in particular. Then people got up from their seats and bowed to Ashley raising their coffee cups, coffee mugs, and tea glasses up in the air for air toasts. Girls jumped for joy quickly screaming so high it was like they were trying to break some Guinness Book Of World Record record for screaming. Guys high-fived, beat the tables with their fists, roared like they were at a football game and their favorite team had just scored the winning touchdown. It was like the entire café had won the lottery. A million and up jackpot each. A teen dressed like a sexy elf then jumped and called out to Michael Myers, "Michael! Michael kill me up against the wall. Stab me!" She pleaded smiling throwing herself up against the plastic covering in which the blood ran down the walls. Michael eagerly charged over knife raised and brought it down in close proximity to the girl who made a show of being fake slash murdered. She screamed in horror despite smiling giddily. She tossed her head left and right as if trying to fight away her attacker. She cried, "He's stabbing me! He's stabbing me!" As she mimicked choking on her own blood. Michael was having a joyful time pretending to really do as Michael would do and kill a young girl as people watched. The only difference was people were cheering him on. And the girl was not really going to be killed of course. *Okay. Two differences.*

The teen sexy elf outstretched her arms on the bloody walls and slowly slid down the wall to the floor as Michael kept on stabbing. "Oh! Oh! Oh!" She exclaimed with each thump of the knife on her back. "It's my blood!" She screamed. "It's my blood. It's my blood. It's my blood!" She exclaimed over again whilst throwing her body from side to side. "I'm dying. I'm dead! I'm deeeeead!" She fell back revealing a wide satisfied grin. Michael then raised his knife to each corner of the café slowly as if threatening that he would be their slasher next. He and the sexy elf were given a round of applause for their impromptu performance art.

Sierr and the girls stood silently.

"Welp." Carmen said purses lips.

"Mm-hmm." Sierr bit her bottom lip to keep from laughing.

"Hmm." Willow twisted one side of her mouth to the side. "Well what were you saying, Sierr?"

"I have no friggin' idea." Sierr replied.

"Imagine if moments like this could be captured forever and shared and commented on by thousands of likeminded individuals on a shared domain?" Carmen said thoughtfully. Her wheels clearly turning.

"What do you mean?" Willow asked.

"Like sure we think it's all kinda silly, but what if there was a place, a community, online where people could post spontaneous events in their lives with limited space to describe how it made them feel, ya know to keep the domain short and sweet, and everyone who shared their same interests could like follow their lives and keep up with them online? Like a website where thousands and millions of people did this globally. Connecting people near and far with posts and clicks. A network of some kind."

"Huh." Willow replied.

"Hmm. Maybe." Sierr mumbled.

Decades would pass and Carmen would still go on to believe that Jack Dorsey was the mystery guy in the Michael Myers costume and that he had overheard her idea. She would insist that it was she who was the true inventor of Twitter.

Meanwhile Michael Myers and the sexy elf took a bow to more applause and some crazy dude shouting, "Encore! Encore!" And just as the über excitement for dripping red paint down a plastic sheet over a shiplap wall died down nearly as soon as it got started, business was back to usual in Ashley's. Ashley handed out free coffees to Sierr and the girls as well as some other patrons including Michael Myers and sexy elf and Sierr and the girls headed to the Plaza.

A zombie bumped into Willow on the sidewalk, "Excuse me." She said to which the zombie replied, "Uggggggghhhhhhhhh?"

"I hate Halloween." Willow declared.

"Because it's the devil's holiday!?" Carmen piped up.

"No, it's just so stupid. I just can't stand it." Willow grimaced annoyed as fuck.

"Some parts are…okay." Sierr said reluctantly.

"Like what?" Carmen asked.

"Pumpkin spice." Sierr smirked taking a sip of her Pumpkin Spiced Latté.

"You can make anything pumpkin spiced year round. It's just cinnamon, nutmeg, ginger, and allspice. What else do you like about Halloween?" Carmen pressed.

"Some of the costumes. Dressing up in characters is kinda fun."

"We ought to do that one of these years. Go all out!" Carmen smiled brightly.

"What? From the person who keeps reiterating that it's the 'devil's holiday'?" Willow's eyebrows shot up.

"Yes! And I'm going to tell you why. One day unfortunately probably soon, we're not going to be the same trio in Downers everyday hanging out with each other."

"We don't do that anyway. We don't hang out everyday. We hang at school. Church. Sometimes after school. Catch a bite to eat with each other. Yeah. But, not everyday. Especially not Sierr. You know how much she hates humanity." Willow states casually.

Sierr gasped, "I do not!"

Carmen waved a hand, "Anyway, our lives on the very brink of changing forever. We're going to be going off to college. Who knows one of us could actually have a boyfriend at some point. We may take a gap year and travel the world. We may find our soulmates and get married and started having babies!"

"Oh Lor." Sierra said in a whispy British accent. She then winced the word, "Offspring?"

"I'm with you, girl." Willow nodded at Sierr wincing at the thought of getting pregnant and giving birth.

"It could happen!" Carmen insisted. "And because it could happen we should spend our last few years with each other just being carefree girls right here in Downers as fully as possible doing stupid things, doing memorable things, do things we'll remember forever!" She beamed.

"Doing memorable things AND doing things we'll remember forever. Ya hear that, Sierr? Doing *memorable* things AND things we'll *remember*." Willow grinned.

"Yes. I'll have to write those two completely separate ideas down to make sure I remember to make a memory of them." Sierr also grinned.

"Yes, to keep those things to remember memorable!" Willow snickered.

"Ha. Ha. Carmen can't talk. That's hilarious." Carmen bobbed her head around dramatically. "An-y-way. So, are we doing it?"

"Doing what? Halloween?" Sierr asked before sipping confused.

"Yes! The way it's supposed be done. Costumes the works! And not just that we have to do everything we can together before everything changes." Notes of sadness came alive in Carmen voice.

"Well I think we've done everything in Downers twice already." Sierr hunched a shoulder.

"What? No! That's impossible." Carmen insisted.

"Small town woes."

"Hey-Ya." Carmen said in the saddest voice either Sierr or Willow had ever heard come out of her.

Sierr and Willow shared a sympathetic look.

"Well gosh, Carm." Willow patted her on the shoulder.

"How long you been thinking about this?" Sierr asked.

"Oh, I don't know this morning? Afternoon?" Carmen tilted her head up to the sky thoughtfully. "One of those."

Sierr and Willow shared another look. Sierr finally sighed and said, "Okay, we'll do the devil's holiday. Just once. And do it up right. The traditional way."

"Yes, eat bats. Burn witches. Sacrifice infants. You know the traditional way." Willow said casually a little grin twitching to life in her cheeks.

"Uh-huh. What could go wrong?" Sierr feigned agreement. "And then we have to add more plans to the list about stuff we can do together because Halloween is just not enough."

"No way. Not even close to being halfway enough." Carmen and the girls walked deeper into the crowd entering the Park at the Plaza. People with alternate identities dressed for alternate realities strolled across the cobblestone road of Sweet Pique and up into the plush, squishy grass of the park. Many different tents were set up which had raffles the largest of which was for a cabin in the hills and a brand new Rolls Royce to get there all curtesy of Angelica McCord Costume Designs. There were amusement park games, arcade games, food venders, cider tables, Angelica McCord fashion show which was in the program being passed out to attendees by volunteers, the entire gazebo was dedicated to featuring Angelica McCord Everyday Wear, and tables for pagan rituals such as fortune tellers who attendees of the Bash did not know were paid specifically to give spooky and cryptic fortunes in the spirit of Halloween.

Fog machines kept the ground hidden by a layer of fog which whipped up around attendees feet like the steam from a caldron.

Willow lead her friends to a tent by the sound stage where Angelica was set to address the crowd in a few moments. Two employees of Angelica's were standing there scribbling in a heavily scribbled in notepad presumably about the evenings event plans.

"Hello." Willow slipped her backstage pass around her neck for the two employees to see. "Is Angelica backstage?"

"Nope. She won't be here until just before she steps on stage." The Asian woman, Royal Ho, in a tight wool turtleneck said. Fake black tarantulas hanging from her black gothic tutu. She was Angelica's personal assistant.

The man, Jame Gumb, chirped, "You know the old girl likes to make a show of her entrances!" Sierr noticed that he had a thick stubby penis which he oddly where up the front of his sequence pants bootcut pants. Usually men wore their members to the left or the right side angled down or angled up higher on the thigh. Most men did not strap the their penis into their belts. Sierr wondered what else the man did that was weird. She tilted her head to side and examined him from top to bottom. *Hmm,* he chews his nails she made note seeing his mangled fingernails and bloodied cuticles. Wonder if he drank his own urine or suffered from OCD or something like that too. His entire presence didn't set well with her anymore.

Apparently Jame was Angelica's longtime lackey. Graduating from her errands boy to her house manager in a few years. He handled her schedule and affairs of her manor in the hills. Was her right hand man if she ever needed a right hand man.

"Alright. I'll go see what help the gazebo needs?" Willow asked.

"Sounds good. When Angelica gets here you'll come over here with us, Okay?" Royal said.

"Kay." Willow turned to Carmen and Sierr. "We'll be able to hangout after the event is underway." The girls nodded and she headed over to the gazebo.

"Do you two need an itinerary?" Royal asked already holding out two itineraries for Sierr and Carmen.

"Oh yes. Thank you!" Sierr replied taking hers as Carmen took the other.

The two began walking deeper into the crowd of make believe and horror. Hideous goblin half turned into wart covered tree men hobbled slowly through the crowd. "Well let's see." Carmen frown at her map. "We could go to the arcade games or sign up for the raffle before the line gets too long. Or get some food. Are you hungry?"

"I actually am. I didn't eat breakfast."

"Lemme guess only coffee?"

"Yeah."

"People die like that you know."

"Yeah." Sierr nodded.

"I'm thinking raffle. Before the line gets too long. Then corndogs shaped like ghosts?"

"Cool."

"Great."

When Carmen and Sierr arrived at the line for the raffle they were greeted by a line of people which wrapped around the raffle tent three times. "What do you know? People really want a free car and a free house." Sierr hunched a shoulder.

"Or $100 VISA gift cards. Or $500 VISA gift cards. Or an all expenses paid trip to L.A. with tickets to the Celine Dion concert. Or free entrees at La Marie."

"Man, I want some of that stuff." Carmen pouted. She was an heiress of a prestigious line of renown attorneys and yet always wanted free gifts. It wasn't because she could not get things herself, but she liked the concept of winning.

"So, in the line we go." Sierr stepped forward and Carmen followed closely behind. The girls took their places in line.

"Stay here I'm going to go get food." Carmen elbowed Sierr in the forearm.

"Yes, be a huntress of mythical creatures, Madam Carmen."

Carmen mimicked shooting a bow and arrow at Sierr. She turned back in the direction of the corndogs stand and almost crashed into a Freddy Kruger, a "homemade Freddy Kruger". His stripy shirt the complete wrong set of colors. Blue and green. His pants were red, but still cropped. His mask was perfect, even looked homemade. He had on a straw hat, but you barely even noticed it and he was just as thin as the real Freddy. His claws were the only thing that weren't quite right. They looked like a kitchen knives swing on a thread. Silver winter glove covered in metal shards with kitchen knives dangling off each finger. It looked rather silly really, but Sierr could always appreciate when someone tried their best at something even if they failed miserably while at it.

Soon enough Sierr had made it a full 20 spaces forward in line and Carmen was just returning from the corndog stand with giant ghost shaped corndogs in hand.

"Whoa, what kind of meat is this?" Sierr asked eyes wide and stomach growling loud.

"I asked and they told me they are Sweet German Sausages wrapped in a honey butter crescent rolls cut with a cookie cutter to look like a lovely ghost!" Carmen said taking a bite and handing Sierr the other.

"Yum!" Sierr licked her lips and dug in. "Mm, oh Lor I forgot to say grace."

Carmen chuckled licking her lips. "Hey, look at that guy." She pointed in the direction and Sierr met her gaze.

Sierr has do a double check at the guy Carmen was referring to. The lean black guy with the long dreads strolling through the park in a light pink silk nightgown with matching oversized light pink silk pants in light pink three-inch Eden Heel Pumps. His hands were in his pockets, his hair swinging in his face. Sierr checked his penis size and shape so obvious through the thin trouser. It was thick, long about eight inches, uncircumcised by the look of the tip. Nice. Wait, subconsciously her brain pulled from her mental catalog of penises in town and suddenly she realized, thick, eight inches, uncircumcised, medium toned black guy with jet black dreads? "Is that JSF?"

"Can you imagine rubbing a hand up and down a man covered in silk? Kinda hot when you think about it." Carmen breathed. "On someone who's not JSF of course."

Sierr watched as he strolled through the crowd trying to ignore that absolutely on display juicy penis. "I'm gonna say hi."

"Hi!" Carmen waved at Sierr enthusiastically like a very eager doof. Sierr waved back just as enthusiastically before spinning on her heels towards JSF.

"Who are you?" She approached him noticing tiny dots of red on the front of his shirt and his brand spanking new nice smooth beard oiled, shaped, and trimmed. He had been growing it in for a few days.

"I'm Norman Bates." He smiled.

"Oh meh Gosh. That's genius."

"I know right? I'm Norman Bates as…"

"Mother." They both said in unison.

"Who have you just killed? Whose blood is this?" Sierr pointed to the red dots. "Marion's?"

"It's up to your imagination! How are you?" He asked. He grinned, "Feeling cold?

"What?" She checks her nipples.

He snorts, "Ha! Made you look." He made it sound like it was all a joke, but Sierr wondered if he was just trying to get a look. Something charged in his tone and something hungry in his gaze. Then she thought *nah, it's all just my wishful thinking projecting itself on my MOST platonic male friend.* Most platonic to say the very least.

"Now one of these days I'm gonna trick you into touching your lady bits for me in public now that, now that I would deserve an award for."

"What kind of an award?"

"You know what. You have to watch porn with me."

"Uh-huh. Get thee behind me Satan." She said as casually and breezy as someone ordering donuts at the bakery. Original Glazed.

"I just wanna see what you'll think of it. How you'll react to it. What cha know."

"I know enough for now. I'm not even sexually active I think I know more about sex than other girls at school."

"Like what?" He stood in front of her cutting her off. Towered over her. The smell of some Cocoa Butter based lotion wafting from his smooth skin.

"You want me to go through a list? I just know some of the things girls at school talk about is nuts and I would know how to do better." She side stepped him. He took one long step in front of her and cut her off again. "You're such a cartoon character."

"I thought I was a football?" He said innocently again.

"Good heavens. Okay, so Abby said that the best way to give head is to deep throat a guy as fast as possible and then get him to cum as fast as possible. But, anyone with any knowledge about sex would be able to tell you that going slow and steady can build up the tension in the body and make a man or a woman's orgasm much stronger, right?"

"Why ya asking me?" Sierr gave him a look. "Sierr, is this you accusing me of pleasuring myself and/or not being a virgin? My Lord. You dirty girl." He said in a high pitch southern belle voice. A hand fluttering up over his heart for added effect.

"Ha. Ha." She laughed dryly. "So, tell me if I'm right? I am aren't I?"

"Lemme put it like this. *You* should test it. Then you'll know first hand. Or with both hands...whatever you like." He grinned pleased with himself. "Or you could ask for some help."

"No. No. No. Fornication? It's not right. It's sin."

"I've heard. Try it on yourself then."

"N...no. I'm not sure if that's okay either."

"Sweetness. Does the Bible say a person shouldn't masturbate or should a person not look at 'stimulating entertainment or motivation' to fuel their masturbatory habits? You have to read the Bible closely, Angel Baby."

"Wait a minute? Norman Bates." Sierr slapped a palm over her heart in the most flamboyant fashion. "Are you actually trying to corrupt me....on Halloween?"

"While Halloween is the perfect holiday to corrupt someone, I firmly believe in all the same things that you believe. I wouldn't try to corrupt you. I love you."

"I love you too, compromising Mr. Bates."

"And I'll admit when I'm compromising. The pot I know that's a compromise. The porn that's a compromise. What I am telling you I honestly do not consider a compromise. Just thinking out loud."

"Also known as making a suggestion."

"Are you gonna take it?"

"I don't think so."

"That's not a 'no' I'm hearing." He grinned. She wacked his arm playfully. "It might help you stay celibate as long as your planning too. Until marriage."

"I can pray for strength to do that!"

"I believe that."

"Okay? So?"

"Not so…however. If giving yourself a little rub is okay why not soften the wait time then?

"Because you don't know for sure that's why. I'm not okay with compromise. Once you start compromising in one area it's a slippery slope soon you'll be compromising in ten other areas than twenty more areas." They strolled in front of the arcade games seeming to glow as the sky darkened more.

"I've only compromised in two areas."

"Lemme ask you this. Which one of those areas did you compromise with first?"

"The porn."

"Uh-huh and that compromise lead to what?"

"The pot." He sighed.

"Uh-huh. Slippery slope."

"Well if I'm escalating at this rate I'll be a serial killer in no time!"

"Aww, everybody knows potheads aren't violent." Sierr elbowed JSF with a grin.

"What? I though I was a football?"

Sierr laughed until she couldn't breathe. "Are you really going to keep saying that forever?"

"Probably."

"Well you're definitely the smartest football I ever met."

"Sierr, I think you have just uttered the words that are destined to be engraved on my tombstone someday." He threw an arm over her shoulder and gave it two squeezes. "Hey?"

"Yeah!"

"What does the center of our Milky Way Galaxy smell like?"

"It smells of Raspberries and Rum."

"Ahh, you've already heard of it." JSF snapped his fingers once.

"Because at the center of our galaxy is a giant cloud of Ethylene Formate which is the chemical that gives Raspberries their taste and Rum it's smell."

"You got it, pipsqueak. I like walking around in pajamas. I gotta do this more often! Maybe I just like not having on any underwear."

"You don't wear underwear anyway."

"Oh my goodness control your gaze, Madam Blake." He said with perfect enunciation with the accent of a perfect southern gentleman.

"Control your junk and I will, Master Fitzgerald." She spat playfully.

"Sierr!" Carmen screamed from the raffle line waving her scarf in the air like she was surrendering herself to war criminals. She was next in line.

"Oh I gotta go." Sierr gave JSF a hug and kiss on the cheek before turning to meet up with Carmen. "Happy Halloween!" She yelled over her shoulder.

"Happy Halloween!" He yelled charging after her.

"Are you coming with me?"

"Looks like I am!" He hunched his shoulders mid-stride. JSF then reached out and tickled Sierr. Threw his arms around her waist and almost swept her off her feet. Sierr laughed and screamed. For a second she could smell marijuana on his person, but she soon forgot all about that when her arm got caught between his legs and his penis smacked up against her forearm. She felt the overwhelming urge to grab it. Squeeze it. Maybe even kiss it a little. Sierr quickly snapped out of it shaking her head vigorously as if it were an etch-a-sketch which she could just shake memories and ideas away.

Sierr and JSF hobbled towards Carmen in line for the raffle. Their stomach muscles still cramping and aching from laughing so hard. They panted and started laughing with each other again. They were next in line, were handed six blank sheets of paper each, printed their names on the paper pieces, and drop each of the six paper pieces into each individual fishbowls full of other raffle entries in order to be in the running for all the prizes being offered.

"We did it!" Carmen jumped for joy as she often did.

"Hopefully we'll win something!" Sierr said.

"I'll say a prayer that we do." Carmen nodded proudly.

"Me too." Sierr added.

"If one of us wins anything of greater value than the $100 gift card we should share with each other." JSF suggested.

"How about this if you or Sierr win anything of greater value that the $100 gift card than you two can share it with me!"

"Whaaaat?" Sierr exclaimed.

"It makes perfect sense." Carmen insisted.

"How?" JSF smirked.

"Helloooo. Math." Carmen stated like it was obviously obvious whatever nonsense it was that she was talking about.

"Math? That's your answer. What math? What formula?" JSF asked.

"The kind that gets people to share their gifts with you." Carmen cocked her head to the side.

Before Carmen could answer the lights on the sound stage dimmed and ethereal music on the grand piano began to play. Jame Gumb's buttery voice came over the microphones positioned around the park.

"Ladies and Gentlemen. Boys and Girls. Characters from fiction and beyond." His voice echoed and reverberated in chests. "The woman of the hour is a trailblazer. A self-made success. The AM over which admiration itself fawns." *Really?* "The Cord that brings a cohesive quality to our lovely town of Downers Grove." *Huh?* "The moment you have ALL been waiting for…" Actually everyone was really just eager for the announcement of the raffle winners, but *sure* let's act like Angelica is the main attraction here. Jame's long dramatic pause ended with an emotional explosion of the words, "ANGELICAAA." He gasped for air. "McCOOOORD!" He belted the words out so hard and forcefully that his face stretched like it could hardly even fit that woman's name in his mouth and he almost sounded like he was about to cry in utter worship of her grace…lessness. He outstretched his arms facing the street just as her horse and carriage arrived at the entrance of the park and the Spotlight shined on her.

Shock of all shocks the song, "There She Is Miss USA" began to play as she waved swaying a stiff hand, all fingers firmly sealed together side to side like a real pageant girl to the crowd of mostly confused looking attendees. They didn't know that Angelica was a failed Miss USA contestant and a failed pageant beauty queen. Her youth had been spent trying to get famous off her looks. When that failed she used what connections she had made in the modeling world that never accepted her looks to make looks her peers would purchase to wear from her. Guess her Halloween costume was a version of herself that her younger self would have died to become. Which when you really think about was pretty Halloween forward. She was a beauty queen all the way down to her red sparkly ballroom gown and sash that said "Miss Everything" on it in cursive writing. Her hair a walking PSA for how much hair spray is too much.

Angelica's carriage was white and spun with red, sparkly fringe that matched her gown and robotic black crow which *Caw Cawed* periodically each caw making their throats and eyes that flamed with the red of the demon possessed. Her twin auburn Arabia Mares wore red sparkly bridals and trot trotted into the park dutiful to their masters command. They were not her only minions, no, today Angelica McCord's minions took form in both adult, animal, and child. Four children specifically who rode alongside Angelica in her carriage. Two boys and two girls. All wearing jet black from head to toe. The boys in black three-piece suits with slicked back hair and the girls sparkly black velvet dresses with choker collars that had spikes on the sides. Their hair slicked back into long ponytails.

The Spotlight followed Angelica into the crowd as attendees were cleared to make room for the Mares and their owner's transport.

Just then a flock of men in khaki pants, loafers, and button downs or T-Shirts came running. Alongside them a smaller, but equally energetic float of woman in slacks or dresses that fell in that awkward area below the knee and above the perfect tea length dress zone. Among them all the flocks had many tings in common they were all household names, they were all devoted to their work, all received a call from Jame Gumb that they should want to get first dibs reporting on the greatest event of the year hosted by the one and only, Downers most famous well-known face, Angelica McCord, they were local news reporters mic in hand cameraman already locked and loaded to take his or her shot through the lens.

Angelica then stepped from the carriage with the help of Jame as the mob of reporters ran into the crowd in the park. She then bowed to the cameras, smiled at the children as if she loved them, and helped each one out the carriage. Cameramen and camerawomen captured her best side just as she wanted them too. Without pausing she took an offered microphone from Jame.

"Oh Great Halloween my dear friends!" Her husky, über proper voice echoed over the crowd. Her hands movements embellishing the emphasis in each and every word she said. They spun, twirled, danced, and waved in the air like the hands of a dancer during her greatest routine just because Angelica was speaking. She always did everything she could to make sure she seemed like the most amazing person in the room. The world really. The hand dancing was just one of the many quirks about her. "We've come together on this fine evening to celebrate what we all have in common, what makes it clear that we are all alive, and what we all find a little elusive…and for some addictive…" Her turned and looked over her shoulder at the crowd, arched eyebrow, overly pursed lips, sucked in cheeks. She oozed all the drama she possibly could to purr the word, "Fear."

*Ohs* and *ahs* from the crowd. JSF couldn't help, but snort with Sierr.

"Tell me my friends. What separates the living from dead. A heartbeat? No. Fresh meat? No. Love? No. No. No! No! My friends it is fear that separates us from the dead! For the dead no longer have anything to fear, they have met the worse and either prospered or met the flames of HELL!!" Suddenly flames shot up from the top of the metal structure which created the stage. The fires roared to life. Wind took up the bottom of Angelica's gown creating a whirl of red sparkly fabric all around her body. She spun around slowly posed like a ballerina figurine in a jewelry box. The look on her frozen face was one of maniacal laughter and a shout. Her eyes wild. Left arm crooked above her head, again for added effect, her left hand looked like spider legs with fingers flexed and clenched.

Cheers and applause from the audience. Hooting even. And Howling?

Sierr spied the source of the howling, but instead she found herself locking eyes with Abby's face intentionally held in a position that translated to boredom. Eyes dimmed. Lips parted ever so pouty. Cheeks sunken in. Was that from her parted lips or from a diet? Suddenly her face went into a full snarl as if simply looking at Sierr had disgusted her somehow.

Sierr looked away. JSF's boney elbow jabbed her in the ribs. She squirmed away.

"Don't let the bitches get you down." He said super close to her face so she could hear over the noise of the crowd and the flames shooting from the stage. His breath smelled like potato chips. A fart mixed with onions. Sour Cream and Onion Lays? Sierr didn't mind…that much. She liked it when he spoke into her face like that. It was comforting somehow. Despite the stench.

She giggled as Angelica took to the stage. Revealing heels that rivaled all others, bedazzled in red rhinestones, red velvet bottoms which was the farthest thing from practical on moist autumn grass in a park of all places, and they were platform on top of platform on top of the platform at a ridiculous 7 inches. No wonder she was walking so slowly. Apparently it wasn't just the drama of it all.

She turned back to the crowd holding the microphone to her thin lips, "Let me take you on a tour of what it means to be alive! To fear what is true and what is only conspiracy! To fear what threaten us in reality and what is only the subject of nightmares! To fear…." She winked at the cameras and curled her thin lips into a grin. "…Is what it means to be alive. It is our innate process to maintain our safety, be protected, nurtured. To have concern about losing those things is to have warm blood in our veins. So, as the freaks come out and night and terror descends upon us!! Live and Let Live my friends!!"

Cheers and applause again. Most of the attendees didn't even know what they were cheering at they were just hyped up that they would be getting drunk later on and being scared shitless between then and now by some creep on the street liberated on the one night of the year they could let their freak flag truly fly, some

Halloween Trick, or some horror movie screening into the wee hours of the morning. That new Scream movie didn't look so bad at first glance. To them Angelica was just some old lady talking about scaring people. But with what? The haunted house? The occasional jump scare from a few of her employees dressed like deformed hunchbacks of Notre Dom? Granted the dressed up Costume employees were getting some screams it was nothing truly fearful or frightening.

Hailey, dressed in a jet black crinoline tea-length skirt and a matching fitted sleeveless jet black midriff and black studded biker boots, strolled pass Abby and Damian as they did shots with the rest of The Controversy Crew from plastic cups. The vodka flowed from a silver rhinestone studded flask. Abby's for sure. She's the only person in Controversy who would just die at the sight of something shiny.

"Oh look Hailey came dressed as death. Oh wait no she just does that year round for attention!" Abby clucked to the amusement of her peers.

*Don't pretend like you know me. You don't even know that I'm fucking your dad, prissy bitch.* It almost came out of her mouth. It almost flew out of her mouth like a fly ball, but Hailey bit her tongue. Not for Abby, but for Daddy. Instead she turned to Abby flipped her the bird and kept walking. Never breaking stride.

"Hails!" JSF waved her over to he and Sierr. They were holding smoking witches brew mock-tails aka virgin cocktails that actually had a lower sugar intake.

Alcohol: 0 Mocktail: 1.

Sierr's was pink with a pink smoke that plumed from the brim while JSF's was grey with a grey smoke that he breathed in like it was pot haze.

"What is that?" Hailey wrinkled her forehead at JSF's drink. Her almost perfect, to die for hairline visible with all her hair pulled back in a sleek high-ponytail. A hairline is not something you would normally consider pretty, to die for, or appealing in any certain form at all, but a really beautiful one like Hailey's with jagged edges that cut out her diamond shaped face like a perfect little puzzle piece and that dramatic Widow's Peak could really make a person see that some hairlines really are special somehow.

Sierr always loved pulling her hair back, revealing her own Widow's Peak, but tonight she wore her hair low-heat flat-ironed straight. She had used just enough heat to relax her curls, but low enough to leave some fullness. Her second favorite style. It tickled the bottom of her butt cheeks and JSF loved it.

JSF took a puff of his drink smoke and responded to Hailey, "It's a Grey Matter Flurry. Like the Grey Matter of your brain."

"I got it." Hailey smirked and nodded.

"Befittingly macabre." Sierr took a sip of hers. Inadvertently inhaled some of the steam through her nostrils and sneezed.

"Bless you." Hailey said sounding like a grown ass woman. Gosh, Sierr wished her voice sounded as mature as Hailey's. She always sounded so young and....polite.

"Amateur." JSF smirked at Sierr. "Taste like raspberries." He added. "And something else. Tell me what you think the other flavor is."

Hailey took her offered sip. Smacked her lips two times giving the flavors profile some deep consideration. "Chocolate."

"Oh raspberries and chocolate that nice." Sierr sipped her drink.

"What's yours?"

"Pink Mist tastes like Citrus. Like Lemon, Lime, and something berry-like." Sierr took another sip careful not to inhale this time.

"Is it super sweet?" Hailey asked. Just like everything about her she was older than her years in taste too. Never liking anything too sweet. Even her taste buds were mature. Sierr had a sweet tooth like a kid, but her weakness wasn't candy. It was pastries. Sweet delicious pillow goodness. Donuts. Cakes. Pies. Cookies. All the different kinds she had every tasted from her family's international palate, she couldn't get enough. Thank Heavens her naturally fast metabolism kept her thin despite her poor eating habits when it came to sugar.

"No more than Sprite." Sierr responded. She knew Hailey liked Sprite so she would probably be okay with the sweetness of Pink Mist.

"Cool. I'll have to try it." She eyed the group of misfits from Heisenberg High all huddled together on the other side of the street, adjacent to the park.

"You know them?" Sierr asked.

"The goth freaks?"

"I think they're called The Fringe." Carmen chirped.

"Well we don't hang." Hailey check her hair for split ends. "Too cold and cryptic for my style."

Wasn't her style also….goth? Sierr and JSF tried not to look too perplexed. Hailey finally said, "Yeah I know I wear all black and everything, but they like totally hate the world. They're kind of cult like. I dunno there's something about them." She left out the fact that she heard the goth gang had weeknight voodoo séances. She didn't care to participate in idol gossip it was rather juvenile and she had no proof to confirm the rumors so she dare not spread them.

"Yeah, they creep me out too. Granted they creep out everyone, but each other. Like minds and all that. But, if they tried half as hard to look as sexy as you do I might give the girls a chance." JSF hunched a shoulder and grimaced.

Hailey and Sierr shared a look. "Did you just imply that Hailey tries to look sexy?"

Hailey flipped her ponytail behind a shoulder with a smirk.

"Wha…it was a compliment ladies!"

"No. No. Maybe it was intended to be a compliment, but it didn't come out that way." Sierr replied.

"What's wrong with saying that somebody puts effort into looking good?" He asked genuinely.

"Oh JSF." Hailey shook her head. "What if I said to you sure did try to look tall today with those heels on."

JSF's eyes got wide. "Well first I'm already tall without them and second um… mean much."

"I know that you're already tall. I wasn't implying that you weren't, but you see the backhanded undertone of the remark correct?" Hailey asked.

"I think you're very pretty that's what I was saying!" JSF puts his palms up in surrender.

"Yes, I'm so pretty I have to put effort into looking sexy?" Hailey asked raising that eyebrow as high as it could go.

"You know what you're problem is. You just wanna tease people. Just like you're teasing me right now." JSF nodded like a bobble head.

"I'd rather be the one turning people down rather than being overlooked exaaaaaactly."

"I feel the same way." Sierr nodded. If only she had the draw that Hailey had to be able to attract men to turn down. Oh the joys of being the most invisible person on the planet. Maybe it's because she walked like a penguin?

"And then when you two get attention what do you plan to do with it? Or do you just wanna drive guys a little crazy." JSF asked.

"You wanna go first or me" Hailey asked. She already had a man, this little game of pretending what she would do IF she had the attention of a man was just that...play.

"I haven't really mastered the art of the tease yet. I don't think I have enough experience to say what I would do." Sierr sighed.

"Girl, you don't have to give a guy a lap dance to become the thing that he thinks about within every waking hour. Just have an heir about you. Confidence. Self-assurance. Self-awareness. And a little something pleasant yet mysterious."

*An heir. Confidence. Self-something. Pleasant yet mysterious.* Sierr didn't know if Hailey was really giving her a rundown of how to become desirable, but she took mental notes just in case. Sierr just nodded didn't even realize she was breathing through her mouth.

"It's true. You don't have to lead with your experience giving blow jobs and putting your tits on display like 'little miss originality' over there baring it all." JSF pointed with his pinky with the same hand he held his Grey Matter drink to Abby and the rest of The Controversy Crew removing their sequence blazers and revealing body paint advertisements for a Halloween Masquerade Ball that Abby was throwing in exactly 365 days. Was it tacky to be using Angelica McCord's event to promote her own? Sure. Was it kinda of too soon to be advertising for a Halloween event that wasn't even happening this Halloween? *Yep.* Did Abby care about either one of those things? *Nope.*

So, off came layers of clothes and before attendees knew it all of Controversy was in nothing, but blood stained swimwear and body paint ads. Oh, so they did a wardrobe change from zombie business class wear to zombie swimsuit models. Boy, that's genius. *Not.*

They downed more shots and struck a pose. Abby took the lead saying, "The Halloween Bash not what you'd hoped it would be? Wish this bash was more fabulous? Want to rub elbows with the Glitterati of Downers Grove next Halloween? Well then put on your best mask and come to mmmmyyyy Halloween Masquerade Ball happening in 12 M.O.S.!" M.O.S. had become Abby's new "thing". She knew there was a gap, also known as an entire year, between this Halloween and next Halloween, or what she liked to call it "Her Halloween," and saying the word "months" made the length of time seem sooooo loooong so she decided that saying the abbreviation for months, M.O.S., would make the time span seem shorter and somehow more chic. As if waiting in M.O.S. was better and more faster and more funner than waiting in months. It was utterly ridiculous and so Abby Windsor.

It made Hailey's skin crawl every time she heard Abby try to manufacture a new English language with these little nicknames for already established words. Sierr's attention was elsewhere. The goth group were joining hands and forming something that looked like a prayer circle in their same place on the sidewalk adjacent to the park. She squinted at them trying to get a better look at them. They wore all black sweatsuits. Hoods on, pants rolled up, eyes lined with dark makeup, even the guys. They all had fuzzy keychains hooked onto the sides of their waistbands. Sierr couldn't quite make out what it was. Each one was a slightly different shade of fuzz. Or fur? Rabbit's foot. That's what the keychains were. Rabbit feet. Either fake or real.

Abby shouted while sashaying through the crowd in stiletto heels, "Like the prom, but much better! Better clothes, better food, better drinks, better entertainment, better hosts…" she paused and smirked, "…A better organizer with better style!"

There were laughs. Okay, even Angelica McCord didn't deserve this. Shaded at her own party. By a teen attendee. Just tacky.

The Ladies of Controversy strutted their stuff up and down the crowd showing off the ads for the Halloween Masquerade Ball painted on their bodies. Let guys in the crowd touch the paint even though it was obvious the hormone charged boys just wanted to touch the skin of a pretty girl. Some dorks touched Raven and snorted before catcalling at her. She ripped her arm from their grasp. Swatted away a third before Tim rescued her by putting himself between her and the boys. Tim lead her to model in front of different people in the crowd. The rest of the Jocks of Controversy unfolded a sparkling banner with the same advertisement for the Halloween Masquerade Ball printed on it and they modeled the banner and their bare skin through the crowd.

Abby shouted, "Imagine a party that spans the length of Downers Grove! Up and Down Sweet Pique Lane from Heisenberg High to the Plaza! A rolling Halloween Themed party and scavenger hunt to outdo ALL other Halloween theme events you have ever seen or been to! Wear designer gowns, beautiful costumes, and our best masks! And crack the Riddle before your friends or foes do to win one of many prizes! All are welcome even, unfortunately this is America." She slipped that last part in for good measure. "Again in just 12 M.O.S.! Tell me if you're excited to paaaatry!!" She laughed and cheers answered her.

Abby and Controversy did another round of shots and the majority of the crowd rallied around her and her friends. Three other jocks dressed as Disney dudes. The jocks, all white guys, thought it a fab idea to paint themselves with makeup two shades darker than their skin tone in order to wear Aladdin and Jafar costumes. Sierr, Hailey, JSF, Willow, or Carmen were the least bit surprised. Of course members of The Controversy Crew would not bat an eye at the idea of obvious blackface for a Halloween costume. These were people who had no consideration or sensitivity for anyone outside their very close circle. The Disney rip-off white guys all lifted Abby up on their shoulders and chanted her named over again. It would be her ultimate saving grace to rebuke their rude and uncouth makeup choices, but she was too busy being the object of everyone's affections. Sick.

"Welp." Hailey looked on at the celebration that was, at least for the moment, overshadowing the Halloween Bash by Angelica McCord. "That was nauseating."

"Would you go?" Sierr asked.

"To a party thrown by Abby Windsor?" She left off the words *'my arch nemesis'* from the end of the sentence because it was common knowledge.

"Halloween is your favorite holiday. It could be fun."

"Nothing is worth that. I can very happily celebrate Halloween alone. I mostly like Halloween for the endless horror movies and mystery Thrillers and watch I can easily at home by myself."

"That new prison movie The Shawshank Redemption is awesome. Have you seen?" Sierr took a sip of her drink, flipped hair off her shoulders. Then replaced the hair because the layer of strands on her bare skin added warmth.

"It's not getting ticket sales it deserves, but total classic in the making." Hailey nodded.

"Undoubtedly."

"I liked it. Top ten favorite movies." JSF added. "Number one Stephen King story."

"Even more than Misery?" Willow trotted up.

"The ghouls and goblins don't need your services right now?" Sierr asked.

"Oh, the head goblin is having a fit backstage because of Abby's little stunt stealing her shine." Willow waved a hand. "So, she sent everyone but Jame out and told us not to come back unless she specifically sends for us. So, I guess since I'm just the intern and probably won't be needed you guys have got me for the rest of night!"

"Where'd you guys get your drinks?" Hailey asked Sierr and JSF.

"At the brain freeze stand." JSF lead the way.

Carmen plucked a hair from her candy apple. Took a little force since the hair was literally glued to the apple with the sticky Carmel. She curled up her mouth, "I swear the world is getting dirtier and dirtier by the day! Is there no customer service anymore! News flash hair is NOT edible! I'll have my mother sue the costumes off these people!" She pouted. Her glossed lips twinkling under the stadium lights. She flicked the hair into the grass like she was casting aside a dawn on her clothes. Then she chunked the apple into a trash can nearby.

"Wha…a thought you wanted to sue?" Sierr asked turning around while walking careful not to spill her drink on her clothes the last thing she needed was to have to walk around looking like a little girl with a stain on her dress.

"I do!" Carmen insisted passionately.

"You just tossed away all the evidence!" Willow wailed laughing.

Carmen stopped dead in her tracks. "Aww, man!"

"Are you sure you want to be a lawyer sweetie?" Sierr half-joked.

"No. I've changed my career goals. I've decided that I want to be an investor."

"Meaning?" Willow asked.

"Meaning she wants to make some investments sit back and make money while she does absolutely nothing." JSF grinned. "Correct?"

"Correct." Carmen replied proudly.

"Yeah, screw hard work!" Willow shouted and Willow then pumped a fist into the air and turned to a random group of girls and yelled, "Wooooo!"

They all "WOOOOOOOOOed!" In response raising their glasses and champagne flutes.

Sierr laughed, "A long 'woo' at a gathering like this is like ...... Sounding an alarm!" Sierr and her friends cheered again screaming "Wooooo!" Again the random group of girls yelled "Woooooooo!"

"What else do you think we can make them say?" Willow chuckled.

"PEEEENIIIIIIIIIIIIIIIIIIIIIIIISSSSSSS!!!!" JSF screamed at the top of his lungs and the majority of men in the crowd screamed or hooted it back with gusto. JSF turned back to Sierr and Company and smiled, "I win."

"It wasn't a competition, Fitzgerald." Willow rocked her head throwing her hands on her hips.

"And yet I still won." He replied.

Sierr gasped cocking her head looking at her itinerary, "Oh my goodness Diddy Kong racing in the arcade room!" Her eye bulged with glee.

"I wanna play!" Willow exclaimed.

"Okay, but afterwards we go to the Apple Bobbing!" Carmen declared.

Sierr turned JSF couldn't help, but notice Hailey talking to The Fringe on the other side of the street. It looked like they were wrapping up some conversation. There were head nods, pats on the back including Hailey's, and small timid almost shy waves. Just then a dark, antique car with a hatchback pulled up close to the sidewalk right next to The Fringe. Sierr thought the car looked like a hurst. She couldn't make out the driver it was far too dark and shady, but it was clearly a man. Hailey hopped into the car and it drove away. Sierr realized that JSF had noticed too. "She didn't even say goodbye."

Then as if every member of The Fringe had all gotten a memo saying that someone was watching them from behind, they all turned to Sierr and JSF. Titled their heads to the side eyeing the overly curious teens. Sierr turned and walked away. JSF followed suit. Soon their minds would be taken off the oddities of The Fringe and Hailey's friendly mingling with them and the black hurst looking van pulling up to whisk her away from the crowds. Sierr and her friends all flocked to the arcade tent to play the new version of pac-man with pac-woman. PAC-woman was very new, kind of a big deal in the gaming world.

Willow battled Sierr, both of their competitive sides coming out. Willow's a little more fierce than her friend's. Willow learned to channel her intense competitiveness in Fencing which she was the school champ in. Had traveled for many Fencing events and been a name tossed around For Olympic try-outs, but fashion was the name of her game. Fencing was great, but fashion was destined to be her life. Her life would be in style.

In the arcade, Sierr played Diddy Kong six times, won four times, and taught Carmen how to play three times. Carmen still didn't quite get it and quickly lost interest. JSF Battled Sierr as Willow and Carmen watched keeping score. JSF beat Sierr twice. Had no problem jumping for joy with his kitten heels on. He handled then remarkably well. Next, was PAC-man Carmen had already lost interest in the gaming and filed her nails while standing by her friends supportively. Sierr played twice, Willow four times, JSF also twice.

After PAC-man came bathroom breaks in El Cantinori. On their way to the Apple Bobbing stand they notice that ... caters were sampling insect shaped food. "We gotta get in on some of that." JSF grinned.

"Noooooooo. Carmen whined. "I'll never eat again. I'm still recovering from my random hair Apple!"

""Recovering?" JSF annunciated slowly.

"Yeeeeesss! Recovering, Fitzgerald!" Carmen pouted throwing her hands on her hips.

"Okay. Whatever." He put his palms up in surrender.

Gathering food samples again and buying Hot Chocolates with extra, extra marshmallows. Then it was time for Bobbing for Apples. Or rather watching others bob for apples neither Sierr or her friends were about to get in water or dip their faces into water where random strangers had already dipped their faces, or eat a cold apple on a fall night, or mess up their hair or makeup. Sierr and Willow wore very little makeup to get simply a glowy, natural look, but they still didn't want it messed up. Watching was good enough and that was all they intended to do.

So, sipping on their Hot Chocolates the girls and JSF in heels watched the competition. It seemed a blonde fairy with a pixie cut was a shoe in for the win, but a African-American naturalista angel as was beating her apple bobbing game. Sierr took a sip of her Hot Chocolate.

*Wonder why Hailey was talking to those goth Fringe people? What was she doing with them? Maybe she was telling them to stay away? Yeah, right Seraphim?* Sierr scolded herself for being so silly.

Tabitha appeared in Sierr's line of vision. She was dressed as a Ariel the Mermaid. Her red hair the perfect addition to the costume her bra cups were iridescent blue sea shells, her belly covered in a flesh toned body suit, and her mermaid tail a blue, green scale covered fitted skirt with a fishtail end. She wore flesh toned heels and sparkles on her cheeks where blush would be. "Happy Halloween, Sierr!"

"Hi Tabitha. Did you get yourself some Hot Chocolate? It's really good. Warming."

"No, I did not. I was curious about this smoking witches brew mocktails, though. Any good?"

"Tasty. Cold."

"It's okay. I'm already cold. I'm a fish out of water you know!" Tabitha gave a twirl to show off her costume. "It's an Angelica McCord original!"

"Oh really."

"What are you?"

"I'm a fallen angel."

"But, you're white?" Tabitha looked shocked.

"I'm..." Sierr trailed off.

"Ya know. You're wearing pure white everything a fallen should be something like I dunno. Orange."

"Orange?"

"Or lime green. Something like that because you're no longer a good angel."

"It was just symbolic to be human. Like the angel became human and humans are not as pure as angels so I walk now. I can't fly."

"I walk now. I can't swim." Tabitha beamed motioning to her mermaid costume.

"You're still a mermaid?"

"Huh? Oh yeah. Well I can almost swim. Anyway have you seen Kerry?"

"The journalist guy? No. Although I might not recognize him even if he were standing right in front of me."

"Gorgeous man standing in front of you that looks like Clark Kent? You'd notice." Tabitha nodded confidently. "It's so weird. He gave his pager number said to call any time. I called twice already and no answer. I haven't even seen him around town either."

"Maybe he's catching up with his father?"

"Maybe I wanted to start planning our date." She pouted.

"Start planning it. You'll just have to let him know the deets later." Sierr hunched a shoulder.

"Yes! That way at least I can surprise him!" Tabitha threw her arms around Sierr.

Sierr hugged her back managing to spill Hot Chocolate on her dressed. There it was an oval shaped stain on her. In her mind it symbolized what a ungraceful doof she was. It wasn't a big spill, but it was noticeable. She felt like an idiot.

"Oops. Oh well. Now you really do look like a fallen angel! Hey, where do I find the Witches Brew Fog-Tails?"

"Oh we can take you there after the contest." Sierr offered attempting to dry the stain with paper towels. "It should be over soon."

"Okay." Tabitha turned to the Apple Bobbers Apple Bobbing.

Sierr couldn't help but notice the dunkee's long penis in his loose swim trunks sitting up on his elevated dunking seat. *Very nice.* Sierr thought. *Bet he'd go for the pretty girls who don't spill food on themselves like an idiot.*

The contestants quickly collect their apples and start throwing them at the bullseye underneath the dunkee. Some threw so hard and with such force they push out grunts and shouts. Soon enough the Naturalista Fairy threw an apple right in the center of the bullseye. Sent the dunkee into the water with a big splash. He emerged from the water to applause for the fairy. The water made his clothes stick to his body to the point that he looked completely naked. *Very nice.* Sierr thought again.

"Okay, let's go get you a Mocktail!" Sierr said to Tabitha.

"You gonna get the girls?" Tabitha asked.

"Yes. Right. Of course. Wait here." Sierr went the five feet to the right to collect her friends hoping that they would not put up a fight about hanging with Tabitha.

"Tabitha will go to any length to show some skin." Carmen rolled her eyes to Sierr after eyeing Tabitha.

"She has on a body suit." Sierr noted. "Wanna come with us to gather more Mocktails?"

"Sure." Carmen hunched a shoulder. Willow followed close behind.

"JSF?" Willow called back.

He trotted along behind the girls nearly cracked an ankle finally suffering a stumble in those heels. "Phew!" He said gathering himself. "I almost died."

"Don't worry we'd make sure everyone knew you wanted to be buried in that." Willow cocked her head to the side.

"Snarky bitch." JSF said without skipping a beat.

"Snarky bitch." Willow replied casually.

Approaching the Mocktails booth on the outskirts of the park the group could see children and tweens Trick-or-Treating in the Plaza in their ghoulish and animated costumes. The Carpenter Man lunged out of the alley way between his home improvements shop and the antique store scaring a host of parents and kids, rendering them shaken and screaming. They then laughed how he got them good. Except for Mrs. Sinclair a mother so uppity anyone who say her coming expected some new fresh hell she was bound to raise. In her book the world was against she and her children, the Tibby Twins, and the world would not rest until she spoke to the manager about it.

Sierr could hear Mrs. Sinclair giving Mr. Carpenter man a piece of her mind. Head rocking. Hands on the hips. Shouting at the top of her lungs about how he was tainting Halloween. Sierr got a little chuckle. Did Mrs. Sinclair not know that this was the devil's holiday already? It made her wonder for the millionth time why she had even agreed to participate in this pagan ritual of sin and soul death? Then she reminded herself she was being a good friend. Surely that made her hypocrisy better?

*Nah, definitely not.*

Just then the lights on the stage went off and spotlight came onto a point on the stage where the two sides of the velvet curtain met in the middle. The keys in the music changed. Angelica McCord, apparently feeling better and a little less jilted, emerged from her hubris break and back on to the stage. Arms outstretched as if having her arms wide would help her to better soak up the praise of her adoring fans and the media who welcomed her back to the stage and the center of attention where she always needed to be. She changed from her red sparkly assemble to a fitted midnight blue sparkly dress with a matching black cape with midnight blue trim flowing behind her. Her shoulder pads, silver armored plates on top of her dress, lit up with florescent blue lights with jingling tassels.

She greeted the crowd, "Hello all. Again. Now is the time for the announcement of the first round of raffle winners." She pronounced each word and all their syllables perfectly.

The crowd cheered. Whoop-whooping. Screamed with drunken bliss. Some guy in the crowd gave a loud version of Outcast's new trademarked catchphrase, "O-Kaaaay!!"

"Everyone. Everyone gather 'round the stage. Com'mere. Com'mere." Angelica said curling a bony finger towards herself on stage.

Everyone maneuvered themselves around the stage. Still hyped that they were about to win free stuff although only like four people in the entire crowd were actually winning anything during this round of raffle announcements.

"Oh my gracious!" Angelica laughed. "I forgot the envelopes! Oh silly me." A wrinkly old hand fluttered to her chest as she used her best northern enriched southern belle accent to pardon her, intentional, forgetfulness.

"Building suspense?" Sierr said to Carmen.

"Maximizing the drama as the dramatic do." Carmen replied throwing on a pair of her Dolce & Gabbana shades even though it was dark outside.

"Oh Jame. Jame. Yoo-hoo darling. Mind delivering the envelope to me with the winner's name enclosed? Thank you, dear." She sing-singed into the microphone. "Let the cameras through, please." She addressed some audience members who were blocked her moment in the spotlight by not allowing the camera crews to get through the thick crowd. A bit of stifled laughter responded back to her, but she was too busy fantasizing about her impending televised glory.

"What type of Mocktail did you get, Sierr?" Tabitha asked eyeing the menu written in curly letters, in different colored chalks on a small cloud shaped chalk board at the Mocktails tint. The bar set up behind the counter was stocked with fresh fruits, juices, nitrogen on tap, artificial flavor bottles which JSF was suspicious contained toxic poison which is why they were conspicuously labeled, and glass decorum as in Himalayan Pink Salt and Dyed Crystal sugars matching each Mocktails drink for ascetics.

"Pink Mist. Like a berry essence infused Sprite." Sierr answered.

"Hmm, could I mix that with the white chocolate one?" Tabitha asked thoughtfully tapping a manicured nail on her lips.

The mixologist confirmed that she could and started making her drink. Willow walked up to the counter and ordered an Almond and Blueberry Fog-tail.

JSF stood behind Sierr and whispered, "They should call that combo The Sierr. A mix of different chocolates and fruitiness."

"Oh yeah? You think I'm fruity?" She turned to him and asked rhetorically.

"What would be mine?" He asked eyebrow arched.

"A mystery flavor."

"Oh!" He said intrigued.

"Something that keeps you guessing."

"I like it already." He nodded smiling.

"Fig. Fig Fog." She stated plainly with a straight face.

"Fig F…Girl." Sierr cracked up. JSF snorted. "Are you kidding? I gave you chocolate and fruit and I get dead wasp mush that's not even sexy or…fabulous?" He rocked his head and use a nasalized voice to say the word 'fabulous'. It was always a word he teased and it was always people who used that word that he teased.

"Fig has a mystery taste."

"No, it don't."

"Tell me right now what is the difference in flavor between: Fig, Quince, Dates, and Strawberry Jam. If you can point out to me the specific distinctive flavor profile of Fig from those other similar flavors, I will think of another JSF worthy mystery drink."

He thought for a moment then pursed his lips hard, made his bone structure stand out even more when he did that, "Okay, ya got me. I am fucking Fig Fog thank you very much. Fig Fog at your service!" He grinned.

"Nice to meet you, Fig Fog!" Sierr said cheerily extending a hand like they just met. JSF met her hand and couldn't help but laugh at her quirkiness.

"Nice to meet you, Chocolates and Strawberries."

"Fantastic!" Angelica exclaimed from the stage as her lackey Jame Gumb ran to her on stage with the envelopes neatly stacked in a pile that was tied with a ribbon like a gift. "Okay!" Angelica snapped her fingers like a mariachi band member right before the next set, "On to the winner announcements!"

Cheers erupted once more and another randomly place Outcast style, "O-Kaaaaay!"

Angelica began to open one of the first letter, "For our first prize which is: a Designer Handbag, one year of free coffee from Ashely's Café…"

Willow whispered to Carmen, "More free coffee from Ashley's."

Carmen giggled into her palm.

Angelica continued, "…a priceless yellow-gold Charm bracelet perfect for our young adults out there, and a signed copy of my Coffee Table book featuring professional photographs documenting my incredible rise to greatness in the fashion industry." She added that last totally humble part for good measure. She ripped open the first letter with her acrylic nails and whipped out the embossed card inside with the winner's name. "Our first winner is: Ryan Chamberlain! Where are you, Ryan?" Angelica put a hand over her pencil thin brow and peered into the crowd following the direction of the spotlight. It finally found Ryan near the middle of the crowd with a petite girl on his arm.

"Oh let's get a microphone to him everyone!" Angelica used a shooing motion to her personal videographer to run, literally run, and go interview the first winner of the raffle prizes. So, ran the videographer to Ryan who received the cheers of the crowd proudly even flexed his muscles for the half-shallow, half-drunk girls of the crowd.

Willow, Carmen, and Sierr gave a collective, "Blech!"

"Oh congratulations, Ryan!" Angelica clapped in the most pretentious, irksome manner. Hands raised by her ear, fingers straight, one hand vertical, the other horizontal, the only part of her entire hand actually meeting for the clap: her fingertips. "Best to you dear! Now our next winner of a wonderful prize. An all expenses paid getaway for a weekend in the city of angels…" Angelica trailed off allowing the crowd to react with bliss and excitement as she opened the second letter with the second winner's name in it. "Okay. Listen closely…" Angelica squinted at the name on the card unable to frown with all the fresh Botox effectively paralyzing the muscles in her forehead. She gaffed, "J…is this a joke? JSF? Are these initials? Who is JSF? JSF? Yoo-hoo?"

Somebody snickered in crowd at the sound of Angelica "Yoo-hooing" to a mystery person.

Sierr smiled at JSF who watched uncomfortably as the spotlight tried to find him in the crowd, the way a mustang tenses when the red hot, sizzling branding hook inches closer to their hide. "You won, JSF!"

"Ugh, if I knew this would happened I would have never signed up." He groaned and dropped his shoulders like he was being prepped for an enema.

"Oh it's fun! You're the last person who needs to be winning things though. You've got enough money to buy the town. As a good member of the 1% you would opt not to take your winnings." Willow nodded with her arms folded pleased to be taunting and goading JSF some more.

He smirked at her and replied, "I never even wanted to win ya know. I only signed up because I stood all that time in the line to sign up with you people."

Willow gasped deeply widened her eyes with fake shock and asked gapping, "Yoo-who? Asians?"

Carmen put a hand on her hip, "Filipino-Americans?" After a pause she glanced at Sierr and said with a grin, "Whatever all Sierr is?"

Sierr, visibly offended, folded her arms over her chest and replied, "It's not like it's a list or anything!"

"Everyone done now?" JSF asked in a monotone voice. Suddenly the spotlight found JSF in the crowd. He turned his back as the videographer and news crew came running. "Oh dear God."

"Oh there he is. Kind sir? A penny for your thoughts? What do you think about this prize that you have won, sir? Is JSF your *real* name?" Angelica fanned the air towards JSF from the stage.

JSF seeing cameras coming at him from every direction, ducked behind Sierr. The width of her big curly mane hiding most of his upper body in entirety.

"Oh so you don't mind me being on camera is that it?" Sierr said accommodating JSF by keeping her back to him and her face to the cameras.

"Not if you don't. Be fair warned though. Governments being able to find people just by using a snapshot of their faces? Very big thing coming in the new millennia!" He actually seemed worried still hiding behind Sierr.

"Oh my Lord." She breathed. "Don't worry I'll protect you." She gave his arm a pat just as Angelica McCord's personal videographer and the local news crews approached her with microphones and bright lights.

"May we speak with the winner?" The videographer asked.

"I….will be his spokesperson. He is a very private person. Hence the name. Some think it's a bit much, but I think it avant-garde! Ask me anything!"

"Has the mystery man ever been to Los Angeles?" A newswomen from channel 3 news asked. Sierr had seen her reporting before always the fluff pieces like interviewing winners at a Halloween Bash, but Sierr was sure she would work her way to the top.

"Oh no he has not. He's not much of a traveler. More of a homebody. A philosopher. Astronomer in his own mind kind of like me! Kind of like Sir Issac Newton once said, 'A man's imagination is endless when broadened to ponder the makings of matter and time!'"

"Oh very charming!" The newswoman replied glowing.

"He is lovely!" Sierr beamed proudly. JSF wrapped his arms around her and hugged her from behind.

"Is he artistic or an actor or anything this could be a trip that offers him the chance to reach new pastures as they say!" A bubbly young newsman with a plaid hoodie on asked his spiky blond hair sticking straight up in the air. He always had a feminine air about him. Just enough to reel in prospects, but not broadcast 'I'm super queer!' to his colleagues at first glance.

"Nah, he will probably find a quiet place away from the city lights and city noise and star gaze oh of course hit the beach!" Sierr laughed.

"And eat the food!" Willow popped her head into the shot.

"And visit the sights!" Carmen giggled popping in next, gave her hair a flip.

"What kind of food does your friend like?" A brunette reporter who spoke through a tight smile asked. He smile as much the result of effort as his career level.

"Fish!" Sierr said.

"Pie!" Carmen said.

"Fruit!" Willow hunched a shoulder. "Dude, eats fruit y'all. Can't go wrong with a cold orange." Willow added with her index finger pointed towards the camera and her head nodding like she was teaching kids at home a fact of life or something. "That's what I always say!"

"That's what you always say!" Carmen laughed with Sierr. "Yep! That's right!"

"Oh and hot chocolate!" Sierr declared.

"Yogurt with honey and nuts!" Willow squealed.

Everyone looked to Carmen for the next answer. She gave a stiff smile and said, "Uhh...." She stammered with a blank stare, then threw her head back letting out frustrated, "Agh!"

Everyone burst out laughing.

Sierr said the words, "Cheeto Puffs!" like a two-syllable cheer at a pep rally.

"Dr. Pepper!" Carmen squealed hopping up and down and clapping. The girls giggled as they started firing off answers as fast as they could.

"Hot wings and bleu cheese!" Willow laughed.

"Froot-loooooops!" Carmen gasped for air from laughing so hard.

"Fondue!" Sierr screamed through tears of joy and making emphasis with her hands.

"Roasted Corn!" Willow barked her competitive side emerging through the silliness of the game. It may have been all fun and no one may have been keeping score, but just the same she still wanted to win.

"Ahh, sweet corn fritters!" Sierr exclaimed while clapping excitedly.

"Zucchini fritters!" Carmen screamed unable to contain herself.

"Fried Broccoli!" Willow lunges forward and screamed passionately wanting make sure she was heard getting the answers right.

"Steak!" Carmen hopped up and down again this time with her arms outstretched by her sides.

"Chili with cheese and saltines!" Sierr squealed beaming like a light.

"Ladies! Ladies!" The newswomen from channel 3 news interrupted with a chuckle. "We got it. You know your friend very well!"

"We do. He's been a fixture in our lives since childhood...like a pet...turtle." Sierr grinned. She could feel JSF shifted behind her. She had gotten to him and she loved it.

"Which is so fitting for him because he is hiding right now! Like a turtle in its shell!" Carmen grinned eyeing JSF behind Sierr. She saw him whip his head towards and before she knew it he had shoved her nearly off her feet. Suddenly dangling in the arms of Willow, who caught her just before she would have hit the ground, Carmen lifted herself back in an upright position and marched back towards JSF. "You could have killed me! You should know how vulnerable wearing heels makes a person! You almost fell earlier remember, Norman Bates?! And that happened to you without someone shoving you!"

JSF put up his palms in surrender with his arms looped into Sierr's from behind. Then he not-so-subtly pointed at Sierr as if implying that she was the one who shoved Carmen. The girls scoffed and rolled their eyes all at once.

"Liar, Liar pants on fire! No more candy for you!" Sierr pouted with her arms folded.

"May I ask what is everyone's name for the broadcast?" The bubbly newsman asked moving his microphone towards Sierr.

"Uh Seraphim Blake future Entertainment Specialist."

"Willow Koi! Future stylist of the stars!" Willow popped her head into the camera view.

"Carmen Cameron! Your future best friend!" Carmen poses for the camera and blew a kiss.

"Thank you girls for your candor." The videographer put down his camera. The News Crews followed suit and they were on their way. Angelica McCord continued on congratulating JSF before moving into her next raffle winner.

"Wow, I love how you girls act like you're high as kites even though you're all sober." JSF grinned. "Makes me wonder how lit y'all would be with tainted blood."

"I love how you almost pushed over a female on national television with your meat hands." Carmen widen her eyes and cocked her to the side at him.

"Aww, you three know how much I love you...all three of you nut jobs." JSF straightened Carmen's cat ears.

"Prove it. Buy us stuff." Carmen's eyes twinkled.

"Or let us crucify you." Willow smiled purely as an angel.

"Aww, maybe another time." He replied through clenched teeth.

Sierr hopped in-between Carmen and Willow and threw her arms over their shoulders. "You can totally make it up to Carmen by inviting her along with her two best friends on your trip to Los Angeles! I know I like that idea very much!"

"Ooooh, yes! Agree to that and all will be forgiven." Carmen smiled.

"I dunno. I may not be going." JSF said.

"What? Why not?" Willow asked.

"I just don't wanna go." He said casually.

"But, it's a free trip. It seems like someone as frugal as you would love a nice trip that you don't have to pay for!?" Sierr inquired curiously.

"Yeah, you'd think but I'm just not excited about it. I might let someone else have it ya' know? That's another reason why I didn't want to be on camera accepting the gift. Because I might not take it." JSF hunched a shoulder.

Sierr took a long look at JSF. Something was wrong with him. She had slowly noticed his change in personality and energy level for the last few years. His patience a little shorter. His eyes a little more dim and distant. His fire weakened by the rain from the invisible cloud over his head. How long before she could subtly nag the truth out of him? Not yet. She wanted him to feel like he could trust her enough to not feel obligated to put on a front with her. She wanted him to see her as a safe space because that was what she was to him. Something was bringing her friend down both physically and emotionally and she felt the need to heal and help him. She loved him dearly. She always would.

"Well I would just like to let you know that I would be more than happy to volunteer as the sacrificial lamb to take the trip off your hands." Carmen offered... humbly.

"I'll help." Willow interjected.

JSF shut his eyes and took a stabilizing breath.

"You know what?" Sierr jumped in, "We should totally start making our way over to the stage for the fashion show."

"Oh yes. It starts in like..." Willow took a peak at her wrist watch. "7 minutes."

"Perfect." Sierr said as Carmen and Willow walked together and she hooped her arm into JSF's.

"Ya know." He slowed to a stop. "I think I'm going to go on home."

"Why?" Sierr looked deeply in his eyes almost wishing they would tell her whatever it was that he was hiding.

"I'm just tired."

"Well d...don't you wanna see the fashion show? You're dressed like a queen anyway. This is your scene!"

"Hmm, well thank you for that, but you know me. I've never been seen at a party. I'm just not the type. I only came here to support Willow. I think I've done that. Now I need a break from people."

"I know how that is." Sierr smiles warmly at her friend. "Well let's meetup over the weekend. I'll make you something yummy, kay?"

"Something sweet?"

Sierr took his hands and spread them wide initiating The Twist with him. "Whatever you like. How about-" Just then a hard force knocked her to the ground.

JSF lifted her up and shouted at the figure dressed in an all black, hood on, head down who elbowed her to the ground, "Hey where do you think you're going!? Fuckin' little punk!"

"Who was that?" Willow asked running back to check on Sierr.

"How rude." Carmen frowned trotting up in her heels.

JSF protectively pulled Sierr close as she tried to gather herself. She stretched her neck to see if the goth group was still hanging out on the other side of the street. They were gone. Then she noticed another person in all black walking with their head down too. A rabbit's foot keychain dangling from their pants belt loop. "JS..." She started. His leaned down to hear her. "Look, it's the..."

Another person in all black, with a rabbit's foot keychain, and their head down hissed within hearing distance, "They're coming."

To other attendees of the event other members of the goth group did the same thing, pushing past people forcefully hissing, "They're coming." "They're coming." "They're coming."

One pushed past Abby this one growled, "They're here."

"Wha?" Abby winced pissed that anyone, *anyone* dare take the Spotlight off her. A buff dude from The Controversy Crew grabbed one of the goth group members by the arm with a tight fist and spat at him, "Hey who do you think you are shoving people around! Piss off!"

The guy just smiled back. "Soon it won't even matter!" His eyes twinkled

"They're coming." Hissed through the crowed in unison. The crowd grew silent. People spun around in circles trying to identify who was disrupting their night with cryptic whispers, violent shoves, and intrusive entrances. A female member of The Fringe shoved past a tatted vampire bride who shoved The Fringe girl to the ground. Another member of The Fringe charged at the tatted vampire bride screaming bloody murder. Tatted vampire bride's tatted Dracula came out of nowhere and pushed the charging goth back. "Don't make this worse" He shouted maneuvering himself in front of his bride.

The same member of The Fringe who pushed past Abby and was confronted by her jock dude, snickered at her. Abby yelled, "Freak!"

"Oh you have no idea how true that is, precious!" The Fringe girl staggered towards her. A jet black matted greasy looking dread lock falling into the The Fringe girl's pale face and smacking her in the nose. Her eyes were wild like she was some kind of feral child all grown up. The Fringe girl *hisssssssed* Abby's way and then cackled like a crack head. A Jock of Controversy shoved him again. "Dude, I'm warning you!" Jock balled his fingers up into a fist and raised his arm. But, before any other confrontations could be made and any punches thrown all eyes fell on the West and the crowd grew utterly and completely silent.

From the West, a layer of fog rolled down the mountain like a calming avalanche. Howls seemed to be carried on the winds with it. The fog over Mangroves and Carrs slithered between houses and condominiums. The buildings of the Arboretum rendering them mere indistinguishable shadows. The fog crashed over the park. From the park it crawled onto the front lawn of Heisenberg High, the football field, and the parking garage next to the school. The fog creeped like the wave of death did through The Prince of Egypt cartoon. In-between each level of the parking deck. Cars were engulfed. Supporting columns hidden behind thick murk. The air turned wet with moisture. Warm from the mist, yet cold as the night autumn air cooled the dampness on your skin. Hot and cold confused the senses.

The crowd, The Controversy Crew, Sierr and her friends all stood motionless with little to be seen in their limit line of vision and they listened hard for any cues or clues about what was going on. Surrounded by thick white soup in the air the kind can wonder. Is it poison? Will it start to burn? Is this a cover for some horrifying crime currently taking place? Is this a distraction from something terrible happening close to them right now? Is this a Halloween prank?

Whispers grew from The Fringe again. They continued hissing their line, "They're here." "They're here." "They're here." First, one at a time. Then, three at a time. Then in unison like chants from another realm. The dark and ominous place beyond mankind. Howls from the wolves sent chills up the spine of all.

Voices from other members of the crowd grew from light whispers to panicked screams, some tried to make a run for it for fear they would be killed or eaten alive if they stayed put. People running blind tripped and fell at Sierr and her friend's feet.

The loud footsteps of a female darted past Willow and we're almost immediately halted just a few meters away. A scream coming from their direction. Carmen let out a shriek and threw her arms around JSF. JSF held Sierr tighter trying to squint through the cloud of fog with no luck. Willow took a strong stance ready to throw a punch at anyone who got near her. She toughen her face and tighten her fist. She was a black belt and she was ready. Sierr tried to steady her breathing so she could hear what was going on beyond what her eyes could see. Howls again. Were the wolves coming down out of the mountains? Were they stalking new prey. Were they close enough to start plucking people off one by one? Sierr's heart was pounding in her ears. Her hands flew up to her head. If only she could just hear what was going on!

A loud thud reverberated in the crowd members eardrums and chests. Screams as gasps erupted. Sierr whipped her head towards the noise. JSF did the same. Just then like a ship finally leaving behind the fog over a dark ocean and heading towards the glow of a light house, the glow of the lights on the stage got brighter and brighter. A cool breeze met the skin of everyone to the right of the stage as a giant wind machine blew the fog in that direction away. In the wind, the grass whipped at the feet of anyone with open shoes, an itchy feeling. Tents blew nearly off their posts, dirt particles blinded those who could not even see past the fog to begin with. Pieces of makeshift costumes, disposable cups, hats, scarves, raffle tickets, and any of The Controversy Crews signs - that were not painted onto their bodies - blew up into the air.

Sierr could see Angelica McCord walking towards the microphone stage, but only if she squinted past all her vision blurring curls which blew in her face from the wind machine.

"Friends! Attendees! Whatever this is...get out while you still can! Go!" She shouted into the microphone. "GO!" She pointed to Sweet Pique Lane to the right last the camera crews who perched in the same direction. "Run if you have to! RRRRUUUUUUUUNNN!

The crowd wasted no time charging for the park entrance/exit which connected to Sweet Pique Lane. Bolting towards news camera crews, the stampede couldn't believe their eyes when they saw a bloodied, wounded half naked man stumble into the park entrance/exit. The crowd stood in shock as he fell to his knees and screamed bloodied murder. He had been brutalized, beaten, patches of skin peeled away from his torso and forehead, his arms and legs cut up like a strong, beastly animal had used his limbs as a scratching post, his eyes blood shot, his hands delicately cradling a stab wound just under his rib cage.

The News Crews aimed their camera at the action. Journalists in fear for their lives still trying to get the scoop.

Sierr, breathless and unblinking, pulled Willow close not even realizing that she was still clinging into JSF's bicep and that his arm was wrapped firmly around her waist. Carmen clenched and clung the hem of his satin robe like a life preserver in stormy, rapid waters.

The man screamed an agonized wailed of a cry, "They got me!! They got me! The animal...brothers!! The boys! They came after me!" He crumbles to all fours, blood steaming from his stab wound.

The Fringe all turn to the man like a hungry pack of animals spotting wounded prey. Some with teeth bared. Eyes wide. Nostrils flared. Their hair stood on edge the chill in the air replace by pure energy. Another female Fringe member said breathlessly to herself, "The boys are looking for a sacrifice."

"Their power is immense and extraordinary!" Another member of the Fringe cries with glee as he charges towards the brutalized man at the park exit/entrance.

The other members of the Fringe follow suit chanting in high pitch hisses, "They're here! They're here! The Boys are coming! The Boys Are Coming Home!

Nearly leaping off the stage past gapping, crying, hyperventilating attendees and exuberant members of The Fringe, came Angelica McCord. Her own crafted gown dragging in the dirt she frantically threw herself towards the park exit/entrance. To the ground she went heaving and sobbing at the same time as she crawled towards the cameras and their lights and her bloodied lackey, Jame Gumb, who lie on the grass bleeding and bloodied.

"Jaaaaaaaame!"She sobbed. "My darling! My love!" She finally made it to him and wrapped her arms around him. Cradled him into her bosom.

"They tried to eat me…aliiive! The Boys!" He cried. The camera crew zooming in on his face distorted both with pain and mutilation. "The Boys." He repeated weaker this time. His eyelids fluttering. Eyeballs rolling into the back of his head.

"The Boys?" A newswoman, standing halfway in the view of her cameraman's camera, asked no one in particular as did some other frightened attendees.

"They're Coming. They're coming." The Fringe breathed almost simultaneously watching Jame closely from the crowd. "The Boys Are Coming Home!"

Sierr and her friends eyed the wild-eye Beckwith brother fanatics suspiciously.

"Jesus! Baby! It's going to be alright! It's going to be…okay." Angelica sob wailed. "Somebody call 911!" She screamed. "Get a phone!! Call 911!!!"

# Chapter 7: The Boys, The Boys, The Boys

*October 31, 1994*

I n the mountains high above Downers Grove where the fog had came and since returned, Halloween had come and gone without celebration or acknowledgement. The only hint that Halloween had even existed at all was the sight of the town festivities through the shared binoculars that the boys inherited from the old man. The boys made it a habit to look in on the doings of the Downers. Holidays were always the most curious events. They always came with Downers peculiar activities and artificial lights which brought an extra glow to the town, decorations that went with either ghostly Halloween or serene Christmas.

Traditions were lost on the Beckwith Brothers. For they had none and they never had any. Watching the people below fall in line with set traditions to eagerly put such time into celebrating whatever meaning they found in their holidays was a sight to be seen. Like watching animals in their natural habitat. And the boys loved to watch the animals…

As the autumn stole away the lush green of the leaves in the tree canopy the boys watched as the leaves turned crisper and became deeper shades of burgundies, sienna, and browns, the boys kept their eye on the Downers below as they always did. Never close enough or consistent enough to watch any one person gallivanting from store to store doing trick-or-treating or putting up ghoulish decorations to delight or scare fellow citizens. Yet, they did know some habits of the whole.

It was Fall right now which meant that the Downers were assuming and easily falling into their common Fall mannerisms. The boys could see the Downers once again roaming around gardens full of pumpkins with their mates for life and their offspring as they always did this time of year. They were always jolly as they circled particular pumpkins over again, took pictures posing with the pumpkins, sipped their lattes and chai teas as they admired the pumpkins, hugged pumpkins as they carried them out of the pumpkin garden with the joy of a cougar dragging a kill home to hungry kittens. It was a spectacle to say the least. Almost as bad as the event they made out of picking apples off the trees in their little town. That was like a party in and of itself.

At least the Downers did not put the apples they picked on display around town like they did with the pumpkins. After many years of witnessing the Downers adding their layers and seeking out and displaying only the best, most perfect pumpkins, the twins came to the only logical conclusion that these people had to be obsessed with pumpkins during this time of year. It was maddening.

Besides that another thing the twins had trouble understanding about the Downers below was their fascination with the concept of fear. Many wore elaborate, scary costumes as they acted out scenes to frighten other Downers in the middle of town in a leaf covered park, others donned masks to enter what the twins remember Eric refer to as "haunted houses" where spooks were set up to scare the visitors who dared to come through its doors. It seemed the dumbest thing on the planet to the twins. Honestly, how can anything be scary that is already being anticipated? Furthermore, the other humans senses should be able to pick up on any disturbances before they get close enough to scare. Eventually; however, the boys would have to remember that the civilized were often plagued with dulled senses. It was a shame really. That entire communities would let themselves become so vulnerable like that. It's a surprise some invasive predator had not come in and eaten them all alive yet. It would certainly be easy and they had opened the door for attack by collectively letting their guards down. Even herds of deer knew better than to do that.

The twins took their eyes off the Autumn obsessed Downers and turned to their brother who was standing on a small elevation above them with tiny Pretty Brown Eyes struggling to keep up by his side. He was strolling through a mulberry bush searching out some sturdy sticks to make a new bow for his bow and arrow with. He could sense the boys attention directed his way so he gave them a quick check meeting their gaze and eyeing their perimeters for a precautionary moment before returning to his activity.

Eric liked to watch the Downers too, but their township had less of an impact on him as it did with his brothers. At times the twins seemed totally fascinated by the other humans and all their rituals, dances, and holidays. But, just like when he was a child, Eric was far more interested in watching the animals. He believed they had souls which spoke to him. He noticed Pretty Brown Eyes stumble over a fallen tree branch, her little mouth quivering in the air from a shiver, a puffed of fog exhaling from her snout. It was a brisk morning. He plucked her up and cradled her in Noah's hide where it was warm. He slid Noah's skull over his thick mane of hair and continued on his search for the perfect branch.

*Maybe I will have to cut down a small tree?* He pondered absentmindedly stroking Pretty Brown Eyes' head.

He checked his surroundings again and went back to his brothers who were still taking turns eagerly peering into the binoculars down at the town.

"See anything interesting?" Eric asked aloud.

He could hear the twins hearts flutter in response, *a lustful yes.* A fluttering heart always meant a lustful yes for the twins.

It meant they wanted something. Covetous lusting. Eric wanted something too. He wanted to see he and his brothers reproduce. The obstacles in their way were too numerous to count. No contact with civilization. No ability to speak for two out of the three of them. No desire to actually leave their safe and comfort place in the forests where they had grown up in and grown up with. Was there another way? Another option? There had to be.

He stroked Noah's hide over his left pectoral bulging beneath the fur. Let his hand settle where he could feel his heart beat. He remembered what it felt like to feel Noah's heart beating. He wished there was another way then. Another option for assuming the role of Alpha Male in the wolf pact other than eliminating Noah. He was a good wolf. Attentive. Nurturing. Strong with good stamina and drive for his wolf family. The ability to produce wolf pups to build the pact and make it stronger over time. If there was a list of ideal pact leader qualities, Noah definitely would have retained most of the items on the list.

Eric had to be that way. Like Noah was. His brothers too.

Eric clicked his tongue twice for the twins to follow him back to the cabin. He decided he would have to cut down a tree. No twig was going to work. He might do so later on that day. Maybe not.

He could hear the twins following him with light steps. Childhood in the forest surrounded constantly by dangers that were made curious by any tiny sound made all the boys rather quiet creatures. Their steps were nearly inaudible. Swallows undetectable without close attention paid. Breathing always steady. And they had all utterly mastered the concept of using their inside voices.

It was good. Comforting in a way to Eric knowing that his baby brothers were able to navigate the forest safely, for the most part, innately even though they still needed him. Eric was still unsettled by the possibility that his dream could come true. Either he or one of the twins bleeding profusely as the snow falls. It was why he wanted to make a new bow and arrow. Perhaps the culprit of the injury was a wild animal or worse…a human.

They needed weapons. More weapons. They had plenty for hunting, but not for a fight. A few hunting knives, butchers knives, mallets made from stones and branches tied together with some torn fabric, and cross bows. However, in case of a drastic emergency and for some reason they needed more weaponry he wanted to give he and his brothers a full supply. And they would get it.

The boys eventually made their way back up to the cabin. Eric unlocked the gate, let his brothers in first, then himself, and locked the gate behind himself all without making a sound other than the unavoidable small *creeeeek* from the old fence. The twins padded up to the garden and plucked some zucchini squash to go with the remainder of the deer for lunch.

The twins were eager for Eric to cook it over the flame the way he always did. Somehow it was perfect every time. Green squash skin wrinkled and burned to just the right point, the inner flesh hot and soft, drippy with its sweet inner waters and fresh out of the flame Eric would sprinkle the perfect amount of salt on the outside.

Eric walked up to the front door, unlatched the bear proof hatch and opened the door. It also gave an unavoidable *creeeeeek* with age. If only he could fix it. The wolves engulf him with pounces, kisses, fur, slobber, and pants of joy.

"Hello. It's only been a few hours, my friends. I'm glad you miss me so." He smiles and greeted each one with a head pat, a back stroke, or a kiss on the forehead.

The twins entered behind him and he shut the door. The wolves gave the twins a similar greeting, but Luke and Lyle were busy shielding the Zucchini from their hungry mouths. Eric whistled twice commanding the wolves to calm themselves. As they always did for their Alpha they respected his wishes and obeyed without hesitation.

"We can all go out after dark and find another deer. But, after lunch I want to go somewhere just the three of us. A special adventure!" Eric said with excitement to his brothers.

Luke and Lyle looked to him with eyes wide, eyebrows raised, mouths turned up in the corners showing hints of eager smiles.

"Where?" Eric verbalized for them. "A place we have not been since we were small. Very small."

Luke took a cautious step back his smile fading. No where they had been as children had been all that great etched with triggers of their abuse and people who would ruin their escape from society. They intended on never being found, never having their lives disrupted by the peering human gaze. And they certainly never planned on returning to anywhere they frequented as children. Lyle on the other hand was still intrigued.

"I feel you both deserve to know where I want to go today. Because it may not be very safe, but I believe that we will be alright. This trip will be rather short. But, necessary." The twins shared a look. "I want to go back to the car. The car that daddy drove us up here in."

The twins faces were etched with confusion. Eric walked towards them slowly. "Listen. He is dead. I'm sure of it. Unfortunately, so is mom. But, the car may have some supplies for us. Supplies that we need."

*We haven't needed them this long.* Luke telephathed.

"You're right. But, there's a change in the air."

*Bear?* Lyle telepathed as a question.

"He may still be out there. Or he could have moved on. I know how to detect his presence. He cannot scare us or sneak up on us. If he's there we'll know."

The twins looked to each other.

"Hey." Eric said putting their attention back on him. "And if he's there. We'll kill him."

With that the brothers ate and shared their food with the wolves and their growing puppy. Nourishing themselves for the half day's walk across the river and towards the scene of their father's bloody killing that fateful day 14 years ago.

The boys had last made this trek with tiny feet and much smaller steps with their wounded mother guiding the way. This time they were returning to the scene stronger in mind and body. The bear could not surprise them again and they were the ones in complete control as long as they remained calm, wise, and alert they would be alright…together.

The boys each bundled up a wad of warm clothes, animals hides, and weapons and walked down to the river. They chunked all their wads over to the other side and began undressing. They would swim across together in the nude. Then air dry on the other side of the river as they put on each item of dry clothing in each of their wads and set off. It was already cool and the temperature was sure to drop as the day wore on. They simply could not make this trek soaking wet.

They were expecting to be home by dusk. This gave the wolves enough time to rest up for tonight's hunt. If the brother ran as quickly as they could, about 30 miles per hour on a slow day, they could make it to the car and back in under two hours, but they decided to take it slow. They wanted to be able to hear, see, and feel their surroundings. The rush of winds when running would ruin their ability to sense their environment and what could be lurking in the trees.

Eric had to know if the gun was still there in the car. They did not want to use a gun for anything, but protection against an unknown foe. Hunting could be done with knives and bows. Eric considered bullets were a weapon solely meant for humans. It was his fear that humans were the culprit of the bleeding in his vision. They were the monsters of nightmares. Only to be observed and not to cross paths with.

The boys walked through the cool river and when they came out the other side it was nothing, but heel-toe, heel-toe, heel-toe to remain as silent as possible trekking through the fallen leaves from the tree canopy.

Luke often thought it funny how the fall seemed to turn the world upside down. The leaves went from being in the sky to being on the ground and tree branches which often covered by leaves now looked like the bare roots that thread into a ground that was covered in something that belonged in the sky.

He could hear the wind lightly whistling through the tree trunks, Lyle too, but not Eric. His hearing was not as keen as theirs was naturally.

The twins were tuned into frequencies higher and lower than the average human. Their ear canal and speech centers of the brain held the secrets to their power. Their abilities beyond the ordinary, but not supernatural. Just a phenomenon of the physiological and neurological.

Eric too was a special case. With the same defect as his brothers only with mildly reduced strength. He's strength lay mostly in survival.

Eric knew the way to the car was like the back of his hand. Not because the trail back to the vehicle was burned into his memory, but because he mentally retraced all the steps he took that day with their mother. He was determined to remember every single last moment he shared with her and those moments happened to be on the trail between the old man's cabin back to that car. He could lead his brothers on the path with his eyes closed. He often dreamed of walking this trail with their mother. Not as she was in her last day alive, bloodied and broken, but healed and beautiful. He could see her smiling, her auburn wavy hair falling over her delicate shoulders in the pink dress from the antiques. She frolics with him through the trees initiating a game of hide-and-seek with her firstborn son. Finally free. Finally happy. Finally at peace. No ax. No fear. No abuse to take her beautiful, carefree smile away this time. Utterly perfect among nature. Her little boy finally able to feel her hugging him once more. But like always the dream ends with no mother in sight and no mew memories to hold onto with her face. Every time he would awaken from a dream about her, Eric would retrace his last steps with her all the way down the entire trail back to the car from the river where he last saw her face.

A pang of anger hit Eric. Not even at the bear for its attack. The bear had the right to protect its territory from invaders. His mother was gone and it was all his father's fault. He utterly hated that man. He utterly hated any man who could be cruel to someone so good and so pure. If Eric could kill Carson twice... he would.

Soon the boys were coming up on the big tree they all took shelter in for safety that night. The tree where mother spotted the smoke bellowing from the old man's cabin's chimney. The tree in which she had saved her sons' lives.

"Momma." Eric whispered reaching out a hand and touching his fingertips to the tree trunk. He hesitated, but wrapped an arm around the tree and then the other holding it close. Wishing it could hug him back. He so appreciated having contact with a piece of his mother's life before it tragically ended. The moment felt like it lasted for hours, but it was just mere seconds. Eventually he felt Luke and Lyle's arms wrap around his body and the tree too. He opened his eyes to them smiling and he couldn't help, but laugh. This was his family. His joy. His comfort. His life. Weren't they enough? Surely they were enough. He loved them and they loved him. He could feel it from deep in their souls.

He ran a hand through Lyle's hair smiling and kissed Luke's forehead. "We're making it. Because we're strong. And we're brothers. We will always make it together."

The twins smiled and nodded hearts fluttering.

Just then a helicopter flew overhead breaking their tender moment. It let a mist out of the bottom of it's metal belly and that mist rained down on the forest below. It seemed incredibly loud in a world that was most often utterly quiet. The brothers shared a look as it went on into the distance. That was a piece of a world that was not theirs. It never was theirs. They weren't born for what was out there. They were born and equipped for life out here. This is where they belonged and it was perfect. It was theirs.

They continued on. Eric assured the twins they were close. Eric slowed his pace to that of a turtle, shoulders swaying from his limp. They were in bear country. He kept his eyes peeled to each and every visible corner of the woods. Easier to see a bear without a ton of leaves shading the forest floor. On the flip side that also meant it would also be easier for a bear to spot the boys in his territory. Easier to chase them. Easier to hunt them down and kill them. The boys could only hope the bear was sleeping somewhere in a warm den…far away.

Each step brought them closer and it became clearer and clearer through the collection of tree trunks ahead of them…the dilapidated old car. It was over ground with vines and covered in layers and layers of leaves from this fall season and by the looks of it at least a half dozen others. The car was rotted. Paint eaten away by the elements. A mix of sun and rain. The tires were dull and flat so dry rotted they had all but crumbled pieces fallen away from the rusted rims. The headlights were shattered by God knows what and the windows were slid down into their slots with a crooked tilt. The windows, the windshield, and rear window were all clouded with dirt, mud, pollen, and the cloudiness that comes with age. But, most importantly it was here and the boys had made it.

"Let me look first." Eric echoed motioning for his brothers to wait behind him. He walked forward carefully. Heel-toe. Heel-toe. He cursed the sound of the crunching leaves beneath his feet. The sound of their dull *Crunch, Crunch* seemed to fill the air with every step.

Making his way to the car, Eric took the 150th quick glance at his surroundings to check for the bear. Then at his brothers standing with their backs to each other keeping watch as well. He gave his bow and arrow a tap making sure everything was in place to be used at the ready. He walked alongside the car amazed for a moment at how big the vehicle seemed to him when he was a ~~cub~~ boy. It was once a giant machine to him which roared and growled like a man-made beast of metal and rubber and fabric. He towered over it now. Able to look down on its roof. Seeing it from a new perspective as a fallen behemoth, reduces to nothing but rot. Like a sequoia which reached its peak and crashed down reduce to dust by fungi and the natural decompositional processes. Finally, he peered inside the old car. Squinted through the clouded windows to see if he could spot the gun. Checked his surroundings again. No bear. Check. Twins standing guard by the wayside. Check.

Eric slipped his hands into the open space where the window had slid down into its spot over time and forced the window down further. He could have broken it easily, but didn't want to make that kind of noise. He opened the door from the inside. Had to use some force. It was stuck, but after a moment he got it. Noticed the smudges in the dirt, mud, and pollen layers on the car from his hands and fingers and no others. He was confident the car had not been touched since that fateful day. Which meant the gun had to still be here.

"Luke. Lyle. Come." Eric echoed. The twins responding with their obedience. Eric began to search the car. It had to be there. "Help me look, please."

Gun? Luke asked in tuned with his brother. Eric knew Luke was too young to remember the gun from childhood.

"Yes." Eric whispered. Checked their surroundings. He tried to crawl into the backseat ripped a tiny hole in his jeans. So, instead he found a lever under the driver's seat and pulled it causing the driver's seat to lunge forward whacking Lyle in the face. He sat down in the passenger's seat nursing his aching face. "Sorry, brother." Eric gave a lock of Lyle's hair a playful tug. Lyle nodded. Just then something caught Eric's eye between the driver's seat and the console. Something that didn't look like it belonged to the car's interior. Eric pulled it up and there it was. The rifle. And a handgun. Luke grabbed the handgun before Eric could stop him and stood outside the car admiring the weapon. "Luke!" Eric barked an echo.

Just then a gunshot at close range. Oh God. Lyle nearly jumped out his skin. Loud noises were the worse for him. Made him jittery and nervous. Eric's stomach dropped. "Luke!" He exclaimed out his mouth to his own surprise…and Lyle flinch again at the loud scream next to his ear.

Eric threw himself out of the car and bolted towards Luke who stood motionless holding the handgun down at his side. To Eric's relief, Luke was unharmed and staring curiously towards the trees. Eric followed his gaze and saw movement in the trees.

"Yaaaaaaaaaa-hooooooooo!" A voice foreign to the boys cried out from just ahead of them. It was a male person.

Another male person laughed hysterically, "Yee-haw! Or whatever mountain people say!"

"Hahahahahaha!" The first male person cackled.

They were running right towards the boys. Lyle hopped out the car. Eric grabbed the twins and pulled them into the quickest hideaway he could find…under the car. He tried to guide the twins under…

The male voices grew closer and another gunshot rang out followed by cheers of a small bunch of idiots. Two? Three people? Then Eric and his brothers spotted them. Three people: two boys and one girl.

Lyle's heart pounded with excitement when his eyes laid on her, He telepathed excitedly and giddily, *I don't believe it. It's...it's....It's a girl! IT'S A GIRL PERSON. THE GIRL PERSON FROM THE BODY BOOK!! She looks just like the pictures!! IT'S A GIRL! IT'S A GIRL! IT'S A GIRL!! IT'S A GIRL!! IT'S A GIRL!! IT'S A GIRL! IT'S A GIRL!!!!*

Luke got excited too. He waves his fingers in the air quickly never knowing quite how to express his emotions in a natural, non-odd way. He telepathed, *I know I see her too! She's right in front of us.*

Eric hushed yelled aloud, "Will you two shut up about it and calm down!! My Lord!!"

Lyle jumped up and down and telepathed, *IT'S A FEMALE HUMAN! IT'S A FEMALE HUMAN!! IT'S A FEMALE HUMAN!! IT'S A FEMALE HUMAN!! IT'S A FEMALE HUMAN!!*

"Be quiet!! I can't think with you screaming like this!!! I can't even hear my own thoughts!!" Eric spin around looking for a place that all of them could.

Lyle was nearly hyperventilating, *IM SO EXCITED! IM SOOOO EXCITED!!*

*Silence.* Eric telepathed. The human's were getting closer and just like that the three other humans disappeared into the forest.

Eric took a breath. *That was close. Way too close. People were way too dangerous to be crossing paths w...*

Then he realized Lyle wasn't next to him anymore.

Eric frantically looked to his left and to his right. He didn't see Lyle on the ground or his feet standing up anywhere. Eric side crawled out from under the car and spun around more times than he even knew. He could hardly catch his breath he was so frightened. Then he saw Luke pointing towards a clearing to the far left just before he darted in that direction. Eric charged after him hoping he would lead him to Lyle. Fortunately, he did. Luke came up behind Lyle watching the college students skinny dipping in a lake. The girl was naked and shivering by the shore. Her hair was wet against her skin and her fair skin pale. The profile of her breast revealed hard tiny nipples. One of her male friends stood behind her, also naked, trying to coax her back into the water.

Lyle stood behind the bushes and a baby tree watching on quietly his penis erect in his trousers. It was hard as a rock and be couldn't do anything about it. Like literally. He was totally frozen by the sight that was in front of him. Luke touched his shoulder. Lyle felt it, but he didn't take his eyes off the girl.

Eric reached Lyle and yanked him backwards. "What the hell were you thinking?" He hushed yelled right into Lyle's face.

Lyle ripped his arm away from Eric and whirled around so he could see the girl again. But, when he looked at where the girl and her friends were they were nowhere to be seen. Just then the boys could see the college students running right towards them jiggling bare skin seeming to lead the way as their giggles quickly filled the air around them all.

With mere yards between the students and the brothers, Eric wrapped his arms around Lyle who was still foolishly trying to catch a peek at the damn girl and threw himself and Lyle into some bushes which unbeknownst to Eric opened up to a ravine that took their balance away and seemed to suck them down into a deep, dark hole in the ground. Eric and Lyle rolled down hard rocks and compacted dusty, dead soil they broke fingernails and skin trying to break their fall on the way down. Eric bit down on his tongue to keep from crying out. It was hard. He almost admired Lyle's inability to scream at all. Almost. They reached the bottom with a hard thud.

*What about Luke?* Eric immediately thought to himself. He actually found some comfort in the fact that at least it was not snowing or else he would be sure that his premonition was coming true. Since it was not snowing hopefully that meant that he and his brothers would make it out of this okay.

He checked on Lyle who was already on his feet. "Are you okay? Are you hurt?" Eric whispered. "Are you…" Eric trailed off. He and Lyle's gaze met the same sight ahead of them. Overlapping, fresh bear tracks and multiple bear beds. Oval pits in the ground just big enough for a bear to curl in a ball inside of. Then Eric saw it. A pale small figure in the corner of the dark hole. A round shaped human skull. Based on the bone structure Eric could even imagine how his father's face once fit over that skull…back when he was alive and uneaten. "Oh fuckin' hell."

Then they heard light thuds approaching them. They knew that was the sound of heavy footsteps slowly approaching.

*Up. Get up there! Now!* Eric said to Lyle in silence.

Lyle obeyed or tried to rather. It was hard to make it back up the ravine the way they came which was steep and smooth. Lyle quickly found a tree root sticking up out of the dusty, dead soil, saw that it lead all the way up the ravine and over the top and grabbed ahold of it using it to pull his weight up the incline with. Eric started behind him when the bear came into sight with an angry roar. It charged towards Eric. He'd never be able to make it all the way up the incline before the bear got to him. He had to make a split second decision. He simultaneously leaped off the incline and let go of the tree root. The bear roared again and turned towards Eric. Growling and revealing his sharp teeth.

*Oh God!* Eric readied his bow, took aim, and suddenly Lyle appeared in the ravine and struck the bear with his own arrow right in the shoulder. It let out a pained guttural howl. Eric struck the bear himself, the bear swatted at Lyle. The bear then turned to Eric and charged at him. Two strides and he was merely feet from Eric. Eric intended now to finish the deed and kill the hungry beast. So, he took another bow and struck the bear in the neck. Then another bow in the head as Eric fell under the bear. With the last mortal strike the bear fell to his death right at Eric's side, collapsing to the ground with a hard, heavy thud in the den.

Eric panted sweat running down his face and down his neck. Lyle stooped down and caught his breath. Eric laid next to the bear observing the power of his own instincts. He stood up and looked down at the monster that he managed to take down. He stepped forward, tapped Lyle on the shoulder, "C'mon let's get outta here. Find Luke."

*"Luke's fine."* Lyle assured Eric silently in his mind.

Eric nodded, used the tree root to pull himself up the incline with Lyle close behind. When they reached the top Luke was standing by the baby tree staring unblinking towards the lake. Eric walked up behind and asked silently, "*Luke?*"

"*They did…bad.*" Luke telepathed in reply.

"*What?*"

"*Bad.*" Luke telepathed again.

Eric stepped forward and saw what Luke was staring at. The college boys were standing over the girl. She was laying on the ground. Nude. Not moving. Not blinking. Her blank stare up in the clouds where they would stay.

Luke exclaimed silently, *The boys chased her back towards the water and then started putting his mouth on her and she pushed him. Then the other one pushed her. She tried to run again, but they stopped her. Smothered her. One with his hands around her throat. The other held her legs.*

Eric didn't know if it was his annoyance with Lyle for causing trouble. His anxiety about the bear or the humans. His anger at his father. His loneliness in general. His tired muscles from the walk. His general…restlessness. Or residual adrenaline from having to kill a territorial brown bear to save his life, but he felt just about fucking fed up. And now he had to learn that more abusive humans were in the fucking forest causing some shit. He didn't quite appreciate that. Not one bit. Not one motherfucking bit. He was so pissed off he felt like he could just cuss. And he never did that. Father did that. And he never wanted to be like father. Ever. No, he would be like his mother and like Noah.

Yes, Noah. Noah would protect his family and his territory. And since Eric just killed the bear that owned this territory in the rules and laws of nature this was now his land. His home that people were defiling. He didn't like that. That was wholly unacceptable.

So, Eric stepped out from the covering of the bushes and the trees and made his presence known to the naked college boys who were fondling the breasts of the dead girl now. Repulsive crooked grins on their faces.

"Hey." Eric called out his deep voice loud and bellowing. He wasn't used to speaking loudly. Barely even recognized his own voice at that level.

The college boys turned around to him. He was a sight that was for sure. A 6'5 grown man, thick eyebrows that happened to be naturally arched, scruffy beard, as always, sun bleached wild yet tamed brown curls down his wide muscular shoulders and puffed up pectorals barely contained in two-toned flannel jackets, never been washed jeans that barely contained his quadriceps or his bulging penis for that matter, fishing boots. His wild, piercing grey eyes that seemed to slice into flesh and open the soul, a large wolf hide which draped over his entire body swinging down to his ankles, and a homemade, yet tediously carved, bow and arrow finished off the look.

The college boys looked him up and down and after a moment had the audacity to *chuckle. At. Him.*

Eric cocked his head to the side as Luke and Lyle emerged from the bushes as well looking equally as outlandish as their brother. The only difference was the twins were both 6'2, although they still had time to grow to Eric's 6'5 later on. Also, the twins' beards were thinner, lighter, and shorter than Eric's, but they had time to grow those in as well.

The college boys looked The Beckwith Brothers up and down and snorted. "What are you guys some sort of mountain men?" One of the boys laughed heartily his sad little penis bobbing with each of his gasps for air.

"Bet you don't even know what year it is." The second boy laughed then he put on a terrible country accent to say, "Bet y'all don't even know nothin' but how to make moooonshiiiine!!" He laughed like that was the funniest thing in the world.

The college boys laughed for a good obnoxious two minutes until their laughter died down. The Beckwith Brothers stared at the boys. Eric's glance fell on the body of the girl and then his eyes settled back on the boys with an undereyed stare. Eric wasn't too pleased that the first voices his ears had heard in years were antagonistic ones from killers of a female person. Or that the first female he had seen in person in years was now dead either. Frankly, it all contributed to his quietly, intensifying fury.

"This has nothing to do with you. So, all three of you backwoods fuckers can just dip back into the darkness where you belong." The first college boy barked.

"This has everything to do with me. This is my land." Eric growled in his gruff voice.

"You own this land? You *bought* this land? *YOU!?!?*" The boy gaffed eyeing Eric tattered shoes and over worn jeans.

"Better. I earned this land. Through blood and battle. Persevered into my possession."

"You're lying. You're nothing but a bunch of stupid hicks! Now shut the hell up and drop dead! Fuckin' weirdo!" The second college boy shouted.

Eric's undereyed stare remained on the first college boy. The vein in the center of Eric's forehead pulsating hard. His skin turning pink then red.

The first college aged boy chuckled again, "What? Got nothing to say now? Wild madman! Mute like those two are you?" The boy sneered gesturing towards the twins.

"Perhaps you should go for a swim." Eric now relaxed, cool, and unbothered verbalized. Just then whilst keeping his own feet firmly planted on the ground and his hands at his side, Eric swept the first college boy off his feet and suspended him in midair. The first college aged boy screamed and then Eric dropped him on his face into the mud on the banks of the lake.

The second college boy shouted, "What the fuck!?!"

Eric was the one laughing now as he calmly dragged the first college aged boy into the lake by his ankles bound by unseen strength and power. The boy pawed at the mud desperately trying to save his life as he screamed, "Stop it! Stop it! Let me go!"

The second boy bolted for the thicket, but Luke quickly shot him in the knee with an arrow. The boy crumbled to the ground the arrow slicing his femur from his shin and shattering his kneecap. It jutted out from both sides of his leg and he screamed bloody murder. A shriek like that of a rabbit being eaten alive by one of the wolves. Both high pitch and guttural at the same time.

Eric held the first boy underwater though he struggled the power of Eric's gift cocooned his body and rendered his movements useless and hopelessly restricted.

Eric tossed and flipped the first boy in the water disorientating him as he screamed for his life. His words mere bubbles breaking through the surface. A trail of bubbles followed the boy to the center of the lake where Eric flipped his body forward so the boy could watch as he was taken deeper into the murky waters and farther from the surface. Soon the bubbles stopped and so did the struggling, but the job wasn't done yet.

Eric turned to his brothers standing over the second boy who desperately crawled away from them. They watched curiously as he tried to navigate a broken leg with an arrow stuck in it and obstacles on the forest floor: fallen tree limbs, rocks, puddles, bushes, more baby trees. It was almost funny. Seeing this wounded person dragging themselves through the mud and dirt to get nowhere fast with the twins following him, looming over him, at a mere snails pace.

A lovely game of cat and mouse. *Ha! Ha!* Eric thought to himself.

Eric walked towards his brothers, but paused. Turned to his right to observe the female's warm corpse. She looked peaceful. Pretty. Soft. Pale. He knelt down and used his thumb to close her eyes one at a time. She was something of interest. Different. Nice. Parts not like his own. Intriguing genitalia without even a little bit of hair. *Odd.* He thought. *But, fine.* He began to think how much he would have loved....just then he silenced his mind. Shook the thought from his head. A crazy thought. Insane. Looney Toons Ridiculous. Then he sighed standing up over her body. Looking down on her, her still wet skin gleaming in the sunlight. He allowed himself to think again, If only I could spoken to her. Just once. To actually speak to another speak to him in a kind voice. Oh to hear a woman's voice again! If only. Her laugh was still clear in his ears. How long before it was gone?

At least the meeting of the other humans lead to ridding the forest of that bear. It was the rightful owner of this land for years, but as the code of the wild says now Eric was king of the forest. King of the wild mountains. A powerful King with no possible legacy.

He needed a code now. A code within himself. As a boy he knew that he would never kill an animal, rob the earth of its beastly beauty and purity, without good cause. Protection. Safety. Hunger. Yet now that he had found himself enjoying the hunting of humans a grand total of Three (3) times now and he felt the need to expound upon his boundaries for taking lives away.

First Boundary for Human Killings: Never kill any females.
Second Boundary for Human Killings: Never kill without provocation.
Third Boundary for Human Killings: …

Well, there was no Third Boundary yet. Perhaps there would never be a Third Boundary. Either way he learned at least two things today: he was the apex predator of both living kinds the human and the animal. His brothers would be too and they would rule with him. Finally, it was because of this that he was certain the three of them were more equipped to survive all things that came against them. Their power was endless. He could sense it. He could feel it.

Eric walked up behind his brothers still playing with their food. Well, playing with their prey. It's not like they would be eating the second boy or anything completely crazy like that. Eric got a chuckle again. Although, this dude would totally fill the wolves belly and then they could all skip going for a hunt tonight. *Hmm, decisions, decisions.*

Eric silently commanded his brothers, *Finish him.*

Lyle removed a hunting knife from his belt and stepped towards the boy. The boy screamed and tried to drag his body a smidge faster. Lyle then raised his knife over the boys head when Luke grabbed his arm as if to stop him. Lyle wanted an explanation. Luke then wrapped his thick hand around his twin's which was also wrapped around the handle of the knife and gave Lyle a nod and grin. Together they drove the knife down into the boy's heart and gave it a twist. He groaned lightly before falling limp in the soil.

"Brothers." Eric put his hands on each of their shoulders. Turned them towards him gently. "We are unstoppable now. Our limits have gone away. No one and nothing is worthy of our fears. Not a bear and certainly not a human. We are powerful. We are the apex predators now. It is obvious. Is it not?"

*"I see it."* Lyle telepathed.

*"I see...us."* Luke grinned realizing that they were not seeing "something," but instead we're finally seeing themselves in brilliant color as of for the first time. Seeing their true potential as brothers as beings beyond the others.

*"I see us."* Eric proclaimed in the corners of his mind.

*"I see us."* Lyle finished.

Soon enough the seasons changed. The boys watched on as the Downers below celebrated Christmas with their usual cheeriness. Sleigh rides in the park where they once built haunted houses. Horse and buggy rides with steaming hot cups of brown liquid and thick blankets to snuggle up in going up and down quiet streets on the weekends when everyone was out and about. The big shopping center, known to the Downers as the Plaza Mall, was full of foot traffic and people in winter wear and carrying shopping bags. Green leafy decorations embellished with either white lights or colored lights and ornaments were perhaps everywhere they absolutely could be: street lamps, traffic lights, park benches, the school, houses, the buggy used for horse and buggy rides, some of the cars, doors of buildings, door frames of buildings, and restaurants such as the shiny silver building, known to the Downers as Metallic. Snow fell and children danced in the streets. The fluffy ice from the sky warranted as much if not more joy from families as the pumpkins did for Halloween.

The Twins had long forgotten the majority of their early lives in civilization, but Eric had not. He remembered Christmas with his family. Snow fall. Making snowballs with his mother. He remembered being glad the snow kept him from having to go to school where the bullies were happy to alienate him from the rest of the school. The quiet boy with the creepy family. The boy whose family were ghosts or killers or vampires or some other manifestation of strangeness which would explain their odd behavior around town. He'd heard enough of the outlandish rumors and remembered enough of them too. People were so small. Few like his mother. Few as wonderful and pure hearted and kind as she was.

He never even really liked Christmas or any of the other holidays for that matter. They all involved people either staying away or coming together. When they stayed away the holiday was bound to end in arguments initiated by Carson. When they came together the holiday was marked by Mother having to fake joy and hide her bruises. Father pretending he was a good dad who loved his sons. No one noticing they were all slowly suffocating to death.

They had a heavy snow this year. Playing in the snow was fun. The Boys would play within the gate of the old man's cabin. They would wear their thick fur pelts, torn pants, and fishing boots which made patterns in the fresh layer of snow outside with their feet. Dove into the deep snow. Felt the snow in their hair and ate hand fulls of it. The boys all chased each other making snowballs and throwing them at each other with gusto and glee. The twins chased Eric and leapt on his back crashing into the snow with him. They piled on top of their older brother and wolves pounce on their backs with a puppy like eagerness. Pretty Brown Eyes, now nearly 20 pounds of long legs and thin torso, frolicked with her new family in the cold fluffy that engulfed her entire body with every leap she took through the snow.

However, hunting in the snow was hard. When the boys stood the snow came up to their knees. Their six-foot plus stature cut into thirds by the snow on the ground. One third in. Two-third struggling to get through. Running through it was tiring. Trying to walk on it quietly to stealthily track prey was another story of difficulty. Not to mention with all the leaves dead finding cover to conceal oneself was nearly impossible, but the animals were the lifesavers in this case. The brothers learned early on under the tutelage of Mother July the tricks to hunting in every season. The boys had observed the order and strategy involved in the wolf hunts before and after they were allowed to join the pack. This order and strategy was key to eating and being top predator and never becoming prey.

Times would come were everyone in the pack's ribs would show through and their legs and necks would slim down, but these occurrences were rare. This winter was rough, but the eating was better. The boys made sure of it back when Eric was still a teenager and the twins not even growing facial hair yet. Eric once heard that humans are the masters of altering their environment and he decided a little environment altering was exactly what he and his brothers, the pack, and young Pretty Brown Eyes needed for a well fed winter.

By mapping out sections of the forest which the boys knew well and intertwining thrones, tree limbs, and vines from within the forest into each other in these sections, the brother successfully created entire channels within the deer habitat which mostly blocked them from migrating too far away from the old man's cabin. No more than 50 square miles give or take. That gave the boys just enough room to not be overrun with deer, especially not aggressive bulls during the mating seasons, and gave the deer enough space to find food to flourish. This alteration to the forest kept a high concentration of food nearby so the boys and the wolves could always have pickings for meals in the colder months. When Spring came they always undid their handiwork to allow the deer the space they needed and redid the intertwining at the start of Fall. It was hard work. A feat to be accomplished, usually took weeks to be fully fulfilled, but it paid off in the long run when colder winters were made easier to survive with a stable food source.

In what seemed like the blink of an eye Downers Grove was shining bright as fireworks popped over the town. They played music loud enough that the thuds of the beat carried on to the mountains. The twins love watching the fireworks and Eric loved to see them enjoy it. Their youthful amusement still a comfort to see. They sat grinning from ear to ear on the edge of a rocky cliff that faced the town below. It's angle leaving the sky full of fire totally visible and open. Nothing to be missed not even the small fireworks that didn't fly too high. Eric sat behind them with a growing Pretty Brown Eyes in his lap. July lay by his right side and Bee to his left.

Pretty Brown Eyes licked his cheek and he gave her a scratch behind the ears. Her white curly fur which grew a little bit longer off the tips of her ears flounced with every scratch.

Later on that night when the fireworks ended and the night was dark and quiet. Mother July stood on the edge of that same rocky cliff, raised her head high, and howled long into the night. Steam from her mouth bellowed into the brisk air like steam from a steam engine like so many wolves in these mountains did before her. Eric cradling his growing puppy in his arms walked up beside Mother July, stooped down next to her, raised his head high, and howled too. His form with Noah's hide on his back gave the appearance that Noah was sitting next to July and that the two were reunited in their rightful place as Alphas of The Halo.

Eric's howl was the same pitch and decibel as his fellow pack mates and when humans below and in far off surrounding areas heard the collective howls into the night they thought, our native wolves are indeed together on this night. Shadowy figures in the darkness that ruled the wild highlands where they belonged and always would remain.

Big ears and fuzzy tails appeared over the wild flowers in the wide open field in just a flash before disappearing into the abyss of chlorophyll colored stems. Occasionally another flash of bunnies would catch their eye. Even a rabbit or two. Undoing one of their many interwoven alterations to the environment, the boys came upon a scene right now straight out of a nature show.

Two bull deers facing off in a field of color. One balks his antlers freshly sharpened and rutted. He is tall at the shoulders. Six feet or so. His coat still shedding excessively thick winter fur. Patches of thick fur still holding on here or there. His white fluffy chest is strong, muscular, bulky, as are his shoulders and his legs. His neck wider than some mature tree's trunks. He ducks his giant head down low to the ground, scrapping his front hoofs on the ground over again to challenge his foe, an equally intimidating bull with even bigger antlers.

The boys are close enough that they can feel the beating of the ground as the two bull encircle one another sizing each other up before taking the first strike, but the bushes gave them just enough cover. The second bull scraped the ground with his hoof two, three times. Snorts and balks as well. Their language unidentifiable yet understood.

Eric always appreciated the commonality between animals and humans in spirit. Even with the many barriers between man and beast there was still an undercurrent of understanding between the two types of beings because the emotions and feelings they both felt were mostly exactly the same.

These bulls wanted rights, legacy, respect, status, and power and were willing to risk life and limb for the ability to obtain the life they wanted particularly females with which to mate. One fight seal could seal their fate. One fight leading to prosperity or the end of life altogether.

Eric and Noah had to come to terms with this reality once before. Now these bulls would have their time.

The larger bull blew out lungs full of air through his nostrils. Urinated on his hind legs as a show of aggression. Beat the ground with his hoofs and charged with all his might towards his challenger. The smaller bull charged as well running towards the larger bull like he would run at a cliff he intended to jump over. Powerful legs sliced through the air in a synchronized rhythm that kept the bulls on their collision course without a single missed step. One hoof beating the ground at a time. The two bulls met in the middle of the field going full speed and rammed each other's antlers into the other was a crack like that of tree limbs snapping clear off the vine when struck by lightning. The impact of the bulls antlers potentially deadly yet they do it again. Once more. Ten times more!

The boys watched through the leaves and twigs in the foliage in front of them, laid on their stomachs watching the fight. There was no longer a need to wear their animal hide coats in the warmer Spring weather. Bottoms and the old man's boots was all the brothers needed to wear. Lyle - jeans and short fishing boots. Luke - unfastened overalls and fishing boots. Eric - flannel pajama pants torn at the knees and steel toed working boots. Eric even provided snacks for he and his brothers to nibble on throughout the long day. Snacks in the form of berries, cucumbers, and carrots from the garden stuffed into his knapsack. Luke popped berries into his mouth while Lyle gnawed on a carrot. Eric played with a blackberry in his dirty fingers too distracted to eat.

The bulls spun around in circles still wrestling antlers-to-antlers. They stumbled their way to the edge of the field and crashed into the trees with enough force to rattle the immediate areas of the tree canopy. Grunting and heavy breathing was the soundtrack to their battle.

Perhaps it was all that extra weight the larger bull was carrying around, perhaps the larger bull was just older and tired more easily, but soon enough Eric noticed the smaller bull was winning. With more stamina and technique the smaller bull managed some good distraction maneuvers. At one point he ran away only to double back and crash his antlers into the larger bulls flank. The smaller bull threw his entire body into the larger bulls legs bringing him to his knees. Then rammed his antlers into the larger bulls antlers just when he finally caught his balance. Confidence withered away from the larger bull along with his strength. His muscles quivered under his skin, shook his head back and forth as if to attempt to shake off increasingly dizziness, bloody drool ran from the corner of his mouth, and still he continued fighting.

There were opportunities to mate at stake. Bloodlines in Jeopardy. Rights to be earned. Failure was not an option. Failure was never an option. And when those females were within the winner's grasp it would all be worth it.

The smaller bull snorted and charged the larger bull again. The impact of their horns echoing through the forest. The larger bull locked his knees as the smaller bull pushed him feet backwards. The larger bull tried to push himself forward, but the smaller bull jumped to the side. Agile as a feline. A good fighter. Then the smaller bull ramped the larger bull in the abdomen. The larger bull's mouth formed a square and he cried out. Jumping back the larger bull, cried out again. Hobbled to the right. Ducked his head down in fear. The smaller bull charged at him, but did not strike. The smaller bull came at him with his horns lowered, aligned to strike his side once more. The larger bull backed up and sidestepped to the right. Kept his head below the smaller bull's in submission. But, the smaller bull bellowed and charged the larger bull again rammed his antlers into the larger bulls neck puncturing the flesh.

The large bull cried out. Reared up on his hind legs and took another antler impact to the stomach. He fell backwards. Crashes to the ground in a hard thud. The smaller bull bellowed once more shaking his head left and right like he were trying to shake off excess water. His eyes wild like a rabid beast. brothers heard his loud loud, rapid panting from their place in the bushes. The larger bull stood and bolted for the thicket. The smaller bull gave chase using his antlers to flip the larger bull's hind legs into the air. That motion in addition to the inertia of the larger bull's running space suddenly halted sent the larger bull airborne. Hoofs over his head, he landed on a forearm crooked in the worse position. That arm cracked as soon as his weight came down on top of it. The pop echoed off the trees and reverberated through the brothers' eardrums. The larger bull screamed as well as bovine lungs could have. A hollow, high pitch bellow of sorts.

Still the smaller bull was not yet satisfied. So, he came around the side of the larger bull, who was unable to move due to his broken limb, and began stomping the larger bull to death. Hoofs to the skull. Hoofs the skull. Once. Twice. Three times. Ten times. Twenty.

Eventually the larger bull stopped screaming. Eventually the smaller bull stopped stomping. The blood that oozed from the larger bull nearly coated the smaller bull from a series of splats, splatters, and smears. The smaller bull took a deep breath in and bellowed as loud as he could, marching around in circles in the field with his chest puffed out proud and his head held high.

Eric was confused. Deer were anything, but the "overkill type". In fact most animals weren't the overkill type except maybe humans. Where was the aggression from? Why? Was this smaller bull just different? Or was he not as knowledgeable about the killing drive of animals as he once thought? Either way Eric knew why the smaller bull was so joyous. His life was in perfect order now. No longer a nomad without a purpose. Now a mature bull with a rightful legacy all his own. It was only a matter of time before he could claim it.

"*C'mon.*" Eric telepathed lifting himself off the ground, rolled his shoulders back to pop the left blade.

Luke obeyed, stood up, dusted dirt off his stomach.

"*C'mon.*" Eric repeated to Lyle. Let's get back home.

Lyle telepathed nothing. Ate the rest of his berries alone on the ground watching the winning bull pace in circles balking victoriously.

"*Lyle, are you listening?*" Eric asked.

"*What?*" Lyle snapped.

Eric stepped towards him, stood over his head. "*I said let's go home.*"

Glaring Lyle replied silently, "*I know where it is. I can catch up.*"

"*I command you to come. Now. With me and with Luke.*"

Lyle dropped his gaze, dimmed his eyes, clenched his teeth, and plastered a look of disgust on his face. Eric stooped down to him. But, Lyle spring up with ease. Eric stood back up.

"*Safety in numbers, brother.*" Eric telepathed.

"*Yeah. Okay. I got it.*" Lyle breathed, turned, and walked off in the direction of the old man's cabin.

Eric sighed, looked to Luke, and followed Lyle.

Back at home Eric gave Pretty Brown Eyes a pat on the head, then picked her up off the floor. Tossed her onto the bed. After landing on her paws, she spun around and gave him an eager lick on the cheek.

"Oh girl. My girl." She peered into his soul as she did as a lost puppy like he was the North Star to her entire existence. Playfully taunted him into playing tug-of-war with her favorite "toy". It was a makeshift toy that Eric made her out of the outfit he arrived at the cabin in, his only remaining childhood outfit all knotted together to a durable enough item for his playful puppy to get all her wiggles and jiggles out with.

She had grown a bit since the pack first discovered her. A little bigger. A little more strength and weight behind her tug on the toy. She got her footing and snatched the toy clear out Eric's hands. She barked and hopped with joy. Stretched pleased with herself. Eric reached out and kissed her snout whispered directly into her floppy envelope ear, tiny fur hairs tickling his lips as he spoke, "You know I let you win, right?"

She tilted her head to the side. Tugged on her toy as Eric gave her another kiss on the forehead and long rubs up and down her sides, he knew she always found that comforting. It made him happy to comfort her because she was always happy to comfort him. Afterwards he made his way downstairs. Didn't see his brothers anywhere. Called for them.

"Luke? Lyle?" Checked the library. The kitchen. The loft. "Luke? Lyle?" Where were they? Eric strolled onto the patio outside. Saw Luke and Lyle on their knees folded over something in front of them by the nearly sprouted pink roses that grew on the fence surrounding their home. Couldn't make out what the something was quite yet until he stepped a few feet closer. Eric ran forward. "Luke! Lyle!"

The twins turned to their brother with tears in their eyes. Eric crouched down between them. Patted the still cheek of what was once like a second mother to him, Mother July. "Oh July. July, my mother. Please. Please don't leave me. Please wake up."

No response. No kiss. No sound. No breathe. Just stillness.

"Oh please." Eric began to cry. "Please. I'm sorry. I'm so sorry." Eric laid his body across hers. "Please forgive me. I wasn't here. I took someone you loved. I pretend to be someone you could trust. After you gave me everything. I'm so sorry. You'll never know how sorry I am. Oh Mother. I'm sorry."

Eric cried into her fur. Luke and Lyle cried silently beside him. Eric could see the rest of the pack, mere blurs figures behind his tears, emerging from the cabin to inspect Mother July's body. Whimpers already leaving their mouths. How did they know so quickly? Why didn't he know? He should have been there. He should've been there with her, the way she was there for him and the twins. He would never let himself forgive himself for allowing her time of need to evade him. Never.

Hours would last and the sky would darken before Eric could peel himself off the ground to bury Mother July behind the cabin. At least she would remain close to her family. Even closer to Noah in the ground.

Eric cried that night with Luke and Lyle and the pack by his side. He cried the longest and hardest he had ever cried in his entire life. He felt a flood of emotion that night greater and stronger than ever before like a surge of wind that overtook him and swept him off his feet. By the time he got it all out of his system everyone else was asleep. His face was wet with tears, his lips salty, his sinuses clogged, his skin coated in oil and dried sweat. His chest hair and beard both still a little damp from either or both bodily fluids. He didn't even know anymore. All he knew was that after the lost of yet another mother, he felt more lost than he ever had before in his life. How could he feel so at home and so far away all at once? Something had died. Something died with July and was buried with her. A part of himself was buried with her. A part of himself was in her grave. Keeping her company tonight. A fairly chilly night. He could tell he *was* laying bed wet with tears and sweat after all. At first he felt good knowing that Mother July and Noah had been reunited in someway, but now he was glad that he was there too. In her grave. A piece of him. An unidentifiable piece of his soul was with her and that made him feel good. She was his second mother. Why should Noah get her all to himself? Eric deserved a share of her even in death and now…he had that.

Just as the sun was rising Eric was finally able to rest peacefully with that thought.

# Chapter 8: Dead Serious

*I*t was the Spring of '95 and it was wonderful. Sprinkled with a rare flow of creativity for Sierr and a comfortable return of some sense of normalcy for Downers. It was good to see her lovely town regrouping after the debacle of Halloween '94. After the attack of Jame Gumb and the cloud of fog rolled over the city angst and paranoia ran rampant. Teens who witnessed the event organized support groups for help healing after such trauma. School Counselors met regularly with students who seemed to taking the effects of the event the hardest. Parents pushed back on such frightening demonstrations during Halloween and advocated in favor of a more kid-friend Halloween from now on. It was not the time to be scaring the fragile children anymore after all. They had already suffered enough.

Townspeople came together to pay the hospital bills for Jame Gumb although he obviously didn't need the help financially. It was clearly a show of support from the middle class. They also designated safe-spaces for anyone who needed emotional support to be able to escape into at any moment on any given day for "mental and emotional recuperation."

The church was designated as one of those safe spaces, not that it wasn't already. Congregation members even went door-to-door in early November offering to pray with members of the community. Carmen, Willow, and Sierr went with a group of congregation members through The Mangroves and were pleasantly welcomed for their efforts although little praying actually took place.

It was right after the events; however, that some members of Downers took a turn for the worse. It was often just chalked up to stress. Some of the boys…and men…the male gender specially, who seemed to take Halloween debacle the worst. Particularly those who were in close proximity to Jame and the cloud of fog. It was like the terror lingered for men and boys. They became rigid, hostile, agitated, aggressive, short tempered, and in some cases even violent. It wasn't all the men and boys, but a good enough amount that the church organized a male only Bible Study Night on Wednesday's to help the men and boys work through their new…issues.

Reports of random bashings, underground fight clubs, vandalism, and even two sexual assaults came across the local news. All boys and men in area apparently assuming whole new identities in the face of tragedy. It was psychotic to say the least. Nearly unbelievable until the "rage" could no longer be dismissed as simple flukes.

The real turning point was an incident involving a teenage boy from Heisenberg High. Turner Holland, 17. He was a normal guy, carefree, easygoing, attended the Halloween Bash dressed as homemade Freddy Kruger. He had since expressed having a deep sense of "inner rage" following Halloween. One that he had never felt before, but couldn't seem to control. His parents took him to see a therapist outside of Downers Grove who suggested he get examined for a "hormonal imbalance" and that a shift in Turner's hormone levels was the only explanation for his sudden change in behavior. However, the Holland family were certain that the term "hormonal imbalance" was code for Bipolar Disorder and that to them was unacceptable. Turner's family just couldn't imagine mental illness as the culprit of anything that could possibly effect their child. Maybe somebody else's child, but not theirs. Trauma. They knew this was trauma. They knew their sweet son just needed time that was all. So, they took him back home and turned in for the night. In the wee hours of the morning, they awoke to their sweet son standing over them covered in blood. A bloody knife in his hand.

"I don't know what happened. I just...couldn't stop." He said a dissonance distorting the entire pitch of his voice.

Mrs. Holland had to squint just to register that this person was even her son at all. After a stunned beat, she wordlessly bolted for the den where Turner's room was. *It wasn't true.* She thought. It's unthinkable. Impossible. To painful to imagine. In the 60 seconds it took for her to run down the stairs and into the den she considered the unthinkable, dismissed it outright, and realized she was already hyperventilating at the chance that her nightmare was true. Finally, she reached the scene of the crime and sure enough her worst nightmare was realized. Her youngest, her six-year-old daughter Little Maisey, was already dead. Mutilated. Almost completely dismembered. From hundreds and hundreds of stab wounds given by Sweet Turner Holland.

Downers were not actually sure if the reports that Little Maisey was stabbed "hundreds and hundreds" of times was fact, but they did know that her stabbing murder was deemed "overkill" and that her head almost came clear off because of the excessive stab wounds.

That was the worst of it though. It had certainly shown the community that trauma was not something to be played with and could cause a domino effects of tragedy and suffering. Most Downers had learned this lesson. Most except for The Fringe who took the events of the Halloween Bash to capitalize on their message that, "The Boys Were Coming Home" just like they chanted that fateful night. They were gathering more members although no one could say exactly who was a member and who wasn't. It was a rather secret...society. Apparently though since the Halloween Bash they had a standout new member who was more mysterious than they were. A member who was no more than a figment. A formless figure. Without a name or a face...yet.

Another effort to support the community was the town-wide campaign to try and cool the outbreak of paranoia in Downers Grove for everyone to commit to, "See Something. Say Something." The tenets of the campaign was that if everyone would commit to that then nothing not a wolf, not a rapist, not a mentally disturbed killer, not a violent men or a violent boy could ever get past them or hurt them again. Problem was Downers Grove was always a lovely place and Downers themselves were notoriously comfortable in their pleasant little town. Nothing was ever what it seemed because despite the last few months Downers Grove was not a place where things went wrong and even if they did everything had an explanation and a solution. Surely.

Now thankfully, the drama and creep factors following Halloween of '94 were all clearing up and some good things were happening now at least for Sierr. She snagged her first directing gig. The next Hallows Eve Church Play. The last one, not surprisingly, was panned by reviewers. Granted some saw the fantastical take on the Adam & Eve story as avant-garde most, including Sierr & Company, saw the play as confusing, without nuance, and well…all over the place. So, Sierr used her amateur public relations skills to convince Becca to let her re-write the script and be co-director of the new play.

Becca agreed reluctantly at first, but after she and Sierr worked through some ideas and a story treatment Becca started to have a little more faith in Sierr's abilities. Honestly, Sierr had surprised herself. Over the last few months she had, for once, managed to tune out the chatter and not allow the recent havoc in their small town to clog or inhibit her creativity. She used retreating to her room for peace and quiet as moments to write to her heart's content. Not just little burst of writing here and there, but day after day she was writing. The words just seemed to flow and not only was the screenplay for the play mostly finished the first entry into the Jessica Daffy series was finally complete.

The story had developed into a trilogy series named, "Dead Serious: The Jessica Daffy Chronicles," about a complex female NARC agent who was being courted by the FBI through her secret FBI Director and her unrequited love, Officer Vaschez, who was slowly falling in love with her and who had dangerous secrets of his own. Sierr felt that the early draft version of Jessica Daffy was too polished, too perfect, too squeaky clean. People may want to be that way, but usually it takes effort live that way permanently. Temptation tempts everyone after all. Sierr knew about that first hand. Jessica had become somewhat of an alter ego of herself. A doppelgänger who functions as she did, but navigated life and love more smoothly and badass-ly. Jessica was a version of Sierr that she knew was in her somewhere and just needed to be found, put on like a suit, and given full reign over specific parts of Sierr's consciousness, particularly her confidence.

It was delightful to be ahead of her schedule to finish Book One by her 18th birthday. She allowed herself to wonder if it was possible to set a new goal to have the book published by her 18th birthday? It would be a feat, but she was hopeful. The thought of directing her first project and publishing her first book felt like stepping into her destiny to be an award winning author and filmmaker of the future. This was only the beginning.

Sierr flounced in a dramatic gown to her vanity humming absentmindedly not really paying attention to the words in her head or coming out of her mouth trailing off occasionally between the lyrics and skipping random lines without any real focus.

"*Hmm, hmm, hmm to catch them is my real test,*

*Wanna be the very best…*

*To train them is my cauuuuuse,*

*DumDumDum!*" Sierr drummed the air and thudded her head to beat. "*The power that's insiiiiide, Gotta catch 'em all!*

*It's you and me.*

*Hmm, dada da…It's my destiny.*"

She plopped down in the chair at her vanity plucked up her chunky The Little Mermaid hair brush from middle school and brushed out her fluffy curls.

"*Hmm you teach me,*
*Da dum I'll teach you…*"

Then using her hairbrush as a make believe microphone, she belted out, "*Pokémo…*!" Just then a familiar shriek from outside cut off her singing and her thoughts.

"SIERR!!" Willow screamed at the top of her lungs from the street. "Open the door!!" Sierr peaked out her window to see Willow running towards the Blake house in cargo pants and a halter top with papers in her hand. Carmen biking close behind in a flower print summer romper.

Willow pounded on the front door endlessly as Sierr galloped down the stairs shouting, "Okay! Okay!"

She threw the door open and Willow breathlessly said, "You are never going to believe this!"

"I'm still pretty blown away myself." Carmen hopped off her bike and whipped the helmet off her head. They both walked inside.

Willow jumped up and down gasping for air, "My life! My friggin flabbergastingly finally fabulous fierce fashionista life is taking us all somewhere very special!"

"Us all?" Sierr arched an eyebrow.

"She would have had to take me anyway. I would have forced her to either smuggle me through her carryon on drag me from here to JFK connected at the ankle."

"JFK? In New York? What's going on?" Sierr asked.

"I have been invited to New York Fashion Week. I have four tickets for me and my closest friends to enjoy two weeks in the big city curtesy of Angelica McCord designs." Willow pulled out four round trip from NorCal to NYC plane tickets.

Sierr gasped with Carmen.

"Why are you gasping? You've already seen them?" Willow asked Carmen.

Carmen hand fluttered to her chest, "They are just as beautiful as they were the first time."

Willow scoffed playfully, "Listen during the trip I have do intern stuff. Angelica is launching her haute couture line and I am going to be helping her do PR from the teen crowds so she wants me, and my friends, to attend some teen events wearing her most outlandish clothes and talk her up ya' know. Market her line and get in touch with the youth crowd."

"We get to model too?" Sierr asked.

"Model!!!" Carmen squealed like she was about to burst. "I might faint." She leaned up against the wall dramatically. "My prayers have been answered!"

"Said the lawyer." Willow chuckled.

"I can moo-del and lawyer." She pronounced the "Mo" in model like "Mooooo" from a cow and the 'del' she pronounced as 'dull' so the word became: Moo-Dul. "In fact I could a moo-del lawyer. I can be anything I want!" She flipped her hair, did a twirl, struck a pose.

"Here! Here! Just like Barbie teaches us!" Sierr cheered. Carmen laughed. "When is the trip! What events will we be going to! Are living expenses paid for too?" The girls walk into the kitchen. Carmen helps herself to Sierr's stash of salted almond dark chocolate bars in the freezer.

"Everything is taken care of. Angelica paid for everything. We will stay in two hotel suites two of us in each room. We get whatever we like from room service. She will give us a little spending money. We will have an escort to make sure we stay safe navigating the city and attending events."

Carmen munching chocolate, "Oh an escort! How fancy!"

Sierr pours them all lemonade. "Ooooh unlimited room service! How fancy."

Willow, "Ditto, ladies. This is a pivotal moment in our lives. We're moving on up…to the east side."

"We finally gotta piece of…" Sierr sang.

The girls all scream, "…Oh thhhhhhhheeeeee piiieeeeee!!"

Then Sierr gasps, "Oh meh Goodness. Do you know what this means!? I can talk to publishers while I'm up there!"

"Is your book finished?" Willow asked fishing Ice Cream out of Sierr's freezer.

"Yes! I finished it this weekend. It felt so good to write the words…The End." Sierr gathered three bowls and three spoons for she and her friends. "And then I realized it has a continuation so I had to delete that. But, it still felt great that the first book in the series is finished!"

"Totally." Willow dug a spoon into the ice cream carton and eat it.

"Hey!" Lux squealed at the sight of Willow eating straight of the ice cream carton. She walked to pantry and grabbed a banana and some peanut butter and vanilla protein powder. "What's all with all the commotion?"

Sierr swiveled on the bar swivel chair as she spoke, "Willow has surprised us with four tickets to New York Fashion Week curtesy of Angelica McCord designs."

"Curtesy of Angelica McCord? Guess that wackdo comes in handy, huh?" Lux loaded all the pantry items into the blender. "It'll be a breath of fresh air to leave this friggin' town for a while. Get away from all the insanity."

"Angelica is eager to get away too. She's just glad that Jame is well enough to travel now." Willow said.

"Are she and Jame a thing?" Carmen asked with a wince.

"I dunno what they are. I don't see him anymore. I mean not that he hasn't been there. He is being tended to by a private nurse in Angelica's mansion in the hills." Willow replied.

"He stays in her house? Oh they're a couple." Carmen states matter-of-factly.

"What if older woman and younger gay man is the kind of madness the new millennium has in store for us?" Sierr said flamboyantly tossing her hair behind her shoulder and popping her tongue.

"Maybe. He. Is. Her. Sex. Slave." Carmen said with the utmost seriousness. Willow, Sierr, and Lux looked to her with wide eyes before bursting into laughter. "I was serious!" Carmen put her hands on her hips.

"Sex slave?!" Willow laughed.

"People can be sex slaves. It happens! It even happens to men sometimes." Carmen said.

"Not by women." Willow said.

"Well it is possible if the woman has leverage over the man, or the woman has some kind of threatening presence in his life, or…" Lux sliced the banana into the blender. "It could be consensual." Sierr and her friends shared a look. "So, who's your fourth person?"

"Hmm?" Sierr cocked her to the side.

"You said Willow has four tickets. Who's your forth person?" Lux asked again retrieving almond milk from the refrigerator and splashing some into the blender along with a squeeze of honey.

"Oh yeah." Willow said thoughtfully. "Who else do we like?"

"Gee no one really." Carmen admitted wide-eyed.

"Well we like JSF." Sierr reminded them.

"No *you* like him." Willow stated.

"Oh c'mon. You really *don't* like JSF?" Sierr asked Willow with a smirk.

"He's tolerable at best." Lux replied.

"I. Was. Asking. Willow. Thank you." Sierr droned.

"He's tolerable at best." Willow grinned.

"Oy." Sierr sighed.

"What about Hailey? We like her." Carmen suggested.

"We are going to invite a gothic, anti-social person to Fashion Week to moo-del clothes at parties?" Willow arches an eyebrow with a grin.

"Well she is a romantic gothic. They know a little bit about fashion, right? She matches textures well. Remember that eyelet lace burgundy corset she had on for the last day of school with those black velvet thigh high boots?" Carmen noted hopefully.

"Angelica has a summer collection. Where does burgundy and black fit into a summer collection? I don't think I've ever seen Hailey in a single bright color. At least with JSF Angelica will have someone male to moo-del her menswear line?" Willow said thoughtfully.

"All I can say about JSF is that he is a child of God….who push me on national television." Carmen scooped ice cream into her bowl.

"National Television? It was local news in a small town. Nothing that ever happens in Downers Grove will make headline news. I guarantee it." Willow rolls her eyes.

"He had no business pushing me! We're not all kids anymore. He has to treat me like a girl now!" Carmen pouted.

"He apologized a million times about that since then." Sierr said.

"Actually it was twice and both times YOU had to drag it out of him and one of those times you had to bribe him with cheese sticks!" Carmen shouted.

"Okay. Sure. Yes, exactly. But, he's still our friend." Sierr said. "He's always been there with us."

"He's our friend." Willow admitted. "Beside I'm sure you and him are a packaged deal anyway." Willow rolled her eyes as Carmen passed her the almost half empty ice cream carton. "Geez how hungry are you?" She asked scooping out her serving.

Carmen hunched a shoulder sucking on her spoon.

"We can invite him, but who knows he may not even come. He turned down his free LA trip." Willow passed the ice cream to Sierr.

"I think that's because he didn't want to be alone." Sierr scooped out some ice cream into her bowl and crumbled quite a bit of the dark chocolate over the top.

"Well he could have given the trip to us!" Carmen states bitterly. "But, noooooo he just had to gave it away to some rando."

Lux turned on the blender. Shouted jokingly that she hoped she wasn't interrupting anything. The girls all smiled and nodded.

After the blender stopped it was silent for a while eating and Lux drinking. Eventually Willow chuckled to herself.

"I must say I bet that hobo had never been happier." Willow chuckled.

Sierr cracked up with Willow and Lux and Carmen couldn't help, but laugh too.

Carmen noted, "I call dibs on sharing a room with Willow."

Lux interjected, "Oh you all are sharing rooms? So, I guess that means you'll be sharing a room with…the boi."

"Uh yeah. I guess." Sierr sipped her lemonade allowing her ice cream to melt into the perfect soft serve consistency.

"Don't you two kids get into any trouble now!" Lux teased sarcastically.

"oH MeH GoOooOsH wE'lL tRy!" Sierr replied sarcastically in the dopiest voice she could muster up. "Heavens just the thought. Eww."

"Double eww." Lux replied warningly.

"Let's go ask him if he'll come." Willow said getting up from her seat.

"Now? When are we leaving? I still have to ask my parents." Then Sierr beamed the words. "…although I know they'll say 'yes'!"

"We leave Monday after the next!" Carmen chirped happily.

"Angelica wants all of our parents signatures before we can go on the trip. Ya know so they can't claim that she kidnapped us or anything crazy like that." Willow grinned.

"Wait I gotta change into something!" Sierr trotted up the stairs and quickly changed into Jean capris and a blouse.

The three girls make a right out of the Blake's driveway and walking deeper into the Mangroves to meet up with JSF at The Fitzgerald's Estate. Soon a convertible pulled up beside them from deeper in the Mangroves.

"Ladies!" Abby sing-songed from the passenger's seat with oversized shades shield at least a third of her face from sunlight. Damian was driving the car in a pair of gold rimmed, navy blue aviators. "Heard you three are going to the big apple with me!"

"With you?" Willow's eyebrows shot up. "We're going with Angelica McCord."

"Well so am I!" Abby flashed her super bleached teeth. "I met your boss and told her how faaaaabulous I thought her clothes were aaaaannd how our age group would simply love wearing stylish haute couture in the halls aaaaaannd how I would be so proud to model her clothes in front of aaaalllll my friends and guess what she did? She invited me to come to New York to introduce her line to the '95 runway! Is that not the best news you have ever heard?!" Abby was the personification of peppy. It was so unlike her.

Carmen and Sierr shared a look.

Willow just squinted at Abby Windsor or rather this peppy person who pretended to be Abby Windsor. "Sooooo, you're gonna walk the runway?"

"Yeah and of course attend all the events with you guys! OhMehGod it'll be so fun! So modelly!"

"Can't wait." Carmen mustered up the fakest smile and fakest happy tone of voice possible.

"We'll see each other everyday....Just like at school." Sierr smiled. Hers a better fake than Carmen's. If Sierr knew anything about herself it was that she was a princess of counterfeit smiles. It was a trait learned by the best introverts after years of being asked if they were secretly depressed or on meds or suffering with something or whatever. Sierr had even managed to train herself to make her eyes crease in the corners when delivering counterfeit smiles as it made them much more authentic looking.

Abby gasped, "I know right! Well there's sooooo much to do to get ready for my runway debut. Toodles girls!" She then sing-songed, "Oh and remember, if you see something say something!" Abby blew Sierr & Company a kiss and Damian drove off.

"Okay what the hell just happened?" Carmen watched as Damian and Abby disappeared down Sweet Pique Lane.

"Potty mouth much." Willow stated.

"What just happened here warrants a cuss word. Even the Lord would sympathize."

"He would?" Sierr arches an eyebrow.

"One Thousand percent! Because we are going to have to spend our vacation with Abby Windsor now." Carmen replied marching forward.

"Does this mean Angelica got over Abby one upping her at the Halloween Bash?" Willow arched an eyebrow. "Maybe she has an ulterior motive?"

"I cannot imagine that woman ever getting over a slight." Sierr pondered aloud.

"Wait where is she going to stay?" Carmen asked. "Never mind I'm sure she has her own room. She is walking the runway after all. That's a...special position." Her nostrils flared. "I'm so glad JSF is coming."

"*Now* you're glad he's coming?" Sierr said surprised.

"Yes! Cause he knows how to knock her down a few pegs when she gets out of line. I mean I do too...mostly. But, ya know." Carmen hunched a shoulder. "He's tougher than us all put together."

"Speak for yourself!" Willow dropped her shoulders in disappointment and deep offense. "I can handle myself and Abby!"

"Hey-ya. Wait, no! I retract that 'Hey-ya' because you'll be interning. He'll mostly be hanging with us." Carmen replied.

"Moo-deling!" Sierr chirped.

"Moo-deling." Willow repeated. "Carmen, make this your mantra. 'I will be my own attack dog.' Mkay?"

Carmen nodded her head vigorously with a vulnerable look on her face, "I'll try."

"Whose a good girl?" Willow said through a full pout like one would do when rewarding a pooch. Carmen smiled with relief.

They come up on a section of The Mangroves where the houses were even bigger and the lawns were twice the size and each house was separated by 10 ft tall black rod iron fences and evergreens for added privacy. A group of mommy joggers, wearing different colored versions of the same style of sweatsuits, padded the ground on the other side of the sidewalk shouting motivational quotes at each other with gusto and fervor.

The white bricks in the ground were laid in a swirly pattern and the mailboxes had swirly embellishments too. The girls approached a large stone house with a black gate in the front. It was open and the girls walked in. A dog frantically started barking inside the house. It was Tiffany Fitzgerald, the Fitzgerald's award winning Yorkshire Terrier.

JSF was puffing on a joint and tending to the garden in the front lawn. He used one hand to pull weeds and the other to hold his joint between puffs. He wore two oversized lightweight jackets with some jeans. One pant leg rolled up to the knee.

"Hey landscaper! I got a few weeds you can pull!" Carmen shouted across the lawn.

"What does that even mean?" He shouted back. Tiffany continues barking in the house. "TIFFANY! Hush." He shouted at the window she was yipping in front of. She panted, her little pink tongue hanging out, before she trotted away. He turned to them with bags under his eyes.

"We have a proposal for you! Ms. Koi?" Sierr said turning to Willow.

"Mr. Fitzgerald I have been cordially invited to a little event called…" Willow cleared her throat dramatically. "Fashion Week and we are all going as very important members of the young adult fashion society…"

"Young. Adult. Fashion. Society." JSF smirked sarcastically.

"Let her finish! You're so rude!" Carmen spat.

"Do you still hate me, baby girl?" JSF smiled like an ass.

Carmen folded her arms over her chest and looked away.

"As I was saying young adult fashion society and we would like to invite to be the fourth member in our group." Willow concluded.

"Me? At fashion week?" He asked.

"Yes, you do have to do much really. Just attend some events with us wearing items from Angelica McCord's menswear's line. And we'll be doing the same thing except we'll be wearing the womenswear line. And it's all prepaid so we don't have to buy anything ourselves!" Sierr explained further.

"You'll all be there?" JSF asked.

"Yes. And Abby." Carmen said.

"Abby got invited too?" He said.

"Yeah but she will have her own suite. We're going to be split between two." Willow said.

"Oh who do Iiiiiiiiii get to sleep with!?" JSF's grinned with wide eyes.

Sierr punched him in the arm and tucked a curl behind her ear.   "I already volunteered. So, are you coming or not?"

"Okay. You don't need to beg." He whipped the hair wrap off his head and threw his hair to the side gave it a hard tussle.

"We weren't…" Carmen cut herself off. He was too much at times. JSF cut his eyes to Carmen and looked her up and down with a sinister little smirk. She backed away from him. "W…what?"

"Oh nuthin'." He said strolling towards her with the watering hose from the garden in his hand.

"Don't…don't you dare." Carmen trembled.

Willow was already laughing. Sierr cracked up too.

"What? A black man can't walk towards someone in his own lawn?" JSF said as innocently as possible continuing to approach her slowly. "I just think you need to cool off."

Carmen back away from JSF watching him, watching the hose, watching him, watching the hose. In a fit of panic she screamed, "Willow do something!"

Willow screamed back in a fit of hysterics, "Save yourself, woman!"

"Ahhhhh!" Carmen screamed like a manic as she turned and bolted for the exit. JSF sprayed her in the back. She screamed like a person being stabbed. Crumbled to the ground like she had a severe injury and was suffering major blood loss. JSF sprayed her again with pulsing rhythms. She crawled and screamed incoherent gibberish at him.

JSF thought he heard her wailing that he was a "sexist pig," but he couldn't quite be sure. Besides he was laughing so hard he was crying and he didn't really care about Carmen's drama either. Sierr ran to Carmen and helped her up off the ground. JSF sprayed her too and growled at her with a smirk, "Traitor!"

"Oh you are so dead!" Sierr calmly said.

"You know I'm actually close to believing *you*." JSF admitted wiping his eyes from the tears.

"Believe this!" Willow snatched the hose out of JSF's hand and sprayed his face. He lost his balance and buckled to his knees.

"It feels good to….hey wait my joint!" JSF exclaimed realizing she soaked his joint too.

"Ha!" Carmen shouted throwing her neck around.

JSF charged at Willow and she sprayed him with perfect aim and precision. He managed to get ahold of the hose and wrestled with Willow for it. He wrestled with her from behind and front to front. Eventually her firm demands for him to let go and back off dissolved to a fit of giggles and hysterically laughter as she herself got soaked.

Sierr and Carmen laughed in the background and JSF now soaked from head toe retrieved the hose from Willow whose was also soaked from head to toe, her pencil straight black hair stuck to her perfect fair skin. He calmly stood in front of her towering over her petite frame with a creepy little grin. He turned the hose off. Willow struggled to catch her breath.

He panted, "You know what I hate?"

Willow panted, "What could possibly hated? You caused this hoopla!"

He adjusted his grip of the hose like he was holding a pistol, "I hate that one of us is still dry."

Willow's expression changed, "Sierr ruuuuuuunnnn!"

JSF bolted towards Sierr chasing her towards the house.

"Dude! Don't you da…..nooooooo!" Sierr screamed as JSF caught up to her wrapped his arms around her waist spun her in the air and sat her on the ground with a thud. He straddled her on the ground and pinned her down where he sprayed her from the hose by holding the hose near his genitals and shook the hose up and down, thrusting towards her, as it streamed like he was taking a giant whiz on her face and chest. "That's so uncalled for my goodness! The Rudeness!" Sierr shouted when he finally stopped.

"Don't act like you didn't get a kick out of it." JSF chuckled.

"You made it look like…oh forget it!" Sierr rung out her hair like a towel.

"Like I was relieving myself on you?" Then he lowered his voice, leaned in close to her, and sing-songed. *"Wouldn't be the first time!"*

"Oh Lord. What were we back then? Four? You're almost a full man now! *Almost.*" Sierr respond with a sneer. "You're obviously still a child upstairs!"

"You liked it back then too." JSF said in the most feminine voice he could muster up.

"Shut up!" She started towards the gate of the Fitzgerald's Estate with Willow and Carmen.

"Go dry your panties off ladies!" JSF sing-songed/screamed across the lawn waving wildly like he was trying to guide in a couple planes.

"Go sober up!" Willow shouted back bitterly.

"Wait! When do my parents need to sign the permission slip?" He walked towards the girls.

"How presumptuous of you to assume that you're still invited after your rude treatment of us." Carmen replied.

"I'm a friend of the family." JSF smiled and glanced at Sierr. She pursed her lips hard, hiding a hint of a smile.

"I'll come by with the slip. Your mom or dad can sign it. I'll give it to Angelica and that's all you need to do." Willow said cordially.

"A'ight." He responded.

"A'ight….Jerk." Willow playfully whipped her body away from him as did Carmen and then Sierr and then girls left the Fitzgerald's.

JSF watched the girls walk away before calmly strolling back into his quiet house with a soggy squish, squish in every one of his unbothered steps.

Abby Windsor walked hand and hand with Damian into the Windsor Estate. The house was marble upon marble. Marble floors. Marble walls. A grand foyer with a chandelier and grand staircase greet all who enter. It was well lit with warm lights and accent plants and flowers lined the path to the kitchen to the left. With Mocha Frappuccinos rom Ashley's in their free hands, Abby and Damian strolled into the kitchen and there staring her face-to-face the face of death, or as most people referred to her, Hailey in all black as always. Hailey leaned on the marble island in the kitchen. Ran a hand through her hair and casually met Abby glare.

"Uh what are you doing in my house?" Abby gave Hailey a sharp once over.

Hailey looked taller somehow despite wearing flat black combat boots paired with a black dress with a thigh high split. She looked down on Abby as if Abby was intruding on her turf somehow…in Abby's house. She had a womanly energy to her stance. A confidence. A mysterious radiance.

She didn't even bother to answer Abby's question as if it would be beneath her to even dignify a question, any question, from Abby with a response. Abby's nostrils flared with outrage and fury. How dare that bitch come into her home and then disrespect her?! The nerve! What was she doing here anyway?

Just then Daddy Windsor trotted down the stairs with papers in his hand. "Okay. Ms. Francesca. Here are the class notes you asked for." He handed Hailey the papers and she flipped through them revealing detailed class notes and a chart of some sort. Abby peaked over her shoulder to see.

"Thank you, Mr. Windsor. I just completed blanked during class and I don't even have an explanation really." Hailey chuckled lightly tucking a lock of straight slick hair behind her triple pierced right ear.

Daddy walked Hailey past Abby and Damian as if they were both invisible as guided his prized student to the front door with his hand on her lower back well within waist territory, "That's quite alright." He replies to Hailey opening the door for her. "I'm understand that school can be demanding of students. I try to make it a point to be as supportive as possible. It's my job to help you kids in anyway that I can especially right before finals." He stood over Hailey in the doorway.

She nodded and thanked him walked down the drive way. Daddy closed the door and walked past Abby again without speaking to her. Plucked a Golden Delicious apple off the island in the kitchen, threw it up in the air, and caught it in his hand again before taking a bite.

"What was Hailey here for?" Abby squinted her tone accusatory at best.

"I gave her the class notes she wanted to be prepare for finals next week." Daddy crunched on the fresh, crisp, sweet apple.

"Why didn't she just ask a student?" Abby frowned. Daddy noticed Damian squirm.

"Well I'm not sure she would trust another student's notes. I know I wouldn't. Perhaps it's because she doesn't really have friends to ask. I've noticed she's a bit of a loner." Daddy munched.

"Well she's a freak." Abby stated matter-of-factly.

Daddy sucked his teeth, an almost predatory look crossing over his face he replied, "When the only interaction you have with a person is snarking at them in passing you're not really in the position to judge who they are."

"Have you seen her?! She's…" Abby's chest nearly heaved with anger.

"She's your age you know. Do you really want to be one of those girls?" He stared dead into Abby's soul. "One of those girls who attacks her peers and finds pride in being a social pariah? One of those girls who pushes others down without even considering their humanity? One of those people who will eventually push everyone so far away because of their narcism that they end up old and alone with only liquor and superficial relationships to keep then company? Because that's the path your headed down." He turned on his heels and ate his apple walking into another room.

"Where's mom?" Abby stepped forward dropping Damian's hand. He immediately began rubbing it as if nursing a pain.

"She's on her way to Angelica McCord's house in the hills to give her the permission slip for you to go to Fashion Week and to give her the substantial payment that Angelica requested in exchange for you to have this opportunity after that disrespectful, distasteful stunt you pulled at *her* event on Halloween." Daddy walked out of sight.

Abby glared at the spot where Daddy was standing before turning back to Damian seeing him rubbing his hand. "What are you doing?" She snarled.

"You…you can't dig your nails into someone's skin like that. It hurts." Damian said with wide-eyes.

Abby took his hand in hers and apologized, "I'll make it better for you." She guided him up the stairs where another chandelier greeted them. They walked towards a white door with a glass doorknob and entered her room. A crystal covered abode that closely resembled a winter wonderland. Crystal blues, frosty whites, glass makeup cases. Her room large and wide with her elevated bed right in the middle on a white shag rug. She had to walk up three stairs just get into bed it was lifted so far off he ground. She pulled Damian up on the bed with her. They make out.

Damian notices the door to Abby's room is still open, "Oh we forgot to close the door." He starts get up, but she pulls him back on top of her kissing him.

"I don't care. Let him watch. I don't care about anything anymore." Abby says in between kisses on Damian's ear.

"Well…I kinda do." He chuckled. "I'm gonna close it." Damian got up to colors the door. Abby sat up and looked out the window thoughtfully.

Damian climbed the three stairs and crawled back up into her bed. Kissed her neck and started removing his shirt. She was still obviously distracted. Something else occupying her mind. She kissed him back and removed her paisley button top. She grinned.

"What?" Damian smiled. "Don't finish without me." He joked.

"I want to finish."

"I can make that happen." Damian moaned kissing her.

"I want to finish my dad." She breathed in his ear. A wide smile growing across her heart shaped face.

Damian's expression changed. He laughed. Abby laughed too. He asked, "What are you talking about?"

Abby cocked her head to the side. Hoped off her bed and retrieved a pink rhinestone encrusted flask from the drawer of her white dresser. Took a few dramatic steps back towards the bed and struck a runway pose. Smirked flirtatiously at Damian and took a swig. She skipped to the door, opened it, and peaked out. She close the door again. Took another swig and threw herself back in the bed. "I wanna kill daddy."

Damian looked at Abby for a while. Searched her face for any indication that this was just a morbid joke. His face broke into a nervous smile, "Are you kidding?"

"Listen." Abby radiated joyful and excited about her new realization. She searched for the right words to use, "He's not family. He's a thorn in my side. And mother's. She hates him. I hate him. They argue all the time. Everyday. There's something. A fight. A dig. An insult. He goes out of his way to separate himself from us. And then he has the nerve to favor his students over me! His own true, biological daughter! He's all over Sierr. He's all over Hailey. Willing to address their concerns and feelings. Well…what about mine? What about my concerns for our family unit? Ya' know?"

"Sure." Damian replied.

"I cannot stand him anymore. I just can't. I don't want to." Abby smiled again. "Wouldn't it be great to make a plan to get rid of him for good?"

Damian paused and leaned in closer to Abby, close enough to kiss her, "Yeah let's make a plan."

"That would be like so…therapeutic for me!" She ran her arms under her hair sexily. Then tongued Damian. "Ugh!" She took another swig. They laid down facing each other. "Should it be bloody or should it be silent! Like a silent killer type thing? Like poison!"

"Uh nah. Let's bludgeon him!" Damian kissed Abby he moaned the words, "Bludgeon him with a hammer."

"Or a steel bat!" She giggled.

"Then we clean up the blood." Damian suggested.

"But not before we christen the scene of the crime."

"Christen?"

"By making love…in his blood. Like his blood will symbolize our new beginnings! Because without him around we'll all be free!"

"Damn girl. You so dirty!" He laughed giving her an Eskimo kiss.

She threw her head back laughing so hard her face stretched and her eyebrows arched in the middle. Developed a demonic look of immense joy.

"Just wait until the disposal process. We chop him up into tiny little pieces and stuff him into trash bags." She continued giddily. "Then we drive him up to the mountains where the wolves can eat him and turn him into the shit he really is!"

"Ha! I bet The Fringe would love it if people think the ghost of The Beckwith Brothers took him and ate him." The two shared a laugh.

Abby playfully hit Damian's arm and noted, "That would be so perfect! The perfect crime! We do the killing and mythical dead little boys get blamed for it!"

"It is perfect. Do you feel a little bit better now?"

"Yeah a little." She smiled.

"A little fantasy makes everything better." Damian kisses Abby on the cleavage.

"I'm serious." Her smile faded. He looked at her intensely. "If I ever needed you like really needed you…would you be there for me?"

Damian looked at Abby thoughtfully for a while, "I would always be there for you."

"Good. Because one day this might be more than just a…plan. You know?" She ran her hands through his hair.

"I understand." He responded dead serious.

# Chapter 9: The Dawning Of A New Era

Luke and Lyle ran together through the trees. Barefoot and shirtless. They ran as fast as they could through a vast field of wildflowers. The occasional buzzing of the random bee or wasp nearby. The head of a bunny rabbit appearing just over the tops of the flowers with each of the bunny's hops. The birds tweeting and singing in the full, green tree canopy above. An eagle circling the field possibly for the bunny? The cool breeze made the warm day all the more enjoyable especially following a brutal winter.

Lyle and Luke had changed over the last few months too. They towered over the flowers two inches taller than they were just weeks earlier. Their shoulders wider and their hair longer. Thick, wavy sun bleached tresses tickled the space underneath their shoulder blades like Eric. Luke ran ahead of Lyle he always liked being the faster one. Just by a few extra strides Luke could lead Lyle any day or any terrain. He doubled back turned to Lyle, cut him off, and tackled him to the ground. They laughed silent belly laughs. Lyle too weak from laughter to fight back, resist control, allowed Luke to pin him to the ground. Luke handed him a daisy. Lyle smelled it and Luke ran his fingers along Lyle's new Adam's Apple. Luke grabbed Lyle's newly sprouted, thicker chest hair which covered his pectorals and grew down to his abdomen much like Eric's already did.

Lyle grinned telepathed to Luke, *"Grab your own?"*

Luke telepathed back, *"I do! We're fuzzy like rabbits now!"*

Lyle straddled his brother, rubbed his chest hair with both hands, and smiled deviously, *"More like wolves."*

Lyle grabbed a fist full of hair on Luke's head and telepathed, *"Hair."* Then a fist full of chest hair, *"More Hair."* Then pulled down Luke's pants revealing his glossy pubes and his uncircumcised penis and laughed, *"Extra hair!"*

Lyle then shoved Luke to the ground and bolted into the field. Luke simultaneous hopped up, yanked up his pants, and charged after his twin with glee. The flowers surrounding them. The forest full of animal life and flourishing plant life again. Their garden had bloomed rather well too. Eric was back at the cabin tending to the strawberries, zucchini, potatoes, tomatoes, Almonds, and oranges. It would be nice to be able to eat good again. Not just meat and potatoes stored in the cold hole. Spring was the best time.

Despite belly laughs making them both weak they still ran with all the force and power that they could. Luke eventually lost Lyle in the trees. Suspecting that Lyle was tricking him, Luke slowed to a stop listening closely to his surroundings. Lyle could not evade him. They were connected within each other's souls. They could keep no secrets from one another for long. Not even where the other was hiding. Luke slinked around in the brush for a while. Could feel Lyle's presence close. Deciding where he was exactly should have been easy. Luke noticed a thick berry bush within a few feet and was sure that Lyle was hiding right in that spot. Luke wanted to surprise him and took light steps to sneak up on his twin. Luke grinned to himself as he approached the bush. He could tell that Lyle was right there for sure. Luke sprang into the bush only to find himself standing in old fur from a dead rotted squirrel. Luke jumped back in disgust. He wiped his feet on the ground dug into the soil and pulled out some moist dirt to wipe off his feet. He then wiped the moist soil off with leaves.

He shook his head. How did he lose Lyle? He had never lost Lyle before. They were always in tune with each other to know if the other was okay or within proximity. What happened? Just then Luke heard the bellow of a bull deer nearby. Curious he followed the sound. Through the thicket Luke walked towards the sound of deep heaving, grunting, and snorting. There he found his brother laying on his belly watching the bull mate a female in his harem. Without even looking towards Luke, Lyle patted the ground next to him inviting his brother to sit and watch too. Luke quietly dropped to his knees and laid down next to Lyle watching. The bull had wide, stunning antlers shed of their antler velvet which was blood red and richly nourished from a good diet earned from keeping and also feeding from coveted territory. He dwarfed his mate, a doe with narrow shoulders, the blank look in both of their eyes. Lyle often wondered if animals as dumb as deers can figure out breeding and maintaining a kingdom why couldn't he and his brothers? Maybe the girl people were the key? Maybe he and his brothers needed the girl people? Like kinds needed like kinds. But, obviously that wasn't the rule the books had already showed he and his brothers that sometimes hybrids were best. Like Mr. Tumnus in Narnia. The brains of a man, the arms and hands of a man on top with the strength and majestic beauty of a stallion below.

*Must depend on the coupling.* Luke determined.

The bull mounted the doe and she squealed and spun around. The bull hobbled and hopped around to keep his balance and stay on her back at the same time. He bellowed again and it was over. The bull shook like the wolves did when they had water on their fur and then he ate some grass chewing it like a cow. The doe stood still like she was playing dead or something. One moment intense pleasure and fulfillment of life's purpose and the next nothing. Like it never even happened. But, it did happen. It would only be a few months before fawns would arrive as evidence of the bull and the doe's actions of today.

Luke stood and nuzzled his head on Lyle's shoulder. Lyle stood and watched the deer a little longer. A look of hunger and hatred in his eyes. Why could they have what he could not? Would he ever have what they had? When would it be his turn?

Eventually the twins arrived back at the cabin walked through the gate and locked it behind them. As soon as they stepped inside a roaring grew outside. Luke glances outside the window. Another helicopter, but the boys didn't know that word. They only figured these were the flying cars...promised by The Jetsons. This one dropped a trail of mist, fluid from the skies like many before it. The fluid mist would rain down upon the land as before and evaporated before it hit the ground like it was never even there at all. Eric was weary of the flying cars that encroached upon the airspace over their territory. He saw them as intruders. But only predators were intruders? *Well...*Luke realized, *people are intrusive predators.*

Lyle slowed his pace as the wolves greeted he and Luke with eager whimpers and kisses. Pretty Brown Eyes was perched upon the stairs watching them with her same stoic expression. She had such a humble, docile, and purposeful disposition. Often observed those in her presence may they be human family or part of her wolf family. She could usually be found perched on some high place. It was almost as if she knew that she was the special one at least according to Eric.

Lyle buried his head in his hands and shut his eyes so tightly that no light could come into them. Luke thought he saw his twin wince in agony. Lyle slipped into his dark bedroom and laid down. Luke watched Lyle in the doorway and Eric approached him from the kitchen.

*"What's wrong?"* Eric telepathed walking into the bedroom with Lyle. "Brother?" Eric sat on the edge of the bed and pat Lyle on the back. Then rubbed his back. Eric thought the comfort would nice for Lyle and that he would like it, but instead to Eric's surprise Lyle swung at him. Eric jumped back. *"Wha...? Geez. Calm down."*

Lyle revealed his face to Eric it was red with fury and rage and wet with a mixture of tears and sweat. His mouth formed a rectangle as he seethed. He turned away from Eric. Eric stood perplexed by Lyle's bed for a while before walking away. What was happening to Lyle? He was much more likely to be irritable and aggressive in recent months. What pain was his brother suffering from? Eric wanted to help. To hold him. To read to him. Make him feel better, but instead Eric walked out of a Lyle's room, clearing the wolves and Bright away from the door as he closed it behind him. Maybe a little solitude would help Lyle. He reassured Luke that Lyle was just a little sick and that they could cook together.

In the kitchen, Eric and Luke cooked in the old man's pots zucchini sautéed in animal fat and strawberry simmered until reduced down to a sweet, rich jelly perfect for snacking on between meals. The boys had such a savory diet anything remotely sweet offered a much desired treat for the tastebuds.

Luke flipped each zucchini over in the pan of sizzling animal fat, tediously trimmed from Canadian Geese, with a fork. The zucchini's little bottoms golden brown and their pale tops the only side left to cook. Eric kept a close watch on Luke, his cook habits over the years proved to be hazardous at best. Since they were boys, Luke had acquired many bad burns and cuts on his hands and forearms from cooking incidents. He was always a little clumsier than his brothers and wore the scars to prove it. He never cared about the pain though. Pain was inevitable in the wild and as long as he could eat and the food was good all burns and cuts would soon be forgotten.

Once cooled, Eric transferred the strawberry jam into a glass jar. Chipped and stained and it's gasket all worn down to nothing but a sad, squishy little disk, for the average person the glass was well past it's lifespan, but the boys were masters of resourcefulness and recycling.

Eric gave the pot, coated in strawberry jam, to Luke to lick clean before it got its salt scrub and a quick rinse in the river. Luke happily lapped the pot squirming away from Pretty Brown Eyes and the rest of the pack.

Pedigree body shoved Dee. Growled angrily at her his hair standing up on his thick shoulders. She cowered to him normally this type of reaction would cool the aggressor in a wolf pack, but instead Pedigree growled even more harshly at her, bared his teeth, and snapped at her. Pretty Brown Eyes immediately started barking in Dee's defense. Atlas then came to Pedigree's defense and lunged at Pretty Brown Eyes suddenly Eric's arm came across Atlas' neck and shoved him back into a wall. Eric barked at Pedigree, "Stop!" The wolves whimpered and cowered in fear and anxiety as Pretty Brown Eyes continues barking. Pedigree growled and snarled like a rabid animal. Bee and Eee started barking too. Eric smacked Pedigree on the nose as hard as he could. Pedigree did even flinch. Just stared Eric down growling ready for blood. Eric grabbed his muzzle and jerked his head from side to side. Pedigree snapped at him and Eric stood over Pedigree, licking his own teeth, and cornered the wolf challenging the animal with his stature. Pedigree finally broke his aggression, put his ears back, closed his mouth and stopped growling, and sat down. Eyes to the floor. Eric grabbed Pedigree by the flesh on the back of his neck and dragged him squirming, snarling, and barking out onto the porch where Eric intended for him to stay for the rest of the night. Just as Eric turned his back to close the door, Pedigree spun around and bit Eric in the fleshy part of his calf muscle. Eric roared in pain, growled at Pedigree kicked the animal in the teeth and slammed the door. Eric then grabbed Atlas by the tuff of fur on the back of his neck and ushered him outside on the porch too.

"Damn dogs.." Eric mumbled to himself limping back into the kitchen through the pack of anxious canines. *Didn't they know he was king?*

Luke helped Eric sit down in a chair at the kitchen table. Luke eyed the blood and gave Eric a long look.

"I know." Eric said back aloud resting his head on the table. The other wolves leaping on him and giving him comforting kisses.

Pretty Brown Eyes paced trying to slip through the cluster of furry bodies. Eric patted Cee and Bee and gently moved them to the side to make way for Pretty Brown Eyes. She galloped towards him with her long legs and he helped her into his lap.

*"Let me help you."* Luke telepathed reaching for a fairly clean rag on the kitchen counter.

Eric could feel the blood running down his leg. He tapped it, bouncing Pretty Brown Eyes on his knee trying to distract himself from the pain. One of the wolves bumped into his leg. He grit his teeth could feel the wetness of his blood dribbling into his boot. He pulled Pretty Brown Eyes closer to him and cradled her as he stood up. He said aloud, "I...I...I'm going to go into the library. I'm okay. I'm okay. It's okay."

Eric left Luke and the wolf pack in the kitchen and carried Pretty Brown Eyes into the library. He closed the door behind them. He always found the library as he and his brothers cozy place. always smelling of old paper, dust, oak, and something else they could quite put their finger on that was oddly stale. Books lined the walls and stories that took their mind away from their fear of the unknown in the wilderness when they were boys surrounded them. Back then Eric knew that the stories could serve as a source of comfort for his baby brothers and it was his belief that creative material was the few doubtlessly, positive results of humanity. Anyone who could create joy from words on paper and was able to make people see worlds beyond with mere ink deserved immense appreciation.

Eric sat Pretty Brown Eyes on the floor and she walked a circle around him. He grabbed a fairly clean piece of fabric and wet it with the water from a mug on a small round marble and leather trimmed coffee table. Sat down in the leather lounge chair busted at the seams except for where gold studs held the treated hide firmly in place. He tended to the bite wound and took a breather.

Pretty Brown Eyes sniffed around the door of the library before turning back around to Eric. Eric nursed his leg and watched Pretty Brown Eyes gliding towards him. Almost a year had pasted since she found Eric and she had quickly matured past the flat headed, envelop eared puppy and grown into a longer and taller version of her elegant, lean form. She was a doe like specimen. Her distinctive curved back, long about nearly a full five feet in length from nose to tail, big brown eyes that bulged from her narrow skull all remained and while her features were the same they seem to fit her better now. Like she had grown into herself. A perfect friend. The curly hair that only grew long off the tips of her ears and on the underside of her body almost touched the floor.

She approached Eric again and rested her head on his lap. Eric stroked her warm, furry head and purred to her. Sent a long steady exhale of air from his lungs through his mouth to reverberate his tongue.

Eric laid his head back. He didn't want his brothers to see, but all the bickering in the house was catching up to him. His head hurt at least a few times a day, he could barely sleep any longer, he every itch of his body ached at times. Was it an illness? Did they pick up something in the forest? He removed his shirt. Was he hairier? His chest and abs were nearly covered with a smooth layer of brown hair. His legs were totally covered and arms too. Maybe this is what puberty did to people? Wasn't he too old for puberty though? That should be done for him now. At least that's what the Old Man's copy of Grey's Anatomy made it seem like. That puberty stops for male humans after 16. Or…was it 18? Maybe it was 25? If it was 25 then he couldn't be finished yet. That would mean he had a good four years of physically maturing still left. He was already much bigger than his father ever was.

It was funny to Eric how much a monstrous giant his younger self thought that Carson was now he had reached and surpassed his stature and build. Now he was the monster or in other words the fittest. The most equipped to survive. He wouldn't mind being even bigger. Bigger wasn't always better in nature, but it certainly contributed to intellect. Brains plus brawn. Smarts plus strength.

He stood and limped to the bookshelf. Selected a book he and his brothers read often. Pinocchio. The story of a lonely man, living in a cabin, amongst the things that made him the happiest, who decided to create his own heir…and succeeded. The boys knew what they wanted was possible…with innovation. Just like Geppetto!

Eric hobbled back to the chair and plopped down into it. Smiled at Pretty Brown Eyes who seemed pleased just to watch him quietly flip through the pages. He scratched her behind the ears and despite holding the book in his hands Eric started reciting the story from memory doing a folksy, thick Italian accent to deliver the lines of Geppetto and doing a kind, childlike voice to deliver the lines of Pinocchio. Eric enjoyed hearing conversation aloud so much that he just kept going. He went on to recite entire scenes between Geppetto and Pinocchio. Then Pinocchio and Jiminy Cricket, whom got a nasally voice from Eric. Pretty Brown Eyes panted watching Eric speaking to her in words she didn't understand like she could listen forever. Eric looked into her big brown eyes panting her head and smiled.

"You know you are my sweet girl? Right?" She tilted her head curiously to the side. "Yeah of course you know." Eric let her lick his fingers. She could smell the scent of zucchini and rabbit fat under his nails. He couldn't help, but let his mind wonder for a moment. He quickly shooed the thought away. Yet, he couldn't suppress it for long. Again it arose in his mind. He sighed and eventually whispered, "God, I wish you could just talk to me. I'd like to believe that maybe you can and we just don't know it yet. Is it possible? Huh?" Eric leaned towards her. Pretty Brown Eyes gave her master a long stare. He looked at her. Allowing himself to hope. Allowing himself to wonder. After a few moments passed his gaze fell and he sunk back into the chair. "I figured. Animals don't do the kind of stuff that's in the books. At least I've never seen it. It's okay, though. It's okay, girl. It's not your fault. I'm sure you'd have a lovely voice…If you could speak to me."

Just then Luke coaxed Lyle into the library. Luke pointed at Eric while glaring expectantly at his twin. Lyle exhaled looking completely spent and worn out. Approached Eric. Leaned over Eric and gently kissed his forehead. Lyle rested his head on his older brother's. His protector's. His care-taker's. His teacher's. Eric received the gesture by pinching Lyle's fuzzy chin. They shared a smile.

Luke ran his fingertips along the spines of the many books on the shelf. Selected one of his favorites. The Chronicles of Narnia. He extended his hand with the book in it to Eric for him to read. Eric took the book. Traced the embossed title letters with his fingers and grinned. "Hmm, What will this be? The millionth time?"

Luke nodded happily his hair flouncing with each bob of his head up and down. If his tongue had have been hanging out he'd looked like a puppy receiving a treat. He sat crossed legged on the floor. Lyle joined him laying down on his back, his head in Luke's lap. Luke scratched his head playfully nuzzling his nose.

Eric started from the beginning, but trailed off when he sensed the twins disappointment. They cocked their head to the same side and simultaneously imagined events in later chapters. Like we're particularly found of Jiminy Cricket.

Eric said, "Ah. I see." So, he took his time to find the right chapter where Jiminy first appeared and began reading there. Eric could sense the twins' inner persons radiated with contentment and joy and that made Eric happy.

In his bed that night, Pretty Brown Eyes asleep by his side, Eric felt anxious. He and his brothers had a connection to humanity. With one foot in the wild and one foot back in Downers Grove. He felt a stirring and a pulling inside. Was he doing he and his brothers a disservice keeping them up here in the mountains? He was more equipped to society than the twins. They had no positive experiences with other people besides him and he was the only one who could speak to them and understand the way they needed.

He remembered his mother's words, *"One day...you'll have children of your own. You'll see that it will become the meaning to your life. You'll understand that type of love and passion one day."*

*Would he?* The meaning of his life would have to culminate in reproduction. Having offspring of his own, from his own loins, with his own blood, to continue his legacy, and his brothers too. That is how it was supposed to be. That was was who they were meant to be.

*"The miracle of reproduction. The meaning of life and living for the alpha male."* He could still remember the voice of the nature show narrator.

Whatever it took even if that meant take a trek back down that mountain where strangers roamed in Downers Grove. The idea was ridiculous. People would never accept them outright. Their own father did not even accept them and that was before they became products of nature and the wild. He and his brothers would need a cover if they were really going to go that route. He looked over at Noah's hide which lay on a wooden chair in the corner of the room.

*People were strange creatures.* Eric thought. He knew that there was just one time of the year where strange was welcome out in the open.

# Chapter 10:
# NorCalifornia Dreamin'

S he heard the pilot come over the intercom moments ago, "Please fasten your seatbelts as we come in for a landing."

Yet, Sierr could not take her eyes off the view below. Manhattan just beneath her feet. Iconic landmarks. The Big Apple. The Metropolis of the present and the future. She could feel JSF reach over her lap and pull something from under her leg. Delayed, she looked around to see him buckling her seatbelt for her. She felt so refreshing and impossibly fresh looking in her 50s style tulip dress. Light blue with white polka dots and a white collar. Her curls pinned up on top of her head with approximately 30 pins give or take, some always mysteriously went missing.

"Thanks, you." She cheesed.

He smiled back sweetly and said dreamily, "If you ever die in my sight I at least want it to be Carmen's fault and not mine."

"JSF!" Carmen leaned forward in her first class seat with ample leg space just behind them. Her lip gloss covered mouth dropped wide open. "If anybody would kill us it would be all him. He's a maniac ya' know?"

"My guess is a paranoid schizophrenic." Sierr said making her face a combination of pouty and fake serious.

"Definitely paranoid." He winked at the girls flashing his white teeth in a grin.

"At he's willing to admit he has a problem." Sierr noted looking out the window again as the ground got closer and closer.

Willow admires the view while managing to say, "I dunno I've always been worried that Carmen's cooking might kill us one day."

"Oh my Lord." Carmen plopped back down in her seat. Folded her arms over her tiny breasts just little bee stings under her spring green dress with fringes on the end. "LordForgiveMeForUsingYourNameInVein. It is Willow's fault after all." Carmen grinned deviously at her friend sitting next to her in overall shorts, a midriff, and a trendy bucket hat.

"My. Cooking. Is. Fine. That ceviche was totally safe." Carmen insisted.

"Except for the fact that you don't serve pork chops ceviche and you certainly have to cure ceviche-d meat for much longer than 3 minutes." JSF said.

"Says who?" Carmen challenged him seriously.

"Uh the CDC, honey." JSF replied smoothly.

"Oh did they?" Carmen nodded sarcastically.

"I think this where you're supposed to say, 'hey-ya'." Willow said matter-of-factly, tilted her head towards Carmen.

"Hey-No way." Carmen snorted.

"Ah, c'mon." Then JSF lowered his voice, "This plane could still crash just before landing. Wind gush. Mechanical malfunction. Belly roll due to pilot error. Missile strike."

"Missile. Strike." Sierr said slowly mocking JSF while turning around to look at her friend girls. "Is that one of those common threats we should be worried about?" Sierr arched her eyebrows at JSF.

"The point is we could totally die and you want your last moments to be dictated by pettiness?" He asked Carmen.

The next second the wheels of the plane met the ground with a tire screech and a hard thud for the passengers. Carmen yelped as did many others. The entire frame of the plane body rattled. Oxygen masks ejected from the ceiling. The plane finally came to a stop. Sierr only just realized that her nails were dug into the armrests. *Willow exhaled a breath she didn't even know she was holding.* Carmen unbuckled her seatbelt just as the pilot came over the intercom saying, "Bit of a bumping landing. All's well however. Enjoy your day and welcome to New York, New York!"

Passengers stood to retrieve their carry-ons including Sierr & Company. Carmen snatched her carry out of the overhead bin causing JSF's to tumble down into his hand chunkily. "Oh and by the way...Yes. Yes, I would." She pushed past him.

"Does she need an exorcism or what?" JSF chuckled.

"My little duckling's learning." Willow gushed beaming and following Carmen.

"Learning what?" JSF asked Sierr.

"To be her own attack dog." Sierr smiled and waved him to follow along as she and her friend girls exited the plane.

"So, is Angelica meeting us?" Carmen asked Willow.

"Nope. She was too concerned about her quote 'endless fans swamping her' in this quote 'motley airport.' Willow replied as they all wheeled their luggage, two luggages each, in the same direction that Willow marched in. Willow could never be a model. Not unless her walk was tweaked. She always looked like she was charging along in slow-motion on the front lines of some battle. A solider in the gender war in her own mind.

"Motley? It's JFK?" Carmen's kitten heels clacked ever-so daintily on the tiles before the floor met some commercial, blue carpeting. Carmen was the only member of Sierr and Company besides Hailey, who actually managed to naturally walk with a feminine, effortless sway.

Sierr's glass slipper look-a-like three-inch pumps clacked to, but not without effort from Sierr. She always struggled to be as graceful as Carmen and most of her peers. She often felt like a clunky sack of door knobs parading around as a girl trying to seem delicate and soft while failing miserably in the process.

Sierr was more lean than her friends, more bony structure and solid muscle than soft curvy, female flesh, and rosy skin. She had to focus on her femininity. It did not just come naturally. It wasn't just a part of her existence like most girls. She had to acquire gracefulness over time and still it fit her like a shoe that was either a half-size too big or a half-size too small. Why couldn't it just be who she was? If she was just naturally the way she wanted to be she could feel more comfortable in her own skin instead of timid and rather shy.

As she walked in her heels she reminded herself over again not to take too long a stride with each step. Not to land too hard on the foot extended ahead of her. Not to walk so pigeon toed like a penguin. Instead she needed to glide, have good posture, sashay even. She had never been able to sashay. Never. Not once. Ugh!

"Sierr!"

Sierr blinked hard to see Willow waving a hand in front of her face quickly.

"Huh?" Sierr asked mouth wide open.

"Hellllloooo? Earth to Ms. Blake are you there? Do you know what year you're in?" Willow asked.

"Where'd ya go?" Carmen snorted head tilted to the side.

"Oh I sorry. I was thinking back to that crazy landing. Scary. Even worse because we have to get back on a flight to get back home. Double scary." Sierr laughed it off.

"Double scary for sure." Carmen's eyes widened with sympathy.

"It'll be okay. Planes hardly ever crash. What are the statistics? Ten Thousand to One?" Willow asked rhetorically.

"1 out of every 836 flights." JSF stated almost absentmindedly looking around the airport atmosphere.

"Always looking to scare people, huh?" Carmen narrowed her eyes into mere skits looking over at JSF.

"I don't think I am." JSF replied.

"We're going to live and walk away from both flights." Carmen said to Sierr.

"Sierr, baby. Usually at least one person walks away from each documented plane crash so what Carmen is saying is totally plausible." JSF noted with a grin. The girls give him blank stares. "Now. I'm trying to scare you."

"We're bursting at the seams Stephan King." Willow remarked to which JSF rolled his eyes and head in the most dramatic fashion.

The group walked on when Willow frowned, "That's not who I think it is? Is it?"

"Jame Gumb?" Sierr gasped. "He's our escort?"

"Maybe just back to the hotel?" Carmen suggested never once taking her eyes off the man just yards ahead of her. She started at him like he was ghost or a corpse unearthed from a grave and propped up in the middle of the airport holding a little white sign that said "Willow Koi: Party of Five" in violet purple marker dusted with teal sparkles.

He smiled his same close mouth, stiff lipped smile. A smile that said something naughty and mysterious all at the same time. Sierr could never quite her finger in what it was about Jame that sent her soul stirring, but she knew well enough her intuition was never to be ignored. It was always wise to listen to that inward voice of detection. She had an inkling where the notion came to her that Jame was detestable in many unknown ways. He looked like the kind of guy who would portray himself as the perfect gentleman, but then make rude and lewd comments about people behind their backs. A man with a dirty mind and an even more foul soul. A manipulator. A liar. A fiend. A two-faced fox with a devilish grin.

As Sierr and Company approached Jame he stepped closer and his visible, but healed scars from his attack could be seen in the afternoon sun which glowed through the floor to ceiling windows at the airport. A large one from his left ear to his upper lip distorted his features on the left side of his face. A small shift in the arrangement of his face from the apparent tension put on his skin as the scar was healing over the last few months. The same for the scar on his right temple which ran through his right eyebrow, slicing it in two halves. One half slightly higher on Jame's forehead than the other half. He wore a breathable turtleneck, presumably to hide some of his other scars, although the scar from the gash that was gaping wide open on his neck at the Halloween Bash was clearly peaking out over the top of the collar.

His outward wounds were a picnic compared to his internal injuries from the attack. Everyone heard from media leaks about the extent of Jame's injuries: flesh wounds, cuts, gashes, bite marks, stab wounds to the liver and kidney, punctured intestines, and a nicked aorta. He nearly bled to death and went into shock soon after arriving at the ER that night. To see him walking around, supposedly escorting people around New York City, was peculiar at best. Like…why?

"Hello Willow. Ms. Blake. Ms. Danahue. Mr. Fitzgerald." Jame began in his utterly perfect proper voice, enunciating each and every syllable you probably did not even know was there, and clasped his hands behind his back. "Of course you know that I am Jame Gumb. Personal Assistant to Angelica. I will now in many ways be your personal assistant too. All of you. I will be your escort. Your connection to Angelica. At your beck and call. Is everyone ready for the events of the next two weeks?"

"We sure are. Very excited. Good to see you again." Willow replied.

"Glad to you are making a quick recovery." Sierr said extending her hand to him. He met it with a single firm shake.

"Likewise. We were very concerned about you after the Halloween Bash." Carmen added.

"Yeah man. We weren't sure if you were going to make it." JSF tossed his long braids over his shoulder with one swift motion.

"Well like all of the greatest fashion pieces nothing ever truly goes out of style. When something seems like it is gone for good…just wait. It will be back." Jame gave the teens his stiff smile wrinkles in his face molded to the smile like a butt print in an old leathery chair. "So thank you for your well wishes. If it is alright we can head to the Ritz Carlton to get you all settled into your suites."

Sierr and Company all shared giddy smiles as they followed Jame to two Angelica McCord company cars, both Champagne colored Rolls Royces. A driver, Alexander Gaston, in a three-piece white linen suit stood by the second Rolls Royce. He was a pale, dark haired pretty boy. Looked like the type who wanted to have a career in choreography, but deigned to hold a regular job until he could really break out into his dream vocation. Jame greeted him and helped him load the teens luggage into his car. Then Jame let the teens into the first Rolls Royce. Sierr and Company loaded into the first row and second row of backseats. Jame hopped in the front seat and slid the partition up between them. He turned on some music. In the back of the Rolls Royce Sierr and Company helped themselves to Sparkling Ciders and a pyramid of freshest eclairs.

Sierr and Company toured New York City with Royal and Jame as their guides. They explored the sights: the Statue of Liberty, 5th Avenue, they didn't do anything on 5th Avenue they mostly just looked at and took pictures. The pictures were endless. Each destination got about 59 pictures each, but it was okay because Sierr made sure to bring hundreds of rolls of film. They visited the Brooklyn Bridge, the Stock Exchange, the Empire State Building, and the city communications headquarters, the Twin Towers. The latter JSF refused to go into citing the multiple serious threats on the buildings and the '93 terrorist bombing with injured over 1,000 people just two years earlier. Even Carmen informing him to what he already knew that the twin towers were the tallest buildings in the world would not change his mind. Willow joked that he cannot be afraid of everything to which JSF replied he is only afraid of legitimate threats. The girls and Jame decided that it should be totally safe especially with the increased security following the recent bombing. So in true JSF fashion he gave them all a creepy wave as if he was bidding them a final farewell and the group went up to the 110th floor, feeling like they were on top of the world, to view Manhattan on the surveying deck of the North Tower. JSF very contently enjoyed people watching on the solid ground below.

Every stop was the same ritual: figure out where to go, what to do first, second, third, etc., pose for pictures at various interesting areas and over any interesting views, then Jame Gunn because he was clearly very disinterested in the tour and would often wander away. It got annoying after a while, but everyone looked past it. Sierr and Company had Royal after all and she was patient and responsible as always.

The smells of the city was a mix of emissions, old food, hot pizza, and on certain streets coffee. It was noisy, as expected, full of noise pollution including car horns, construction, music playing from unidentifiable places. The sun was shining and the city was warm. The group had lunch at Serendipity. Jame whipped out his jumbo Motorola cellphone as big as a clutch purse and walked off. JSF excuses himself to go to the bathroom. He made his way to the men's room and to a urinal stall. JSF unfastened his pants and peed looking out the one way mirror that looked over the parking deck of the building. JSF could see Angelica exit a glossy Powder Blue Rolls Royce on the top floor of the parking garage. Jame approached her outside. He wrapped his arms around her as she smoked a cigarette.

JSF always knew she was a smoker. He could just feel it.

Angelica did not hug Jame back. That would have been too affectionate for her taste. Instead to greet him, she motioned for him to stick out his tongue, which he did gladly, and she put out her cigarette on his tongue. JSF peed on the floor.

*"Oh geez!"* JSF gasped putting his penis away. He couldn't believe what he just saw. He wanted to tell the girls, but figured he'd let them have their fun for the day. He had already been to New York lots of times since childhood, but girls had not. He wanted them to have their fun. Still he would not forget what he witnessed and he would definitely be telling people at the right time. Something about Angelica and Jame just didn't set well with him at all.

Later on, the Ritz grew larger as the gang approached the building. Jame bypassed the line of check-in guests and used a badge of some sort to open a separate gate for elite, long-term residents. The two Rolls Royce's entered the parking garage and soon enough Jame and Gaston were loading a wheelie cart into a gold accented elevator.

"I feel so at home." Carmen squealed as the doors on the elevator closed and took them into the sky.

Jame and Gaston lead the girls and JSF down the long carpeted hallway and past many, many oak wood trimmed doors. "Angelica and myself stay on this end of the building." He said.

"On this floor?" Sierr asked before thinking.

"Heavens, no!" Jame cleared his throat uncomfortably regaining his composure. "No." He said stiffly with a nose so wrinkled you'd think someone farted right on his face. "We stay just beneath the penthouse. But, it is on this side of the building."

"Why not stay *in* the penthouse?" JSF pressed. He hated snooty people. His family was considerably richer than Angelica McCord would ever be, and apparently so was the person who actually could afford to stay in the penthouse and not "just underneath" it, and yet here her personal servant was acting like she and he were king and queen of the whole Western Hemisphere. It as absolutely, positively…nauseating rubbish.

Jame shot JSF a hateful glare. Like JSF was world largest stink bug who dared to squirt its funk in his direction. Carmen, always eager for some light drama and heavy gossip, fought back a laugh which was clearly a losing battle for her. Willow grinned at Carmen and then locked her eyes on the floor. Jame didn't even bother to answer JSF as he unlocked the door to room 305, Willow and Carmen's suite.

The two girls stumbled into the suite chocking back a fit of ever growing giggles. Carmen stopped abruptly in her tracks eyes wide and mouth dropped wide open. "Do you see this place?"

"No. I walked in here and simultaneously went blind." Willow replied dryly with dimmed eyes.

Carmen took in the view in the suite and the view of Central Park below all at once. "This. Is. The. Most. Luxurious. Place. I have ever stepped foot in, in my life." Her voice was breathless. "I may cry."

"It is pretty and…is that a room service menu?!" Willow nearly screamed zeroing in on Sierr who was holding the gold trimmed, lamented room service menu between her finger tips.

"It's a room service menu." Sierr confirmed in a serious voice.

"A Ritz Carlton room service menu?" Willow eases closer as if fearing that if she approached Sierr with the menu too quickly it might scared and fly away never to be seen again.

"THE Ritz Carlton room service menu." Sierr confirmed even more seriously this time and widening her eyes for effect.

"Oh my goodness." Willow to a flying leap towards Sierr.

"I don't think I have ever been this excited to hold a piece of plastic before." Sierr said.

"Open it." Willow's voice shook.

Sierr did just that and they both moaned with delight just reading the appetizers. "Oh the Fried Ravioli with Alfredo Sauce."

"The lobster pot pie." Willow breathed.

"The giant Cobb salad with balsamic and Dolce Bleu!" Sierr threw her head back dramatically.

Carmen continued to wonder around the suite like she was floating on a cloud and living in a dream.

JSF strolled over to Willow and Sierr and put his arms on their shoulder. Read the menu over their heads. "Bourbon, Brown Sugar Salmon and Feta Quiche? Hmm. I'm actually curious about that."

"There's vegan deep conditioners in the bathroom!" Carmen screamed at the top of her lungs; yet, her voice sounded like it was on the other side of a house sized space.

"Mmm, my mom made Bourbon Brown Sugar Salmon once."

Willow gasped, "No way."

JSF widen his eyes and said, "Really?"

"Oh my Gosh! The bathtub is a jacuzzi! I cannot believe this." Carmen screamed again.

"What vegetable did she pair it with?" JSF asked Sierr.

"Buttery, Sweet, Vanilla, Cinnamon Sweet Potatoes and a Danish salad." Sierr replied to which Willow made a hungry animal sound.

"Oh do you think she'd make that if we fly home right now?" JSF asked half serious.

"If I asked her to she probably would." Sierr replied entirely serious.

"Bet she could cook that in time for our flight to land back in Cali." Willow suggested.

Just then Carmen marched back into the living room and stood right next to her friends. Hands on her hips she stated, "Are you people completely insane?"

"What do you mean?" Willow asked her stomach growling.

"New York has more to offer us than expensive food. Or is that just my belief?!" Carmen's arched her thin eyebrows.

"Of course it does!" JSF grinned. "The Smithsonian with the bones of the Elephant Man is also here."

"Oh now that I'd like to see." Willow lit up.

"Do they serve food at The Smithsonian?" Sierr asked innocently.

"Oh my God." Carmen breathed with disgust spinning around on her heels to finish taking in her elegant surroundings.

Later on that day, Willow and Carmen were comfortably settled into their shared suite and JSF and Sierr were mostly unpacked and relaxing from their flight next door in suite 306.

The line trilled in Sierr's ear as she waited for her mother to pick up on the other end. Sierr admired her salmon-apricot nail polish color while she waited.

"Bonjour. Knish, Darling." Her mother answered in her usual pleasant tone.

"Hey-ya momma. We're settled into our suites. It's so beautiful here."

"And busy. New York City is a wonderful place. So much to see. So much to do. Lots of activity 24/7."

Sierr breezed into the kitchen of the suite and grabbed a fruit infused water from the fridge. She cracked the seal just as JSF strolled into the kitchen playing Super

Nintendo. She looked helplessly around the kitchen when JSF plunked a canister of Raw Sugar at her side on the counter. "Ah. Thanks."

"Mm-hmm." He strolled on plucking up a granola bar and starting a pot of coffee in the Krups coffee maker with the Ritz Carlton logo on the front.

Sierr poured sugar into her fruit water. "So, we don't have any plans tonight. Just gonna relax and enjoy the new surroundings. The New York air. The New York flare. Taste the pollution, listen to the taxis being hailed on the streets below, the cars honking, and the smell of a million restaurants which sell probably only ten different varieties of foods!"

"Alright, Judy Blum." Michelle replied a smile in her voice.

"What's your plans with dad?" Sierr gave her bottle a vigorous shaking to melt the sugar into her drink.

"Dinner. Conference call with a potential buyer in London. The usual. You will have a much more interesting night than we will."

"JSF and I will probably watch Jurassic Park or The Matrix again!"

JSF mouthed, "The Matrix."

Sierr mouthed back, "We'll See." He shook his head with a smirk.

"Oh and of course order room service!" Sierr added to her mother.

"Ok, sweetie. Hope you two have a good night. Oh tell J he will be seeing one of my paintings a little more often. His father bought one today...for his room!"

"Oh wow he's going to love that." Sierr shot JSF a look. "Talk to you in the morning, ma."

"Kay, bye. Stay safe honey. Stay with your escort around the city. It's dangerous there."

"Well to be fair Downers Grove has, has it issue recently."

"True. But, New York is a haven for the strange and the ugly."

"Indeed. We'll all stay safe."

"Ok. Love you."

"Love you too." Sierr hung up. "So, guess who can look forward to my mom's art watching over him at night?"

"What? Not me." JSF looked horrified.

"Yes you are the winner of the art lottery!"

"Oh good heavens. I told my dad. I told him. No art in my bedroom. No art from Victoria."

"He probably felt obligated. Ya know us being *neighbors* and all."

"Yeah that's definitely it." JSF replied sarcastically.

There is a forceful knock on the door. Sierr bounces to the door and grabs the door knob to open it, when JSF side steps her from behind, removes her hand from the door knob, and looks through the peep hole. "Girl. Folks get bum rushed just opening their doors to random knocks. You gotta check who it is."

"Sorry." She joked rolling her eyes.

"Great." He whispered. "Now we know to pretend we're not here." He began leading Sierr away from the door.

"Wha...who is it?"

"Fuckin' Abby." He sighed.

"Oh. Well we can't avoid her forever. We're all moo-dels together." Sierr ducked behind JSF and trotted to the door. JSF dropped his shoulders miserably. She opened it to Abby who was dressed in a black mini dress with shimmering silver and gold fringes hanging off the front, back, and sides. She had on high heels and perfectly toned, tanned legs, "Hey, Abby. What room are you in? And...where ya goin'?"

"Uh where are *we* going." Abby replied with a scoff, throwing her hand up on her hips.

"I'm lost." Sierr arched an eyebrow.

"First, get dressed. Second, get your groupies. We're attending the first official Angelica McCord Designs event tonight on the rooftop. We're VIP guests." Abby whipped the gold VIP badges out of her clutch purse and grinned. "As we should be."

Sierr smiles at JSF who looked wholly unamused.

Thirty minutes after 7PM and sure enough the event on the rooftop was full of haute couture dressed attendees and amounts of food so minuscule a bird might even leave hungry. Sierr and Company walked into through double doors which lead to a stop-and-repeat featuring the logos of Angelica McCord Designs and her corporate sponsor for the evening, Fuji Water. The girls took clicked pictures on their individual Nokias to preserve the moment.

Sierr was wearing a satin burgundy blazer with extra thick shoulder pads, a cinched waist, a stiff white collar meant to be popped up. She wore the blazer as a dress, how it was made to be worn, which stopped mid-thigh, it had a pleat in the back which she had perfectly ironed and wore matching red stilettos to complete the look. Her curls were flat ironed and pulled back into an ultra sleek, shiny pony long enough to swing at her waist. She just hopped she could attend the event and make it back to her suite without frizzy too badly from the moisture in the air. Her makeup was she usually wore it which went along with her look...clean and minimalist.

Willow went for a professional fashion look with a white suit for women with some violet pinstripes for added couture flare. The suit had super wide legged slacks with a high waistband a matching midriff length blazer. The blazer had an off the shoulders collar and a sweetheart neckline which accentuated her delicate sloping shoulders. Her hair was in its usual state curled under her jawline, bangs fluffy. She opted for violet eyeliner to match her suit's pinstripes and even used a little to line her Cupid's Bow. It was a risk, it was alien, and it was fashion.

Carmen wanted her debut red carpet wear to be a dress and she wanted it to be flowy. She certainly got her wish as she floated down the red carpet in a gown that popped. It was white with extra fabric just to make sure the person wearing looked like they were flying on clouds of white. The dress dragged the ground behind Carmen's white kitten heels which could not even be seen under the dress. The dress itself with embellished with different sized blue, green, and yellow gems on the breasts and they gradually gave way to a corset of faux peacock feathers which accented Carmen's hourglass waist. Her naturally wavy hair was still perfectly groomed and not at all frizzy under a crown of blue, green, and gold gems and more faux peacock feathers which fit atop her head. She looked like some kind of Queen of the Tropics.

Abby looked disgusted by the childlike silliness of Sierr and Company and opted to take pictures alone delivering only slightly different versions of sultry pouts and over the shoulder poses for the camera. Her fringes swaying dizzyingly for the cameramen and made Abby look like a feast for the eyes. Her hair was teased into a big and shocking mess of frizz and man-made curls she looked like a crazed moo-del just like she intended.

The girls made their way inside the event which was a rooftop nightclub style party

"Wow, the celeb treatment! I am just beyond right now!" Carmen exclaimed.

"What I don't understand is why did Abby know about this event before I did? Like I'm Angelica's actual intern not her. So, like how does she get the heads-up and don't?" Willow sneered eyeing Abby who was flipping her hair at some Mohawk wearing dude across the roof.

"Oh maybe Angelica wanted her to just pass the info to all of us?" Sierr offered.

"The woman. Gave. Me. A. Two Thousand Dollar. Cellphone. So that I could be on her on her list of people to get information first. Who is Abby? Does Abby Windsor have a two thousand dollar cellphone with the words Angelica McCord engrave on the back in gold trim? I don't think so! So. Who. Is. She?!" Willow fumed.

"You're mad? And you took such happy looking pictures too." Carmen said thoughtfully.

"They were fake!" Willow entire body rattled with anger.

"Well let's not let Abby ruin the night for us." Carmen said.

"Totally." Sierr agreed.

"It's not Abby's fault! It's Angelica!" Willow screamed.

"Calm down!" Sierr yelled back. "Just like breathe. Okay? It's okay. Maybe she just went stupid today."

"I need something the eat." Willow looked exhausted.

"There's no food here. It's just water." Carmen said.

"Sponsored water." Sierr noted.

"Excuse me!?" Willow winced like someone just told her she had to eat dog food for a week.

"There's no…" Carmen started.

Willow put a hand up. "I don't need to hear it again. Thanks. Gotta be friggin'…." She trailed off too disgusted to even speak shaking her head in complete outrage."I better go find Angelica and thank her for putting us on the list." Willow tone was like that of someone ready to kill.

"Where's…the boi?" Carmen asked.

"He'll be here later. Wanted to skip the 'hoop-la' as he said." Sierr subconsciously checked her ponytail for poofing. It was only a matter of time now. The night air. Her genetics. Her luck at events where she was supposed to look effortlessly beautiful.

"Where do you want to go tomorrow?" Carmen said.

"I dunno. We should totally check out that women's conference at Madison Square Garden. It's supposed to be a night of faith and fun." Sierr suggested as the two girls opted to sit down two bar stools at the bar.

"That will be fun! Hey we'll get matching church hats to take more pictures in!" Carmen suggested.

"That'll be great. I hear Virgin Pina Coladas are yummy." Sierr said as the bartender, a gorgeous Latin man, approached. He had to have been no more than 24.

"Hey let's see if we can get the bartender to ask one of us out!" Carmen swiveled eagerly in her stool.

"O…okay?" Sierr hesitated. Great. She thought. Didn't really feel like being rejected today, but what's one more guy to not show interest in me? "Sure."

"Hi!" Carmen spoke bubbly and perked up in her seat as the stud, err bartender, greeted them with a smile surrounded by dimples.

"What can I get for you ladies?" His voice was like butter. South American butter.

"Two Pina…." Sierr started, but Carmen cut her off mid-sentence.

"Well we're not too sure." Carmen tossed her head to the side and dropped a shoulder. "Do you have suggestions for us? We need something opposite of alcoholic."

"Ok I'm thinking of all our anti-alcoholic drinks, now!" He chuckled.

"Oh you see how bad I am at this!" Carmen giggled like a silly school girl. Sierr didn't know it was possible to admire a person and be annoyed by them all at the same time.

"Well do you girls like fruit? Like-a fruity drinks?" He smiled and stepped closer showing a willingness to be helpful.

"Ooh well let me ask my friend. Sierr?" Carmen turned to Sierr like she just appeared next to her. "Would you like a fruity drink or something else?"

"Um fruity drinks sound nice. Refreshing!" Sierr smiled. Smiling it was her only default. Her default in conversation. Her default when meeting someone. Her default when flirting. Her default when she didn't know what to say. Smile. Just smile. *Just keep smiling then no one will be able to know that you're a doof.* Unless of course constantly smiling makes a person look like a doof? Ugh! Carmen was such a natural at this flirting thing. Sierr wondered how she could be more like that despite how annoying it was to even listen to.

"So, what kind of fruity, *anti-alcoholic* drinks do you have?" Carmen smiled brightly and smoothed her hair although it was already perfectly smooth. Suddenly as if rising from a slumber, Sierr realized she was just sitting there expressionless with her hands in her lap like a lump.

"How about a Virgin Mojito or a Virgin Pina Colada?" He suggested smiling warmly at Carmen.

"So, hard to decide! What's your favorite!" Carmen leaned in towards him.

"I enjoy a nice Pina Colada every now and then. The virgins ones taste just as good, in fact depending on who you ask, the Virgin Pina Colada tastes better because it is sweeter and more fruity with the bite of liquor in it." He rolled ever single "rrr" that left his tongue.

"OhMehGosh, I think you've talked me into wanting a Pina Colada!" Carmen gushed.

"Really!" He exclaimed motioning his hands like he had gifted her with a surprise.

"What about you, Sierr?" Carmen asked.

This was her moment. She would use this very moment as an opportunity to be impossibly bubbly, cutesy, and flirtatious with the Latin man. It had to be just right. Not too much, but not to little. She had to do something that would leave an impression of freshness and fun and a dash of ditziness just like Carmen. And she had to make her voice go high and low just like Carmen did. This was it. Here it goes. She readied herself. "I'll DO a Pina COLADA, anti-ALCOHOL!" She worked each shoulder for added effect and emphasis every time she raised her voice for every other word in the sentence. Then she let out a disconnected high pitch giggle so far from the pitch of her actually voice she didn't even recognize it.

There was an awkward hush. Then Carmen quickly directed attention back to herself, "We'll do two Pina Coladas and one Mojito. I'm still curious about how it tastes too!"

"Indeed. Ladies. I'll be right back." Then Henry walked away his gaze settling on Sierr a few extra seconds like he felt the need to make sure he kept an eye on the…err…loco one.

"Excuse me while I go die in a corner somewhere." Sierr swiveled her bar stool around to get in position to run, not walk, but run away. Carmen grabbed her arm before her butt could leave her seat.

"Stop." Carmen said. "That was just practice. I picked him for us to play the game with because he's off limits. Doesn't matter if we make fools of ourselves in front of him because he's older. We weren't actually looking to date him anyway."

"But, if he really did want to date one of us it would definitely be you." Sierr replied subconsciously checking her ponytail for frizz again. Was it thicker than before? Was the frizz already starting? At this rate she'll be surrounded by a brown-blonde afro by the time the after party begins.

"That's because you were tryin too hard."

"Of course I have to try too hard! I'm not naturally like you are!" Sierr burst.

"And how am I?"

"Like Abby!" Sierr exclaimed.

Carmen gasped extra exaggeratedly, "That…spawn of Satan?" She slapped her palm on her chest dramatically. "What did I do to deserve this sort of an insult from my best friend!?"

"You're flirty! And girly! And guys like those things! I'm the one who sits there like a lump and when I do talk nobody cares what I have to say! They just dismiss me!"

"I'll be me and you be you!"

"Easy for you to say! Guys automatically like you! Even Damian wanted you first."

"That *other* spawn of Satan isn't even worthy to lick our shoes! The sole of our shoes at that! What does he matter!"

"Because good guys and bad guys like the girls like you! And not me! Never me! I always feel naked and stupid everyday! I know my features aren't even that ugly and yet I get treat like some kind of humenculous!" Sierr had reached a screaming volume at this point. "And I hate it! It drives me nuts! I can't wrap my head around it! Except that it's me! Me! Me!"

Just then Sierr heard a clunk next to her. It was Henry putting their order of drinks down on the bar in front of her and Carmen. He had heard everything. She saw the freaked out look on his face and Carmen's and her fight or flight instinct took over. Bolted she went into the crowd. Thankfully the music and constant chatter at the event saved her from the further embarrassment of other people hearing her outburst. They were none the wiser. But, still she was. She wanted to erase the moment and erase the feelings of inadequacy she had for herself, but she couldn't. She needed to prove herself wrong. Prove it without a shadow of a doubt. That she was good enough.

Walking blindly in a haze of emotions and deep thoughts she ran into a body. Somebody tall and familiar. His grasp on her a feeling of home and comfort. "JSF?" She looked up at him. He looked more groomed and prom than she had seen him since they were kids attending Easter service at church together. In his Angelica McCord Designs three piece suit. Metallic colored scales that reflected blues, greens, ambers, golds, and silvers covered the suit, outward shoulder pads made of metal armor like material draped gold chains down his biceps, similarly matching chains draped from the belt loops in his pants down to his calves. He wore a choker collar which was somehow really complimentary to his masculinity.

"Sierr! Hi I'm roasting in this thing." He replied like he was introducing himself to her for the first time gave her hand a vigorous shake and everything.

"Hi I don't know how to talk to people." She said like she was introducing herself also.

"What?" He squinted. "Sure you do. Whaddaya talking about?"

"Nuthin'. Never mind." She flicked her wrist like she was shooing away a fly. She meant it to come off as casual, but wasn't sure it looked as natural as she hoped. She dropped her shoulders. "When did you get here?"

"Just now. Thought if I dodged the cameras I might be able to evade the feds at the same time. You know one day you won't ever be able to escape the reach of the government. They'll be watching us in our homes and through our phones soon enough."

"Yeah?"

"You heard it from here first."

"Meanwhile they couldn't even arrest The Menendez Brothers without them telling on themselves first just last year."

"Step One to a life of crime snuff. Out. Your. Soul." JSF took her hand and lead her to bar.

"Wait. I can't." She stopped him.

"Why not?"

"Because I..." She wanted to say *because I'm a doof who can't help, but embarrass myself day after day.* Instead she just said, "I left Carmen at the bar and I just realized I didn't bring money for my drink. Could you go over there and give her what I owe?"

"Sure." JSF replied without hesitation. "After that you wanna get out of here?"

"And go where?" Her eyebrows raised with anticipation. She'd love to get out of there. She was much better one-on-one with friends. JSF especially. Dude was legit fam.

"To our luxury suite downstairs without all the people and the cameras and the noise. Just us. What do you say? We can pig out on room service."

"How could I say no to that!" Sierr beamed.

"Kay, I'll go pay and we'll blow this joint!" JSF made the rock and roll gestures with his hands, stuck his tongue out, bit it, and wrinkled his nose for added effect. It made Sierr laugh.

JSF approaches the bar where Carmen was sipping her Virgin Pina Colada she had all three drinks in front of her as if contemplating whether or not she could finish them all.

"Hey." He said slipping up beside her.

"Hey, can you help me finish these?" She said.

"What are they?" He looked at them unamused.

Virgin Mojito and Virgin Pina Colada. Sierr and I were supposed to shared, but…" she trailed off. "Well one for you?"

"Which one would you rather have, girly?"

"I'll do half the other Pina Colada. You can have the Mojito. To minty for my taste."

"Kay. Sure thing." He started taking gulps of the Mojito while digging in his pants for money. He pulled out a $100 and tossed it on the counter like it was nothing.

"Wha…do you want change?" She looked shocked at him.

"Nah. Today and only today I'll be philanthropic." He grinned finishing the drink. A small burp followed. He excused himself. "See ya later, okay? Where's uh…where's Jame?"

"I dunno actually. We haven't seen him since this morning."

"*Some escort.*" JSF breathes with disdain. "These uppity bitches can't be trusted to do anything right. C'mere." He stepped aside.

"Where are we going?" She asked.

"Me and Sierr are going to go back to our suite. But, I can't leave you up here alone. You're underaged and you're supposed be being looked after by your escort. So, we need to find your escort."

"Willow's here. It's okay." She insisted still sitting on the bar stool sipping her drink.

"And where is Willow?" He asked stepping back towards her, digging his hand in his pockets.

"Well…um…" She trailed off looking every angle into the crowd.

"Exactly. She's doing work and you need your escort. There's adults here. We're in New York it's dangerous. You shouldn't be alone."

"Thank you, JSF." She looked up at him and smiled warmly.

"Are we friends again?" He smiled.

"Of course. I could never not be friends with you. You will forever be my oddest friend ever." Carmen said proudly.

JSF kissed Carmen on the forehead and grinned, "Damn straight. Now let's get Sierr and find Jame."

She hopped up out of her chair and followed JSF like a little duckling to Sierr. "Hey. Sorry I left Carmen."

"It's okay. You just needed a minute. That's okay. We all need minutes sometimes." Carmen sipped.

Sierr smiled. She had the best friends in the world. It was hard to find people who truly care about you and she had many people in her life who truly cared about her. That in and of itself was a testament to her character. Her beautiful character.

"We're going to find Jame. He shouldn't need to be hunted down to do his job, but I guess 12-hours into this trip that's already where we're at." JSF lead the girls towards the VIP lounge and they entered with their VIP badges. This area was air conditioned with a separate bar, hooka tables, a glistening overlooking much of the Manhattan skyline, and starved moo-dels who looked like they kill for maybe…an olive. As if unable to stop moo-deling, they sat with their Fuji waters and alcoholic drinks in bikinis and swimsuit covers pouting subconsciously and strutting absentmindedly through the area. They looked brainless yet beautiful.

Carmen pointed out one of the moo-del's stylish shoes to Sierr who gushed over them too. They both looked to JSF who seemed unconcerned and unfazed by all the cleavage, bony bodies strutting around in heels, and glitterati which surrounded them as he walked ahead scanning the crowd for Jame and Royal. Soon enough he spotted them over by the pool with Angelica who had a crowd of other middle aged fashion designers and label makers around her along with Willow. She was in a black one piece bikini with a diamond studded black swimsuit cover with hung to her loose skin covered thighs. Her wrinkled old feet in a pair of blue sandals. JSF actually made a face when he saw her, but quickly re-directed his attention to Jame. Jame and Royal stood off by the end of the pool area seemingly in a heated discussion. Jame obviously felt the most powerful his demeanor was cocky at best. He smirked at laughed at her as she seemed to speak passionately about whatever it was they were talking about. Royal eventually stormed away in her sandals her face red and her eyebrows furrowed. Willow noticed her upset disposition from her perch by Angelica. JSF walked past her along with Sierr and Carmen and he approached Jame.

"Hey, Jame. I believe you said that you're the underaged girls escort during this trip. So, I just wondering when your escorting duties kick in?" JSF at 6'3 looked down on little Jame who was a mere 5'7.

Jame looked JSF up and down and delivered a sinister smirk. He laughed at JSF, then side stepped him. Willow approached. JSF stepped towards Jame who whirled around to him in a defensive stance. "Don't walk away from me, man. Why did I find the two them alone on a rooftop party with liquor being served and adults everywhere without you in sight? Huh? Is that what our parents signed that permission slip for? For us to expect to be abandoned public places?" JSF calmly stated.

"You people were not abandoned." Jame started.

"We certainly weren't *escorted* either." JSF replied.

"Look! Do you have a death wish or something?" Jame spat in a flash of restrained blistering hatred and anger. His eyes revealed how shocked he was at himself for letting his true feelings slip out. His pupils shrunk and his eyelids twitched. He caught himself as soon as he glanced at Sierr and Carmen's stunned expressions.

He swallowed hard and smiled his same cool, fake ass smile. Popped his collar back in perfect place. Smoothed his tie. He had to appear put together at all time. "Listen, don't take it all so seriously. There is strict security here. It is the Ritz Carlton after all. Everything is fine. The girls were going to be escorted by me all night." He paused a muscle in his face twitching harshly. "So." He clenched his teeth. "I suggest. You watch yourself, kid." Jame's face went blank like print paper as he turned and walked away.

"I've never seen him like that before." Willow whispered just loud enough for her friends to hear.

"I think he has seen himself like that before. You see the look in his eye. Like he was forcing himself not to get...out of control." Sierr observed. If anyone knew body language it was her. She spent dozens of hours at the Heisenberg High library, which doubled as the library for all of town and stayed open even on the weekends, just researching ways to make the characters in her Dead Serious Trilogy as realistic as possible. Body language was only one of few character traits she studied to get her fictional friends just right. She knew what words would be used to describe Jame Gumb's rattled demeanor: aggressive, controlling, hot tempered, and narcissistic.

The next day Sierr and JSF hung out as they usually did. Sierr and JSF had just toured the MoMa museum in downtown Manhattan. Now it was time to eat and drink brown gold. They walked into what was considered the largest Starbucks on the East Coast. Two floors of coffee smells. Two floors of hippies and yuppies working amongst one other in perfect harmony bonded by their love of lattes and free WiFi. It was all wood. Everywhere from floor to ceiling different types and different stained woods made up a woodsy ascetic inside the building.

Sierr peered into the pastry case JSF standing behind her so close she could feel his breathing on his neck. "They have the Apple Fritters here! You know the one I was telling you about!"

"I remember them distinctly from your vivid descriptions. I'm dying to try it. Two please."

"Warmed." Sierr smiled at the cashier baristas who happily keyed in their order. "Aaaaaaaand well have triple grande iced vanilla Macchiatos with no ice in Venti cups filled to the top with Cinnamon Dolce Sprinkle/Cinnamon Dolce Syrup infused Cold Foam with Flat Lids."

The barista's fast fingers types in each variation to the drinks in no time and gave Sierr and JSF the total. JSF paid with his debit card.

After receiving their customize drinks and warmed Apple Fritters. Sierr and JSF strolled through the café admiring the painting on the walls. It was like exploring a gallery of rare and hard to interpret art.

They stood before a bedazzled beetle with cat eyes, the wings of a butterfly, and a brief case.

"So like its obvious, right?" JSF grinned after swallowing some velvety Cinnamon Dolce infused Cold Foam.

Sierr smiled at him immediately catching onto his sarcasm, "Totally."

Just then an outburst of laughter erupted from a long table high in up in the balcony of the second floor. Sierr and JSF migrated up there to see what other art they could find.

"I wanna see some erotic art. Where's the penis sculptures and ambiguous vulva department?" JSF said casually in a normal volume. Sierr walked him in the arm. "Hey!" He laughed nursing his arm. "Everyone here has to have one of the other, am I right?"

"Stop it. Dirty boi."

"Oh my God how long did it take you to grow your braids that long?" A curious voice said from the long table to JSF. JSF turned around to face a blonde haired, blue eyed preppy gay in plaid shorts and a sweater thrown over his shoulders. Basically the white version of Carlton from The Fresh Prince.

"Like 12 years." JSF hunched a shoulder.

"Oh my God." The preppy gay said then he turned back around to his friends group. "See that's the look I'm going for!"

"So much to be said." Said a rather unwashed looking brunette woman said from the other side of the table before taking a slurp from her Quad Mocha Cappuccino.

"How about, 'Yaaaassss, Dennis you will look great if you feel great!'" The preppy gay responded with playful outrage.

"Excuse our dear Friend. He's trying out different styles and I suppose yours has spoken to him." A bald, skinny dark skinned smooth talking black man in a turtleneck said. Sierr could imagine him as a poet.

"I want to reinvent myself for publishing season '96! It's an entire year away. I would love to emerge talking about the next big Young Adult author as a whole new me!" Dennis's said with big hand gestures for even greater emphasis.

"Publishing season '96?" Sierr perked up. "Are you all literary agents?" Her eyes widened.

"Why yes! We are." A black woman at the table in a knee length pencil skirt and a satin blouse answered. "Are you an author?"

"Well…" Sierr recoiled.

"Yes, she is. A very talented one. Not published yet. Not influenced. Not inhibited. A pure, blank slate ready to create and learn. Isn't that right, Sierr?" JSF looked to Sierr for the only right answer.

"Yes." She said nodding hard forcing herself not to sink into the floor and/or die of embarrassment.

"That's wonderful." The unwashed looking brunette smiled.

"Another Young Adult Female in Publishing is a great blessing." The smooth black man said.

"What do you write?" The black woman said.

"I'm working on a Young Adult Spy Thriller." Sierr said wondering if she sounded stupid.

"Oooh la!" Dennis said sipping on his Carmel Macchiato.

"Where do you all work?" JSF asked giving Sierr and gentle nudge forward to her ideal mentors.

"Sibion & Sean." The black woman stated knowing how much weight the mere name of her employer carried.

Sierr's heart skipped a beat.

"You know we are just visiting the city. Internship for school. We actually live in Northern California, but I'm sure Sierr would love to just spend an afternoon with you all and learn all that she can from people in the industry that she loves." JSF stated without a shadow of a doubt that his persuasion skills were paying off big time.

"That would be fantastic." The black woman said.

"So Sierr. What is that like one of those trendy names? You know, Sea- Air? Like Apple?" Dennis said with expressive hands again.

"Oh it's a shortened version of my actual name, Seraphim. Like the Seraphim angels." Sierr replied.

"Seraphim Angels. Write that down that sounds like a title for a New Adult mythical creature story." The black man purred to a wide eyed almost fresh faced looking Hispanic girl who looked about college aged. She sat with her legs crossed a fruity beverage in front of her and a green cardigan to accentuate her olive undertone. "Well I am Howard Sharp. Specializing in New Adult Fiction."

"Annalise Tate, Young Adult and Mystery/Thrillers." The black woman smiled and waved.

"I'm Dennis. I like style. Officially I work in Woman's Fiction and Comedy." Dennis blew an air kiss towards Sierr.

"Middle Grade, Coming of Age Stories. Janice Barrow." The unwashed Brunette said.

The Hispanic looking girl observed all the greeting until Howard motioned for her to introduce herself. She looked hesitant. Could I? She mouthed. Howard smiles and nodded, "Of course. You're a Partner here too."

The girl lit up and smiled, "I'm Gabby Hernandez. Marketing Assistant."

"I'm so excited to meet all of you and I would love to have the opportunity to be under your tutelage." Sierr gushed.

"We'd love to have you under our tutelage, Sierr." Annalise said. "Give me your number so we can set up a meeting. You said you write Young Adult, right?"

"Yes!" Sierr answered.

"Wonderful. Let's talk, *Seraphim Angel.*" Annalise preceded to write down her phone number and walk over to Sierr with her hot red velvet spiral planner in hand. She greeted Sierr and JSF warmly and took down their numbers. "How long will you be in New York?"

"Until next Friday." Sierr answered feeling more relaxed by Annalise's friendly face.

"Oh Great let's shoot for THIS Friday to meet. I have some free time before an event later on that day at Sibion." Annalise scribbled down her appointment with Sierr in her planner with a felt pen. She was a southpaw.

"Oh my God this is so amazing. I am so humbled and grateful to have the opportunity to be poured into by all of you." Sierr smiled brightly.

"We'll get your info from Annalise and send you over some helpful advice, steps to publishing, how to get your foot in the door." Dennis added.

"We'll put you in contact with our favorite Manuscript Editor let her look over some your work walk you through drafting the best, most standout query letter!" Janice smiled.

"Oh my Gosh! This is so exciting!" Sierr said excitedly. She could not believe what was happening this was a blessing. Beyond a blessing, a miracle. Beyond a miracle, Providence! Beyond providence, ordained by God, Himself, she could feel it!

She could feel it so strongly she talked JSF's ear off about the entire encounter all the way back to their hotel suite.

JSF took off his jacket as Sierr excitedly reiterated every moment from the chance meeting. JSF smiled listening to her willing to put up with all her annoying quirks and habits. He sat down and listened to her quietly. When she finally tired herself out she plopped down on the sofa next to him. She fell on his arm and hugged it tight.

"What was that for?" He asked.

"For being the bestest boy-person ever. If it wasn't for you I would never have this opportunity at all." Sierr replied.

"Carpe Diem, baby."

"Carpe Diem." Sierr nodded. "I'm going to be going to this meeting without an escort ya know."

"You can do it. You can do anything." He kissed her forehead.

She often wondered why JSF was the only male who could tolerate her presence for long periods of time. He liked her for her. He didn't just accept her, he loved everything about her. Why couldn't she find an eligible guy like that? Some one who thirsted for her presence. Someone who needed her in their life. Maybe she was crazy. Maybe her sister was right. She was too young to be thinking about these things. Girls her age in other countries were planning their weddings, but it wasn't like that in America. Teen girls shouldn't be thinking about having all-consuming romances like what Sierr truly wanted. Which is why JSF was the best guy for her. A perfectly platonic boy/girl relationship. She loved it and she loved him so much.

# Chapter 11: A Lie Can Make It's Way Around the World While the Truth is Still Putting Its Shoes On

K erry Thomas drove C.C. up to the darken building sitting atop a hill like a great answer to a prayer. It was stone and cement. Good at keeping peering eyes out and the fits and frights from the mentally disturbed within.

The Hill was acres of lush green grass a few dandelions managed to grow in the distance despite the lawn being well manicured. Kerry figured the staff probably only did just as much as they had to keep the grass healthy and maybe that was the same attitude they took to heal their patients as well.

This was John Jhang Institute of Mental Health Care a state funded psych ward where a strange woman lived for an unknown period of time. The name of the building was engraved on its giant brass double doors. Kerry was here on a lead provided to him via a mysterious pager message. He did not know what to expect, but as always he hoped it would lead to more clarity on The Beckwith Brothers and what key their unique brains held for all of humanity and future psychological research.

Kerry put his car in part, pushed his glasses up on his nose, gathered his notepad, pen, and started his trek up the dozens of stairs leading up the front door. He could the steal bars on the patient's windows as he trekked. The atmosphere was cold, haunting, ominous. Like the ghosts of tortured souls were here, lurking, waiting, maybe even warning him what horrors were possible to be suffered here. The air even felt cool despite today being mid June.

Kerry raised his hand to knock on the sturdy brass, engraved double doors. The eyes of the statue of Psychologist John Jhang seeming to follow his every move. A hoard of crows erupted from behind the building, fly over the top, and towards the horizon. Cawing and wings flapping drown out the sound of the giant double doors opening at the hands of Psychologist Shannon Rigel.

"Kerry?" Shannon said with squinted eyes and a small grimace beneath the fluff of his ruby red mustache. "Bird watching is the peace of the anxious. Is this an admission?"

"No." Kerry grinned. "Not at all. My spirit burns, but my nerves are calm. That's what my father always used to say."

"Do come in." Shannon motioned for Kerry to walk in past him.

Kerry smelled into the stone mansion which had a stone spiral staircase leading up to a second floor from the first. Long Floor to ceiling windows lined the front of the mansion which was grey hued even with all the windows open. The walls were stone, the floor was concrete, and the accents such as the rod iron railing of the staircase were the only other visible color and they were black. It is chilly in the building and screamed something was not welcome here. Negative thoughts? Old habits? Family and Friends? Onlookers? Seekers of the truth?

"I was surprised to hear that she had a visitor when no one knows who she is." Shannon said his verbose voice rumbling through chambers of Kerry's rib cage and the stone walls of the building.

"Jane? She never had one visitor?"

"Only doctors. See what they can find out about her. See what she can find out about herself."

"What circumstances surround her arrival? How did she come here?" Kerry asked as they walked into a dreary kitchen with appliances from the 80s and cooking instruments that looked like they came from the 1880s.

"This is our kitchen." Shannon said motioning his thick hand towards the obvious kitchen that was obviously theirs. "We cook the inmates three squares a day. Give them a balanced diet of fresh fruits and vegetables."

Just then a nurse in all white and pill box hat fluttered into the kitchen did not even glanced the way of Kerry and Shannon and threw open two cabinets in a rush. Seemed to be looking for something with haste. She eventually ripped a drawer open and pulled out a syringe before running away and disappearing down a grey hallway.

Kerry could not hide his perplexity and concern.

Shannon glanced over at his him, "Sometimes the patients need to be calmed. Fits are common. A little tranquilizer does the job."

The job?

Kerry dropped his gaze wondering what kind of a fit some patient could be having that could not be heard. The entire mansion was ghostly still and silent. "What year did she arrive?" Kerry refocused himself to his main objective. The woman in room 8.

"She arrived in '78 with amnesia, a punctured lung filled with water, a broken nose, a ruptured cornea, a busted lip, and several broken fingers. She was quite the mess. She had nearly drowned and was sent here by Bounty Hospital just north of here. They are the ones who received her when a Good Samaritan alerted the hospital that a nearly dead woman had washed up on the banks of a stream around those parts." Shannon and Kerry walked down a corridor adjacent to the kitchen.

"Bounty figured that perhaps we could break the spell she was under, the memory lost, with our mental health care methods and team of psychologists."

"Besides her physical condition how did her mind seem? Her demeanor. Had she simply forgotten her life?"

"No, this was far more serious than that. This was a state of a traumatic event causing severe PTSD which was exacerbated by lack of oxygen when she nearly drowned. It is possible that we may never know who she really is." Shannon and Kerry arrived at room 8. Shannon smiled warmly at Kerry. His warmth almost seeming practiced or rehearsed. "But still the oddest thing about our Jane Doe is the stories she makes up about herself. A mother with three sons who had supernatural powers and a husband who was eaten by a bear. We've all heard it. She cannot remember her life, but she always remembers that story." Shannon retrieved a master key from the pocket of his blazer with a pinched index finger and thumb and he unlocked her door.

Kerry stepped inside her basic room. Concrete walls painted a shade of eggshell, matching floors, a nightstand where a plastic tea cup sat to be refilled with water, and a cot like bed in the far corner. Guess the workers at John Jhang did not think that the healing and hurting needed anything to particularly brighten their lives.

Then he saw her. She blended into the background almost perfectly. A flat figure amongst flat objects and even flatter colors. She arose from the bed in her grey John Jhang issued track suit, grey like everything else, her hair was long and merely a full reminder of what lush, shiny mane used to flow from her head all those years ago.

He eyes gaunt as well as her cheeks which dropped long before their time. Her lips parted when she spotted Kerry at the door. He looked like Superman. Like the real superman. Maybe he could save her? Bring her the clarity she had been begging and dying for?

Kerry marches aged towards her. Now that they were in the same room he would not hold back. He would ask the pressing questions not the fluff him dished out to Shannon. The first being, "June? Is that you?"

June leaped from the bed as if it were on fire and Kerry was the puddle that could save her life. Her eyes were wide like a crazed woman, but she was calm. She opened her mouth to speak. Kerry was ready he whipped out his notepad to take notes. Pen firmly in his left hand.

"Her name is Jane. Not June. Jane." Shannon steppes forward peering down at June who shut her mouth in terror. Shannon turned to Kerry and narrowed his eyes, "Kindly do not confuse the patients during your visit, Mr. Thomas.

Kerry swallowed hard. Blue balls was less frustrating than what just happened here. She was about to say something important before that Shannon butted in! Then Kerry gathered himself he would just have to change his approach. "May…may I hear your story, *Jane*?"

June nodded slowly easing back down on the bed. Her eyes followed Shannon as he positioned himself behind Kerry and by the one window in the room which was guarded and obstructed by rod iron bars on the window.

Her lips quivered. Her gaze settled on Kerry. "They could kill."

"They who?" Kerry's heart quickened.

"My boys." Her voice was lower and more focused than Kerry imagined it would be. This was a far away woman, lost to injury and time, he imagined that her position in life would have shrunk her down into a whisper. A hollow sound. A mere flicker of light. A shell of who she once was or ever could have been. But, this woman sitting before him was not that…she was stronger. Intense. Sure of herself despite the looming figure positioned over them both.

She cut her eyes to Shannon then back to Kerry.

"She is fresh off her medication, Kerry. We took her off of her meds just to she could be coherent enough to speak with you today. I warn you now that her delusions are merely uninhibited right now and that means they can flow very freely during this time."

"I would like to hear her story if that is alright, Doctor."

"By all means." Shannon exhaled looking out the window.

"Go on, Jane Doe." Kerry nodded to June willing her to feel safe and comfortable with him.

"Halloween was coming and they still couldn't talk. So, he…." June searched for the right words her eyes rolling around in her head. "Kept hitting me. Threatened their doctor."

*My dad's friend the twin Beckwith's pediatrician.* Kerry thought writing down a quick note.

"He was also so secretive about his life. His early life. Hated women and young people. Hated weakness." June began shaking like a leaf. She would gently pound her thigh with a balled up fist as she spoke like she was trying to beat her words out the way some would beat wine out of grapes. "He never could accept the boys. So, no wonder they found their own language. They were just trying to be heard. They were all they had forever and ever."

"You hear her? She's nuts." Shannon squinted.

"Jane, how do you believe that your sons communicated if they could not speak?" Kerry asked ignoring Shannon.

"They heard the voices. Not other people's voices like people around here in this building do, By they specifically heard each other in their heads not their ears. Not. Their ears." June nodded forcefully. A muscle in her face twitched twisting her face into a distorted warpness. The spasm eased and her face returned to normal, but Kerry couldn't help but remember that sometimes Electrotherapy can cause people to have random muscle spasms for life.

"When did you last see your boys, *June?*" Kerry pressed he couldn't imagine Shannon would let this go on for much longer.

"Her name is Jane Doe. Please do not confuse her or project another identity onto her!" Shannon's voice grew deeper.

"Answer me." Kerry demanded.

"When he killed his scary daddy." June breathed eyes drifting off into the distance.

"He who?" Kerry asked.

"The one beyond this world. The special one." June replied.

"What was his name?" Kerry asked.

"She hasn't made up a name for those boys she speaks of yet." Shannon interjected.

"Where did he kill his father?" Kerry asked.

"His father killed himself. With his backwards thinking and his evil ways. He drove himself to the grave. My boy just gave him the keys to the car."

"Where is that car right now?" Kerry asked literally asking where is the family car from that faithful day when the boys went missing.

"In the mountains with the trees and the bear and the old man." June replied looking lost all of a sudden.

"What old man?"

"The old man who tried to save me. The one who died. That's where they are! My babies! That's where they are! They'd be so happy! They'd be so happy!"

"Jane calm down! Jane. Calm yourself." Shannon barked.

June gasped in another hopeful outburst. She restrained herself and literally bit down on her tongue to prevent any further excitement. She dropped her head and lifted it back up her hair in her face now. "They would be so happy."

"Why would they be happy? Without you? Without their friends? Without their town?" Kerry asked.

"They are all each other need. They are all each other have ever needed. More than their mother. More than their father. They would be happy because they were at home in nature. Loved fishing. Loved nature shows. Loved animals. Even loved plants. They always admired the powerful creatures. The lions and tigers and bears." June chuckled at herself and added, "Oh my!" Just like Dorothy in the land of Oz.

"What do you think they want?" Kerry asked.

"To rule. The be kings of the forest. Be Alpha and Omega. The snakes that everyone cowers to." June suddenly look tired. "Oh I suddenly feel very weak." Her hand fluttered to her forehead.

"What makes you think they are alive?" Kerry sat forward.

June looked thoughtful for a moment. Eyes glistening behind a veil of wheat looking hair. She opened her mouth to speak when a forcefully pounding on the door interrupted them all.

"Dr. Rigel! Open the door!" A loud voice roared from the other side of the door. Fists pounded on the door so hard it shuttered on its hinges. Kerry stood. June covered her ears with her hands like a frightened child. Shannon charged towards the door and threw it open

"What in God's name!" Shannon shouted at the two men who stood before him both dressed in all black suits.

"You're coming with us!" One if the men marched inside the room and headed straight for Kerry.

"Me? What is this about?" Kerry said taking a step back. The man clamped a meaty hand on Kerry's shoulder.

"Just know that you are in very big trouble young man." The second man in Black came inside the room baring handcuffs for Kerry.

"Excuse me?!" Kerry winced. "You cannot arrest me. Who are you people?"

"Your worst nightmare." The first man in black grinned inches away from Kerry's face. The men in black then handcuffed Kerry and escorted him from the room. He caught June's eye just before exiting the room. She looked scared, unnerved, and hopeless as the door closed she and Shannon in the room together. He looked to her like he had plans for her that she wouldn't like.

Kerry learned a few things during his trip to the John Jhang Mental Health Care Facility. June Beckwith was alive and mostly well. She seemed to know for a fact that Eric, Luke, and Lyle were all alive even if she could not retrieve their names from the reserves of her mind. Shannon was mighty unnerved by June learning who she really is and the outside world. Also, John Jhang was more than ready to lie to the public about a variety of things from the well being of the patients to the food they ate.

This was a mirage in the desert. Kerry knew that from the moment that zippy nurse who was on the hunt for that syringe opened the cabinets in the kitchen where the staff supposedly prepared "nutritious meals" for the patients and he saw that all that was in the cabinets were cans of off brand dog food.

As Kerry was being thrown into the unmarked black Crown Victoria by the men in black he had a chuckle to himself. If June and the other patients have been having a diet of Dog Food you would think June's mane would look better. Kerry choked back a laugh.

"What are you laughing at? Huh? What's funny?" The second man in black said.

"Never mind what I am laughing at who are you? What division on the government are you with?" Kerry spat from the backseat veins in his neck popping.

"Divisions of the government?" The first man in black said glancing at the second man in black. His gazes settled back on Kerry and a smirk crawled across his muscular face, "The government ain't got nuthin' on your daddy, son."

Hours in the backseat of the car left Kerry's legs cramped and achy. When the car finally stopped at his father's house in Downers Grove Kerry was just happy to get the hell out of his temporary wrongful imprisonment. "Who's going to go back and get my car?"

"Someone will bring your car back to this very spot if that is what you want." The second man in black said.

"I would like that. My car is important to me." Kerry said as the first man in black opened the door. "Surely the cuffs can come off now? I am not a prisoner. Where is my father?"

"Wow, he is full of questions." The first man in black said leading Kerry towards the house.

"I'm a journalist." Kerry said.

"Wannabe journalist." The second man in black said.

"Amateur." The first man in black laughed.

"I'm getting the answers I've been needing." Kerry stated knowing now that the tape recorder in his pocket had already probably ran out of space in the memory, but still maintaining a shred of hope that it hadn't.

As the men in black lead Kerry to the door, it opened. There Horacio Thomas was standing in the doorway.

"Dad. Why did you do this?" Kerry squinted.

"Son, a person should be able to muster up a thank you when someone saves them from themselves. Shouldn't they?" Dr. Thomas took a sip from a glass of water in his hand. Kerry stared in disbelief at his father. Speechless. Dumbfounded. Confused. All at once.

Dr. Thomas said, "Thank you gentlemen. You can un-cuff him now."

The men in black did as they were told. The second man in black said, "Yes, sir." The two walked to their unmarked car and drove off.

Kerry stepped inside the house. "I cannot believe you. I truly cannot believe you."

*"Thank you father for keeping me shielded from the consequences that could easily come from my own insanity. Thank you father for trying to make some sense of this utter disaster that I have been poking and prodding at for months now."* Horacio said sarcastically.

Kerry whipped his body around to his father. "Dad, you cannot control and butt into my life like this and you certainly cannot keep me from revealing the truth about The Beckwith Brothers or what's happening at John Jhang. That place is creepy in the daylight and I suspect a nightmare when the lights go out at night. The public deserve to know the truth."

"Guess what it is not your call to make to tell them that truth. Son, someone is trying to draw the boys out. Townspeople in the mountains have been making reports. Lurking figures. Low flying planes. The Fringe group in town laying the groundwork for a Beckwith Brothers return. Do not ignore all of this. When those boys come home you do not want to be in the middle of this train wreck and that is exactly what it will be."

"Dad, June Beckwith is alive." Kerry stepped towards him father. "I saw her. I sat with her. I talked to her. She seems to believe that her three sons were abandoned in the woods and could communicate...through their minds. She was just about to tell me why she was sure that they too are alive when your goons came and got me."

"I believe they are alive too because of Eric. He would know how to insure he and his brothers' survival. He would have the endurance and the strength to as well. Let me ask you a question. How do you think June has been classified as a Jane Doe all these years? Or why?" Horacio shoved his hands deep in his pockets and squinted at his son seeming to know something Kerry didn't know.

"Those people in that facility." Kerry replied.

"Actually son you're wrong." Horacio motioned for Kerry to sit down. "Please sit down, Kerry. I don't want to fight with you. I want to help you understand." Kerry exhaled and sat down at his father's wishes. Horacio sat down on the coffee table in front of his son. "John Jhang is a government facility for the criminally insane."

"Wha..." Kerry started.

"It masquerades as a mental health care facility when it is not. It's tenets identities are sealed for their own protection and the protection of those who work there."

"But, June Beckwith is not a criminal and when she went missing she wasn't insane!"

"Her secret however could hurt a lot of people. It has hurt a lot of people. Do you know how many in the government are monitoring June making sure she is drugged up enough to either be disregarded or silent? Do you know what has happened to those who tried to sell her story to the media? How much blood has been spilled and how many have died?"

"Someone who knows about her and her secret who wants the story out is alive and well and free. Who do you think gave me the tip about her?" Kerry showed his father the pager message from before.

"You notice how hey kept their identity anonymous? Whereas you are out here trying to expose the truth with your real name and your real face?" Horacio smirked.

"That's journalism, dad! People putting themselves in the line of fire to set the record straight and make things right. To help people. To speak the truth. Which is exactly what I am doing."

"Kerry....You have a story. If that's what you wanted you've got it. You know about the mysterious woman who has an unknown past and who has a tale of great interest. You have the townspeople accounts of low flying planes and figures in the forest. You have a cult in a small town and myth of magical boys. I beg of you to just let that be enough. Go forth with that and end your investigation. Take what you have and know when to stop. You have dodged many bullets with what you have done thus far. I beg of you. Be done. Submit what you have. With what you have many more journalists will have piqued curiosity of The Beckwith Brothers and they will continue the search for answers. You will be recognized for your contribution. That way the truth can still come out and you don't have to be front and center when the backlash comes down. And trust me son....it will come down."

Kerry could tell how serious his father was, he appreciated that, but what he was asking was unacceptable. Is journalistic integrity still fulfilled if only partial segments or hints of the real story are told? If the larger chunks of the truth are left up to implication? Could Kerry bring himself to be that person? Did he really want to give up his position as lead investigator either? This was his chosen case. His chosen assignment. The answer to each of those questions and possibilities was clear he didn't even have to think about it. No. Absolutely fucking flat out NO.

"I...will think about it." Kerry said stiffly. Horacio narrowed his eyes at his son.

"Kerry...promise me. That you will truthfully honestly think about this. I need...I need to know that you will do as you say and think about it." Kerry's eyes fell. Horacio swallowed hard and shifted his weight one leg to the other. "I need peace of mind." Kerry was silent eyes shifting back and forth as if trying to decide between two ideas at once. "Just come back home."

"I want to come back home." Kerry finally said.

"Then come back. Before you left you were all ready to move back in and then months you were just gone."

"I was following my lead."

"Don't you have enough leads? Just report a simpler story. This is not the time to go all out. Just promise me that you'll think about it."

"I will, dad. I will." This time Kerry meant it.

Kerry meant it all the way up to his bedroom, in the shower to wash Mental Institution off of himself, getting dressed for bed, pondering if he wanted to make something in the kitchen downstairs. He even meant it when he heard his father turn in for bed. This house was pretty, but the walls sure were thin. Kerry was glad that his father remained chronically single after his mother died. He certainly couldn't live at home if he could hear Horacio having hookups through the walls. *The trauma.*

Kerry meant what he said as he crawled into his bed and flopped down on his stomach. Then he remembered an offer made to him by a girl with a very important connection. The Petite, Fast, Fitness, Freaky Red Head…Tabitha Banks. The source of one of the best orgasms he had ever managed to give himself and there were some personal records to be beat. No pun intended.

She had offered to be of any help to him that he needed. To repay the favor of saving her life from that malicious, murderous hot dog wiener. The daughter of a Downers Grove lieutenant! Could he pass up her offer? Could he let go of all the wealth of information she could give him access to about the cover ups and the happenings surrounding The Beckwith Brothers and the Fringe and the government secrets. What about murders to silence truth tellers like himself? Could he resist? Kerry plucked up his pager and texted her number. He'd saved it his handy dandy notepad. The one he took with him everywhere. He grinned to himself, he was like Steve from Blue's Clues. Ha! He slid his black glasses on just to make sure that he could see straight.

He typed so fast. He had to re-read his words five or six times just to make sure he didn't have any typos. He was a Grammar Nazi after all. It was perfect. He hit send on the message that said: Tabitha. It's Kerry Thomas. Thought we could meet up. Were you serious about that favor you offered me for saving your life? I may have a very important assignment for you. Try not to make me wait although we agreed how much waiting makes a better finale.
~ Kerry

Kerry removed his glasses in one swift motion using his index finger and thumb. He flicked a wet curl from his forehead and slid down in the bed. Laid there with his boxers on. Let his legs fall open. His limp member fell from the inner seem. Kerry used his palms to smooth the few little hairs on his tummy. He wondered how testosterone injections could improve his lack of chest hair? Crazy thoughts. He scoffed to himself. Everyone knew that synthetic testosterone could be deadly. He had enough body hair really, but he always wanted more. To be more bear and less smooth. He had hair on his legs, pubic area, forearms, a few hairs on his chest and torso, could grow a full beard, and his head was full and lush. He could be happy with that. It was all well and good.

Then breaking his focus on the minute, vane things she responded. Kerry put his glasses back on to read her message. It put a smile on his face.

Tabby B: It's been so long. Wondered if I'd ever hear from you again or see you. I am totally at your service. Let me know what you want me to do.
Xoxo, Tabitha

*Sometimes a mirage is the real deal.*

The next day Kerry rose with the sun and had his morning coffee. He looked through the paper to find wars and rumors of wars. An update in the Oklahoma City bombing investigation revealed that the Taliban had their eye on New York City. A heat wave killed nearly 800 elderly people in the streets of Chicago in one day. Kerry wondered if the climate really could become as unstable as the lesser known scientists of the time were warning the world? 8,000 were slaughtered in Srebrenica which was being called The Bosnian Genocide.

In better news, "Toy Story" was getting rave reviews as the newest delightful addition to the Disney collection and as the first entirely computer generated film of all time. Kerry made a mental note to check it out in the theater at The Plaza. Maybe he could go with Tabitha?

"Troubling times." Horacio came into the kitchen eyeing the newspaper in his son's hands. He poured himself a cup of coffee.

"Thank God for the journalist who bring us these events so we know about what's going on the world." Kerry said. Horacio cut his eyes to his son.

"If only they knew about all that goes on out there. Some try, but they are too often killed." Horacio stated casually with a smirk.

"What do know about the rage killings that happened here when I was away?"

"Not much. I just know some unfortunate women were assaulted and a poor little girl was killed by her own brother."

"What...do you think would cause something like that? Because those things don't usually happen here. As a person with medical training, what are your ideas about..."

"Is that off the record?" Horacio sipped his coffee.

"Of course!" Kerry was hurt. "I wouldn't trick you into giving me information for a story. You're my dad!"

"Kerry you won't even protect *yourself* for your stories. We've certainly had that conversation before."

"That doesn't mean that..."

"This is off the record?"

"Yes." Kerry's voice went small.

"In my personal opinion what you are implying sounds like you think this town was poisoned or otherwise influenced on a mass scale. I think that is a dangerous idea which you should leave alone because only dangerous people would do something like that. In my medical opinion, rage is often considered a result of mental illness, but that is often a farce. Rage is beyond emotions and psychology. Rage is something that originates in your physiological system. It is so strong. So powerful. So mentally and physically all consuming. I'm sure you've heard of the concept of blind rage. Rage is usually a byproduct of hormonal imbalances. So, for a mass group of people to experience rage one would be logical assume that they all received a dose of an excess of hormones. Particularly testosterone."

"Oh."

"What are you going to do? Test the water in every house in this town now?"

"Well not the water. The water probably would have undetectable levels of whatever caused the rage at this point. But, maybe the pipes would have residual residue. Minerals in the pipes might have absorbed deposits of what was in the water that once flowed through it."

"What are you going to do rip somebodies pipes out? You can't do that."

Kerry looked thoughtful then hunched his shoulders, "Oh well. Too bad. So sad. Thanks for the medical opinion anyway, dad."

Horacio shook his head, annoyed, and walked away.

Kerry gathered his necessary supplies from the garage and made his way to Sweet Pique Lane. He passed The Metallic where he met Tabitha and Tabitha met the hot dog, and he turned down into The Carrs housing development. He navigated the identical row houses, unknowingly passed Willow's house on the left, and continued onto a brick townhouse in the very back of the development. He pulled C.C. into the driveway. Put her in park. This was the house where it happened. He looked at the pristine house with the groomed lawn and imagined the heartache that took place right here in this place. When little Mangled Maisey Holland was transported to the Morgue from her home.

Kerry walked up the driveway and took a breath. He knocked on the door. The house had a two car garage so it was impossible to know if someone was or was not home. Although he suspected at least Mrs. Holland would be home she was rumored to have become a shut in since her daughter was killed by her son two months ago. Kerry could see the light from the peephole in the door go dark. Someone was inside. Looking at him from the other side of the door. A moment passed. The door opened. Just a bit. Mrs. Holland opened the door looking like a soccer mom. She was bathed, her strawberry blonde hair was blown dried and pinned up. She looked tired, but that could just been because she didn't have on any makeup and was middle aged.

"Can I help you?" She asked pursed lips.

"Yes, ma'am. My name is Caleb Riley. I wanted to ask you about event leading up to the night of May 17 this year."

"You mean the day that my daughter was murdered in the basement?" She frowned at Kerry the way someone would when the sun is in their eyes.

"Yes ma'am."

"No." She started closing the door.

"Ma'am What you know could save many more lives." Kerry waited for her reaction. She paused then took a breath. She let him inside.

She poured them both Chamomile teas in blue mugs in the white on white farmhouse style kitchen. A glass rooster was positioned by the bread box on the far off counter and a window was over the sink. Kerry was reluctant to drink anything from the pipes in this house, but he was willing to risk his life to get he answers he needed. He hope he couldn't be poisoned from tiny sips. They sat for a while before Kerry asked about Tyler.

"It was right after Halloween when he started getting the headaches." She said "He complained of splitting headaches. He had mood swings. He would snap. Be more disobedient, but he would always apologize after. His father and I thought maybe it was just growing pains? We thought maybe he got hit in the head by a soccer ball even. He loved to play soccer." She smiled remembering the good old days of taking her son to practice before their lives went all wrong. "Then he started to have the fits."

"When was this? Do you remember?"

"Um, maybe it was around like February. He started having temper tantrums like small children would. That was when his behavior got more alarming to his father and I. He would pound things with his fists. He would have such pain in his head. So we took him to doctors and therapists. We feared he may have had a brain tumor or something, but he didn't. Nothing was physically wrong with him. So, we took him back home. Everything was fine for a while until we got a call that he had exposed himself to a group of girls at his school, Heisenberg High. And that he tried to jump on one of the girls. Those animals at that school tried to say that my son wanted to rape the girls. I don't believe that *my* Tyler could *ever* do that."

Tyler slaughtered his own baby sister, but rape is what Mrs. Holland cannot believe her son would do. It wasn't that much of a stretch. Kerry thought to himself counting how many sips he was taking from the poisoned mug. Just enough not to be rude and hopefully so few that he too would not experience any rage fueled fits later on.

Mrs. Holland continued, "Then came May." She paused rotating her blue mug back and forth nervously. "I don't want to talk about what happened in May." Then she looked thoughtful. "Who did you say that you're with again?"

"Uh, The San Francisco Times. I moved down to be with my partner he's working in Silicon Valley. May I use your bathroom?" Kerry said with a straight face.

"Sure. It's up the stairs and down the hall to the right."

Kerry thanked Mrs. Holland and made his way up the stairs and to the bathroom trying not to let the tools in his jacket rattle on the way.

He found the bathroom and locked himself inside. He lifted the toilet seat. Not sure why. Habit he supposed. He didn't actually have to go. He was there on a mission. He stood in front of a white Pedestal Sink. Pipes visible underneath. Bingo. Kerry stooped down and carefully removed various tools from his dad's toolbox that were in the inner pockets within his jacket and placed them on the floor. He didn't know how he was going to do this as quickly as he needed to. Peeing didn't take this long and he hadn't even started taking apart the pipes yet. Kerry took a wrench and started untwisting the gasket to the pipe under the sink. He opened it. It was clean inside. Kerry picked up the little sample cup, which was actually a small salad dressing container, he swiped from the pantry of his dad's house. However, there was nothing to collect. The pipe was clean. *Damn.* He needed an older pipe. One of the ones in the wall. He couldn't come this far and get inside this woman's house and lie to her to take a sample from her pipes just to find nothing. No! No. He needed a bigger, older pipe. One of the pipes in the wall? Yes. So, Kerry, without even thinking smashed a hammer into the wall behind the sink. He hit wood. *Fucking wood.* He hit the wall again and found drywall. *Hallelujah.* Kerry used his hands to pull the drywall back. First little pieces then big chunks. Kerry got his flashlight and clenched it between his teeth. Used the light to see inside the wall.

He almost jumped out of his skin when Mrs. Holland knocked on the door. "What's going on in there? I heard banging."

"I…I fell off the toilet!" Kerry wailed like he was mortally injured.

"OH MY GOD!" Mrs. Holland screamed like she was on fire. "Are you Okay?"

"I'm hurt!" He screamed. He didn't know where he was going with this.

"Oh my…I can't stand nobody else dying in this house!!! Why's the door locked?!?"

"I need…I need an AAAAMBUUUULLLLLAAAAANCE!!" He screamed further borrowing into the wall using his screams as cover for the noise. He finally found a bigger pipe in the wall and yanked at it during that last scream for an ambulance.

"What is that sound!!!"

"I'M TRAAAAPPPED!" He screamed so hard spit went flying from his mouth.

"Oh My GAAWWWWWWDDD!" She shrieked. "I have to MOVE! I can't be HERE!" He could hear Mrs. Holland run away screaming something he couldn't make out. He assumed she was fleeing the house in terror that her house was haunted or out to get her or maybe she was calling an ambulance like Kerry needed. *Or actually like he said he needed.*

Wait, if it was the latter that meant…Oh shit. The ambulance and probably the police were coming. Kerry had to hurry. Oh God. The guilt was setting in for what he had done here. First, he tricked her. Then he lied to her. Now he had officially exploited and terrified the mother of a dead child. *Yep.* He thought. He was definitely the devil.

He yanked in the pipe again. That little bitch was in there good. He'd have to saw it out. Very well. He pulled out a small saw and started sawing the metal. He had to apply way more pressure than he anticipated at this angle. It was awkward and painful. He was getting cut up and down his arms digging in the wall. He sewed faster and faster. He was halfway through and could already seem a build up of sediment and minerals in the pipe. To anyone else the sight would have been gross, but to Kerry he had struck gold. He kept sawing. Sweat beading off his forehead. For some reason his glasses were fogging up. He was breathing heavy. Man, this was a workout. Well at least he could skip the gym today. Then finally it popped off and he caught the piece with his other hand. He removed the piece of pipe from the wall. Now he just had to make his way back downstairs, dodge Mrs. Holland, and get out of The Carrs before the police or the ambulance came.

He stuffed the old pipe piece and his tools back into his jacket and peeked his head outside the door. He could not hear or see Mrs. Holland. He darted into the hallway and made his way downstairs. The front door was wide open. Did she leave? Maybe she really fled the house in fear of some malevolent force in her house that she felt was going around killing people.

Kerry could not let her see him leave. So, he ran as fast as he could to his car without dropping anything. Then she spotted him.

"HEY! What are you doing!? WHAT ARE YOU UP TO?" Mrs. Holland screamed running towards him from a whole block away with Tabitha and off duty Officer Ginger Banks, also known as Tabitha's mother, close behind.

Kerry threw himself into C.C., cranked the engine, threw the car into gear, floored it in reverse, threw the car into drive, and fled the scene burning rubber the whole way.

The women stopped in front of the Holland house.

"What just happened? That's the victim you were talking about?" Ginger asked Mrs. Holland.

"Yes, or I thought he was a victim. He was in my bathroom screaming that he fell off the toilet and he was tuck and he needed an ambulance immediately and I thought you're right down the street. So, I ran out and came to get y…oh my God. He was in my house alone." Mrs. Holland ran inside with Ginger and they both bolted upstairs. Mrs. Holland screamed at the top of her lungs at the sight in the bathroom, "WHAT THE FUCK?! WHO DOES THIS?!"

Tabitha knew exactly who did that, but she didn't say a word. She spun around on her heels and trotted home. She had a meeting that evening to prepare for with culprit of this debacle.

Later in that night, Tabitha was fixing her lip gloss in her palm pilot in a booth at Metallic waiting for her date to arrive. She adjusted the sweetheart neckline of her top to sit as low as possible without showing her nipples.

She caught her breath when he walked in the door. Kerry approached her and she immediately said, "I believe you've been naughty boy."

"I was." He admitted sitting down.

"How could you?" She grinned.

"Uh desperate times calls for desperate measures." He answered bashfully.

"Must be. So as much as I liked receiving your message I am very curious what was this important assignment that you needed my help for?"

"Well I need some information."

"Lemme guess from the police?" Tabitha licked some whipped cream from the end of her straw.

"Yes. There's only so much I can find out through my" he cleared his throat comically, "very professional sleuthing. And as of the events of today, I need a laboratory on short notice. That will test something that I have without asking too many questions."

"Ah. So you need an inside person? Is that right?" Tabitha leaned in close.

"Yes, that's exactly right."

"I can be that for you. I can be whatever you like actually." She smiled and he believed her. "So, let's go."

"Go where?"

"Hello, the lab at the station. I know a tech who works there third shift. We have a few hours."

So, they made the short drive to the station with the canopy of C.C. down. Kerry glanced over at Tabitha, the night air blowing through her vibrant red hair. She tossed her head back and then smiled at him. "Hey watch the road big guy." She said. He obeyed her.

They made their way to the police headquarters where the Crime Laboratory was located. It was a stucco building eight stories high with lots of windows. It had a spire on top. The front side was where the police station was and a surplus of parked police vehicles and the back side was where Tabitha and Kerry were going.

Kerry parked in a fairly empty, dark parking lot and Tabitha stepped out of C.C. and told Kerry to come when she signaled him to. Kerry was disappointed that the police department would have such a dark, spooky parking lot. They should of all people should know better. There could be criminals just lurking back here in the shadows. Kerry watched Tabitha sashay up to the backdoor of the building. She knocked and a young adult blond male opened the door. He smiled and hugged her. She kissed his cheek and waved Kerry to come in. So, he did.

Inside the building was shiny tiles and to the immediate left was the technology lab. Daniel Kias was the blonde. He was so bubbly to be around death and murder all the time. "Welcome to my lovely abode." He greeted them and ushered them into the laboratory. "Where I work and where I play." He eyed Tabitha with that last line. Tabitha giggled. Kerry suddenly felt like a third wheel.

"Daniel, I have a friend here with and we have a favor to ask you." Tabitha stepped forward.

"Sure. What is it? It's not too illegal is it?" Daniel joked…or maybe he wasn't joking at all. Kerry wasn't sure.

"Not this time!" Tabitha laughed.

"You remember or lovely celebration?" Daniel pulled her close.

"Of course!" She giggled like a silly school girl. "I remember showing you my technology lab!" She and Daniel both cracked up like Dave Chappell was giving them a personal show.

Tabitha then got serious, "Daniel, honey, I need something tested. Something important. We apologize for the short notice."

"Okay. What is it?" Daniel asked. Kerry presented the piece of pipe.

"The deposits inside we just need to know what all is in there." Kerry said.

Daniel put on a blue glove to protect the evidence and took the pipe from Kerry. He examined the sponge inside. "Now if I knew what I was looking for this could go a lot faster."

Kerry looked to Tabitha. "It's ok." She nodded.

"*You can trust me. I'm the police.*" Daniel said sarcastically already knowing that people don't often trust cops.

Kerry grinned. "Hormones. Real. Fake. Anything that could alter a person's hormones."

"Very interesting." Daniel grinned. "Give me an hour. Go back to your car. Grab a bite. Come back I'll have some answers for you." Daniel shook Kerry's hand. Kerry and Tabitha did as they were told. They hung out in C.C. the next block over on the highest point of Downers Grove. It was closest thing to a Lovers Lane the town had.

"So, this is part of your investigation of The Beckwith Brothers disappearance, right?" Tabitha asked.

"Yes. Maybe preparation for their reappearance. I dunno." Kerry said.

"Seriously? Where would they come from?"

"From where they've been. All along."

Tabitha readjusted herself in her seat. Subconsciously looked around her surroundings. "Do you really think they would come back?"

"I think they should be found."

"What if they don't want to be found? I mean if they are out there. They just know we're here. They must see. They may be looking down on us right now. From the mountains. They could just walk down and reveal themselves, but they don't. Who knows maybe they're dead." Her eyebrows shot up.

"They have something to offer us that they are afraid to share. Maybe despite all they have survived their greatest fear is the force of mankind. I know I will find the truth. I feel like I am on the cusp of a breakthrough."

"And your career will be solidified? Big amazing journalist, Kerry Thomas!"

"I'll try. I'm trying now."

"Trying hard. What was that earlier today?" Kerry started laughing with Tabitha. "I see what you were going for, but won't she find you?"

"I told her my name was Caleb Riley with The San Francisco Times. Oh yeah and that I was gay!"

Tabitha gasped playfully. "This is a bombshell. A bombshell!"

"Yeah right! So, there's a Caleb Riley out there who may not be having a great day."

"Naughty boy indeed!" She wacked his arm. "Who are our suspects" Tabitha put her feet up in the window. Her skirt crawling far up her thighs. Her butt angled towards Kerry.

"Our?" He arched an eyebrow.

"Of course. I'm your sidekick now aren't I?"

"Abso-freaking-lutely."

"Ha! Who watches Sex and the City?"

"This guy." Kerry said shyly.

"Hmm, maybe you are gay!"

"Shut up!" He smacked her ass.

She sat up and leaned so close to his face that they could feel each other breathing. She acted like she wanted a kiss. A passionate kiss. Kerry was ready. He leaned into her, but she turned her head away and checked her watch.

"Time to go." She flopped back down in her seat and put on her seatbelt. "Safety first."

"Safety first." Kerry our his seat belt back on, cranked up C.C. and made his way back to the Crime Lab.

He looked confused and suspicious. Daniel eyed Kerry the most. As if somehow Kerry was the culprit here. "So, where did the pipe come from?"

"A house." Kerry said.

"From...where?" Daniel asked.

"San Francisco." Tabitha lied. "Gay couple's apartment. Poor guys."

"Who do you work for?" Daniel asked Kerry.

Kerry paused. He was going to lie again, but Daniel was Tabitha's "in" at the station which meant Kerry needed him...bad. He may have some other piece of damaged and stolen property he needed tested for poisoning one day. Who knew? He needed to nurture this relationship and to do that he needed to be honest. He looked at Tabitha. She nodded.

"Listen I believe that something bad and wrong is happening in this town."

"Of course there is." Daniel admitted.

"I'm trying to get to the bottom of it. All of it. Part of the mystery in front of us is what made people here in Downers Grove turn violent after Halloween. Now I have gotten a medical opinion…which has informed me that a possible reason for the rage killings could be an influx of testosterone. The water system is the only mode of delivery that makes sense. This pipe could give us a lot of answers."

"From San Francisco?" Daniel arches an eyebrow.

"I told her to say that. Blame me." Kerry said.

"You sucked my dick in this very room. You don't think you can trust me?" Daniel said über casual to Tabitha.

*This very room?*

"I do. I didn't want to say anything that would ruin Kerry's investigation." Tabitha said.

"Look, I will help you. Do you see anything on the report that speaks to you?" Daniel passes Kerry his report.

Kerry lowered it enough for Tabitha to see. Their eyes zeroed in on two words: Artificial Testosterone. "300% increase?" Kerry asked.

"It means that the saturation of testosterone in that one place is just that much more than the average amount that it would usually in the location which was tested." Daniel explained. "Just below that is a booster to testosterone. Do you see it?"

"Steroids?" Tabitha frowned. "500% increase?"

"Oh my…" Kerry said.

"Do you all know who did this? Honestly?"

"We honestly don't know." Tabitha said.

"Do you have an idea? Because what happened here in Downers, if the assaults and the murders were a result of someone tainting the water system that is an act of terrorism."

"Not…literally, right!?" Tabitha was shocked.

"Yes, literally!" Kerry and Daniel responded.

"I am keeping a portion of the pipe. You can have the rest. But, just in case something…bad happens. To you Kerry. You may be investigating some dangerous people. I need to know where the pipe came from."

Kerry took a deep breath, "I stole it right out of someone's wall. You all may have gotten a call about it today, I dunno." Kerry nervously hunched a shoulder.

"Oh wow so…you're like *crazy* crazy?" Daniel said like he just realized this.

"Pretty much." Tabitha grinned at Kerry.

"General area? I won't tell." Daniel asked.

"The Carrs development." Kerry admitted.

"Got it. That's plenty. No one will find out what you did. I have my ways. Tabitha can vouch for that!" Daniel smiled. Tabitha gave him a bear hug and a cheek kiss.

"One more question. Is there anyway that we could find out where someone would get enough testosterone and steroids to poison an entire town?" Kerry asked.

"Oh I'm sure the feds already know. That much? They know." Daniel nodded with confidence.

"How can we know?" Kerry asked.

"Word of mouth. Know a guy. Find the source and find a way to hack into their servers. That last one I wouldn't suggest because it's *illegal*." Daniel used air quotes around the word 'illegal' like he did not consider the word illegal to be set in stone.

Kerry shook Daniel hand, "Thank you, Daniel. Thank you so much."

"Thank you, Daniel." Tabitha curtsied.


Kerry and Tabitha made their way back out of the building.

"You remember what I said about Angelica McCord?" Kerry said.

"She's your person of interest?" Tabitha went all into detective verbiage.

"Who else has that kind of money in Downers to order a surplus of anything to make this percentages?" Kerry held up the report.

"I can't think of anyone." Tabitha sat straight up in her seat.

"I'm taking you home. I need you to do another favor for me."

"Anything!" Tabitha effervesced.

"I need you to just keep your ear to the ground about anything you hear your mom, or her cop friends, or anyone else regarding Angelica, The Fringe, and The Beckwith Brothers. Anything. Absolutely anything you hear, let me know."

"It would be an honor, sir!" She said in the same pitch that Rudolph the Red-Nose Reindeer did in the classic television special.

"And Tabitha…"

"Yeah?"

"I cannot even thank you enough for what you've done today."

"Oh Kerry. Don't make me blush. I'm red enough already." She smiled.

# Chapter 12: I <3 NYC...Kinda

Carmen always wanted to "arrive." She never was able to articulate exactly what that meant, what it meant to her, or exactly what all it entailed, but today was the day that made her feel closer to that ever evasive mark. In her mind she had arrived. Being here in New York City was one thing being a moo-del of Haute Couture was another, but being the honored guest of Jean Jesus French Tipping & Sipping Manicure AKA The Place Where Only the Wealthy and Famous Go To Get Their Nails Come was a whole different animal that made Carmen's head explode with glee, bliss, and excitement. Jean Jesus catered to all even his hyphenated first name was chosen to embrace to cultures which were not even his own: Language of Love and the Language of Passion and yet he was an Italian American who was orphaned at 2 and raised by Hasidic Jews.

Originally the invite was for Willow, but being a Tom Boy to the bone getting a manicure just wasn't her ideal afternoon in the Big City. It just was anything but. So, after making some arrangements Willow realized that she could use her afternoon to attend the behind the scenes meetings and fittings for a small fashion show held by a friend of Angelica's. Being a fly on the wall at a fashion house big enough to have a following and small enough to give her a personal tour of the show, introduce her to the moo-dels and the whole process was too good an opportunity to pass up. Manicures were the least of her concerns. She gave her tickets to Carmen who she knew would love the gift more than she. Carmen was still a minor, so true to the promise of Angelica McCord to the teen moo-dels' parents the girls were not left to fend for themselves, thusly Alexandra accompanied Carmen to the spa.

It could have been Sierr, but she was elsewhere. She was meeting with the agents of Sibion & Son and they were wonderful. They were just as funny, supportive, kind, and modern as before. They listen to Sierr and gave her pointers to get into the industry she loved. They gave her tips on her query letter which they had previously requested and since reviewed. Then they delivered the biggest news yet. They were interested in keeping Sierr as their collective, ongoing mentee until Dead Serious was right where it needed to be to reach publishing. The goal was modify the manuscript and Sierr under their tutelage until she graduated high school. Then they would meet back up again in New York to discuss how to bring Dead Serious from a Work In Progress to the Best Sellers list.

Sierr was ecstatic. Hopeful. Thankful. She had always wanted to be guided through her inspirations and ideas and now she would have that way sooner than she had ever imagined. She had to tell Lux, her parents, JSF, her friends, the whole world, and of course Downers Grove. This was the absolutely best news.

Sierr arrived back at the Ritz and entered her shared suite with JSF. She called out for him, but he didn't answer. She immediately picked up the phone and dialed Lux.

"No friggin' way. Sierr, I am so happy for you!" Lux squealed Sierr could hear Toni Braxton's "Unbreak My Heart" playing in the background.

"Are you doing some kind of romantic dance class, right now?"

"Yes, I am. Slow dancing. The art of seduction. The works." Lux smiles in her voice.

"I need to take your classes that's for sure." Sierr said. "Give me all those sexy talents."

"Sexy talents?" Lux echoed her sister. "Watch me name a class that and it sell out and I'll be all like I have my 16-year-old sister whose never even been kissed to thank for it."

"Soon to be seventeen!" Sierr reminded her.

"You got four months, missy. Until then you're just a sweet sixteen."

"Kay, I'm gonna call you later. I have a call waiting."

"Bye."

"Bye." Sierr clicked the line over. "Hello?"

"Does a gay man ogling anorexic women in thongs and tube tops flattering or rapey?" Willow said into the receiver squinting at Jame Gumb doing that exact thing to moo-dels at the moo-del fitting she was at.

"Uuuum, rapey. Just because he likes men doesn't mean he can't also like and potentially rape women. Especially pretty women."

"Angelica's not particularly pretty and he likes her." Willow stated.

"Are we 100% sure that Jame isn't being raped by Angelica?" Sierr snugged up her nose.

"Good question." Willow replied.

"Aaaand is willfully being someone's personal slave equate to liking them?" Sierr pondered aloud.

"Maybe he wishes he was one of the moo-dels?" Willow said.

"Nah, he likes his penis too much to want to be a woman." Sierr said. "He places it too perfectly in his pants."

"Someone's been looking."

"Only because it was so noticeable." Sierr lied not willing to admit she had a crouch gawking habit. "Do you ever feel like you could be sexual?"

"Nah."

"What if we took a class in seduction then how do you think you would feel?" Sierr arched an eyebrow eagerly waiting for Willow's reply.

"It depends. Would we be dancing with each other? Or men?"

"Men. Or maybe my sister. Or maybe her business partner, Marnie, actually I'm not sure. Maybe we'll be dancing by ourselves. Like learning motion and rhythm moves?"

"Get all the details and get back to me."

"Will do."

Sierr and Willow hung up with plans to continue their conversation later. Then JSF came out of the bathroom first looking ill, then rolling his shoulders back and easing into the living room with Sierr.

"You'll never believe what happened!" Sierr rejoiced.

"Lemme guess they all loved you and your book?" He smiled.

"Yes! And I'm so proud of myself. I went all by myself. And I did it. I was afraid, but I did it! I went and I talked and I feel so good that I did it!"

"You survived an interview and the streets of New York. And just a wee baby too." JSF pouted.

Then in the voice of a damsel in distress Sierr continued, "I left here thinkin' 'how ever will I survive?'"

"Know some rhythm and motion." JSF grinned.

"Oh heavens." Sierr laughed.

"Then maybe you can feel sexual."

"Oh gawd." Sierr put her face in her palms. JSF couldn't help but laugh at her and Willow. "You know what you really need? Some defense moves."

"Defense Moves?" Sierr cocked her head to the side like a perplexed puppy.

"Defensive moves."

"Uuuuhhhhhh…like hiya?" Sierr did a karate chop towards JSF.

"Nah chicka. I mean like real moves. Like the deadly basics. Stuff you can do to kill people in one swift move." JSF stood up.

"What like a donkey kick? Wadda ya talkin' about?"

"Stand up." JSF waved her towards him. She obey and greeted him with a pouty, "Okay. Mr. Bossy."

"I'm not bossy. I'm the boss. Now. Stand with one of your legs positioned back behind you for strength and leverage." JSF demonstrated. Sierr followed his cue, "Then put your hands up to protect your face and then throw a punch."

Sierr tries to mimic JSF's demonstration. He stops her. "Never have your thumb in when throwing a punch because you can break your own thumb that way from the impact. Hold your hand like this." He showed her his fists with his thumbs over his knuckles and she successfully took the right stance.

"Watch me use that move to put Skeeter, Jeremy, and Kev and the other skateboarders in their place next time they come for me and my girls." Sierr laughed.

JSF started to undress, "Take a bath with me!" He grinned.

"12-years-ago that would have worked. But, I am smarter and wiser now, Fitzgerald."

"You can't be sexual you said." He scoffed. "You ought to hear how Damian Jacobs likes to talk about the ways in which he wants to screw you."

*Excuse me.* "Excuse me?"

"Puh-lease. Like you don't know that Damian's been crushing on you since middle school." JSF removed all of his clothes besides his boxers and T-Shirt. "If you'll excuse I'm going to scrub the germs from the outdoors off of me." JSF dismissed himself.

Sierr was so deep in shock, JSF had time to go and take a hot bath, scrub his skin, floss, and brush the espresso off his teeth before Sierr could even think of all the follow up questions she had for him about this bombshell that Damian who hates her and who she totally couldn't stand might actually like her. Waiting for JSF to finish sterilizing himself would take too long so she showered, Witchhazel-ed her skin, ate a banana. Then she tried on a satin, flora dress curtesy of Angelica McCord trying to see how it hung on her shapeless body. During this entire time she pondered very hard.

Her thoughts could focus if the smallest things and magnify them. She knew this little detail about herself for years. Was clear to her when she could obsess over the smallest sentences in her writing and still feel that nothing is good enough. It was also clear to her when she would try to count the hairs in the rug on the bathroom mat of her parents bedroom. So, she knew she was beginning to obsess. She was partially disappointed in herself for focusing on a jerk like Damian when perfectly lovable people just love bombed her and offered her help and kindness at Starbucks...the place where good coffee happens.

Despite that as soon as JSF got out of the shower and joined her in the kitchen of their suite. Sierr just couldn't help herself...

"So...what other boys are secretly into me at school?" Sierr asked as JSF dried his braids and plucked a water from the fridge. He wore only a pair of pajama pants. No underwear. His penis was too all over the place for underwear to have been anywhere in the vicinity of his crouch.

"Oh meh gawd. Gurl. Please. Don't get carried away, okay?"

"I just wanna know." Sierr states calmly.

"I love how you can look so calm when your so obviously busy...like in your head. It's almost scary like one of those people with multiple personalities."

"Who. Likes. Me?"

"No one you should ever want to be with. End up like fucking Hailey some unattainable guy just because he's attractive and forbidden."

"Hailey! You know who Hailey's engaged to?" Sierr's eyes got huge.

"Who else? Mr. Windsor!"

"Huh?!" Sierr practically screamed.

"Abby's dad."

"I know who Mr. Windsor is." Sierr could never not remember the owner of the 8 inch penis she got to ogle three days a week in her favorite class. Who could not know Mr. Windsor?

"He's a predator."

"But he's really nice. And married."

"You didn't think that marriage was healthy did you?" JSF plopped down on her bed.

"No." Sierr looked thoughtful. She wailed, "But he's so nice!"

"Yeah. He's just great." JSF smiled wide with deep sarcasm. "I bet even Hitler had his moments."

Sierr stammered, "Hitl...Wh...Well geez."

"He is fucking a child, Sierr."

"But he's Mr. Windsor!?" Sierr exclaimed again.

"Have I ever steered you wrong?" JSF grinned. Sierr plopped down on the bed next to him.

"Bet that's why Hailey's been so…confident."

"You don't have to have a guy, or an older guy to feel confident. Please tell me you don't think that."

"Well it would be a confidence booster!" Sierr pouted unintentionally.

"You could have been with guys by now. But I don't think that's something that you wanted. They would have corrupted you. I wouldn't have wanted that either. The guys who like you at school they don't want what's best for you because they don't appreciate your values. They want to be your first just to be able to have that to claim, ya know? The rest of the guys just don't know how to approach you because of your…how do I put this lightly…Bible Thumping."

"Bible thumping? They think I'm a Bible Thumper? What exactly even is that? Do they think that I'm a prude?" *Ha! If only they knew that she had her townsmen's penis shapes and sizes before their faces! Like circumcised, eight inch length, girth at least two inches, always to the lower right in dress slacks surrounded by well developed quads was also known as Mr. Windsor.* At least in Sierr's mind it was.

"Yes and they can tell that you're different in other ways too. Sweet wifey material. You're not the girl people just date. They know that you'd want more… deepness. And caring."

The sun was setting now. With this information Sierr finally knew why she felt so cursed. By day break she could have all the answers she need to finally make herself desirable.

"How can I fix it?" She flipped her hair determinedly.

"Fix it! There's nothing to fix! There's nothing about you that needs fixing." JSF looked at Sierr deeply like he really wanted her to know that what he was telling her was the truth.

"Well then what's wrong with me?"

"Nothing!"

"The guys. These guys you speak of in school. Why don't they talk to me?"

"They know that you would want more from them than their willing to give you right now. The other girls they're okay with being temporary. Everybody knows basically going after you would be a waste of time. So, quit worrying about yourself. You're perfect."

Sierr scoffed and hunched a shoulder all at once and winced at that she was anything but perfect. "I don't want to be so good that nobody wants to be around me either."

"Don't let the world jack you up just to make you more acceptable to trash people. Fuck them people. Be who you are. If you were close to them they would do nothing, but distract you anyway. So, be happy you don't have tons of people in your life to steer you the wrong directions."

Sierr looked thoughtful. He had a point. She wanted to be well liked and desired, but it wasn't worth compromising herself. "I should be glad I have you to cuss me into lunacy again?"

Sierr laid down next to him.

"Exactly, cuz!" JSF slips a blunt out of the pocket of the designer jeans he left on the floor as casual as someone would retrieve a bag of chips from the pantry.

"Dude. Are you seri…."

"Sis, breathe." He laid down next to her. The room got dark quickly with no lights on and the sun setting outside.

"I thought I was supposed to be myself." She smirked as he lit up.

"You do you, baby."

Sierr watched as he took a long drag. The glow from the tip of the blunt casting a red hue over his golden skin. Dark skin was so attractive. Sometimes Sierr wished she took after her mother a little more. Than she would look like JSF. Mocha. Carmel. Carmel Mocha. A smooth blend of deep, richness and soul. Baked by the earth to something unique, pure, untapped.

JSF exhaled a white cloud fumes from his mouth and nostrils. His eyes slowed dimmed and then shut altogether. Sierr likes it when people closed their eyes around her. Then she could study their features in close proximity without having to play it off or gather enough visual data in small glances. Piecing together their appearance in small parts like a puzzle. Just to have opportunity to look at someone. It was an intimate act. That was what she really wanted to be intimate with someone. Intimate beyond the physical. Beyond sex. In the realm of soul touching. Sharing emotions. Being in love.

JSF took another long drag his eyes still closed. He ran a hand through his dreads and in one swift motion brushed them out of his face. He features in full view now. He exhaled long again. A cloud of the fumes surrounding him.

Suddenly Sierr was feeling remarkably peaceful and relaxed. Like her whole body was at ease. The world slowed to the pace of molasses or honey or maybe amber like the amber that the mosquito in Jurassic Park got caught and preserved in. Something thick and smooth. Her flesh was honey. It was warm and slow. Glued to the bed. If the entire suite self-combusted and went up in flames Sierr wasn't quite sure she would have even had the will to move, get up, and save her own life. So relaxed. It was lovely. She blinked watching JSF. He was watching her now. She was oddly aware of her breathing. Lungs expanding slowly. Air pacing through her nostrils slowly. Rinse and repeat.

"What are you looking at?" She smiled.

"What are you looking at?" He grinned back.

"Watching you." She said.

"Watching you more." He puffed.

She giggled. He giggled.

He took another drag a shorter one this time. "I better get going. Gotta shower. Change. Stupid shit ya know?" He crawled off the bed and stood over her.

She looked up at him. Laughed again. "Me too."

"Mm-hmm. Then get some rest pretty girl."

"Oh yes. I will. I feel rested already." She smiled still holding his gaze over her head.

He stood for a while looking past her eyes and in the distance. Not that distant though. Sierr wondered if he was till looking at her just not at her face. Maybe another part of her body. Arm? Legs? Maybe he was admiring her dress? No that would be silly! Wait? What…What was she thinking about again? Oh yeah JSF…he was glowing. He was so pretty.

"G'night." He said strolling away arm outstretched swaying in the air like a child playing airplane. He went to his half of the suite.

Sierr willed herself to get up. Arise from the bed, put on her pajamas, maybe have a snack. Just needed to get up. Instead she was fast asleep.

"Hey." She eventually heard a voice say. "Hey. Wake up." JSF whispered in her ear. Her eyes flew open. She gasped.

"What time is it?" Did I miss breakfast?" She rubbed her eyes and her hand came away smudged with makeup.

"No, you must have fallen asleep." JSF said standing in the same position over her head now in his pajamas, a pair of plaid pants and a T-Shirt. He handed her a damp towel. *That must've been strong pot to give ol' girl a contact high.* He grinned to himself.

"Oh. Oops." Sierr lifted herself up from the bed stronger and more herself again and got into a sitting position. Wiped some of the makeup off her face and hand.

"Here let me help you." JSF got back on the bed on his knees and helped Sierr unfasten her dress. She got on her knees on all fours and helped JSF take her dress off. She crawled under the covers in just her matching baby pink bra and pantie set and JSF tucked her in.

He laid down next to her. Wrapping his arms around her. Kissed her cool, damp cheek. "Hey!"

"Yeah?" She replied her voice muffled by the plush pillow her face was enveloped in.

"Which one is more likely 1984 or Back to the Future?"

"1984." JSF could hear the smile in her voice in the dark.

"Why?" He nodded.

"Because the government isn't meant to be trusted for too long. Their failures will bite us before science will." She mimicked his voice as best as she could. Making her pitch deeper and more…skeptical?

"That's my girl." He chuckled. Sierr laughed with him. "Hey some humans aren't fully humans, you know why?"

"No? Aliens?" She supposed.

"Nah. No aliens. Neanderthals. They mated with our ancestors. Had offspring. Statistically that means those hybrid humanoids offspring would have lead to a strain of humanoids that look just like us and talk just like us, but that have non-human DNA!" JSF widened his eyes in the darkness.

"Don't tell Abby. She's probably a hybrid that's why she's so mean."

"That's why she's always grooming, plucking, and smearing things on herself it's in her DNA."

They laughed and he pinched her torso playfully just before they both fell fast asleep.

The next morning Willow and Carmen were in the dining room of their suite enjoying a lavish spread of fruit, pastries, jellies, jams, nuts, and spreads and assorted beverages including juices, protein drinks bar, and coffee. They sat at each end of the table like the man and woman of the house. Willow giggled, "I so enjoy preparing a large meal the children, Ward."

"Oh yes, June. Beaver and Wally will have their fill and then off to school the both of them so I can bend you over the kitchen table like we do here in burbs on Thursdays." Carmen replied in a low, man's voice.

"Oh Ward Clever you naughty boy!" Willow replied in a voice much higher than her own.

The girls had a laugh. Carmen turned the TV onto The Price is Right just as Plinko was beginning. She turned the volume as loud as it could go without drowning out her conversation with Willow. Carmen scooped up her plate and sat down next to Willow on the other end of the table. "Does Angelica have any plans for us tonight?"

"Jame and Royal are coming over and will give us a rundown of plans for the day. I think they are tossing around a few ideas. Party over there. Clubbing over here. I dunno. I suppose I am privileged enough, *today*, to get a heads up about the goings on *before* Abby." Willow selected only the juiciest cubes of honeydew melon for her plate.

"Unless she already knows." Carmen arched an eyebrow.

"Oh God." Willow rubbed her eyebrow.

"I'm sorry. Sorry. I don't wanna be a wet blanket. Maybe yesterday was just a minor oversight. That's all. I'm going to see if Sierr is awake. I'd hate for her to have to come in after Abby gets here."

"Kay." Willow sipped her orange juice.

Carmen knocked on the adjoining door between her suite with Willow and Sierr's suite with JSF. She used her keys to access the room. "Hello!" She called out happily. She tip-toed inside playfully peaking her head around every corner to try and spot her friends. She continued on into the suite, "Hello? You two can't still be asleep in here. You're gonna miss everything. Nobody sleeps in, in New York. It's too friggin' noisy." Carmen peaked her head in JSF's room. It was super quiet in their suite. They had to be somewhere. Carmen wondered if they were in Sierr's bedroom. Maybe getting dressed? Carmen eases towards Sierr's bedroom door and knocked lightly. "Sierr?"

Carmen took in the sight of JSF spooning Sierr, only in her bra a panties, in the middle of tussled 4000 count sheets.

Carmen could feel herself frowning and then reminded herself to stop before she gave herself wrinkles. She swallowed hard and backed out of the room. No. That was not at all what it looked like. She thought. Nope. Sierr was her best friend who would never compromise herself just because of mere convince of having a suite away from home. Freedoms wouldn't just make Sierr lose her mind and do some craziness with JSF. Especially not JSF.

Carmen walked back into her suite with Willow. She resigned within herself not to say anything to Willow. The last person she needed to be gossiping about was her best friend. Especially when this was obviously a misunderstanding.

"So, are they coming?" Willow stirred some cream and sugar into a mug full of coffee.

"They were in bed together!" Carmen hush yelled. *Welp, so much for her decision not to say anything.*

Willow paused, stunned, and gaping. Then she broke into a laugh. "Well that couldn't've been what you thought you saw!"

"Well they weren't naked. Sierr only had on her bra and panties though." Carmen said thoughtfully.

"Did they act suspicious when you caught them? Not that they were doing anything to *catch*."

"They didn't know I saw. They were still asleep."

"Carmen." Willow shook her head slowly looking weary.

"I know! I'm sorry. I…think I just got carried away. That was a little shocking."

"We've all slept in beds together. We've all even taken baths together with JSF."

"Yeah, but that was when we were younger. And when we've slept in beds together older we at least had our clothes on. Why is Sierr undressed? She has plenty of clothes."

"Carmen, I'm sure there's a reason. Never mind us knowing how Sierr is and that she would never go wild just because she was away from home and that a little freedom wouldn't get to her like that. Were talking about her and JSF. He's all the way off limits." Willow laughs sitting back in her chair. "She would never cross that line. That's crazy talk! Don't you see?"

"Yes." Carmen nodded having a seat in her chair next to Willow. "Yes, you're so right. I don't know why I…"

"It's fine. No biggie. We just don't know the whole story that's all. I'm sure there is a perfectly logical explanation." Willow opened the newspaper. She looked like she was studious and enjoyed being informed, but really she was just reading the Funny Pages.

Carmen took a bite of a chocolate croissant. "You're right."

What they did not know is that Abby was already inside their suite and she had heard everything they discussed about Sierr and JSF.

Soon enough Jame and Royal arrived and joined the girls for breakfast. Royal sipped her coffee in a Dolce & Gabbana black dress which clung to her bony figure. She clutch her coffee like it was the only thing she'd consumed in days. Like a life preserver which was there to save her from the depths of complete starvation in the name of skinny girl fashion.

Sierr and JSF emerged from their suite freshly showered and in dressed in matching linen outfits which made them looked like refresh fraternal twins. "Morning." Sierr smiled at everyone.

"Hey." JSF sat down and immediately started serving himself Bear Claws and Almond Butter.

Jame slowly turned his head to glimpse JSF from the other end of the table, the chair Carmen sat in as Ward Cleaver. He strummed the table his his stubby fingers.

JSF met his gaze and stuck his tongue out revealing chewed Bear Claw to Jame in a show of ultimate disrespect. Jame winced. Sierr got herself a coffee. Abby re-entered the suite and sat at the table near Carmen and Willow. "Good morning."

"Hey." Carmen flopped her hair.

"G'morning." Willow replied.

"Now that everyone is present we can go over the itinerary for the day." Royal said. "So, this evening there's a party. A Teen Magazine party. You all are already on the guest list."

Abby let out an excited gasp. Her polished nails gleefully fluttering to her lips.

"Now there's just one thing. This is a mature costume party, ok? The doors do not open until midnight, understand?" Royal opened the invitation and read from the gold trimmed envelope. "This party may be for teens, but it's not for kids. So, use this time before the doors open to rest up because the night..." She pauses for dramatic effect taking a moment to blink her almond shaped eyes. "Is young." She finally said.

"Rest up? I will be pampering myself from head to toe. Massages. Spa treatments. Hair care treatments."

"Personality transplant. The works." JSF smacked from the corner.

Abby sent daggers his way, readjusted herself in her chair and then turned to Sierr, "So, Seea-aaairrr. A lot of girls feel that pampering boosts their confidence perhaps with a little more effort you could be prettier like some of us."

"What shifted the stick up your butt, Abby?" Sierr spat.

"Sierr, ignore her." JSF said.

"I definitely don't appreciate the accusation that I am lazy. I mean what gives?" Sierr winced she was so suddenly furious.

"Girls." Jame spoke up holding his Mont Blanc one like a cigar in his fingers.

"What kind of sour ass person are you to talk to Sierr like this? She's always been nothing but kind and nice to you. Always!" Willow shouted.

"It's just the truth. Whiny little girls can't see the truth. They are just a bunch of posers."

"Abby just get out." Carmen said.

"Gladly. I have to go enhance myself." Abby stood proudly.

"Good luck with that." JSF said. "While your at it make sure you know that you're not connected to any posers before you go throwing that accusation at someone else."

"And what posers do I know? Hmm? Tell me right now who?" Abby squinted at JSF.

"Just wait and see."

"Aww, more empty threats and cryptic one liners from the conspiracy theorist. What else is new?" Abby smirked.

"Don't talk to him like that." Willow said evenly.

"I bet he actually believes there's alligators in the sewer!" Abby scoffed loudly.

"He's a better person than you'll ever be." Sierr yipped.

"Be careful you might actually grow a pair, Blake." Abby waved goodbye to Sierr like a princess and exited the suite.

"What in the world got into her?" Carmen bucked her eyes wide at dinner plates.

"Sour milk kinda shite she is." Willow stabbed a cantaloupe with a fork and a clenched fist.

"Shite? Is that how church taught you how to say 'shit'? How....adorable." Jame said in a tone as dry as sandpaper. "Dramatically Dramatic Drama-fueled

Differential Damned Damsels doing Deplorable Deeds Doubling the trouble within their Difficult Days. Now is that what you girls really want?"

JSF cut his eyes to the girls. The girls cut their eyes to each other. Everyone stared back at Jame. Was there even a response for what he just said?

Jame looked at them expectantly. He clasped his hands together. "So. Go onward and be about fashion. We will see you tonight."

He and Royal gathered their jackets, purses, and briefcases and trotted out like the gay men they truly were inside.

"He moves well for a person who was recently mauled." JSF commented looking thoughtfully.

"How even dare, Abby." Willow scowled.

"What did you mean about she's connected to posers?" Carmen leaned forward towards JSF.

"That circle of friends she has. Her crooked family. Well known information." JSF hunched a shoulder eyeing Sierr. She knew he was talking about Damian and Daddy Windsor specifically.

"Why come I didn't know?" Carmen flounced back in her seat.

"I'm going to take a nap." Sierr rose from her seat. "Enjoy the breakfast." Sierr did just what she said. She quieted her mind and fell straight to sleep. It was the only time she ever truly felt rested for even her quiet moments were etched with the business of her mind. Doubts, fears, self-consciousness. Presently she was angry at Abby. Now was a time for sleep. She laid down and slept for hours.

She dreamt about the grass and the trees. A small, wooden cabin looked like it was build by inexperienced hands by a stream. Blue lights reflecting in the night off every surface in the forest. Flashlights being frantically waved back and forth. indistinctive shouting from men in the distance. Dogs barking. Wolves howling. A stunning crown of rubies, pure gold, emeralds, and rubies being lifted from its protected place of preservation by scarred hands. She could have slept even longer if it were not for Carmen and Willow literally shaking her awake.

"Wake up!" Willow screamed excitedly into her face.

"Wegotplansthatyouneedtobeapartof!" Carmen shouted illegibly.

"Huh?" Willow frowned.

"Just get up!" Carmen said.

"What is it? What time is it?" Sierr asked groggy and a little confused.

"It's five o'clock." Willow answered.

"Oh the party isn't until midnight. Now is the best time to sleep." Sierr rolled back over.

"No!" Carmen "We found something fun and interesting to attend."

"What the party?" Sierr asked.

"No! An Escape Room!" Willow nodded with wild eyes.

"I don't think I want to be in a place that I have to escape from." Sierr said.

"See that was my first thought too, but then I realized that there is a prize if you win!" Carmen looked dazzled and did some Jazz hands for effect.

"What's the punishment if you lose? Do you die?" Sierr did her own Jazz hands for effect too.

"No! You just leave. But, guess what the prize is?" Willow asked.

"Uh…What like a…." Sierr flounced her hair a little dried out from sleeping on a pillow that wasn't covered in a satin pillowcase.

"It's a $1,000 prize for each member of the groups that participate!" Carmen blurted excitedly.

"But you're already rich?" Sierr squinted. "In fact…I'm already rich."

"It's still fun to win stuff!" Carmen said.

"Aww, I wanted to see what she would suggest." Willow pouted.

"I'm sorry I got really excited." Carmen put her hands up in surrender.

"$1,000 for each player? That's pretty cool." Sierr said.

"Right! But, I was thinking since I'm rich and you're rich we could just give the winning to Willow to thank her for being us along on her special trip!" Carmen yanked the covers off Sierr.

"Oh! Really?!" Willow exclaimed.

"Of course. You deserve it. This trip is the best. We're in New York, we're moo-dels. I went to the best spa in the country. I have arrived and it's all because of my best friend!" Carmen three her arms around Willow and gave her a big bear hug.

"Now that idea I can get behind." Sierr got up and joined the hug. "What about JSF?" Sierr asked.

"He took a page out of your book and went to sleep. He put on his noise canceling headphones and said not to wake him. He said he'll be ready for the party tonight though."

"Okay." Sierr stretched. "So, let's go."

The Escape Room was set in an old 1960s Mansion an hour outside of Manhattan. Sierr was a little weary about being so far away from the city when they had to be back at a certain time for the party and there was no telling how long it would take them to escape the escape room with only their combined wits.

The taxi drove up the long winding grey colored brick road which lead up to the house. Each side was lined with hedges that were trimmed in a variety of odd and interesting ways. A perfect square here, a hexagon there, a cluster of balls which ambiguously looked like the way a poodle's hair is often cut if the bare shaved parts were not keeping each balls of leaves separate. Three sets of Three-Dimensional Triangles ended the trail of odd shrubbery and the driveway opened up to a circular roundabout where other Rolls Royce's were parked after presumably delivering other players to the game.

Sierr and Company were dressed in yoga outfits. Their gowns for the party were carefully placed in the back of the Rolls Royce just in case they would be running late to get to the Teen Vogue event later on in the evening or technically tomorrow morning.

Sierr wore lavender. Willow ruby red. Carmen blush pink. They exited the Rolls Royce and bid their driver farewell and gave him thanks. "Okay." Willow said. "We each have our gamer aliases. I'm Clemency. Carmen you're Death Row. Sierr you're Jailbait. Understood?"

"Understood." Sierr nodded firmly. Carmen too.

Before them was a grand staircase made of petrified stone leading to the gigantic black framed crackled glass double doors. The stair railings, on both sides, began with bronze statues of Zodiac Signs. The railings ended, at the top of the stairs with a placard that said, "The Place Of No Return".

As the girls walked up the stairs were other attendees were also making their way into the building. Two of the attendees were a gothic looking man and woman, young adult aged, they had upside down star outline tattoos on their chests…the logo for The Church of Satan. The girl had the tattoo on her cleavage and the guy had the tattoo on his bare chest which was visible through his open jacket. The other attendees looked either satanic or plain gothic too.

Carmen stopped where she was, "Maybe this wasn't such a good idea. We compromise too much. This is just like Halloween all over again."

"We didn't know that it would be like this before we got here." Sierr noted.

""Besides this is our year of doing fun and exciting things together. This is fun and exciting." Willow said. "We're not Satanists. We don't actually follow Zodiacs or Horoscopes."

"We're not supposed to! That zodiac stuff is hocus pocus kind of stuff and we don't believe in it." Carmen said.

"Of course not." Sierr said.

"I bet 20 years from now they'll discover that they marked the years wrong for the Astrology calendar and suddenly realized there's supposed to be a 13th month and throw off the whole system! Then everyone will know it's fake." Carmen exclaimed.

"That's super specific, but okay. We don't have to believe in it just because we're playing the game." Willow said.

"Doesn't it though? Isn't what we're doing wrong somehow?" Carmen looked helpless.

Sierr stepped a few steps down to her friend. She put her hands on Carmen's shoulders and said, "There is no need to be scared. We are all in this together and when it's over we are going to give Willow and awesome present, right?"

All the girls looked towards the house as four spotlights beamed up to the sky. A crisp female announcer's voice came over the speaker located just outside of the Mansion which said, "Welcome to the Escape Room. A place where fear is the greatest possible authenticity and your intelligence is your saving grace. Enter now for the game…has begun."

The words, "Enter Now" illuminates from the front facing windows of the Mansion welcoming all souls aboard this wild ride. Sierr turned to her friends. Carmen looked reluctant. Willow grabbed both of their hands and said, "Let's do this and win the friggin' thing."

Sierr squinted at the house. It *was* intriguing. Carmen took the lead and lead her friends into the house with the other attendees.

The attendees gathered in the foyer of the Mansion. All other exits and entrances were closed. Apparently locked since no one had wandered any further into the house not even out of curiosity about this house of secrets needing to be unearthed by the game players.

Carmen pushed on the front door just behind her and realized that it was locked from the outside. She whipped her body around to her friends who watched as a projector started playing and projecting on the ceiling.

"Benicia, California 1969 was a wonderful place." The narrator said in a voice like of one of those 1960s commercial about soup companies which showed the dutiful wife preparing canned meals for her family like she was fulfilling some standard of motherhood and being a wife. "A town where everybody knows your name, the birds never cawed, the water was clean, and the only time doors needed to be locked was on that special Thursday."

The guests laughed and cringed at the thought that some folks actually set a day of the week for sex.

A slideshow of old time-y images showed Benicia Vallejo, California, Napa County, California, and San Francisco circa 1969. Family picnics. Family dinners. Blinded haired, blue eyed. School girls in black and white. The high school football team. Apple pie. Smiling groups of lily white people. Young. Old. Baby. Student.

"Benicia, California. It was a beautiful place. A place where there were lovers lanes, meatloaf dinners, all around joy and bliss. Until the truth came to set them free."

The projector stopped on a clip of a family with a daddy, a mommy and their two point five kids all waved on the lawn of their perfect house on a perfect street. The projection stopped. All the lights went out. The guests gasped. Sierr could feel Carmen's nails digging into her arms.

The female announcer with the crisp voice came over the speakers again, "now select your partners and listen for your first task. What is weak, but also strong? What is a nuisance strong as steel? What have I got that you ain't got? For this first task you have 10 minutes to get the correct answer and find the next clue. Remember there is a thousand dollars for each player on the winning team at stake here. Ponder wisely"

Then just as the announcement ended the lights powered back to life and all the door except for the front door automatically opened via mechanism. Each team of players immediately began scattering looking for clues and whispering ideas amongst themselves.

Sierr and Company stood like a bunch of slow dopes who didn't know what way was right or left. Willow bumped into Sierr and Sierr snatched the map away from Carmen who was just standing with her hair in her face still jiggling the door handle of the front door trying to free herself. "Ladies listen up. I think I know the answer. So, we need to find something, anything having to do with spiders."

"SPIDERS?!" Carmen gasped loudly.

"WILL YOU BE QUIET! YOU'LL GIVE AWAY THE ANSWER!" Willow hush yelled at Carmen. Willow whipped her head to Sierr what makes you think the answer has to do with spiders?"

"What is a nuisance as strong as steel? Spider webs. They're strong as steel and they annoy humans." Sierr said. "The attic." Sierr pointed to her map after studying it for a half second.

"What about it?" Carmen asked.

"Where do spiders like to hang out?" Sierr grinned.

"Let's go." Willow said determinedly.

The girls charged up the stairs of the rickety old house. The winding staircase like something out of a Hitchcock movie. The girls charged down a long hallway of black and brown doors. Each with a word written on it that was part of a single combined message that said, "Everywhere you go I'll find you."

The girls charged ahead. The hallway was barely lit and the dark green curtained which shield each window from being able to give off even the tiniest morsel of sunlight or moonlight.

Sierr herself let out a shriek when a male player stepped out in front of them. The girls cowered not sure why they were afraid. *Oh yeah...their competitors seemed like devil worshippers.* That was why.

The player smiled and obviously fake smile and cocked his head to the side, "Where are you three headed?"

"All you need to know is where your team is headed." Carmen frowned gripping Sierr's hand so hard Sierr wasn't sure if she was breaking the skin or not, but she powered through the pain.

"Exactly." Sierr said.

"You know only the strongest survive. He knew that well. His spirit lives on in those who are worthy of it." The player squinted all hints of fake kindness gone to the wayside and replaced by a cold glaring hatred. The guy scolded at Sierr and Company before pushing past them and heading back down the hall.

"Where's the attic?" Carmen said her anger at the player fueling her determination to continue on.

The girls continued on their path when music began filling their ears. Thudding downstairs broke their concentration trying to decipher the words of the song. It sounded like people were trying to break into a room that was shut or downright throwing chairs and other shite. Chants echoed through the house followed by crazed shouting. Just then Sierr realized she and her friends were standing under the hatch to the attic.

Carmen looked freaked, but her instinct wasn't to run, but finish sooner. "What can help us get up there?"

"Keep in mind we don't want to kill ourselves." Willow said.

"There has to be an answer hidden around here somewhere. We're supposed to use our brains." Sierr said.

"I think the word is *intellect*." Carmen replied.

"Thank you." Sierr firmly responded not truly thankful.

"Wait, look up there." Willow squinted at the ceiling. Sierr and Carmen followed suit and squinted as hard as they could. They all read together, "Look within."

"Within what?" Willow asked.

The girls looked around. Spinning in one direction before spinning around in the other when they all settled their gaze upon a little black box on a gothic looking clown table in the hallway. The fighting match downstairs was certainly getting out of hand as the ruckus grew louder and louder. Money was on the line here. To the girls this was just a fun experience to share together before their lives changed next year. Before school and God knew what else could take them away from each other. To the other competitors this was a war for a commodity that ran the world. People will kill each other over $20 in a pocket what little would it take for them to kill each other over $1,000 per team member.

The girls wanted to leave, but that wasn't an option any more. They made their choice. Their choice was to play the game. If they could win, the doors would be opened sooner and hopefully everyone could leave without injury. To Sierr the high stakes…made the game all the more fun and she was surprised at how much fun this had become for her. Her heart was pounding from fear and intrigue and anticipation. *What a rush!* Maybe Angelica was right maybe fear was life. Hmm…Sierr thought. *Funny the announcer also said something like that when the players entered the house?*

The girls stepped towards the box together.

"Should we open it?" Sierr asked already knowing the answer.

"Do you want to die?" Carmen hushed yelled using hand gestures for emphasis.

"Do you want to get out of here?" Willow asked bluntly.

"I'm sure we're not total hostages, you know." Carmen stated. "They can't just kidnap us for a stupid game. People go to jail for that sort of thing."

"Not *total* hostages." Sierr smirked.

"Ma'am…so not funny." Carmen shook her head.

"Hey-ya. Let's just open the box. What do you think is in there? A bomb?" Sierr asked.

"Those crazy ass people will be up here soon to presumably also rip us to shreds." Willow stated forehead wrinkled.

"We're cussing now?" Carmen said.

"I'm opening it." Sierr stepped forward.

"WAIT!" Carmen wailed, but it was too late Sierr already lifted the black velvet lid from the black velvet box. What was revealed was not what any of them imagined. It was stunning. Breathtaking. Illuminating their entire selves. This was beyond. The entire box was lined if cylindrical lights which made the box glow from inside out. The entire lining of the box was pure gold sturdier than stone and brighter with the lights that surrounded it. The underside of the lid was studded with pink diamonds which made the lid very heavy. The box itself was too heavy to even move. The entire container contained just one precious item a piece of tissue paper with hand inscribed gibberish words and symbols addressed to the New York Times.

A single line of direction in English was printed below the handwritten words: *What am I? Say it out loud and enter the chamber of legends.*

Here is a clue: *I am what I am and I am also the name of a character in The Matrix.*

"What is what? The message?" Willow squinted.

"Characters in The Matrix." Sierr mumbled to herself.

"I haven't seen it." Carmen shook her head.

"NEO!" Willow nearly shouted at the box.

"Shh, don't alert the mob." Sierr commanded.

"Neo means new this isn't new this is a language." Carmen said.

"What other names?" Willow was frantic.

"I'm trying to think." Sierr held her head dramatically.

"Morpheus?" Carmen shook her head.

"It has to do with words. Symbols. Font. Code." Willow said. The shouts from downstairs got closer like they were coming towards the bottom of the staircase.

Men and women were shouting. Whatever those people thought that they were onto they were obviously wrong and when they discovered that three teen girls were beating them at the game for thousands Sierr and Company was doomed. Time was of the essence now.

"Code. Coded language." Carmen thought hard. "Anagrams?" She tried. Nothing happened no fireworks. No secret doors opening. No, *Yay here's a thousand dollars*! No nothing.

"Pig Latin?" Willow tried. The shouts were getting closer. The girls could hear footsteps coming up the stairs.

"Wait the character that tried to sabotage Neo." Sierr started. "What was his name?"

"I don't remember." Willow's eyes widened.

"Calligraphy?" Carmen said just throwing out any type or form of modified written language she could think of.

"Think. Think!" Sierr pleaded to Willow and also to herself.

"I'm trying!" Willow was frantic.

"Calm down! It'll help you both get your thoughts together!" Carmen shouted.

"It was the bald guy! The one who was hairy and small!" Sierr yelled. All volumes were high without any regard for who heard. They were on the brink. Voices were coming towards them from the hallway. Running feet were closing in.

Willow looked like she had a revelation, she pushed her hair back, "Cypher. CYPHER!" Willow shouted into the box.

Just like that the hatch to the attic clicked and a tiny little staircase dropped down from the ceiling. Simultaneously the box closed itself back up and locked shut. The girls gasped with delighted and charged up the staircase. It soon closed behind them melding again with the ceiling just as the other players arrived at their same spot none the wiser.

It was dark up in the attic. The air was cool. The girls could feel wood floors beneath their sneakers. They walked some ways towards a small yellow glow coming from around a mound of furniture and old fixtures covered by sheets and plastics. Willow rounded the corner to see a small circular window letting a small amount of moonlight into the room.

Sierr whispered, "We're on the third floor now."

"But, this isn't the upper level and this isn't the attic." Carmen added.

"But, it looks like an attic." Willow noted.

"Maybe that's the point." Sierr said her features made more dramatic when shaded by the darkness in the attic-like room.

Up here the music playing through the house was more clear. The lyrics were clear; "Everywhere you go I'll follow you down." It was the new hit by the band Gin Blossoms. Stalker-ish in tone. It in and of itself seemed to be a clue.

"Look. Over there!" Sierr pointed to a cluster of spider webs which may or may not have been real. The girls reluctantly eased towards the cluster.

"Gross." Carmen curled up her upper lip.

"Shh." Willow hissed. "It may not even be real."

"It may be real." Carmen replied softly.

"Let's not touch it then. Maybe there's a clue somewhere near it." Sierr tried to find a compromise.

So, the girls eased closer to the cluster of spider webs. As they got closer they realized that it was actually a giant fake spider web which was canopied around a shrine of Benicia Vallejo, California, Napa County, California, and San Francisco circa 1969 collectibles, lit tea candles,  The girls decided to open the canopy no longer afraid that it was a real spider web.

They stepped inside the canopy of white threads and took in the magnitude of Killer worship that lay before them. The shrine was made up of pictures of men and women who had red "Xs" over their faces.   Clothes that were torn and bloody spattered which were laid out the same way in which a bride would lay out her gown for her wedding. Placed gently and purposefully. The candles were an alternated mix of gold yellows and whites burning brightly in the darkness. Willow jumped back from a beige leather colored display case full of 37 bloodied knives strapped into place for viewing. Carmen pattered her back for comfort. Sierr zeroed in on the centerpiece of the shrine which was a giant framed statue of a faceless man with a striped shirt on. He was actually faceless meaning he had a head, but absolutely no features. No nose. No eyes. No mouth. No teeth. No eyebrows even. Just a tuff of dingy brown hair covered the top of his head.   Nothing about him was notable expect for the results of his actions. Above the shrine was dirty torn linens hanging above and read as the word, "Fear Everything. Fear Nothing."

"What kind of a…Where's the riddle?" Carmen asked folding her arms over each other like she was chilly even though she wasn't.

Sierr stepped towards an ancient looking leather bound dictionary, a first edition Merriam-Webster, that lay at the bottom of a wooden slope that came from under a small curtain at the base of the statue of the faceless man. Seemed like the best place to find a riddle to get to the next level of the game. She opened the aged pages, yellowed over the decades, her curious friends peeked over her shoulders to see for themselves.

"Any riddles?" Carmen asked.

"Not yet." Sierr said flipping through the pages.

"What would be the clue to which page the riddle might be on?" Willow asked.

"Hmm, slasher?" Carmen arched an eyebrow and grinned at the display of bloodied knives.

"Okay. Let's try that." Sierr grinned flipping to the Ss. She found the Sls next. Dragged her finger down each page to find the definition of the word, "Slasher". Sierr and Company leaned down to the dictionary and squinted hard at the words before them.

They read aloud together, *"The merely innocence is altered by my intentions. A knife. A blade. A walked down memory lane. A trip to lovers lane. I lurk. I stalk. I taught the feds that I can't be caught. I am as illusive as the stars in the daytime. You will be mine."*

"Creepy." Willow smiles a toothy grin.

"Yeah!" Sierr agreed totally inthralled at this point.

"Devilish. Just Devilish!" Carmen said so hard the ends of her hair shook.

"So, what's the clue?" Willow asked again.

"Let's go to Stalker." Sierr started flipping pages.

"I feel like as though I've been sucked into Jumnji." Carmen groaned.

Sierr found the definition for Stalker. She read aloud, "What about the Slasher who kills and the Stalker that hunts can be summarized in the title of THIS classic piece of literature? You only get one chance." Suddenly a smaller electronic device slid from under a curtain at the top of the wooden slope and slid down to the bottom. Thudded on top of the dictionary.

Willow and Carmen looked confused. A small smile grew across Sierr's face.

"Waddaya smiling about?" Willow asked with a wrinkled forehead.

"We're enclosed in a giant spider web, the first clue was a spiders. What classic piece of literature has to do with a hunt, a stalker, a killer, and spiders?" Willow shook her head and Carmen just stared waiting for the answer. "Along Came a Spider." Sierr grabbed the pager and started typing the answer quickly. She double checked for typos and hit send.

"ACCESS GRANTED." The woman announcer's voice sounded out over their heads in the pseudo attic.

The girls gasped and squealed together rejoicing and celebrating together. Jumping up and down and hugging each other when a hidden passage way opened up behind the shrine. A bookshelf hid the secret door like something out of an episode of Scooby-Doo. Purple smoke spilled out of the secret passageway. A golden light illuminated the smoke from deeper in the passageway.

The girls held hands and walked into the passageway a little more confident and a little more secure. This was just a game not a death match. It was like playing a game of clue. They were simply unearthing the mystery of the perp or suspect or something for the prize!

Inside the passageway were violet colored shag carpet rugs over hardwood floors which lead the girls down a long hallway toward a thicker concentration of purple smoke and a hexagon shaped room. Vases of black roses sat on top of tiny tables situated in each corner of the hexagon. Dark purple colored, a thick curtain hung from floor-to-ceiling all the way around the room even thought it seemed that there were no windows in here. Various spotlight shined down on a tall and wide chaise chair in the middle of the room. Under the chaise chair was a hexagon shaped red shag carpet. On top the chaise was a girl. Her skin black, dark black, but it glowed golden under the golden lights from above. She wore a tiara, violet dominatrix type lingerie complete with a bustier, fishnet tights, Thigh High boots, a corset, gold buckles, belts, buttons, and garter belt. Finally, the girl had on a sweeping cape the same color as the curtain that lined the room. It clasped in the front with gold tassels and looked very expensive.

The girl arose from her luxurious lounge chair and positioned herself at an angle where those who entered would first see her profile only.

"Stop where you are!" The girl commanded Sierr and Company who obeyed immediately some of their original fear quickly returning. "Come correct for you have entered the sacred and holy ground of The Zodiac."

"Who is…" Willow began.

"Silence!" The girl shouted.

"If the Wizard of Oz was a female ho…that's what this feels like." Carmen whispered. Willow shhed her.

"He lives. He's here. He needs to come out and play. Let him play with you. Let him play with you. Let him play with you." The girl said quickly while smiling like a crazy person. The girls grew increasingly terrified. She laughed maniacally then threw her head back and spoke normally. "What would you do with all the power in the world? With a gift that passes all understanding? I'll tell you what you would do…you would be the person to amaze the world. I want that." Then she said emotionally and softly, "I want that…for you, *baby*."

"Um there's three of us…" Sierr started.

"Silence!" The girl shrieked.

"Love transcends. Life now let's his legacy…live…on." The girl continued "He was born anew when he made his first kill, he names himself The Zodiac Killer for people like me and you to understand him. To understand that he is one who cannot be understood. Alpha and Omega!" The girl breathed with awe and wonder. She raised up her hands to the lights and let her fingers create light rays over her body as she smiled wildly and exclaimed, "The GREAT ONE! Revealer of truth. Prevailer of the ones without vision…The Embodiment of Greatness!"

Sierr and Company took a step back and then as if she could sense their flight mode activating she turned her entire body to them. Moved like a cat or some other feline creature maybe a Jaguar. "Tell me do you believe in spooks?"

"Told ya. Wizard of Oz." Carmen breathed eyes full of terror.

"Carmen please." Sierr whispered gripping her friends hands tighter.

"What if I told you he did have a name, a family, a past, and a future? What if I told you he had…sons. All his own. With his same taste for blood and magnificent gifts too impossible to understand. What if I told you his sons were lost, but that they were coming home. What if I told you that life as you know it…"

"Oh my Gawd!" Willow squinted through the smoke, ripped her hand away from Sierr and Carmen, stepped up to the girl, and said, "HAILEY?!"

The girl flinched and stop moving around like a cat. Her confidence broke and she stood silently. Sierr and Carmen marched up too and looked the girl up and down.

"Hailey. What are you doing here?" Sierr asked.

Hailey Francesca just stood there pivoting from one foot to the other. Ankles occasionally wobbling in those thigh high boots which were somewhere between 5 and 7-inches high.

"Why did you say The Boys Were Coming Home?" Willow squinted.

"I…didn't." Hailey raised an eyebrow, her eyes shifting.

"You said his son's were lost, but they are coming home." Carmen steppes forward able to be defensive knowing that she was certainly she wasn't dealing with the supernatural.

"That…that doesn't mean anything." Hailey croaked and hand nervous fluttering up around her corset.

"Are you a member of The Fringe, Hailey? Is that what you're doing here? Are you making more converts into that cult?" Sierr said forcefully then she dropped her shoulders and softened her tone, "Don't do it, Hailey."

"Look this is not what you think it is. I swear." Hailey insisted the girls almost believed her that time.

"Is this what The Fringe believe in? The Zodiac Killer is some sort of supernatural power and that The Beckwith Brothers are *his sons*? Are these people worshipping the spirit of a serial killing murder!?" Willow ask eyebrows raised high.

Then Hailey rolled her shoulder back relaxed her face, stepped towards Sierr and Company and uttered the words, "Have not you heard? *I am* The Zodiac." Then she walked off.

"Wait! You can't just walk off like this. Those people are violent." Carmen shouted.

"Don't support then, Hailey. You can stop the madness." Sierr pleaded. Was Hailey the new standout member of The Fringe? The one who was more mysterious than The Fringe itself. The member who was no more than a figment? A formless figure. Without a name or a face?

Hailey popped the end of her cape and flounced out through another secret door on the other side of the hexagon.

"Did…did she just lock us in here?" Carmen asked eyes wide.

"Why would she do this?" Sierr was so confused. It was like Hailey was a totally different person. "It's like she didn't even know who we were. I considered her a friend and she just…"

Carmen cut her off, "Did she just lock us in here!"

"I don't know!" Sierr yelled back.

"We won didn't we? Isn't it over?" Willow said throwing up her hands.

"I'm sure they hear us." Sierr said.

"They who?" Carmen asked like the last hour never even happened.

"Everyone who's listening! The people *beyond here!*" Sierr said in all seriousness. Her level of seriousness made her sound extra insane.

"Now you're really turning into JSF." Willow said like she was observing a mutating specimen in a Petri dish.

"They've been hearing everything we say." Sierr said. Then she shouted to the ceiling, "You can let us out now! Whether we won or not we're done. Finished! Finito! No more games. We're through. You need to let us out now!"

A few moments passed. The girls waited in silence. Soon enough the sound of latches disengaging filled the small hexagon and eventually the walls to the hexagon facing the front of the mansion open to reveal a second staircase to the outside. There to greet them was all their competitors and a man wearing a striped shirt and a homemade mask. He stood at the top of the stairs where Sierr and Company slowly, reluctantly exited the building and then competitors applauded them from the ground below. Sierr half expected that she and her friends to be shot on site due to sheer jealousy and animal instinct of their competitors. Then she noticed that two of team members from two different groups were missing. Where could they be? Just sitting the conclusion of the night's game out?

"Congratulations on winning the game, Escapee Clemency, Death Row, and JailBait!" The masked man said. "I hope you all are proud of yourselves for using sheer will, intelligence, and determination to make your way out of The Escape Room! Let me ask you did you enjoy it?"

"It was an adventure." Willow said after she realized that she might have been talking to a killer himself. This whole night's events topped off with finding Hailey stumping for a cult left a bad taste in all the girls mouths. Something about these people just weren't right.

"Thank you we are so happy to have won!" Sierr smiled politely.

"I'm sure it is a lovely and exciting experience to win big sweet girls!" His voice was muffled by the mask. "Because you are our victors of this challenge please take thee these trophies as you cash prize will be delivered to you." Then he leaned in closer the sound of a smile in his voice, "Because you'd hate to have this angry mob steal your real winnings, *amiright*?"

The girls just nodded quietly wanting to get out of this place and away from their angry mop competitors.

"So, if all the loser can agree with me…Until next year folks!" The masked man teased the crowd. They glared at him and Sierr and Company with the fakest smiles in the world plastered on their faces.

The girls were then taken to a private car where they were given their checks for $1,000 each. The ride back to the city was quiet. The air was thick. The girls had so much to say to each other, but the driver was listening. He was quiet, but he was listening. Soon enough they dropped off at the front door of The Ritz. Sierr and Company walked inside hand-and-hand and made there way upstairs. When they reached their floor they still had not spoken a word to each other partly because there was so much to say and partly because they were still paranoid that they were being watched and listen to even though they were alone now. They also believed that somehow once they were in their suites they would have privacy. As they made their way down the hall to their adjoining suites a young, tall pretty guy walked up behind Willow. He looked like a moo-del himself, looked like a stiff breeze could blow him over, but his mere presence caused Willow to nearly jump out of her skin. He kept walking to a nearby suite door. It was Abby's suite.

Sierr used her card key to open her suite, Willow and Carmen stood close behind, and stepped inside with her. They all peaked their heads out as Abby opened her door to the pretty guy. She planted a sloppy, wet kiss on him and pulled him by his shirt collar inside her room.

Sierr and Company gasped before ducking back into her and JSF's room.

"Holy moly!" Willow bucked her eyes wide her jet black hair flounced in her face.

"Abby's cheating on Damian!" Carmen gasped. She didn't know how to explain it, but a little gossip did something to rejuvenated her soul. *Sweet, sweet gossip.* Suddenly she felt like she could smile again.

"Of course she is." JSF walked up in a pair of slacks rolled up to just under the knees and a button down that wasn't buttoned. He sipped on a can of pomegranate sparkling water.

"You knew!" Sierr asked.

"Abby's not the faithful type. Neither is Damian. I hear he looks at other women." JSF eyed Sierr.

"Wow." Sierr seemed sad.

"What are you surprised that true love didn't prevail with the two worst people we've ever met?" Carmen stated.

"No! I just…I'm surprised that's all." Sierr replied. "She's full blown cheating. That's…I dunno. I'm just surprised."

"Well she missed out on the real fun today." Willow hunched a shoulder. "We won $1,000 each today while you were snoozing." She said to JSF.

"Oh yeah? Who'd you three rob?" JSF asked.

"No one." Sierr said.

"Oh multiple people? Was this a heist type thing?" JSF arched an eyebrow.

"We played a game. We escaped an escape room." Carmen pulled her flouncy dark brown hair up into the perfect messy bun.

"It was Zodiac Killer themed." Willow said.

"Hailey was there." Sierr added washing her hands and pulling open a bag of cheddar cheese popcorn. "She was a fixture within the game."

"She was acting…kinda crazy." Carmen said. "She reminded us of The Fringe back in Downers."

"Reminded us of The Fringe?" Willow said. "She was talking like she *was* The Fringe. Like for real. Not only that she was saying things about how she felt that The Beckwith Brothers were the sons of The Zodiac Killer and that they were coming back with the spirit of their murderous father. It was way far out."

"The Zodiac Killer was never found. A lot of people think that the Zodiac Killer has blended back into society having quenched his blood thirst. It's not crazy to think that he would have children. Those children specifically being The Beckwith Brothers that's unlikely. What did she think about Carson Beckwith? He was The Beckwith Brother's dad…Does she think that he was the Zodiac Killer?" JSF asked.

"We didn't get that far. We asked her question then she said that she WAS The Zodiac and ducked into some secret door." Sierr munched on her popcorn.

"A secret door?" JSF asked looking back and forth between the girls. "Are you sure it wasn't some kind of secret hatch in the floor or a time travel machine?"

"Are you mocking us, Mr. Fitzgerald?" Willow cocked her head to the side.

"I suppose I am. You three and your outlandish outings." JSF grinned.

"So, you wearing that to the party tonight?" Carmen smirked.

"Nope. This is my napping clothes." JSF responded.

"You know the theme is Gender-Bending, right? Have you seen the invite? We're all wearing some form of menswear from different centuries." Carmen said.

"Huh? What am I supposed to wear a dress or something?" JSF wrinkled his forehead.

"Nah, I'm sure a skirt will suffice." Willow grinned.

"I'll figure something out." JSF said.

"Man." Willow frowned. "It's crazy how comfortable Hailey looked talking about The Fringe."

"Well we don't know for sure if she is actually part of The Fringe." Sierr said.

"I keep wondering where I heard the announcer's voice?" Willow said thoughtfully. "Was that Hailey's voice?"

"Too mature." Carmen said. "What do you think?" She turned to JSF. "Oh Wait you weren't there never mind."

"Always ready to give my opinion." JSF smiled.

"Goodness, don't we know it." Carmen rolled her eyes.

"I can't figure out if everyone was being creepy for the game or if they really did believe what we were hearing from Hailey." Sierr said.

"I think it was real and that those people are the same breed that lurk within our very hometown waiting for the brothers to emerge from the forests. Talkin' about fear like it's key to life or something." Carmen said.

"It's going to bug me." Willow stated. "Where I've heard that voice from." Willow stared at the floor for a while thinking hard and when she looked back up she noticed JSF staring at her intensely. Like he'd just seen a ghost. The look sent her blood running cold, but before she could ask what he was so afraid of he stepped away and ducked into his bedroom.

Later on that day or rather that evening the girls were dressed and ready to Gender-Bend for Teen Vogue. In Angelica McCord tapered linen suits with shoulder pads, pointed pumps, neutral colored makeup other than their dramatic eyes, thick eyebrows made wooly and wild by the power of a fluff brush, and hair pulled back into slick ponies, the girls were the epitome of androgyny. Their car with Jame would be arriving downstairs in ten minutes.

"Where's JSF?" Willow asked giving her already slick pony another quick smoothing for good measure.

"He went to the library. Said he needed to find a book." Sierr hunched a shoulder. "Have you seen Abby?"

"Saw her walk down to the car." Carmen said checking to make sure her bracelets were straight.

"How?" Willow squinted.

"I was looking out the peep hole." Carmen replied.

Sierr laughed and teased, "It's funny how nosy you are."

"HaHa." Carmen replied dryly. They had a laugh together. Soon enough they were all headed downstairs.

At the party was thousands of people, paparazzi, and size two moo-dels everywhere. This was by far the largest and most significant event the gang had attended since their New York trio started. This Teen Vogue the Mecca for high fashion and youth. Entertainment Tonight was here and so were the hottest young adult celebs all clustered on and maneuvering the red carpet. InSync was here and so was JoJo. The Olsen Twins were fashionably late and Raven Simone had already made it to her seat inside.

Sierr and her friends were ushered from their limousine by Jame Gumb and Royal Ho. They were all wearing Angelica McCord originals and they told every paparazzi and correspondent that as well. Royal wore a pink flowing femme version of the garb only male Royals of Chinese Dynasty were permitted to wear. Being able to embrace her Chinese roots and also the theme of the event at the same time made her pleased. Jame was in black spandex with a bejeweled floor sweeping vest. He wore elbow length gloves and round, rose colored glasses. His shoes, much like elf shoes at first glance, matched his vest.

"This Thursday you Four need to clear your schedules, okay? Because we have a lesson for you four about your runway walk for Angelica's Fashion Show, Okay? So, the four of you...wait." Then Royal squinted her already narrow eyes at the girls. "One. Two. Three? Where's four?"

"JSF?" Carmen asked.

""Yes the boi?" Royal replied pivoting from her left foot to the right.

"You know you are all supposed to present at these events. There is no such thing as being fashionably late when you are a model." Jame walked with arms folded over his chest. He actually said the word "model" and not "moo-del" which rubbed all of the girls the wrong way.

"He's not late...he..." Sierr almost went into detailed explanation for why JSF likes to avoid big crowds: pathogens, government monitoring in the media, terrorist attacks, biological warfare, the general noisiness that comes from having a bunch of people in the same place at the same time. Instead she just said, "He planned to meet us inside."

"He's supposed to be a model. A model on the Red Carpet for Teen Vogue!" Jame barked a venomous seething hatred boiling in his eyes. He immediately switch personalities like a car changes gears when a photographer aimed her camera his way and smiled the most genuine looking fake ass smile in the world. Sierr was certain Jame was a friggin' madman.

Inside the event it was like an explosion of pink and all hues of pink. Pink sparkles studded the black marble floors, pink curtains were strung from the high ceilings, pink lights shone from the ceiling, pink drinks were being served by waiters wearing tapered suits and long gloves who weaved through the crowds. The stage near the left was engulfed by pink smoke and the chairs around the stage were draped in black and pink.

Angelica strutted up to the girls in a dramatic diamond studded tapered suit with outlandish, haute couture dinosaur like metal plates up and down the back and horns off the tops of the shoulder pads. "Gulls! Gulls!" She clapped. Gave Willow a hug first then the rest. "Jame, darling. Could you refrain from speaking for the rest of the night, dear?" Jame smiled quietly as if eager to please and more than willing to obey his queen. "Oh you know I'm just joking. Speak! Talk! Promote the line! And most importantly...have fun!" Angelica spoke with her flashy hands and almost danced her words. "Willow darling. Come, come! I have someone very important that I want you to meet. Does the name, Anne Taylor mean anything to you?" Angelica purred.

"That name means everything to me." Willow breathed.

"She's here. Let's introduce." Angelica said whisking Willow off. Jame followed close behind.

Royal got a phone call on her cell phone. She put the clunk decide to her face. It was nude colored and looked like a giant tumor growing from her cheek. It was ugly. Hideous. Standing next to her was Carmen who was close enough to overhear someone on the other end of the line shouting frantically, "Where are you! Where are you! I've been trying to call you for hours!!"

"I've been preparing for an event." Royal replied taken aback.

"THEY KNOW! Do you understand! THOSE GIRLS! THEY KNOW HAILEY PERSONALLY! It's only a matter of time before they figure everything out! Get Angelica!!"

"I...What do you mean?" Royal stepped away covering the earpiece on her phone a little too late.

Carmen turned to Sierr who plucked a pink drink from a waiter's tray. "Did you hear tha...you know that's probably alcoholic, right?"

"Ya think?" Sierr's eyes widened.

"Sierr."

Sierr took a sip and winced. "Why'd he let me take it?"

"I think teen moo-dels drinking around here is the least of anyone's concern. Did you hear that phone call Royal just had?"

"No." Sierr swirled her drink staring at the pink liquid wishing it was sweet and yummy instead of spiked.

Carmen stepped closer, "They were talking about us."

"Talking about us how? In what way?" Sierr looked Carmen dead in the eyes.

"About us questioning Hailey and being close to discovering something about her and Angelica." A lot ran through Sierr's mind after hearing those words. Knowing how unsettled their trip to the Escape Room made her feel, Sierr couldn't help but be glad that Carmen's gossiping habit was finally coming in handy.

Up on the upper floor of the event location Willow was being introduced to Anne Taylor the powerhouse herself. Although Angelica was doing most of the talking.

"So, I said to her daaaarling you absolutely must know your audience. You have to know how to appeal to your buyers and have that shoppers appeal. And if you do not have a buyer than you make one." Angelica said.

Anna laughed dryly looking uncomfortable and flighty, "Uh well I do not know how one would *make* a buyer."

"Well create the environment where you, not your clothes, but you are needed. The your clothes by default will also be needed, necessary." Angelica said. Jame nodded in support. Was he actually staying mute on purpose?

"Um create the environment where you are needed? Fashion is supposed to represent culture as it is and how it could be. To be the everywomen and everyman and to offer..."

Angelica cut Anne Taylor off, leaving Willow in shock, "Fashion is merely a tool for something greater something more vast and wonderful. Once people are wearing your ideas, they too will wear you. I run my fashion house out of Downers Grove and it is a place where everyone knows everyone's name a place where quint and modest is key so how does one appeal to them when what you make will never be their style? How? How?" Anne opened mouth to speak, but Angelica cut her off again. "You *change culture.* You craft an environment in which their little town will come *to you* to find their new identity. How do you change culture? You either wait patiently or *force change.* You show them why they need you and your ideas by *proving to them* why you are what is best for them, why your style should be their style, why *your truth* should be *their truth,* why your fears...should be their fears."

And then it finally clicked. Willow slowly looked up at Angelica.

Angelica concluded her monologue, "…and the past that you wanted can become their future with new players in the game just like with a new fashion season comes a new visions and interpretations of common wear." Anne Taylor looked offended and unnerved by Angelica. "Do you disagree?" Angelica taunted with a smile.

Anne Taylor squinted at Angelica and said, "I see someone I know. So, if you'll excuse me." Anne walked away in one of her own tan pants suits.

Willow could barely breathe. She was beginning to excuse herself when Jame pulled Angelica in for a kiss. Willow could have thrown up. Instead she spun on her heels and walked towards the stairs. At first she speed walked, which turned into a sprint, before she knew it she was full blown running back to her friends back downstairs. She found all her friends: Carmen, Sierr, and JSF all together by the soda machine in a far off corner of the event space.

"You're never going to believe this." Willow walked up to her friends who all looked serious and terrified. "What is it?"

Carmen and Sierr looked towards JSF who held a satchel full of books and papers. "Willow, there's something about Angelica that you don't know about. She could be very dangerous."

"I think she's the announcer. The one from the Escape Room. I think it's her voice." Willow said expecting the girls to be surprised, but they were not.

"I think she's part of a cult. Not just The Fringe, but something more sinister. I have proof." JSF said.

"Show me." Willow stepped forward.

JSF and the girls got on the floor and he displayed all of his gathered material from the library, "As soon as you said earlier that the announcer at the Zodiac Killer inspired Escape Room was maybe an older woman fetishizing fear I immediately got suspicious that it was Angelica."

"Why her?" Willow squinted.

"I told you all from the start there's something that's just not right about her!" JSF said. "You all thought I was crazy, but look!" JSF showed Willow a picture of a large group of people from decades ago all dressed in sweatsuits standing motionless and expressionless by a still lake. "This is 1970 Benicia Vallejo, California. Where a total of 37 people were murdered by a nameless, faceless slasher who wrote to the San Francisco Times deeming himself, The Zodiac Killer. The Zodiac Killer was so mysterious, so haunting, so threatening many people didn't even want to go outside or live their lives for fear that he was lurking in the shadows and fully capable of killing them without a trace. But…some people were enamored by The Zodiac Killer. They found him to be inspiring, intriguing, sexy, and sympathetic. It's like he was putting the entire community under some sort of a spell. However, eventually something happened. No one knows what. He just stopped. He stopped writing the papers. He might have stopped killing. He may have died. He may have been imprisoned. Soon enough fear of him lifted, but the mystery and the intrigue remained. His followers unified in honor of him and began to meet together to celebrate his life and his murders and his power. They soon committed their lives to him through blood oaths and accountability contracts. Those people…are right there in that picture. That picture was taken where The Zodiac Killer actually stabbed a couple on a picnic…to death. The young woman in the very back of the picture, tell me who that is."

Willow welled up. Fear overtaking her composure. She could feel herself nearly hyperventilating. The girl was fresh faced with smooth skin and full lips. She was a far removed image of her current self the way a fresh grape look next to a raisin, but there was also a clear resemblance. It was Angelica. A young Angelica. "Oh my God."

"There's something else, Willow." Sierr said. "After reports of strange occurrences happening surrounding The Beckwith Brothers including their disappearance that's exactly when Angelica moved to Downers Grove. It's like she was following the power she couldn't understand and felt like they automatically had something to do with the Zodiac Killer."

"She's priming our community to be her next batch of followers for her re-envisioning of the cult she used to be a part of. Except now they worship the sons and not the father."

"The Fringe." Carmen said. "Hailey is a part of it and because we know this now they are warning Royal and Angelica about us. Like we know too much now." Carmen looked more pissed than scared. What kind of a world did they live in where a little juicy gossip could get someone killed?

"This is too much. I need to get out of here." Willow stood up, "I need to quit my internship. I need to…I need to…I need to…"

JSF stood up too and laid his hands on Willow's shoulders. "You need to stay put."

"Huh?!" Willow exclaimed.

Carmen and Sierr popped up off the floor too. "You can't let them think we are taking any of this hogwash seriously!"

"Right. Hogwash! All of it." Sierr said firmly.

"I can't do that. I'm actually scared of her now!" Willow said.

"You have to conquer that fear." Sierr said.

"I mean you should be the one that's uncomfortable. We're the innocent ones here. We all warned you not to take an internship or get close to that woman." Carmen stated casually.

"Oh…my GAWD!" Willow wailed. Her mind was racing so fast she couldn't even think of anything else to say.

"Carmen!" Sierr said shocked.

"We did! We told her to say, 'NO!' standing in the halls of Heisenberg High. Now look at us potentially having an angry cult looking our way!" Carmen responded.

"I think the best course of action is to blame everybody, but ourselves at this point! You are not helping anything!" Sierr said.

"You just had to be at fashion week. Couldn't you have just doodled in your sketch book at home!?" Carmen shouted.

"No one could've guessed anything like this would come up. Everybody just settle down." JSF started. "First of all, if you act like seeing Hailey at the Escape Room was all part of the game Angelica may think we are all just a bunch of dumb kids which is probably best. Second of all, your internship ends in a few months and then you don't have to be around her anymore. Third of all, if she's gonna kill us she's gonna kill us."

"Wha..." Carmen's gapped.

"Don't say that! Are you insane!?" Sierr wailed.

"It's the truth." JSF hunched a shoulder. "When it comes to some people once you've been tagged you've been tagged. There's no escaping it especially when we all have to live in the same town as her it's not like we can hide."

The group was silent for a moment and shared a series of intense looks with each other.

"So wait...does mean this The Beckwith Brothers might actually be out there?" Sierr asked. "You know who would know much more about this than we would? That journalist Kerry Thomas, Dr. Horacio Thomas' son."

"We should stay as far away from anything having to do with The Beckwith Brothers, Angelica, and The Fringe as possible. Oh yeah and Hailey." Carmen hushed yelled.

"And Abby." JSF added.

"Why Abby? What do you know about her?" Willow asked.

"It's more about her daddy." JSF said.

A door to the room opened and Abby stood in the doorway. "What are you all doing in here? I just met Giselle Bunchum! She wanted to know where I got my blazer from so what did I say, *'It's an Angelica McCord original I'm here moo-deling her latest line!'* It was so fun!" Abby gushed. "You four are missing everything! Get out here so I don't have wander around alone! As long as we're in New York we're a five-some! When we get back it Downers then I'll go back to avoiding *you people*!" Abby demanded. She spun on her heels and exited the small room.

Willow said to no one in particular, "Okay, considering Abby's the only one here who's like legitimately white I feel like that was racist."

"I wouldn't be surprised." Carmen noted re-joining the party with Willow.

"C'mon let's go back to the party." Sierr said to JSF, but he grabbed her hand.

"Sierr. I know I say things that are scary sometimes and I know this is scary, but I don't want you to be stifled by fear. Promise me that you won't be."

"I won't. I promise." Sierr smiled and held JSF's hand tight. In truth fear had birthed something new in her. The fear translated into curiosity for the unknown. It was rather intriguing. She had many more questions about the boys too. Questions she intended to get answers to. "I'm going to go to the ladies room."

"I'll go with you." JSF and Sierr made their way through the crowd of moo-dels and expensive gems and high fashion pieces and yet none of it mattered. They had each other and they had their friends. They were whole and in need of nothing else because they had each other. Sierr hugged his arm just as she made it to the bathroom. She opened the door and heard hushed yelling from inside. She peaked in and saw two women inside. Or actually two pairs of women's feet with super expensive shoes on inside the rest of their bodies were blocked by open stall doors.

Sierr knew exactly who the two women were by recognizing their designer shoes: Angelica and Royal. Sierr waved over JSF who quietly approached the door and listened closely.

"I'm not hiding you and Jame's lies anymore!" Royal shouted firmly.

"What lies? What lies?" Angelica said with a sneer and a smirk in her voice.

"Don't you play those games with me because I have seen you two! I know you two faked him getting mauled! Or more disturbingly he actually did get mauled or beaten or tattered or what it is you two agreed to let happen to him!"

"Jame was mauled by rouge humans who descended from those woods where they have been living for 15 years." Angelica stepped towards Royal, "Now are you saying that you intend to mislead people by telling them something other than that happened?"

"And now you're involving children in your schemes." Royal seethed with a tone of judgement and disgusted. "That little Escape Room of yours? Your intern and her friends went there today. Discovered The Zodiac in her natural habitat. Recognized her from Downers Grove. I got a call telling me to warn you. But I guess I know you're gonna find out anyway. That's why I'm telling you right now. I have proof that you're a liar. I have proof about the things that you've done! So, you leave those girls alone or you'll regret it you sick bitch!"

Angelica let out a satanic cackle. The sound from an entire other dimension. A realm far, far away. "Be gone before somebody drops a house on you! You crazed little lackey. Are you feeling a little power hungry or are you craving a piece of fruit for energy?" Angelica mocked.

"People like you get what they deserve. I don't have to make it happen, it just will. I'm just warning you, you have been very open with your sneakiness. And those children should NOT have to suffer because of you. I'm tired of being a part of something evil. No matter what I will be better off in the end for turning away from your wickedness!" Royal side stepped Angelica. Sierr and JSF bolted down a hallway and hid.

They saw Royal re-join the party and soon enough Angelica stomped out of the bathroom on her own cellphone in a panic she shouted into the receiver, "She's gone rogue! Get her! It doesn't matter how! Just do it!" Follow by something incoherent. Sierr and JSF looked at each other and ran to find Carmen and Willow.

As Sierr and JSF re-joined the event space the music immediately picked up. Prince was blaring so loud they could barely even think. Sierr and JSF found Carmen and Willow in the crowd. They were just about to shout the new developments to their friends when Angelica appeared beside them. "Hey!" She said angrily. "You!" She pointed at JSF. "Why are you not dressed?"

Prince went down a few volume levels as if the radio itself was cowering to Angelica.

JSF stepped forward and said, "Howdy! I do believe that I am dressed."

"Not in my label." Angelica replied looking JSF up and down in his slacks, white button down, and blue hoodie. "You're always late. You show up whenever you want. You don't do the red carpet events. What is your problem?"

"Nothing's wrong with him!" Carmen barked.

"And now that I am really looking at you girls why do you three look like lesbian librarians?" Angelica winced at the girls.

"We're wearing your line." Sierr replied.

"That's not my line for one specific reason. The clothes that I make are not meant to be worn like that. My clothes are meant to be appealing. The shirts are not meant to be buttoned up all the way like you have them. AND you need to have bigger breasts to wear it correctly!"

"What...the hell?" JSF said like he was sure he was being PUNK'd. The girls looked at Angelica like she was crazy, but she continued on.

"There are men here who come to these events to see how they would like their models, their actresses, their sugar babies to wear in their outings and projects. I need them to look at you young, pretty babies and see something sexy. Next time dress appropriately!" Angelica turned and walked away.

"Did...that really just happened?" JSF asked through a laugh.

"'*Ya' need to have bigger breasts!'* Can't we sue for this? You can't say that to somebody?" Carmen asked seriously.

"It took everything for me to bite my tongue." Willow said.

"How did you four get on Angelica's bad side?" Abby asked appearing out of nowhere.

"Girls." Jame shouted forcefully to their right. The girls spun around to him. He was accompanied by three older white men. White hair and white beards. All looking hungry and thirsty. "Stand there." Jame then turned to the men, "Now you all are discerning men. Experienced men. Men who know what they like. Please gentleman as you see fit to show these young girls, tell them how they have presented themselves tonight."

"What...the fuck." JSF said like he was doubly sure he was being PUNK'd now.

"I don't see any appeal." The first man who look oddly like Colonel Sanders twin stated first.

"Well what would you know about being a looker." Willow spat.

Jame went, "*Tsk, Tsk, Tsk.* No commentary until *after* the teaching, ladies." Sierr cut her eyes to Carmen. "Men are creatures of dominance. Ladies delicateness. As young women of faith doesn't even your Bible teach this to you? Obedience is key."

"That's not what the Bible says!" Sierr shouted.

"We would know we go to Bible Study every week!" Carmen proudly proclaimed.

"That's right! How dare you try and parade us around to some old pervy men and then try to get us to just stand here and accept it in the name of Jesus! What the hell is the matter with you?!" Willow screamed at the top of her lungs.

"Ooh let's not get all high and mighty." Jame smirked and laughed. "The higher you go the farther you'll fall." Jame walked away floating on a cloud of his own cockiness.

"We're all made in the image of God and have rights in his sight!" Carmen screamed wagging a finger in the air at the back of Jame's head as he walked away. "Do you think he heard?" She asked Sierr.

"He probably won't look it up or..." Then just as Sierr was responding to Carmen one of the older men pinched Carmen's side boob. Carmen gasped and jumped back like someone had smeared sewage on her. The rest of the girls stood in shock.

Then the old man had audacity to start with, "Obviously, what Jame is trying to say is…" But in a flash, Sierr's fist slammed into the old man's jaw and he hit the floor like a sack of door knobs.

"Oh my God!" Carmen somehow wobbled in her heels and hit the floor herself. JSF pulled her up off the floor. Hi-fived Sierr Five, Six, and Seven times.

"I…I did it. I threw a punch!" Sierr exclaimed jumping up and down. JSF jumped and down with her. His entire 6'3 stature and Sierr's 5'7 stature darting up in the air over and over again made it very easy for security to spot Sierr in the crowd. Before Willow and Abby knew it they were both being shoved out of the way by large security guards who grabbed Sierr's arms by surprise in mid jump. She squealed falling to her knees. She quickly got back up and whirled around.

"Hey! She didn't do anything wrong!" JSF shouted angrily stabbing the air towards the security guards with his index finger forcefully.

"She assaulted a guest!" The guard shouted back twisting Sierr's arm in an unnatural position. She squirmed in pain so he tightened his grip.

"She was defending me!" Carmen shouted. "That man pinched my breasts!"

"It's true he did." Willow shouted as well.

"Look lady. We'll have plenty of time to sort this out while your friend is in a cell, Okay?"

"Have you lost your mind!" JSF approaches the guards.

"J…no. Just…Just stop! There's gotta be cameras. Witnesses. I won't be in trouble." Sierr whimpered.

"You don't know that. You don't know what they'll do once they put you in a place where you don't have any power! Let her go!" JSF got closer.

"Hey look, kid! Back off!" The second security guard bellowed. Other guests started clearing the area.

"She was defending me! She was defending me!" Carmen screamed frantically.

"Let. Her. Go!" JSF shouted. "You're making an unlawful arrest! That girl did nothing wrong! You should be arresting that rapist over there!"

"That girl deserves everything she gets!" The old man shouted finally pulling his fat ass off the floor.

"Hey you shut the fuck up!" JSF roared his voice going deeper than Sierr had ever heard before. The second guard charged at JSF and reached for him, but JSF jumped back.

"No! Don't touch me." JSF demanded.

"JSF!" Sierr screamed. "Fitz!"

"Look boy! You clearly don't know what's good for you. I will light you up" The guard growled at him under his breath.

"Boy? Dude, I will ruin you." JSF said only loud enough for the second guard to hear.

The second guard seethed, "Fuck you! What is your name?!" He shouted in JSF's face.

"Ted fuckin' Bundy!" JSF shouted with a smirk. The guard grabbed him, dug his nails into the skin of his arm. JSF head-butted him…hard. Left both of their heads streaming with blood. The guard hit the floor and grabbed his taser from his belt. Sierr and Company were all screaming unintelligible gibberish breathlessly at the guards and JSF. But, JSF was done. Like so done. He was done with Angelica. He was done with the guards. He was done with New York. He was done with having to wear clothes he didn't like and having to obey stupid people's rules. He wasn't having it anymore. He yanked Sierr away from the first guard and stood between her and the taser wielding second guard. He flipped his long braids over his shoulder, bared down on the guard, and said, "Wha cha gon' do?"

The second guard shook with anger and licked the blood from head which streamed down to his lips, the first guard pulled his taser and aimed it at JSF too. But, suddenly a loud thud came from the ceiling followed by shrieking, horrified screams from the party goers.

Sierr and Company, the guards, Abby, and everyone else looked to the ceiling wide eyed and terrified. It was Royal hanging from a noose from the rafters. Her eyes frozen open and her mouth dropped. It looked like she died with a look of shock which froze when she took her last breath. Terror etched into her corpse. She swung and swayed to the beat of LeAnne Rhimes newest hit, "Can't Fight the Moonlight" which played over the speakers.

*No matter what you think; it won't be too long; til you're in my arms.*

It would almost be comical if this wasn't such as serious moment.

*Will it steal your heart tonight?*

Because it was such a serious and macabre moment, people freaked the fuck out. Like not just *fear* was unleashed because of the sight, but a full blown stampede which bumbled towards to two fire exits.

*You can try to resist...*

People crashed into the doors of the exits and set the fire alarm off.

*Try to hide from my kiss...*

It blared with a piercing blare. Still you could hear some of the words to the song over the speakers.

*Deep in dark. You surrender your heart...*

The two security guards immediately got on their walkie-talkies and started shouting commands and pleas for the real police as they left Sierr and Company and charged towards the fallen and injured people within the stampede.

*Can't Fight the Mooooonlight...*

Sierr hugged JSF tight. Tighter than she even intended to.

*No. Nooooo.*

She wasn't sure if he could even breathe she was holding him so tightly. Carmen and Willow held hands and Willow even took Abby's hand. They all hugged and cried.

*You can't fight it.*

"You see that?" Willow asked in a hushed tone despite the fact that they were surrounded by screaming and crying from hysterical guests.

Everyone said, "Yes." They were talking about the words that were burned into Royal's pink garb. Her dress was branded with the names,

*Eric Beckwith.*
*Luke Beckwith.*
*Lyle Beckwith.*

*Underneath the starlight; starlight, you can feel the magic so right....*
*He will steeeeeall your heart tonight*

Hours later the sun was rising over the Manhattan skyline. JSF was being treated at Mount Sinai along with the stampede victims who managed to live. His forehead just needed a few stitches. He was in one of those temporary emergency beds surrounded by more temporary beds each shrouded in the blue curtains.

The trip was official over. Carmen's parents, the great Cameron lawyers, just landed at JFK International Airport ready. To. Sue. *Everyone.* Her dad was a giant Filipino with a big thick beard and her mother a fair skinned curvy little red head. Both had on business casual their usual wear for anything. To them they weren't even dressed up. They'd grocery shop like this.

"Mommy! Daddy!" Carmen threw herself on her parents crying.

"Don't you worry, dear. People will pay." Her dad assured her in his robust, heavily accented voice.

Lux walked around the corner in Thigh High socks, a mini skirt, a sweater, and teased hair. She hitched a ride on the Cameron's Private Jet to the east coast to pick up Sierr and JSF. Willow's tinie-tiny dad scooted down the hallway of the emergency room close behind Lux. He was also a Cameron tag along.

Willow's dad approached her with arms wide open and they hugged quietly in the waiting room. Lux sashayed to Sierr who was too preoccupied watching JSF getting stitched up. "Eww. So after this are you going to do anything else?" Sierr said into the ear of the doctor who's shoulder she was peering over.

"Could you be any more interested?" The doctor mumbled rhetorically.

"No, I'm already soooo interested." Sierr smiled in reply missing the doctor's annoyance.

"Hey you two." Lux said walking up.

"Hey. Thanks for coming all this way. Hope the traffic wasn't too bad." JSF grinned knowing that the traffic was insane following a murder at Teen Vogue red carpet event and a fatal stampede.

"Wow, you can be sympathetic and a jerk at the same time." Lux replied. "Thanks for defending Sierr's honor by the way. You could have been killed." She plopped down on JSF's hospital bed.

"As long as Sierr's good I can die happy." JSF smiled sarcastically.

The doctor finished stitching up JSF and excuse himself to other patients.

"Are you Okay, Sierr?" Lux asked. "Mom, would kill me if I didn't ask. She's already beside herself for being out of the country while you were the victim of... murder witnessing. As if she could have known this would happen."

"I got bandaged up by a very friendly nurse." Sierr showed off her wrist braces for the sprains she suffered from the security guard manhandling her.

"I'm still pissed that man grabbed you. I'm going to get a copy of all your medical records and X-Rays and everything." Lux stood up. "Mr. Cameron will want them for *his* records." Lux flounced out the curtain and towards the information desk.

JSF stood up. The front of his face looking a lot like Frankenstein. He closed the curtains around his bed. "Look we're survivors together!" Sierr smiled sitting in the warm spot from where JSF was sitting. JSF looked somber. He stood over her and hugged her close. He smelled so good. Like freshly washed clothes. Like warmth. Comfort. Love. Kindness. He was the best. The friend everyone needed.

JSF pulled away only slightly and before Sierr knew it he was kissing her softly. Soft lips pressed against hers. He gently parted her lips with his and kissed her upper lip. Then the lower lip giving it a small, tender suck. Tenderly. So tenderly. And warm. So warm. The exact way she always imagined her first kiss would be. The perfect first person to kiss. Her beloved…

Suddenly Sierr's eyes flew open tore herself away from the boi. She was shuddering and shaking. She pleased and disgusted all at once. How could he? Better yet how could she? How could she ever…how could…this was wrong. Wrong on every level! What if her parents found out? What if God punishes her for this? This was unacceptable.

"Wha…What are you doing?" She asked backing away from him and wiping the kiss off with the back of her hand.

"I…I was just…I love you so much, Sierr." He said calmly.

"Please don't say that like that. You can't say that like that. We can love each other, but like innocently! Only! Innocent love, like *family love*, and that's it. No more than that. Because that's much more appropriate." Sierr was nearly gasping for air her heart was pounding so fast and her mind was racing.

"I…I'm sorry. I…just…it felt right." JSF replies softly. His voice barely above a whisper.

"It can't." Sierr said evenly. "And…I…I don't think we should be friends anymore."

"Oh no. Sierr…please. That would…" JSF croaked.

"Please don't." Sierr said. "This is hard enough as it is." She said holding back the tears that were burning her eyes.

JSF stared at Sierr searching for the words to say. Searching for a way to convince her that it was all okay. Searching for a way to explain himself. Searching for a way to go back in time and undue the kiss and continue to hide his feelings if that meant she would be his friend again. His heart was broken and so was hers.

On the plane ride home everyone was chattering about all the events of the last 24 hours except the part about Hailey and The Fringe. They just kept it simple no speculations about cults or supernatural father/son killers. Sierr was quiet. JSF was too. He stared out the window watching the landscape pass by his window.

Sierr wanted to go to him, but it was obvious now that over the years they had grown too close. Sierr was made different after this trip. She found a new confidence in herself. It wasn't the ultimate confidence that Abby had, but it was something that made her feel a little more secure. She was given new opportunities that would usher her into new heights and get her closer to her dreams. Life could be a little bit different now. Downers would be a little different too. Mr. Cameron was on a mission to make Angelica pay for her endangering his precious Carmen and he was dead set on staining her reputation in town. Maybe she would leave. Maybe he would bankrupt her and she wouldn't be able to afford living in Downers not even in Carrs. Who knew. What was important was Sierr would pursue a whole new life now. She wanted to be refreshed about it. She wanted to be excited about it. She wanted to thirst for it.

Maybe all that joy would come later. After she had a chance to cry her eyes out from losing JSF. Maybe after a few cries. Maybe after she didn't feel like her soul wasn't dying. She welled up and couldn't stop the tears from flowing. She just hoped no one would notice. She decided that if they did she would just chalk it all up to the latest events. She could only hope it would all get better from here.

*Even she did not believe that, that was true.*

*Thank you to all the readers!*

*The Beckwith Brothers Book #2 is set to be released Fall 2021!*